# Praise for the authors of
## *Forever and a Day*

### Linda Lael Miller

"Miller tugs at the heartstrings as few authors can."
—*Publishers Weekly*

"Miller's name is synonymous with the finest in Western romance."
—*RT Book Reviews*

"Linda Lael Miller creates vibrant characters and stories I defy you to forget."
—#1 *New York Times* bestselling author Debbie Macomber

"Miller is one of the finest American writers in the genre."
—*RT Book Reviews*

### Lee Tobin McClain

"Fans of Debbie Macomber will appreciate this start to a new series by McClain that blends sweet, small-town romance with such serious issues as domestic abuse…. Readers craving a feel-good romance with a bit of suspense will be satisfied."
—*Booklist* on *Low Country Hero*

"[An] enthralling tale of learning to trust…. This enjoyable contemporary romance will appeal to readers looking for twinges of suspense before happily ever after."
—*Publishers Weekly* on *Low Country Hero*

"*Low Country Hero* has everything I look for in a book— it's emotional, tender, and an all-around wonderful story."
—RaeAnne Thayne, *New York Times* bestselling author

# LINDA LAEL MILLER

## LEE TOBIN McCLAIN

# FOREVER
## and a *Day*

ISBN-13: 978-1-335-01258-6

Forever and a Day

Recycling programs for this product may not exist in your area.

Copyright © 2019 by Harlequin Books S.A.

The publisher acknowledges the copyright holders of the additional works as follows:

Mixed Messages
Copyright © 1990 by Linda Lael Miller

Low Country Hero
Copyright © 2019 by Lee Tobin McClain

This edition published by arrangement with Harlequin Books S.A.

For questions and comments about the quality of this book, please contact us at CustomerService@Harlequin.com.

® and TM are trademarks of Harlequin Enterprises Limited or its corporate affiliates. Trademarks indicated with ® are registered in the United States Patent and Trademark Office, the Canadian Intellectual Property Office and in other countries.

www.HQNBooks.com

Printed in U.S.A.

# CONTENTS

Dear Reader,

I'm delighted to share this volume with a talented writer like Lee Tobin McClain.

*Mixed Messages* is an older romance of mine, first published in 1990. Taking another look at it today, I feel it's still quite relevant in this age of celebrity obsession—maybe even more so—although it first appeared preinternet and pre–social media. The story features a renowned journalist (male), who's interviewed royalty, presidents and movie stars, and an advice columnist with higher aspirations (female). Mark, who'd looked on Carly's little advice column with scorn, soon learns that there's more to her—and more to her writing—than he'd assumed. He also discovers that love is the great leveler…

I hope you'll enjoy this return to what is now a distinctly earlier era. But remember, romance is forever!

With love,

*Paula Eykelhof Miller*

# MIXED MESSAGES

For our Wild Irish Rose,
with love

# CHAPTER ONE

HE WAS A LEGEND, and he was sitting right across the aisle from Carly Barnett. She wondered if she should speak to him, and immediately began rehearsing possible scenarios in her mind.

First, she'd sort of bend toward him, then she'd lightly touch his arm. *Excuse me,* she would say, *but I've been following your career since high school and I just wanted to tell you how much I've enjoyed your work. It's partly because of you that I decided to become a journalist.*

Too sappy, she concluded.

She could always look with dismay at the dinner on her fold-down tray and utter, *I beg your pardon, but would you happen to have any Grey Poupon?*

That idea wasn't exactly spectacular, either. Carly hoped she'd be more imaginative once she was working at her new job with Portland's *Oregonian Times.*

Covertly she studied Mark Holbrook as he wrote furiously on a yellow legal pad with his left hand, while ignoring the food the flight attendant had served earlier. He was tall, and younger than Carly would have expected, considering all his accomplishments—he was probably around thirty-two or thirty-three. He had nice brown hair and could have used a shave. Once he glanced at her, revealing expressive brown eyes, but he didn't seem to see Carly at all. He was thinking.

Carly was deflated. After all, she'd been in the lime-light herself, though in a very different way from Mr. Holbrook, and men usually noticed her.

She cleared her throat, and instantly his choirboy eyes focused on her.

"Hello," he said with a megawatt smile that made the pit of Carly's stomach jiggle.

She, who was used to being asked things like what she would do if she could run the world for a day, came up with nothing more impressive than, "Hi. Don't you like the food?"

His eyes danced as he lifted the hard roll from his tray and took a deliberate bite.

Carly blushed slightly and thought to herself, *Why didn't I just lean across the aisle and cut his meat for him?*

He had the temerity to laugh at her expression, and that brought the focus of her blue-green eyes back to his face. He was extending his hand. "Mark Holbrook," he said cordially.

Carly had been schooled in deportment all her life, and she couldn't overlook an offered hand. She shook it politely, a little stiffly, and said, "Carly Barnett."

He was squinting at her. "You look sort of familiar. Are you an actress or something?"

Carly relaxed a bit. If she was going to recoil every time someone did something outrageous, she wouldn't last long in the newspaper business. She gave him the smile that had stood her in such good stead during the pageant and afterward. "I was Miss United States four years ago."

"That isn't it," Holbrook replied, dismissing the achievement so briskly that Carly was a little injured.

"Have you been in a shaving-cream commercial or something?"

"I don't shave, as a general rule," Carly replied sweetly.

Holbrook chuckled, and it was a nice sound, masculine and easy. "So," he said, "you're a beauty queen."

Carly's smile faded, and she tossed her head in annoyance, making her chin-length blond curls bounce. "I'm a reporter," she corrected him coolly. "Or at least I will be, as of Monday morning."

He nodded. "On TV, of course."

Carly heartily resented the inference that any job she might land would have to hinge on her looks. After all, she'd graduated from college with honors back in Kansas, and she'd even written a weekly column for her hometown newspaper. It wasn't as though she didn't have qualifications. "No," she answered. "I've been hired by the *Oregonian Times*."

Mr. Holbrook's eyes were still dancing, even though his mouth had settled into a circumspect line. "I see. Well, that's one of the best newspapers on the West Coast."

"I know," Carly informed him. "I understand it's a rival to your paper." The instant the words were out of her mouth, she regretted letting on that she knew who he was, but it was too late, so she just sat there, trying to look remote.

Holbrook's grin flashed again. "You're behind on your homework, Ms. Barnett," he informed her. "I went to work for the *Times* two years ago."

They'd be working together, if only for the same paper. While Carly was absorbing that discovery, the flight attendant came and collected their trays, and then they were separated by the beverage cart. When it rolled on by, Carly saw that Mr. Holbrook had an amber-colored drink in one hand.

She felt slightly superior with her tomato juice, but the sensation lasted only until she remembered that Holbrook had a Pulitzer to his credit, that he'd interviewed presidents and kings and some of the greatest movie stars who'd ever graced the silver screen. Because she held him in such high esteem, she was willing to allow for his arrogance.

He'd forgotten all about her, anyway. Now that his dinner tray was out of the way, he was writing on the yellow legal pad in earnest.

The plane began its descent into Portland soon after, and Carly obediently put her tray into the upright position and fastened her seat belt. She was nervous about flying in general and taking off and landing in particular, and she gripped the armrests so tightly that her knuckles ached. Even though she'd flown a lot, Carly had never gotten used to it, and she doubted that she ever would.

When the plane touched down and then bumped and jostled along the runway, moving at a furious pace, Carly closed her eyes tightly and awaited death.

"It's going to be okay," she heard a voice say, and she was startled into opening her eyes again.

Mark Holbrook was watching her with gentle amusement, and he reached across the aisle to grip her hand.

Carly felt foolish, and she forced a shaky smile. But she had to grimace when the engines of the big plane were thrust into Reverse and the sound of air rushing past the wings filled the cabin.

"Ladies and gentlemen," a staticky voice said over

the sound system, "we'd like to welcome you to Portland, Oregon. There's a light spring rain falling today, and the temperature is in the mid-forties. Thank you for choosing our airline, and we hope you'll fly with us again soon. Please remain in your seats until we've come to a complete stop at the gate…"

Mark was obviously one of those people who never listened to such requests. He released Carly's hand after giving it a squeeze, and stood to rummage through the overhead compartment for his carry-on luggage.

"Need a lift somewhere?" he asked, smiling down at Carly.

For a moment she almost regretted that her friend Janet would be waiting for her inside the terminal. She shook her head. "Thanks, but someone will be picking me up."

He produced a business card from the pocket of his rumpled tweed coat and extended it. "Here," he said with mischief in his eyes. "If you need any help learning the ropes, just call my extension."

She beamed at him and replied in the same teasing tone of voice, "I think I'll be able to master my job on my own, Mr. Holbrook."

He chuckled and moved out of the plane with the rest of the mob, glancing back at Carly once to give her a brazen wink and another knee-dissolving grin.

Ten minutes later, when the crowd had thinned, Carly walked off the plane carrying her beauty case and purse. Her best friend from college, Janet McClain, was waiting eagerly at the gate, as promised.

"I thought you'd missed your flight," Janet fussed as she and Carly hugged. Janet was an attractive brunette with dark eyes, and she'd been working in Portland as a buyer for a major department store ever since graduating from college. She'd been the one to suggest that Carly leave home once and for all and make a life for herself on the coast.

"I didn't want to be in the crush," Carly answered. "Is my apartment ready?"

Janet shook her head. "The paint's still wet, but don't worry about it. You can spend a few days at my place—you need to wait for your furniture to arrive anyway."

Carly nodded. In the distance she caught a glimpse of the back of Mark Holbrook's head. She wished she could see if he was walking with anyone, but even at her height of five feet seven inches the effort was fruitless.

"Who are you staring at?" Janet demanded, sensing drama. "Did you meet somebody on the plane?"

"Sort of," Carly admitted. "I was sitting across the aisle from Mark Holbrook."

Janet looked suitably impressed. "The journalist? What was he doing in coach?"

Carly laughed. "Slumming, I guess."

Janet's cheeks turned pink. "I didn't mean it like that," she said, shoving her hands into the pockets of her raincoat. "Did you actually talk to him?"

"Oh, yes," Carly answered. "He condescended to say a few words."

"Did he ask you out?"

Carly sighed. She wished he had and, at the same time, was glad he hadn't. But she wasn't prepared to admit to such confusion—reporters were supposed to be decisive, with clear-cut opinions on everything. "He gave me his card."

After that, Janet let the subject drop even though, these days, judging by her emails and phone calls, she was fixated on the man-woman relationship. She'd developed a penchant to get married and have a child.

They picked up Carly's luggage and had a porter carry it to Janet's car, which was in a far corner of the parking lot. The May sky glowered overhead.

"Well, Monday's the big day," Janet remarked when they had put Carly's bags in the trunk and Janet's stylish car was jetting sleekly into heavy afternoon traffic. "Are you excited?"

Carly nodded, but she couldn't help thinking of home. It was later there; her dad would be leaving his filling station for the day and going home. Since his daughter wasn't there to look after him, he'd probably buy fast food for supper and drive his cholesterol count sky high.

"You're pretty quiet," Janet observed. "Having second thoughts?"

Carly shook her head resolutely. She'd dreamed of working on a big-city newspaper all her life, and she had no real regrets. "I was just thinking of my dad. With me gone, there's nobody there to take care of him."

"Good grief, Carly," Janet immediately retorted, "you make him sound ancient. How old is he—forty-five?"

Carly sighed. "Fifty. And he doesn't eat right."

Janet tossed her an impish grin. "With his old-maid daughter out of the way, your dad will probably fall madly in love with some sexy widow or divorcée and have a wild affair. Or maybe he'll get married again and father a passel of kids."

Carly grinned and shook her head, but as she looked out at the rain-misted Oregon terrain, her expression turned wistful. Here was her chance to live out her dreams and really be somebody besides a beauty queen.

She hoped she had what it took to succeed in the real world.


CARLY'S NEW APARTMENT was in Janet's building, and it was a simple one-bedroom unit painted white throughout. Since the walls were still wet, it smelled of chemical fumes.

The carpets, freshly cleaned, were a toasty beige color, and there was a fireplace, fronted with fake white marble, in the living room. Carly looked forward to reading beside a flickering fire in her favorite chenille bathrobe.

"What do you think?" Janet asked, spreading her arms as though she'd conjured the whole place, like a modern-day Merlin.

Carly smiled, wishing the paint were dry and her furniture had arrived. It would have been nice to settle in and start getting used to her new home. "It's great. Thanks for taking the time to find it for me, Janet."

"It wasn't any big deal, considering that I live in this building. Come on, we'll change our clothes, get some supper out and take in a movie."

"You're sure you don't have a date?" Carly asked, following her friend out of the apartment. They had already taken the suitcases to Janet's place.

"He'll keep," Janet answered with a mysterious smile.

Carly thought of Reggie, her erstwhile fiancé, and wondered what he was doing at that very moment. Making rounds at the hospital, probably. Or swimming at the country club. She seriously doubted that he missed her; his career was the real priority in his life. "Are you in love?"

They were all the way to Janet's door before she answered. "I don't really know. Tom is good-looking and nice, and he has a good job. Maybe those things are enough—maybe love is just a figment of some poet's imagination."

Carly shook her head as she followed her friend into an apartment that was virtually a duplicate of the one they'd just left, except for the carpet. Here, it was forest green. "I wouldn't do anything rash if I were you," she warned. "There might just be something to this love business."

"Yeah," Janet agreed, tossing her purse onto the sofa and shrugging out of her raincoat. "Bruised hearts and insomnia."

After that, Carly stopped trying to win her friend over to her point of view. She didn't know the first thing about love herself, except that she'd never been in it, not even with Reggie.

"AN ADVICE COLUMN?" Carly's voice echoed in her cramped corner office the following Monday morning. "But I thought I was going to be a reporter...."

Carly's new boss, Allison Courtney, stood tall and tweedy in the doorway. She was a no-nonsense type, with alert gray eyes, sleek blond hair pulled tightly into a bun and impeccable makeup. "When we hired you, Carly, we thought you were a team player," she scolded cordially.

"Of course I am, but—"

"A lot of people would kill for a job like this, you

know. I mean, think of it. You're getting paid to *tell other people what to do,* for heaven's sake!"

Carly had pictured herself interviewing senators and homeless people, covering trials and stand-offs between the police and the underworld. She knew the advice column was a plum, but it had never occurred to her that she'd be asked to serve in that capacity, and she was frankly disappointed. Calling upon years of training, she assumed a cheerful expression. "Where do I start?"

Allison returned Carly's smile, pleased. "Someone will bring you this week's batch of mail. You'll find all the experts you need listed in your contacts. Oh, and between letters you might help out with clerical work and such. Welcome aboard." With that, she stepped out, closing the office door behind her.

Carly set the box down on her desk with a *clunk* and sank into her chair. "Clerical work?" she echoed, tossing a glance at the computer system perched at her elbow. "Good grief. Did I come all the way to Oregon just to be a glorified secretary?"

As if in answer, the telephone on her desk buzzed.

"Carly Barnett," she said into the receiver, after pushing four different buttons in order to get the right line.

"Just seeing if it works," replied a bright female voice. "I'm Emmeline Rogers, and I'm sort of your secretary."

Carly felt a little better, until she remembered that she was probably going to spend as much time doing office work as writing. Maybe more. "Hi," she said shyly.

"Want some coffee or something?"

Carly definitely felt better. "Thanks. That would be great."

Moments later, Emmeline appeared with coffee. She

was small, with plain brown hair, green eyes and a r[...]
smile. "I brought pink sugar, in case you wanted i[...]

Carly thanked the woman again and stirred half a
packet of sweetener into the hot, strong coffee. "There
are supposed to be some letters floating around here
somewhere. Do you know where they are?"

Emmeline nodded and then glanced at her watch.
Maybe she was one of those people who took an early
lunch, Carly thought. "I'll bring them in."

"Great," Carly answered. "Thanks."

Emmeline slipped out and returned five minutes later
with a mailbag the size of Santa's sack. In fact, Carly
was reminded of the courtroom scene in *Miracle On
34th Street* when the secretary spilled letters all over
her desk.

By the time Emmeline had emptied the bag, Carly
couldn't even see over the pile. She would have to un-
earth her computer and telephone before she could start
working.

"I couldn't think of a way to break it to you gently,"
Emmeline said.

Carly took a steadying sip of her coffee and muttered, "Allison said I'd be helping out with clerical work
during slack times."

Emmeline smiled. "Allison thinks she has a sense
of humor. The rest of us know better."

Carly chuckled and shoved the fingers of her left
hand through her hair. Until two weeks ago, when she'd
made the final decision to break off with Reggie and
come to Oregon, she'd worn it long. The new cut, reaching just a couple of inches below her earlobes, had been
a statement of sorts; she was starting over fresh.

ady      eft her with a little shrug and a sympa-
        .....  Buzz me if you need anything."

Carly was beginning to sort the letters into stacks. "If there's another avalanche," she responded, "send in a search party."

Her telephone and computer had both reappeared by the time a brisk knock sounded at her office door. Mark poked his head around it before she had time to call out a "Come in" or even wonder why Emmeline hadn't buzzed to announce a visitor.

"Hi," he said, assessing the mountain of letters with barely concealed amusement. He was probably off to interview the governor or some astronaut.

Carly gave him a dour look. "Hi," she responded.

He stepped into the tiny office and closed the door. "Your secretary's on a break," he said. He was wearing jeans, a plaid flannel shirt and a tan corduroy jacket.

"What I need is a moat stocked with crocodiles," Carly retorted with a saucy smile. She wasn't sure how she felt about this man—he produced an odd tangle of reactions that weren't easy to unravel and define. The impact of his presence was almost overwhelming—he seemed to fill the room, leaving no space for her—and Carly was both intrigued and frightened.

She was at once attracted to him, and defensive about her lack of experience as a journalist.

Mark drew up the only extra chair, turned it around backward and sat astraddle of it, resting his arms across the back. "What are they going to call this column now? 'Dear Miss Congeniality'?"

"I wasn't Miss Congeniality," Carly pointed out, arching her eyebrows and deliberately widening her eyes.

"Little wonder," he replied philosophically.

Carly leaned forward in her chair and did her best to glower. "Was there something you wanted?"

"Yes. I'd like you to go to dinner with me tonight."

Carly was putting rubber bands around batches of letters and stacking them on her credenza. A little thrill pirouetted up her spine and then did a triple flip to the pit of her stomach. Even though every instinct she possessed demanded that she refuse, she found herself nodding. "I'd enjoy that."

"We could take in a movie afterward, if you want."

Carly looked at the abundance of letters awaiting her attention. "That would be stretching it. Maybe some other time."

Idly Mark picked up one of the letters and opened it. His handsome brow furrowed as he read. "This one's from a teenage girl," he said, extending the missive to Carly. "What are you going to tell her?"

Carly took the page of lined notebook paper and scanned it. The young lady who'd written it was still in high school, and she was being pressured by the boy she dated to "go all the way." She wanted to know how she could refuse without losing her boyfriend.

"I think she should stand her ground," Carly said. "If the boy really cares about her, he'll understand why she wants to wait."

Mark nodded thoughtfully. "Of course, nobody expects you to reply to every letter," he mused.

Carly sensed disapproval in his tone, though it was well masked. "What's wrong with my answer?" she demanded.

"It's a little simplistic, that's all." His guileless brown eyes revealed no recriminations.

Without understanding why, Carly was on the defensive. "I suppose you could come up with something better?"

He sighed. "No, just more extensive. I would tell her to talk to a counselor at school, or a clergyman, or maybe a doctor. Things are complex as hell out there, Carly. Kids have a lot more to worry about than making cheerleader or getting on the football team."

Carly sat back in her hair and folded her arms. "Could it be, Mr. Holbrook," she began evenly, "that you think I'm shallow just because I was Miss United States?"

He grinned. "Would I have asked you out to dinner if I thought you were shallow?"

"Probably."

Mark shrugged and spread his hands. "I'm sure you mean well," he conceded generously. "You're just inexperienced, that's all."

She took up a packet of envelopes and switched on her computer. The printer beside it hummed efficiently at the flip of another switch. "I won't ever have any experience," she responded, "if you hang around my office for the rest of your life, picking my qualifications apart."

He stood up. "I assume you have a degree in psychology?"

"You know better."

Mark was at the door now, his hand on the knob. "True. I looked you up. You majored in—"

"Journalism," Carly interrupted.

Although his expression was chagrined, his eyes twinkled as he offered her a quick salute. "See you at dinner," he said, and then he was gone.

Thoroughly unsettled, Carly turned her attention back to the letters she was expected to deal with.

Resolutely she opened an envelope, took out the folded page and began to read.

By lunchtime, Carly's head was spinning. She was certainly no Pollyanna, but she'd never dreamed there were so many people out there leading lives of quiet desperation.

Slipping on her raincoat and reaching for her purse and umbrella, she left the *Times* offices and made her way to a cozy little delicatessen on the corner. She ordered chicken salad and a diet cola, then sat down at one of the round metal tables and stared out at the people hurrying past the rain-beaded window.

After a morning spent reading about other people's problems, she was completely depressed. This was a state of mind that just naturally conjured up thoughts of Reggie.

Carly lifted her soft drink and took a sip. Maybe she'd done the wrong thing, breaking her engagement and leaving Kansas to start a whole new life. After all, Reggie was an honest-to-God doctor. He was already making over six figures a year, and he owned his sprawling brick house outright.

Glumly Carly picked up her plastic fork and took a bite of her salad. Perhaps Janet was right, and love *was* about bruised hearts and insomnia. Maybe it was some kind of neurotic compulsion.

Hell, maybe it didn't exist at all.

At the end of her lunch hour, Carly returned to her office to find a note propped against her computer screen. It was written on the back of one of the envelopes, in firm black letters that slanted slightly to the right. *This guy needs professional help. Re: dinner—meet me downstairs in the lobby at seven. Mark.*

Carly shook her head and smiled as she took the letter out of the envelope. Her teeth sank into her lower lip as she read about the plight of a man who was in love with his aunt Gertrude. Nothing in journalism school, or in a year's reign as Miss United States, had prepared her for dealing with things like this.

She set the letter aside and opened another one.

Allison popped in at five minutes before five. "Hello," she chimed. "How are things going?"

Carly worked up a smile. "Until today," she replied, "I had real hope for humanity."

Allison gestured toward the computer. "I trust you're making good use of Madeline's contacts. She made some excellent ones in the professional community while she was here."

Madeline, of course, was Carly's predecessor, who had left her job to join her professor husband on a sabbatical overseas. "I haven't gotten that far," Carly responded. "I'm still in the sorting process."

Allison shook a finger at Carly, assuming a stance and manner that made her resemble an elementary school librarian. "Now remember, you have deadlines, just like everyone else at this paper."

Carly nodded. She was well aware that she was expected to turn in a column before quitting time on Wednesday. "I'll be ready," she said, and she was relieved when Allison left it at that and disappeared again.

She was stuffing packets of letters into her briefcase when Janet arrived to collect her.

"So how was it?" Janet asked, pushing a button on the elevator panel. The doors whisked shut.

"Grueling," Carly answered, patting her briefcase with the palm of one hand. "Talk about experience. I'm expected to deal with everything from the heartbreak of psoriasis to nuclear war."

Janet smiled. "You'll get the hang of it," she teased. "God did."

Carly rolled her eyes and chuckled. "I think he divided the overflow between Dear Abby, Ann Landers and me."

In the lobby the doors swished open, and Carly found herself face-to-face with Mark Holbrook. Perhaps because she was unprepared for the encounter, she felt as though the floor had just dissolved beneath her feet.

Janet nudged her hard in the ribs.

"M-Mark, this is Janet McClain," Carly stammered with all the social grace of a nervous ninth grader. "We went to high school and college together."

Carly begrudged the grin Mark tossed in Janet's direction. "Hello," he said suavely, and Carly thought, just fleetingly, of Cary Grant.

Mark's warm brown eyes moved to Carly. "Remember—we're supposed to meet at seven for dinner."

Carly was still oddly starstruck, and she managed nothing more than a nod in response.

"I take back every jaded remark I've ever made about love," Janet whispered as she and Carly walked away. "I've just become a believer."

Carly was shaken, but for some reason she needed to put on a front. "Take it from me, Janet," she said cynically, "Mark Holbrook may look like a prize, but he's too arrogant to make a good husband."

"Umm," said Janet.

"I mean, it's not like every dinner date has to be marriage material—"

"Of course not," Janet readily agreed.

A brisk and misty wind met them as they stepped out onto the sidewalk in front of the *Times* building, and Carly's cheeks colored in a blush. She averted her eyes. "I know he's the wrong kind of man for me—with all he's accomplished, he must be driven, like Reggie, but—"

"But?" Janet prompted.

"When he asked me out for dinner, I meant to say no," Carly confessed, "but somehow it came out yes."

# CHAPTER TWO

CARLY ARRIVED AT the *Times* offices at five minutes to seven, wearing an attractive blue dress she'd borrowed from Janet and feeling guilty about all the unread letters awaiting her at home.

She stepped into the large lobby and looked around. She shouldn't even be there, she thought to herself. When she'd left home, she'd had a plan for her life, and Mark Holbrook, attractive as he might be, wasn't part of it.

An elevator bell chimed, doors swished open, and Mark appeared, as if conjured by her thoughts. He carried a briefcase in one hand and wore the same clothes he'd had on earlier: jeans, a flannel shirt and a corduroy jacket.

"This almost makes me wish I'd worn a tie," he said, his warm brown eyes sweeping over her with admiration. Another of his lightning-charged grins flashed. "Then again, I'm glad I didn't. You look wonderful, Ms. Congeniality."

Carly let the beauty-pageant vernacular slide by. Although she'd had a lot of experience talking to people, she felt strangely shy around Mark. "Thanks," she said.

They walked three blocks to Jake's, an elegantly rustic restaurant-tavern that had been in business since 1892. When they walked in, the bartender called out a good-natured greeting to Mark, who answered with a thumbs-up sign, then proceeded to the reservations desk.

Soon Mark and Carly were seated in a booth on wooden benches, the backs towering over their heads. A waiter promptly brought them menus and greeted Mark by name.

Carly figured he probably brought a variety of women to the restaurant, and was inexplicably annoyed by the thought. She chose a Cajun plate, while Mark ordered a steak.

"Making any progress with the letters?" he asked when they were alone again.

Carly sighed. She'd probably be up until two or three in the morning, wading through them. "Let's put it this way," she answered, "I should be home working."

The wine arrived and Mark tasted the sample the steward poured, then nodded. The claret was poured and the steward walked away, leaving the bottle behind.

Mark lifted his glass and touched it against Carly's. "To workaholics everywhere," he said.

Carly took a sip of her wine and set the glass aside. The word "workaholic" had brought Reggie to mind, and she felt as though he were sitting at the table with them, an unwelcome third. "What's the most important thing in your life?" she asked to distract herself.

The waiter left their salads, then turned and walked away.

"Things don't mean much to me," Mark responded, lifting his fork. "It's people who matter. And the most important person in my life is my son, Nathan."

Even though she certainly wasn't expecting anything to develop between herself and Mark, Carly was jarred by the mention of a child. "You're not married, I hope," she said, practically holding her breath.

"No, I'm divorced, and Nathan lives in California, with his mother," he said. There was, for just an instant, a look of pain in his eyes. This was quickly displaced by a mischievous sparkle. "Would it matter to you—if I were married, I mean?"

Carly speared a cherry tomato somewhat vengefully. "Would it *matter*? Of course it would."

"A lot of women don't care."

"I'm not a lot of women," Carly responded, her tone resolute.

He shrugged one shoulder. "There's a shortage of marriageable men out there, I'm told. Aren't you worried that your biological clock is ticking, and all that?"

"Maybe in ten years I'll be worried. Right now I'm interested in making some kind of life for myself."

"Which you couldn't do in the Midwest?"

"I wanted to do it here," she said.

Mark smiled. "Exactly what kind of life are you picturing?"

Carly was beginning to feel as though she was being interviewed, but she didn't mind. She understood how a reporter's mind worked. "Mainly I want to write for a newspaper—not advice, but articles, like you do. And maybe I'll buy myself a little house and a dog."

"Sounds fulfilling," Mark replied.

There was so little conviction in his voice that Carly peered across the table at him and demanded, "Just what did you mean by that?"

He widened those guileless choirboy eyes of his and sat back on the bench as though he expected the salt shaker to detonate. "I was just thinking—well, it's a shame that so few women want to have babies any-more."

"I didn't say I didn't want to have babies," Carly pointed out. Her voice had risen, and she blushed to see that the people at the nearest table were looking at her. "I *love* babies," she clarified in an angry whisper. "I plan to breast-feed and everything!"

The waiter startled Carly by suddenly appearing at her elbow to deliver dinner, and Mark grinned at her reaction.

She spoke in a peevish hiss. "Let's just get off this topic of conversation, all right?"

"All right," Mark agreed. "Tell me, what made you start entering beauty pageants?"

It wasn't the subject Carly would have chosen, but she could live with it. "Not 'what,'" she replied. "'Who.' It was my mother. She started entering me in contests when I was four and, except for a few years when I was in an awkward stage, she kept it up until I was old enough to go to college."

"And then you won the Miss United States title?"

Carly nodded, smiling slightly as she recalled those exciting days. "You'd have thought Mom was the win-ner, she was so pleased. She called everybody we knew."

Mark was cutting his steak. "She must miss you a lot."

Carly bent her head, smoothing the napkin in her lap. "She died of cancer a couple of weeks after the pageant."

When Carly lifted a hand back to the table, Mark's was waiting to enfold it. "I'm sorry," he said quietly.

His sympathy brought quick, stinging tears to her eyes. "It could have been worse," Carly managed to say. "Everything happened almost instantaneously. She didn't suffer much."

Mark only nodded, his eyes caressing Carly in a way that eased the pain of remembering.

"How old is Nathan?" she asked, and the words came out a little awkwardly.

Mark's voice was hoarse when he answered. "He's ten," he replied, opening his wallet and taking out a photo.

Nathan Holbrook was handsome, like his father, with brown hair and eyes, and he was dressed in a baseball uniform and was holding a bat, ready to swing.

Carly smiled and handed the picture back. "It must be difficult living so far away from him," she commented.

Mark nodded, and Carly noticed that he averted his eyes for a moment.

"Is something wrong?" she asked softly.

"Nothing I want to trouble you with," Mark responded, putting away his wallet. "Sure you don't want to go take in a movie?"

Carly thought of the pile of letters she had yet to read. She gave her head a regretful shake. "Maybe some other time. Right now I'm under a lot of pressure to show Allison and the powers-that-be that I can handle this job."

They finished their meal, then Mark settled the bill with a credit card. He held her hand as they walked to his car, which was parked in a private lot beneath the newspaper building.

Barely fifteen minutes later, they were in front of Janet's door. Mark bent his head and gave Carly a kiss that, for all its innocuousness, made her nerve endings vibrate.

"Good night," he murmured, while Carly was still trying to get her bearings. A moment after that, he disappeared into the elevator.

*"Well?"* Janet demanded the second Carly let herself into the apartment.

Carly smiled and shook her head. "It was love at first sight," she responded sweetly. "We're getting married tonight, flying to Rio tomorrow and starting our family the day after."

Janet bounded off the couch and followed Carly as she went through the bedroom and stood outside the bathroom door while she exchanged the dress for an oversize T-shirt. "Details!" she cried. "Give me details!"

Carly came out of the bathroom, carrying the dress, and hung it back in the closet. "Mark and I are all wrong for each other," she said.

"How do you figure that?"

Turning away from the closet, Carly shrugged. "The guy sends out mixed messages. He's very attractive, but he's bristly, too. And he's got some very old-fashioned ideas about women."

Janet looked disappointed for a moment, then brightened. "If you're not going to see Mark anymore, how about fixing me up with him?"

Carly was surprised at the strong reaction the suggestion produced in her. She marched across Janet's living room, took her briefcase from the breakfast bar and set it down on the Formica-topped table with a thump. "I didn't say I wasn't going to see him again," she said, snapping the catches and pulling out a stack of letters.

After tossing her friend a smug little smile, Janet said good-night and went off to bed. Carly looked with longing at the fold-out sofa, then made herself a cup of tea and set to work.

Although there was no sign of Emmeline when Carly arrived at work the next morning, suppressing almost continuous yawns and hoping the dark circles under her eyes weren't too pronounced, a memo had been taped to her computer screen.

*Staff meeting,* the message read. *Nine-thirty, conference room.*

Carly glanced at her watch, sat down at her desk and began reading letters again. It was almost a relief when the time came to leave her small office for the meeting.

The long conference room table was encircled by people, and they all seemed to be talking at the same time. An enormous pot of coffee chortled on a table in the corner. Carly poured herself a cup of coffee and sat down in the only empty chair in the room, shaking her head when a secretary came by with a box full of assorted pastries.

She saw that Mark was sitting directly across from her. He grinned and tilted his head slightly to one side in a way that was vaguely indulgent.

*Mixed messages again,* Carly thought, responding with a tight little smile.

The managing editor, a slender, white-haired man with the sleeves of his shirt rolled back to his elbows and suspenders holding up his pants, called the meeting to order.

Carly listened intently as he went over the objectives of the newspaper and gave out assignments.

The best one, a piece on crack houses for the Sunday edition, went to Mark, and Carly felt a sting of envy. While he was out in the field, grappling with real life, she would be tucked away in her tiny office, reading letters from the forlorn.

Mark sat back in his chair, not drinking coffee or eating doughnuts like the others, his eyes fixed on Carly. She was relieved when the meeting finally ended.

"So," boomed Mr. Clark, the managing editor, just as Carly was pushing back her chair to leave, "how do you like writing the advice column?"

Carly glanced uncomfortably at Mark, who had lingered to open a nearby window. *Now's a nice time to think of that,* she reflected to herself, and Mark looked back at her as though she'd spoken aloud.

She remembered Mr. Clark and his affable question. "I haven't actually written anything yet," she answered diplomatically. "I'm still wading through the letters."

Mark was standing beside the table again, his hands resting on the back of a chair. "You're aware, of course," he put in, "that Ms. Barnett doesn't have any real qualifications for that job?"

Carly looked at him in stunned disbelief, and he favored her with a placid grin.

Mr. Clark was watching Carly, but he spoke as though she wasn't there. "Allison seems to think Ms. Barnett can handle the work," he said thoughtfully, and there was just enough uncertainty in his voice to worry the newest member of his staff.

Carly ignored Mark completely. "You won't be sorry for giving me a chance, Mr. Clark," she said.

The older man nodded distractedly and left the conference room. Carly was right behind him, but a sudden grip on her upper arm stopped her.

"Give me a chance to explain," Mark said in a low voice.

The man had done his best to get her fired, and after she'd uprooted herself and spent most of her life savings to move to Oregon, too.

"There's no need for explanations," she told him, wrenching her arm free of his hand. "You've made your opinion of my abilities perfectly clear."

He started to say something in response, then stopped himself and, with an exasperated look on his face, stepped past Carly and disappeared into his office.

She went back to her office and continued working. By noon she'd read all the letters and selected three to answer in her column. The problems were clear-cut, in Carly's opinion, and there was no need to contact any of Madeline's experts. All a person needed, she thought to herself, was a little common sense.

She was just finishing the initial draft of her first column when there was a light rap at the door and Allison stepped in. She hadn't been at the staff meeting, and she looked harried.

"Is the column done by any chance?" she asked anxiously. "We could really use some help over in Food and Fashion."

Carly pushed the print button on the keyboard and within seconds handed Allison the hard copy of her column.

Allison scanned it, making *hmm* sounds that told Carly exactly nothing, then nodded. "This will do, I guess. I'll take you to F&F and you can help Anthony for the rest of the day. He's at his wit's end."

Carly was excited. She wouldn't be accompanying the police on a crack-house raid like Mark, but she might at least get to cover a fashion show or a bake-off. Either one would get her out of the building.

Anthony Cornelius turned out to be a slim, good-looking young man with blond hair and blue eyes. Allison introduced Carly, then disappeared.

"I've been perishing to meet you," Anthony said with a straight face. "I would have said hello at the staff meeting, but it got a bit stuffy and I couldn't *wait* to get out of there."

Carly smiled. "I know what you mean," she said as Anthony gestured toward a chair facing his immaculate desk.

"I saw the video of your pageant, you know. You were splendid."

"Thank you," Carly demurred. She was getting a little embarrassed at the reminders of past glories.

Anthony gave a showy sigh. "Well, enough chitchat. I'm just *buried* in work, and I'm desperate for your help. There's a cooking contest at the St. Regis Hotel today, while the mall is putting on the biggest fashion show *ever*. Needless to say, I can't be in two places at once."

Carly hid her delight by crossing her legs and smoothing her light woolen skirt. "What would you like me to do?"

"You may have your choice," Anthony answered, frowning as he flipped through a notebook on his desk. "Fashion or food."

Carly had already thought the choice through. "I'll take the cooking contest," she said.

"Fabulous," Anthony responded without looking up from his notes. "St. Regis Hotel, two-fifteen. I've already sent a photographer over. I'll see you back here afterward."

Eagerly Carly rose from her chair and headed for the door. "Anthony?"

He raised his eyes inquiringly.

"Thanks," Carly said, and then she hurried out.

After collecting her purse, notebook and coat, Carly set off for the St. Regis Hotel, which turned out to be within walking distance of the newspaper office. She spent several happy hours interviewing amateur chefs and tasting their special dishes, and she even managed to get them to divulge a few secret recipes.

Returning to her office late that afternoon, having forgotten lunch entirely, Carly absorbed the fact that a new batch of letters had been delivered and sat down at her computer to write up the piece on the cooking contest.

Anthony turned out to be a taskmaster, despite his gentle ways, and Carly willingly did three rewrites before he was satisfied. She was about to switch off her computer and go home for the day, taking a briefcase full of letters with her, when a message appeared unbidden on the screen.

"Hello, Carly," it read.

Frowning, Carly pushed her big reading glasses up the bridge of her nose and typed the response without thinking. "Hello."

"How about having dinner with me again tonight? I'll cook."

It was Mark.

"No, thanks," she typed resolutely. "I never dine with traitors."

"I'll explain if you'll just give me the chance."

"No."

"Will begging help?"

Carly shut off her computer, filled her briefcase with letters and left the office. She walked to the department store where Janet was employed and found that her friend was still working.

After consulting a schedule, Carly caught a bus back to the apartment building and was overjoyed when the manager, Mrs. Pickering, greeted her with the news that her car and furniture had been delivered.

"I made sure they set up the bed for you," the plump, middle-aged woman said as Carly turned the key in the lock.

The living room was filled with boxes, but the familiar couch and chair were there, as was the small television set. The dining table was in its place next to the kitchenette.

Carly set her briefcase and purse down on the small desk in the living room, then lifted the receiver on her telephone. She heard a dial tone and smiled. Her service was connected.

Feeling unaccountably domestic, Carly thanked Mrs. Pickering for her trouble and set out immediately for the parking lot. Her blue Mustang, one of the prizes she'd won as Miss United States, was in its proper slot.

Taking the keys from her purse, Carly unlocked the car, got behind the wheel and started the engine. She drove to the nearest all-night supermarket and bought a cartful of food and cleaning supplies, then came home and made herself a light supper of soup and salad in her own kitchen.

She dialed Janet's number and left a message, then called her father, knowing he'd be up watching the news.

Don Barnett picked up the telephone on the second ring and gave his customary gruff hello.

"Hi, Dad. It's Carly."

She heard pleasure in his voice. "Hello, beautiful," he said. "All settled in?"

Carly sat down in her desk chair and told her father all about her apartment and her new job.

He listened with genuine interest, and then announced that Reggie was engaged to a nurse from Topeka.

"It didn't take him long, did it?" Carly asked. She wasn't sure what she'd expected—maybe that Reggie would at least have the decency to pine for a month or two.

Her father chuckled. "Having a few second thoughts, are you?"

"No," Carly said honestly. "I just didn't think I was quite so forgettable, that's all." They talked a little longer, then ended the call with promises to stay in touch.

Carly was feeling homesick when a knock sounded at her door. She had never been very close to her mother, despite the inordinate amount of time they'd spent together, but her dad was a kindred spirit.

She put one eye to the peephole and sighed when she saw Mark standing in the hallway.

She opened the door to the length of the chain and looked out at him uncharitably. "Aren't you supposed to be participating in a crack-house raid or something?"

He flashed one of his lethal grins. "That's tomorrow night. May I come in?"

The living room was still filled with unopened boxes, and Carly was wearing her pink bathrobe. Her hair was probably a mess, too. And this man had tried to get her fired just that morning.

Despite all these things, Carly unfastened the chain and opened the door.

Mark was wearing jeans and a navy-blue football jersey with the number "39" printed on it in white, and he carried a bouquet of pink daisies.

Carly eyed them with a certain disdain, even though she secretly loved daisies. "If you think a few flowers are going to make up for the way you sandbagged me this morning—"

Mark sighed. "I was trying to get Clark to move you to another assignment."

"I'll be lucky if you didn't get me booted out instead," Carly replied. Grudgingly she took the daisies, carried them to the kitchenette and filled a glass with water.

When she turned around, she collided with Mark, and, for several excruciatingly sweet moments, her body seemed to be fused to his. She was possessed by a frightening and completely unexpected urge to bare herself to him, to feel his flesh against hers.

She shook her head as if to awaken herself from a dream and started to step around him.

He pinned her against the counter, using just his hips, and Carly felt heat rise from her stomach to her face as he took the daisies and set them aside. His voice was a low, rhythmic rumble.

"I'm not through apologizing," he said, and then he bent his head and touched Carly's lips tentatively with his own.

She gave a little whimper, because she wanted so much to spurn him and could not, and the kiss deepened. He shaped her mouth with his, and explored its depths with his tongue.

Even with Reggie, the man she'd planned to marry, Carly had been able to withstand temptation easily. With

Mark, things were startlingly different. He had over-ridden her resistance, stirring a sudden and brutal need within her with a simple kiss.

Carly found herself melting against her kitchen counter like a candle set close to a fire. She had a dizzy, disoriented feeling, as though she'd just stepped off some wild ride at a carnival.

With a little chuckle, Mark withdrew from her mouth only to nibble lightly at the length of her neck. He cupped her breast with his hand, and beneath the terry cloth her nipple pulsed to attention.

She moaned helplessly, and Mark lifted her onto the counter. Then he uncovered the breast he had aroused and began to suck gently on its peak.

Carly drew in a swift breath. She knew she should push him away, but she couldn't quite bring herself to do that. What he was doing felt entirely too good.

He traced her collarbone with kisses and then bared her other breast and took its pink tip boldly into his mouth.

Carly gave a strangled groan and let her head fall back against the cupboard door. With one of her hands, she clutched Mark's shoulder, and with the other she pressed the back of his head, holding him close to her.

She clasped his waist between her knees, as though to keep from flying away, and when she felt his hand move down over her belly, she could only tremble. When he found her secret, and began to caress it with his fingers, she started and cried out softly.

"Shh," he said against her moist, well-suckled nipple. "It's all right."

Carly, who had never given herself to a man before, sought his lips with her own, desperate for his kiss. He mastered her mouth thoroughly, then went back to her breasts. He continued his gentle plundering, and Carly's heels rose to the counter's edge in a motion of abject surrender.

Mark kissed his way down her belly and wrung a raw gasp from her throat when he took her boldly into his mouth. He gripped Carly's ankles firmly, parting her legs until she was totally vulnerable to him.

A fine sheen of perspiration covered her body as he attended her, and her hair clung, moist, to her forehead and her cheeks. She writhed and twisted, murmuring nonsense words, while Mark drove her toward sweet damnation.

She cried out at the fiery tumult shuddering through her body, surrendered shamelessly to the searing pleasure. And when it was over, tears of confusion and relief trickled down her cheeks.

Gently Mark released her ankles so that she could lower her legs. He closed her robe and kissed her damp brow softly.

"Oh, God," Carly whispered, as shame flowed into her, like water rushing into a tide pool.

Mark traced her lips with the tip of one finger, and considered her with kind eyes. "Chemistry," he said, and then, to Carly's utter amazement, he turned away.

She scooted off the counter and stood for several moments, waiting for her knees to stabilize. Mark had already reached the door, and his hand was resting on the knob.

Carly cinched the belt of her bathrobe tightly. She couldn't believe it. This man had aroused her thoroughly, had subjected her to a scorching climax—and now he was *leaving*. "Where are you going?"

The insolent brown eyes caressed her as he opened the door. "Home."

"But…"

There was a touch of sadness to his smile. "Yes," he said, answering her unspoken question, "I want you. But we're going to wait."

Carly was finally able to move. She stumbled a few steps toward him, filled with resentment because he'd made her need him so desperately and then dismissed her. "You would have been the first," she taunted him, her voice barely above a whisper.

His eyes slid over her slender body, which was still quivering with outrage and violent appeasement. "I'll be the first," he assured her, "and the last."

And then he was gone.

# CHAPTER THREE

CARLY DIDN'T SEE Mark the next day, but another message appeared on her computer screen late in the afternoon, just as she was getting ready to go home.

"Nice coverage on the food contest," it said, "but telling 'Frazzled in Farleyville' to get a divorce was truly cavalier. Who the hell do you think you are, Dr. Phil?"

Carly sighed. All her life, her view of the world had been pretty clear-cut: this was right, that was wrong; this was good, that was bad. Now she was faced with a man who could melt her bones one moment, and attack her most basic principles the next.

She poised her fingers over the keyboard for a few minutes, sinking her teeth into her lower lip, then typed, "If you don't like my column, Holbrook, do us both a favor and stop reading it."

Mark's response took only seconds to appear. "That's what I like," it jibed. "A rookie who knows how to heed the voice of experience."

"Thank you, Ann Landers," Carly typed succinctly. "Good night, and goodbye." With that, she shut down the system, gathered up her things and left the room.

Somewhat to her disappointment, there were no computer messages from Mark the next day or the one after that, and he didn't appear in any of the staff meetings, either.

Carly told herself she was relieved, but she was also concerned. She worried, at odd moments, about Mark's undercover assignment with the police. A thousand times a day she wondered how soon word would leak out if something went wrong...

A full week had passed when she encountered Mark again, at a media party in the ballroom of a downtown hotel. He was wearing jeans, a lightweight blue sweater and a tweed sports jacket while all the other men sported suits, and he still managed to look quietly terrific.

His eyes flipped over Carly's slinky pink sheath, and instantly her nipples hardened and pressed against the glimmering cloth. "Hi," he said, and the word was somehow intimate, bringing back Technicolor memories of the incident on her kitchen counter.

Carly's cheeks went as pink as her dress, and she folded her arms in self-defense. "Well," she said acidly, "I see you survived the crack raid."

Mark took hold of her elbow and gently but firmly escorted her through the crush of television, radio and newspaper people toward the lobby. "We need to talk."

Carly glared at him. "I think it would be best if we just communicated through our computers. Better yet," she added, starting to move around him, "let's not communicate at all."

He captured her arm again, pulled her back and pressed her to sit on a bench upholstered in royal-blue velvet. He took a seat beside her and looked into her eyes, frowning. "What did I do now?"

She straightened her spine, drew a deep breath and let it out again. "That has to be the most obtuse question I've ever heard," she said stiffly.

"I doubt it," Mark retorted, before she could go on to say that she didn't appreciate his criticism and his nonchalant efforts to get her fired. "Considering that you've probably been asked things like, 'How do you walk without your tiara falling off?' and 'What contribution do you think tap dancing will make to world peace?'"

Carly leaned close to him and spoke through her teeth. "I'd appreciate it, Mr. Hotshot Pulitzer Prize Winner, if you would stop making comments about my title!"

His wonderful, damnable brown eyes twinkled. "Okay," he conceded, "just answer one question, and I will."

Carly was cautious. "Fair enough," she allowed huffily. "Ask away."

"What was your talent?"

"I beg your pardon?"

"In the pageant. When the other semifinalists sang and danced and played stirring classical pieces on the piano, what did you do?"

Carly swallowed and averted her eyes.

Mark prompted her with a little nudge.

"I twirled a baton," she blurted out in a furious whisper. "Are you satisfied?"

"No," Mark replied, and even though he wasn't smiling, his amusement showed in every line of his body. "But I'll let the subject drop for the time being."

"Good," Carly growled, and sprang off the bench.

Mark pulled her back down again. "Lighten up, Barnett," he said. "If you can't take a little ribbing, you won't last five minutes in this business."

Carly's face was flushed, and she yearned to get out

into the cool, crisp May evening. "So now I'm thin-skinned, as well as incompetent."

He chuckled and shook his head. "I never said you were incompetent, but you're damned cranky. I can't figure out which you need more—a good spanking or a very thorough session on a mattress."

That was it. Carly had reached the limit of her patience. She jumped up off the bench again and stormed back into the party.

She would have preferred to walk out of that hotel, get into her car and drive home. But she knew contacts were vital, and she wanted to meet as many people as she could.

She stayed an hour and a half, avoiding Mark, passing out and collecting business cards. Then she put on her shiny white blazer and headed for the parking lot.

She had unlocked the door and slid behind the wheel before she realized that Mark was sitting in the passenger seat. Surprise and fury made her gasp. "How did you get in here? This car was locked!"

He grinned at her. "I learned the trick from Iggy De-Fazzio, a kid I interviewed when I was doing a piece on street gangs."

Carly knew it wouldn't do any good to demand that he leave her car, and she wasn't strong enough to throw him out bodily. She started the ignition and glared at him. "Where to, Mr. Holbrook?"

"My place," he said with absolute confidence that he'd get his way.

"Has anybody ever told you that you are totally obnoxious?"

"No, but my teenage niece once said I was totally awesome, and I think she meant it as a compliment."

Carly pulled out into the light evening traffic. "You must have paid her."

Mark spoke pleasantly. "Pull over."

"Why?"

"Because I can't grovel and give directions at the same time," he replied.

Wondering why she was obeying when this man had done nothing but insult her since the moment she'd met him, Carly nonetheless stopped the car and surrendered the wheel to Mark. Soon they were speeding down the freeway.

"So," he began again brightly, "when you were twirling your baton, were the ends on fire?"

Carly reached out and slugged him in the arm, but a grin tugged at the corners of her mouth. "Is this your idea of groveling?"

He laughed. "Meet anybody interesting at the party?"

"Two or three TV newscasters and a talk-show host," she answered, watching him out of the corner of her eye. "I'm having dinner with Jim Benson from Channel 37 Friday night."

Mark's jaw tightened for just a moment, and he tossed a sidelong glance in her direction. "He's a lech," he said.

"If he gets out of line," she replied immediately, "I'll just hit him with my baton."

Mark cleared his throat and steered the car onto an exit. "Carly—"

"What?"

"We got off on the wrong foot, you and I."

Carly folded her arms. "Whose fault was that?"

He let out a ragged sigh as they came to a stop at a

red light. "For purposes of expediency," he muttered, "I'll admit that it was mine. Partly."

"That's generous of you."

The light changed, and they drove up a steep hill. "Damn it," Mark bit out, "will you just let me finish?"

Carly spread her hands in a motion of generosity. "Go ahead."

He turned onto a long, curving driveway, the head-lights sweeping over evergreen trees, giant ferns and assorted brush. "I have a lot of respect for you as a person."

"I haven't heard that one since the night of the junior prom when Johnny Shupe wanted to put his hand down the front of my dress."

The car jerked to a stop beside a compact pickup truck, and Mark shut off the ignition and the headlights. "I get it," he snapped. "You're mad because I only took you part of the way!"

Carly wanted to slap him for bringing up the kitchen-counter incident, even indirectly, but she restrained herself. "Why, you arrogant bastard!" she breathed instead, clenching her fists. "How dare you talk to me like that?"

He got out of the car, slammed the door and came around to her side. Before she thought to push down the lock, he was bending over her, his lips only a whisper away from hers. "This is how," he replied, and then he kissed her.

At first, Carly resisted, stiffening her body and press-ing her lips together in a tight line. But soon Mark's per-suasive tongue conquered her, and she whimpered with unwilling pleasure, sagging limply against the back of the car seat.

Presently he took her arm and ushered her out of the

car and into the house. By the faint glow of the porch light, Carly could see that it was an old-fashioned brick cottage, with wooden shutters on the windows and a fanlight over the door.

In the small entryway he kissed her again, and the sensations the contact stirred in her pushed all thoughts of their differences to the back of her mind.

"It looks like there's one thing we're going to have to get out of our way before we can make sense of what's happening to us, Carly," he said when the kiss was over. He smoothed away her blazer with gentle hands.

Carly, who had been an avowed ice maiden in high school and college, was suddenly as pliant and willing as a sixteenth-century tavern wench. Her body seemed to be waging some kind of heated rebellion against the resolutions of her mind.

She knew she should get into her car and go home, but she couldn't make herself walk away from Mark.

He led her into a pleasantly cluttered living room where lamps were burning and seated her on the couch. Carly watched as he lit a fire on the hearth, then shifted her gaze to a desk facing a bank of windows. A computer screen glowed companionably among stacks of books and papers.

"I do a lot of my work at home," Mark explained, dusting his hands together as he rose from the hearth. "You can't see it now, of course, but there's a great view of the river from those windows."

Carly was still trying to shore up her sagging defenses, but the attempt was largely hopeless. Mark's kisses had left her feeling as though she'd been drugged.

He left the room briefly and returned with a bottle of

wine and a couple of glasses. Taking a seat beside Carly on the cushiony sofa, he opened the bottle and poured.

Carly figured her chances of coming out of this with her virginity intact were slim—and getting slimmer. The crazy thing was, she didn't want to leave.

Mark handed her a glass, and she took a cautious sip.

"I'm really very bright, you know," she said, feeling defensive. "I got terrific grades in college."

He smiled, set his goblet on the coffee table and swung her legs up onto his lap. "Umm-hmm," he said, slipping off her high-heeled shoes one by one and tossing them away.

Some last vestige of pride made Carly stiffen. "You don't believe me!"

Mark ran a soothing hand over her right foot and ankle, and against her will she relaxed again. "I'd be a fool if I didn't," he answered quietly. "There were over a hundred applicants for your job at the *Times,* and all of them were qualified."

Carly was pleased. "Really?"

Mark took advantage of the sexy slit on the side of her pink dress to caress the back of her knee. "Really," he said.

She put her glass aside, feeling as though she'd already consumed a reservoir full of alcohol. On the hearth the fire crackled and snapped. "I really should go straight home," she said.

"I know," Mark agreed.

"I mean, it's possible that I don't even *like* you."

"I know that, too," he responded with a grin.

"But we're going to make love, aren't we?"

Mark nodded. "Yes," he said, and then he stood and drew Carly off the couch and into a gentle embrace. He kissed her lightly on the tip of the nose. "If you really want to go home," he said, "it's okay."

Carly let her forehead rest against his chest and slid her arms around his waist. "God help me," she whispered, "I want to stay."

He put a finger under her chin and tilted her head back so he could look into her eyes. He moved his lips as though he meant to speak, but in the end he kissed her instead.

Again, she had the sensation of being swept into some kind of vortex, where none of the usual rules applied. When Mark lifted her into his arms, she laid her head against his shoulder.

He carried her up a set of stairs, along a hallway and into a room so large that Carly was sure it must run the entire length of the house. She noticed a fireplace, the shadowy shapes of chairs and, finally, the huge bed.

Made of dark wood, it stood on a U-shaped ledge, dominating the room. It was a place where a knight might have deflowered his lady, and Carly was filled with a sense of rightness, as well as desire.

Mark carried her up three steps and set her on her feet. She stood still as he unfastened the back of her dress and then lowered it to her hips.

The moonlight flowing in through the long windows that lined the opposite wall gave Carly's skin the translucent, pearly glow of white opals, and she felt beautiful as Mark stepped back to admire her. His eyes seemed to smolder in the dim light of the room.

After a while, he bent to kiss the pulse point at the base of her throat, and Carly trembled. She felt as though she'd been created for this moment, as though she'd worked toward it through not just one lifetime, but a thousand.

"Mark," she whispered, and that one word held all her confusion, all her wanting.

In slow, methodical motions, he took away her slip and bra and panty hose and laid her, naked, on his bed. "So beautiful," he said hoarsely, and Carly raised her hands over her head in unconscious surrender as she watched him shed his clothes in the shadows.

"I've never—"

He interrupted her with a soft, reassuring kiss. "I know, sweetheart," he said. "I'll be as gentle as I can." And then he lay on his side on the mattress, caressing her breast with his strong hand, toying with the straining nipple, tracing the lines of her waist and hip.

"Mark," Carly moaned. He had kindled a blaze within her that night in her apartment, and now it burned so hot that it threatened to consume her.

He bent to suckle at her breast, and she whimpered in welcome, entangling her fingers in his rich, glossy hair. He allowed her to fondle him for a time, then caught both her wrists in his hand and lifted them above her head again, making her deliciously vulnerable.

With his other hand he made a light, fiery circle on her belly, sweeping lower with each pass until he found the core of her womanhood.

Carly's flesh pulsed against his palm as he made slow, steady rounds, and she felt herself grow moist in response. She arched her neck, her breath coming in shallow gasps, and instinctively spread her legs.

And still Mark suckled her breasts, first one and then the other. Her nipples were taut and wet from his tongue, and she was sure she would die if he didn't satisfy her.

She began to plead, and he left her breasts to position himself between her thighs. As he had once before, he clasped her ankles and set her feet wide of her body, holding them firmly in place.

By the time he burrowed through to take her into his mouth, the rest of her body was as moist as her hard, jutting nipples. She pressed her heels deep into the mattress and gave a lusty cry as he feasted on her womanhood, and her hips writhed in concert with the teasing parries of his tongue that came later.

She flung her hands wildly, first clawing at the bedspread, then gripping his shoulders, then delving into his hair. The short tendrils around her face were dewy, clinging to her forehead and her cheeks as she strained for the relief only nature could provide.

Passion racked her violently, and her body quivered as she thrust it upward to meet the teasing strokes of Mark's tongue. "Finish me," she pleaded without breath. "Oh—Mark—*finish me!*"

He complied fiercely and wrung a sobbing shout from her, cupping his hands under her bottom, holding her high, supporting her until the storm raging inside her body subsided. When the tempest had ceased, he lowered her gently to the mattress, where she lay trembling and filled with wonder.

"Mark," she wept.

Slowly he kissed her moist forehead, her eyelids, her cheeks. He drank from her breasts again, sleepily at first, and then with growing thirst. When he mounted Carly, parting her legs first with a motion of one knee, she welcomed him, though she knew he was about to change her forever.

She moved her hands up and down his muscle-corded back while he drew at her nipple and, finally, she could wait no more.

She clasped his buttocks in her hands and pressed him to her, and he submitted with a groan.

His entry was slow and careful, and every inch he gave Carly only made her want more. There was a brief, tearing pain as he passed the barrier that had sealed her depths to all but him, but in some strange way it made the pleasure keener.

Moaning when he was inside her to the hilt of his manhood, Mark dragged the pillows down from the head of the bed and stuffed them under her so that she was raised to him, in perfect alignment for pleasure.

His second thrust was gentle, but when she urged him with soft, fiery words, he delved deeper.

Carly encircled his waist with her legs and clenched as if to crush him, and the coupling became a tender battle. Near the end, when they were both wild with need and trembling with exhaustion, he caught hold of her hands and thrust them high above her head. While she cursed him with words of love, he held himself still inside her for a long moment, then made a final lunge.

Carly flung back her head and gave a low, guttural wail as her body spasmed around him. He answered with a shout of amazed ecstasy and filled her with his warmth.

They lay like stone for a long time, neither able to speak or move, and then Mark got up from the bed and lifted a still-befuddled Carly into his arms. He carried her into the bathroom and set her, dazed, on the edge of a deep marble tub.

His body was lean and agile as he adjusted the spigots and fetched two enormous white towels from a shelf. He set them close at hand, then eased Carly gently into the water. When it reached a certain depth, he flipped a switch, and powerful jets made the warmth swirl and bubble around her.

Mark turned off the faucets, then got into the tub behind Carly, his powerful legs making a boundary for hers, his arms resting lightly around her waist. He bent to kiss her bare shoulder.

She tilted her head back and looked up at him, only then able to speak. "If I'd known it felt that good, I'd have been promiscuous," she said.

Mark laughed and then nibbled at her nape. "Me, too," he said, and that made Carly twist to look up at him, a broad smile on her face.

"Come on," she said. "You're not going to tell me that was your first time. Even I'm not *that* naive."

He shook his head, and his wonderful eyes were sparkling at her naïveté. "No, babe—you were the only virgin in attendance. But I can honestly say I've never felt exactly that way before."

Carly settled deeper into the water, leaning back against his hairy chest. "I bet you say that to everybody."

He chuckled and moved his lips against the back of her head. "Wrong again," he replied, and then he dipped a hand into the swirling, soothing water and bathed Carly's breasts, one by one.

It was another beginning.

Soon he was caressing her, and she was surrendering, wanting to melt into him again.

When she had to confront him with her need or perish from it, she shifted so that she was facing him and kneeling between his legs.

"You like being in charge, don't you?" she crooned, taking a fresh bar of soap from a brass dish, dipping it into the water, turning it between her hands until they were slick with suds.

Mark leaned back, resting his head on the edge of the tub, and grinned insolently. "You didn't seem to mind it a little while ago. In fact, my guess would be that it beat twirling a flaming baton all to hell."

Slowly, sensuously, she began to lather his broad chest, making soapy swirls in the down that covered it, teasing his nipples with a mischievous fingertip. "There must be some symbolism in that," she conceded huskily. "But I don't quite see it."

He tilted his head even farther back and closed his eyes with an animal sigh of contentment, and it struck Carly that even surrender required a kind of confidence.

"Think, Barnett," he teased. "Think."

Carly didn't want to think. She wanted to bathe this man, and then turn him inside out, just as he'd done to her. And because of the things he'd taught her, she had a pretty good idea how to go about it.

She took her time washing him, and he submitted, but then he claimed the soap and everything was turned around. Soon every inch of Carly was scrubbed to a delicate ivory pink, and she was limp as the cloth Mark had used to cleanse her.

He got out of the tub, lifting her after him, and flipped off the jets under the water. Then he pulled the plug and wrapped one of the huge towels around Carly like a sling, using it to draw her close to him.

She felt his staff rising hard and insistent between them.

"Oh, Mark," she whispered sleepily, "I can't—not again."

"That's what you think," he replied, his lips against her forehead. And he took her back to his bed, where he dried her and laid her out on the sheet like a delicacy to be enjoyed at leisure.

He joined her beneath the covers, knelt between her legs so she couldn't close them to him, and slid his hands under her bottom to lift her to his mouth.

"I mean it," she whimpered as he placed her legs over his shoulders. "I can't—"

He disciplined her with a few flicks of his tongue, and she moaned as heat surged through her tired body, giving it new life.

Mark chuckled against her hardening flesh. "That's what I thought," he said, and he held her firmly in place while she rode helplessly on his lips, her head twisting from side to side in delirium.

He was ruthless. Carly was drenched with perspiration within minutes, and she locked her heels behind his head when he brought her to climax.

After that she begged him to take her and then let her sleep, but he wouldn't. He put her in a new position and made her perform again, and he granted her no quarter until the last shuddering tremor had been drawn from her and her cries of pleasure had died away in the darkness.

Finally she gathered the strength to take revenge. She

fell to him, like a starving woman would fall to food, and began to consume him.

At last, Carly had found the way to prevail in the age-old war of lovers, and she was no more merciful to Mark than he had been to her. He groaned like a man in fever, and the sound aroused Carly as much as his caresses and kisses had.

When he could bear no more, he lifted her head and held it from him, gasping as he struggled to catch his breath. Then, ever so gently, he pressed Carly back onto the mattress and took her in a long, slow stroke.

Because his pleasure had excited her so much, she immediately began to convulse, the lower part of her body buckling wildly as he made love to her. Through a sleepy haze she heard him rasp her name, and she felt him stiffen upon her in final release. Then they both were still, and the night rolled in like folds of black velvet and claimed them.

In the morning Carly awakened to the sound of a man whistling. Her aquamarine eyes flew open in alarmed chagrin as she remembered where she was and how she'd behaved in Mark Holbrook's arms.

She sank her teeth into her lower lip. It was morning, and she was going to have to go home in her slinky pink evening dress.

Just then Mark came out of the bathroom. He was wearing a towel around his hips and there was a toothbrush jutting out of his mouth. He gave Carly a foamy grin, opened a drawer, took out a striped pajama top and tossed it to her.

She scrambled into it, using the blankets to hide behind, and he laughed and went back into the bathroom.

Carly needed a shower, but she wasn't about to pass

Mark to get one. Knowing a house that large must have at least one more bath, she hurried out of the room. She found what she sought at the opposite end of the hall and, after locking the door, stepped hastily under a spray of hot water.

When she was clean, she put on the bra, panty hose and slip she'd worn the night before. She was about to shimmy into the dress when a knock sounded at the door.

"It's early, Carly," Mark said cheerfully, as though this were a perfectly ordinary morning. "I'll go over to your apartment and get your things if you'll give me the key."

She pressed her cheek to the door panel, embarrassed to be sending a man for such personal items as clothes and underwear and makeup, but she named off the things she wanted. When she was sure he was gone, she stepped out into the hallway, only to find Mark leaning against the opposite wall, grinning at her.

He moved his gaze slowly, possessively, over her figure. "Like I said," he told her in a voice that was as effective as a kiss or a caress, "it's early."

## CHAPTER FOUR

CARLY DODGED BACK into the bathroom and slammed the door, and Mark responded with a laugh.

"Regrets?" he asked.

"Yes!" Carly shouted back. She shoved both hands through her hair. "Go away and leave me alone."

"Cranky," he observed in a resigned tone. "Maybe I should have tried the spanking."

Carly turned the lock, then went to the sink and started the water running full blast. She hummed loudly to let Mark know she wasn't paying any attention to anything he was saying—if he was saying anything.

Fifteen minutes had passed before she dared peer into the hallway again.

Mark was gone then—the house seemed to echo with his absence—and Carly put his pajama top on over her underthings and stepped out of the bathroom.

On her way to the kitchen, where she hoped to find coffee perking, Carly passed through the living room. Once again the computer caught her eye. Since Mark wasn't around to see, she ventured over to the desk, sat down in the chair and squinted at the words on the screen.

Excitement brought her to the edge of the chair as she read backward through what was apparently a stage play. The story centered around the painful demise of a marriage, and it was so gripping that Carly forgot her quest for coffee, rummaged through her purse for her glasses and read on.

She didn't stop until she heard a car door slam in the driveway. The sound brought her back to the present with a jerk, and it suddenly occurred to her that Mark might not want her reading his play. Her heart beating double time, she pressed her finger to the "Page Down" key and held it there until the original material was back on the screen.

She was in the kitchen, pouring coffee into a mug, when Mark came in carrying her garment bag and beauty case. He gave her a curious look, and she had the uncomfortable feeling that he was picking up on her guilt.

*It's a good thing you're not a spy, Barnett,* she thought, reaching out for the things Mark had brought her. "Thanks."

He gave her a light kiss on the forehead. "You're welcome," he answered, and the words had a teasing quality to them.

Carly took another sip of her coffee, then set it aside. If she was going to be at work on time, she'd have to get a move on. "How long have you been up?" she asked idly, remembering that Mark's computer had been on when they came in the night before.

He'd poured coffee for himself, and he grinned at her over the rim of the mug. "A couple of hours. I do some of my best writing before the birds get up."

Carly hesitated in the kitchen doorway. She felt strangely at home in Mark's house and his pajama top, and that was disturbing. "Your piece on the crack-house raid was good," she conceded. The article had had top billing in the Sunday edition, and Carly had marveled as she'd read it.

Mark opened the refrigerator and took out eggs, bacon and a carton of orange juice. "Thanks, Barnett," he said briskly. "I'd love to stand here listening to praise all day, but I've got things to do, and so do you."

Carly felt rebuffed. Until he'd spoken, there had been a certain cautious, morning-after closeness between them. Now there was an impassible force field.

Carly turned around and headed back toward the bathroom.

When she came out, ready to leave for the newspaper office, Mark was at his desk. The play was gone from the screen, replaced by some kind of colorful graph, and he was leaning back in his chair, talking on the telephone.

He dismissed Carly with a wave of his hand—the way he might have done the paperboy or a meter reader—and she was stung. *Apparently,* she thought glumly, *I've served my purpose.*

She gathered up her purse and the clothes she'd worn the night before and went out to get into her car. Her spirits lifted a little when she found a single yellow rosebud lying on the seat.

At the office, another mailbag full of letters awaited her, as well as three frantic messages from Janet.

Sipping the cup of coffee Emmeline had brought to her, Carly dialed her friend's work number. A secretary put her right through.

"You didn't come home last night!" Janet said, dispensing with the usual "hello."

Carly smiled, even though there was a heavy place in

her heart because she'd given herself to the wrong man. "Are you moonlighting for the FBI these days, or what?"

Janet let out a sigh. "I was just worried, that's all. I mean, you're new in town, and there are some real creeps out there—"

"I'm fine, Janet," Carly insisted moderately, getting out her glasses with one hand and slipping them onto her face. Judging by the bulges in the mailbag sitting on her desk, it was going to be a long day.

"You were with Mark Holbrook!" Janet cried, obviously excited at having solved the mystery.

Carly was annoyed. "Janet—"

"I don't mind telling you, I'm impressed."

"Good. I'd hate to think I wasn't living up to my image," Carly said a little stiffly.

Janet made Carly promise that they'd go out for pizza and salad that night after work, then rang off.

Carly immediately set herself to the task of reading and sorting her mail, and her brow crumpled into a frown as she scanned letter after letter berating her for telling "Frazzled in Farleyville" to get a divorce. It was beginning to seem that the public heartily agreed with Mark's assessment of her advice.

She was still reading and disconsolately munching on Cheeze Crunchies from the vending machine in the lounge, when Mark popped into her office at one forty-five that afternoon.

By then she was really feeling cranky. She'd been writing her column for less than two weeks, and everybody in Portland hated her. "What do you want?" she snapped.

Mark grinned in a way that reawakened some of the perturbing feelings she'd had the night before, when they'd somehow gotten past their many differences and visited a new part of the universe. "I came to see if you'd like to go out for lunch, then maybe take in a matinee or something."

Carly took a sip of diet cola and set the can down with a solid thump. "Some of us can't come and go as we please," she replied, glaring at him through the big lenses of her reading glasses. "*Or* take off to a movie in the middle of a workday."

He drew up a chair and sat down with a philosophical sigh. "My older sister is like you. When she gets overtired, and doesn't eat right—" he paused and nodded toward the Cheeze Crunchies "—her blood sugar drops and she takes on the personality of a third-world leader. It's not a pretty sight."

Carly took off her glasses, tossed them aside and rubbed her eyes wearily. "Don't you have to work or something?"

"I'm between assignments," he answered.

The intercom on Carly's desk buzzed, and she pushed the button and said, "Yes?"

"There's a lady psychologist on the phone," Emmeline announced, "and she's hopping mad because you told 'Frazzled in Farleyville'—"

"To get a divorce," Carly finished with a sigh. Her head was pounding. "Put her on," she added with resignation, pushing another button so Mark wouldn't be able to overhear the psychologist's side of the conversation.

He leaned forward to help himself to a Cheeze Crunchy. "It's gonna be a bloodbath," he said, and settled back to watch.

Carly narrowed her eyes at him, then spun her chair around so that her back was turned.

The psychologist introduced herself and proceeded to tell Carly off. "In essence, *Miss* Barnett," the woman finished, "you should be demoted to a position where you can't possibly do any more harm!"

Calling on all her poise-under-pressure training, Carly replied that she was sorry if she'd offended any-one and hung up. When she turned her chair around again, Mark was gone, and the discovery gave her an empty feeling.

Half an hour later she was called into the managing editor's office.

Fully expecting to be fired, to have to go home to her dad in utter disgrace, Carly obeyed the summons, never letting any of her insecurities show.

"We've had some complaints about the way you're handling the advice column," Mr. Clark said when Carly was seated in a chair facing his imposing desk. His ex-pression was sober, and she resisted an urge to bite her lower lip.

She waited in dignified silence.

A smile broke across the editor's face. "And that's good," he boomed. "Means they're reading you. You're shaking them up, jolting them out of their complacency. Which is not to say you couldn't be a little more care-ful."

Carly's relief was overwhelming. "I'll be sure to check with an expert on the trickier questions," she promised.

Mr. Clark was sitting back in his chair now, his fin-gers steepled under his chin. Carly was clearly not ex-cused from the hot seat. "Liked your work on the cooking contest," he said. "How would you feel about taking on more varied assignments like that one? We're thinking of picking up one of the syndicated advice columns instead of running our own, you see."

Carly could barely keep from leaping over the desk and kissing Mr. Clark. "I would enjoy that," she said moderately.

"Good, good," responded the editor as his phone buzzed. As he reached for the receiver, he mused, more to himself than to Carly, "Maybe we'll put you on the fathers' rights piece with Holbrook. Get a woman's side of it."

Carly nodded. She wasn't sure how she felt about working with Mark—God knew, he was a genius and she'd kill for the opportunity to learn from him, but he was also the man who had taken her to bed the night before and calmly turned her inside out. If she did get to share the assignment, she would just have to make damn sure she kept her mind on business.

Mr. Clark dismissed her with a kindly gesture, and she rushed out of his office, feeling better than she had all day. When she returned to her desk, she found a turkey sandwich from the corner deli waiting for her, along with a note. "Eat this that others might live. Mark."

Carly couldn't help smiling. She sat down at her desk and made short work of the sandwich, then spent the rest of the afternoon conferring with experts over the telephone. She was determined that that week's column wouldn't generate a storm of protest like the first one had.

If Mark was still in the building, he didn't come near Carly again, and she was both relieved and disappointed as she caught the elevator to the parking garage at five-thirty. She scolded herself that she mustn't fall into the age-old female trap of expecting too much just because she and Mark had been to bed together. He had probably put a check by her name in his book of conquests and moved on to the next prospect.

The thought made Carly sad, and she was feeling moody again when she got home. There, she dumped her garment bag, kicked off her shoes and exchanged the clothes she'd worn to the office for a pair of stretchy exercise pants and a T-shirt. What she needed, she decided, was a good workout.

After fetching a clean towel from the linen closet, she went downstairs to the building's small but well-equipped gym and began going through the program she'd outlined for herself. When she was finished, she felt better.

She encountered Janet in the upstairs hallway. "You're the first woman I've ever known who looked good in sweat," her friend commented with a shake of her head.

Carly blushed, thinking of the last time she'd been worked up enough to perspire, and opened the door of her apartment. "Gee, thanks," she said with a grin. "And here I thought I didn't have anything going for me."

Janet laughed and set her briefcase and purse down on Carly's table. "Right. You were Miss United States and now you're dating a famous journalist. You're a pathetic case if I've ever seen one."

Opening her refrigerator door, Carly took out two diet colas and set them on the table. "I'm not 'dating' Mark Holbrook," she said.

Janet's lips twitched a little; she was obviously fighting back a smile. "I can't understand why you're so touchy about this, Carly—most women would shout it from the rooftops. After all, the guy is merely sensational."

Carly filled two glasses with ice and brought them to the table, sitting down with a sigh. She shrugged, averting her eyes. "He has this affectionate contempt for me, Janet—I know he sees me as a brainless little beauty queen in way over her head—"

"But," Janet pointed out moderately, "you spent the night with him."

"I don't know how to explain that," Carly said with a weary sigh.

"You don't have to explain it," Janet reasoned. "You're a grown woman, after all."

Carly bit her lower lip for a moment. Janet was right, of course, but she still felt a need to confide her feelings to someone, and she couldn't think of a better candidate than her best friend. "I never had any trouble turning guys down when they came on to me," she said quietly. "Even with Reggie—well, it was just easy to say no. But all Mark has to do is kiss me and I turn into this— this red-hot mama."

Janet let out a peal of laughter. "*Red-hot mama?* God, I didn't think anybody said that anymore!"

Carly flushed. "Janet, this is serious!" she hissed. "That man can try to get me fired, he can make remarks about my title, he can as much as tell me I'm incompetent. And then he just turns right around and takes me to bed! Doesn't that make me a woman-who-loves-too-much or something?"

Her friend was kindly amused. "Maybe it just makes you a woman-who-loves, period. Give yourself a break, Carly, and stop analyzing everything to death." She paused and glanced at her watch. "Are we still going out for salad and pizza?"

Carly nodded. "It'll have to be an early night, though. I've got a lot of work to do."

With that, Janet went to her own apartment to change clothes and Carly headed for the shower. Twenty minutes later she was dressed in gray cords and a soft matching sweater, and the doorbell rang. Tossing her makeup bag into a drawer, she made her way through the living room and pulled open the door, expecting to see Janet standing in the hall.

Instead she found Mark, and he didn't look well.

"What's the matter?" Carly asked, stepping back to admit him.

He moved his eyes over her with weary admiration. "It's a personal problem—nothing you need to worry about."

Carly closed the door. "Then why are you here?"

He shoved one hand through his rumpled brown hair. "I'm not sure. I guess—after last night—I thought I could talk to you."

She came to stand in front of him and looked up into his eyes. "You were right—you can."

"You're on your way out." There was no note of accusation in his voice, only a quiet statement of fact.

"Janet and I are going to a pizza place, that's all. You're welcome to come along."

He grinned in a way that tugged at her heart. "Thanks, Barnett, but I don't think I'm up to snappy repartee."

She laid her hands on his upper arms. "Talk to me," she said softly.

He sighed again. "My mother called me an hour ago.

Jeanine—that's my ex-wife—was in an accident on the freeway. Nathan was with her, and he's in the hospital with a broken arm."

Carly's eyes went wide with sympathy and alarm. "Then you've got to go down there."

"It isn't that simple."

"Why not? Nathan is your son—he's a little boy, and he's hurt—"

"And his mother has a restraining order against me."

Carly was quiet for a long time, absorbing the implications. "You were violent?" she asked in a whisper, and even as she uttered the words, she couldn't imagine Mark doing any of the things that usually prompted ex-wives to take legal measures to protect themselves and their children.

"No, but I was angry—damn angry. And that was all Jeanine needed. She went to a lawyer and told him I was dangerous."

Carly let her forehead rest against Mark's shoulder for a moment, breathing in concert with him, feeling his frustration and pain in a strange, fundamental way. Finally she looked up at him with tears in her eyes. "Do you want me to go with you?"

He smiled, pulled her close and kissed the top of her head. "No," he said. "I just need to know you're thinking about me, and that you'll be here when I get back."

"Mark—"

He tilted her chin up and gave her a soft, hungry kiss, and all the reactions Carly feared so much immediately set in. If he'd wanted her then and there, she would have given herself to him, and the idea frightened her.

"I'll call," he said.

Carly only nodded and followed Mark to the door,

watching him as he left. Janet came in almost unob-
served, dressed in designer jeans and a sweatshirt.

"Looks serious," she remarked.

"Let's go get some pizza," Carly replied.

Although Carly tried to have fun with her friend,
she was essentially preoccupied. She and Janet came
home early.

When she arrived at work the next morning, she
stopped by Mark's office, being as subtle as possible,
and peeked in. The place was spacious and cluttered,
and it smelled of Mark's cologne. And it was empty.

She stepped out, closing the door and wondering how
this man had made her care so deeply in such a short
time. She had too much of herself invested in Mark,
and she had no idea how to back away.

There were flowers waiting on her desk—pink daisies exploding from a pretty cut-glass vase. *It's too soon
to talk about love,* the card read, *but I think I'm seriously in like. With you, of course. I left the key to my
front door with your assistant, just in case you might
want to be there when I get home. Soon, Mark.*

A rush of feeling swept over Carly. She put it down
to "like" and switched on her computer.

When Emmeline came in with the customary cup
of coffee, she brought the key to Mark's house. To her
credit, the woman neither asked questions nor made a
comment.

Carly spent a busy day reading letters and talking
with various authorities, and when her deadline arrived,
she had a solid column to turn in.

She went to Mark's that first night, which was silly
because she knew he wouldn't be there. She walked

through the house, checking to make sure all the doors and windows were locked, then sat down at his desk.

One of the drawers was sticking out, and Carly tried to close it.

It promptly jammed, and she reached inside.

She hadn't actually meant to snoop. Still, when Carly drew her hand out of the drawer, there was a manuscript in it.

Carly realized she'd found a printout of the play he'd been writing, and she couldn't resist flipping to the opening scene. She would just read a line or two, then put it away.

Moments later, however, Carly was in another dimension. She wasn't aware of time passing, or of the dying light at the windows, or the view of the Columbia River. She read, filled with awe and a singular heartbreak, to the very last page.

Tears brimmed in her eyes as she put the play back in its drawer, and just then the phone rang. Feeling like a prowler, but nonetheless a responsible one, Carly groped for the receiver and sniffled, "Hello?"

"Hi." The voice was Mark's.

Carly gave a guilty start and dashed away her tears with the back of one hand, trying to cover her discomfort with a joke. "Your burglar alarm doesn't work," she said.

He chuckled. "I didn't turn it on. I'm glad you're there, Carly—it's almost as good as having you here would be."

"How's Nathan? Did you get to see him?"

"One question at a time, Scoop. Nathan's going to be fine—I think I'm in worse shape than he is."

"And Jeanine?"

Mark hesitated for a long moment. "She's as difficult as ever."

"But she wasn't hurt in the accident?"

"No."

"What about the restraining order? Was there any trouble?"

"I called my parents' attorney when I got here and had it lifted. I'll tell you all about it when I get home tomorrow night."

Carly felt a wifely warmth at the idea. "Maybe I'll stop by after work, then," she said.

Mark's voice was a slow, sensual caress. "Bring your toothbrush."

She squirmed slightly and let the remark pass. "Thanks for the flowers—they're lovely."

They talked for a few minutes longer, then said reluctant good-nights.

During the drive back to her apartment, Carly thought about Mark's play. His talent was truly formidable, and his words had moved her on a very deep level. She should have told him that she'd read his work, she knew, but the truth was she hadn't dared. The play was about a man and a woman and a child, and in it the dissolution of the family had been portrayed with painful clarity.

It didn't take a genius to figure out that Mark had written about his own divorce, or that he felt a tragic sense of loss where his young son was concerned.

The subject of Mark's previous marriage seemed to be sacred ground; Carly didn't know how to broach it. She felt almost as though she'd read his diary, tapped his phone or opened his mail. And yet there was a certain exaltation in her, too, because the play had such a poignant beauty.

Arriving at her own building, Carly carried in her purse, briefcase and mail. There was a wedding invitation from Reggie and the nurse from Topeka, and she rolled her eyes as she tossed it onto the desk with the other things.

After changing her clothes, Carly again went to the small gym to work out. When she returned, she showered, made herself a light supper and started reading the briefcase full of misery she'd brought home from the office.

Although she tried, Carly was unable to keep her mind on the letters from readers of her column. Her thoughts kept straying to Mark, and his play. She wanted so much to tell him she'd read it, and that it was wonderful.

But she was afraid.

The next day was hectic, as usual, and Carly didn't have time to think about anything but her work. At six-thirty she got into her car, where a small suitcase was waiting, and drove to Mark's place, stopping off at a supermarket on the way.

When she reached his isolated house, there was no sign of his car, though the compact pickup was parked in its usual place.

She unlocked the door and went inside. "Mark?" she called out in a hopeful tone of voice, but there was no answer.

Carly carried her luggage into Mark's room, changed into jeans and a T-shirt, then went back to the living room. With considerable effort, she managed to start

a blaze in the fireplace, and she put some music on—
Mozart.

She was in the kitchen, chopping vegetables for a
salad, when she saw his car swing into the driveway.
Her heart leaped with an excitement it wasn't entitled
to, and she hurried out to meet him.

He needed a shave, and he looked haggard, but his
grin transformed his face. "Hi, Scoop," he said hoarsely
when she slipped her arms around his waist.

Carly reached up to touch his cheek. "Aren't you
going to kiss me?"

He laughed and gathered her against him, and when
his mouth touched Carly's, it was as though someone
had draped a wet towel over an electric fence. The
charge was lethal.

She was breathless when he finally released her. "I
hope you didn't eat on the plane," she managed to say,
"because I want to cook for you tonight."

Mark reached into the car for his suitcase and assumed a look of comical surprise. "You cook, as well as
twirl the baton and tell total strangers to get divorced?"
he teased. "My God, Barnett—is there no end to your
talents?"

She gave him a saucy look over one shoulder as she
led the way toward the gaping front door. "I've got talents galore."

He laughed and followed her into the house.

While Carly broiled the steaks she'd bought, and
baked the potatoes, Mark showered and changed
clothes. When he joined her on the little patio off the
kitchen, he was wearing jeans and a football jersey, and
his rich brown hair was still damp.

"I could get used to this," he said, standing behind

Carly and slipping his arms around her waist. His lips were warm and tantalizing against her neck.

Carly pretended to bristle, though the fact was that she wouldn't have protested if Mark had hauled her off to bed right then. "You're a chauvinist, Mr. Holbrook."

"I know," he said, lifting her hair to kiss her lightly on the nape.

She was trembling when she turned in his arms and gazed into his eyes. She had to tell him she'd read his play now, while things were so good between them. "Mark, I—"

He silenced her by laying an index finger to her lips. "Later," he told her. "Whatever it is, please save it until after the food, and the loving."

During the meal Carly and Mark didn't talk about Nathan, or Mark's trip. Instead they discussed some of the funnier letters Carly had received and the answers she'd been tempted to give.

They laughed, and the sound of it healed injured places deep inside Carly. Once, tears came to her eyes because it felt so good just to be sitting across the picnic table from Mark, watching the changes in his face as he talked or listened.

He was rinsing their dishes and putting them into the machine when Carly told him the advice column might be discontinued. She watched closely for his reaction, then felt relief when he grinned and said, "They'll probably find a place for you."

Carly drew a deep breath and leaned against the breakfast bar. "Actually," she said, "they already have, sort of."

Mark looked at her curiously. "Don't keep me in suspense, Scoop—are they sending you on assignment to the White House or what?"

She ran the tip of her tongue over her lips. "I'm probably going to be working with you," she answered, "on a piece about fathers' rights. Mr. Clark wanted a woman's view on the subject."

He sighed, slammed the dishwasher door closed and shoved one hand through his hair. "Great."

Carly went to him and laid her hand gently on his arm. "Mark, I'm not Jeanine," she said in a quiet voice. "I don't have any axes to grind."

He drew her close and buried his face in her hair. "I missed you so much," he said hoarsely.

# CHAPTER FIVE

MARK KNELT IN front of the fireplace, adding wood to the blaze, while Carly sat on the couch, her legs curled beneath her. The white wine in her glass sparkled and winked like a liquid jewel.

"Things are happening pretty fast between us," she said.

He looked back at her over one shoulder. "Is that a problem?"

Carly thought, taking a leisurely sip of her wine. "Yeah, when you consider we don't even know what it is."

Mark joined her on the couch, taking her wineglass from her hand and setting it beside his on the coffee table. "Don't look now, Barnett, but I think it's passion," he said, easing Carly down onto the cushions and then poising himself over her.

He was so incredibly brazen, but Carly couldn't find it in her heart to protest. She wanted to feel his weight pressing down on her, wanted to lose herself in the multicolored light show his lovemaking would set off in her head.

Mark drank the wine from her lips, then shaped her mouth with his and delved into her with his tongue. Carly felt as though he'd already taken her, and an electrical jolt racked her body. With a whimper, she flung

her arms around his neck and responded without res-
ervation.

Mark was gasping when he broke the kiss and slid
downward over her body. Carly raised her T-shirt and
opened her bra of her own accord, and his groan of
pleasure at the sight of her naked breasts vibrated under
her flesh.

She cried out in acquiescence when he caught one
of her nipples in his mouth and grazed it lightly with
his teeth, and dug her fingers into his muscular back.

Before, Mark had taken his sweet time loving her,
but that night there was a primitive urgency between
them that would brook no delays. While he drank from
her breast, Mark was unsnapping her jeans and pushing them down.

She kicked off her shoes, and Mark relieved her of
the jeans. She lay before him in just her underpants,
with her bra unhooked and her T-shirt bunched under
her armpits, and for all the indignity of that she felt
beautiful because his brown eyes moved over her with
reverence.

"Take me," she whispered, letting the backs of her
hands rest against the soft material of the couch on either side of her head.

He bent his head and nipped at her lightly through
the silky fabric of her panties until she was moaning
softly and beginning to writhe.

Then his clothes were gone as quickly as Carly's.
He knelt between her legs, hooking his thumbs under
the waistband of her panties, drawing them downward.

"Don't think you're going to get off this easy, Scoop,"
he teased, finding her entrance and placing himself

there. His eyes glittered with desire as he gazed down into her face. "I plan to keep you busy for a long time."

Carly groaned as he gave her an inch then she clawed frantically at his bare back. "Please, Mark—don't make me wait—"

His response was a long, fierce stroke that took him to her very depths. He cupped his hands beneath her bottom, lifting her into position for another thrust.

"Faster," Carly fretted.

He chuckled. "Does this mean you missed me?"

"Damn you, Mark Holbrook!"

After that, he loved her in earnest, with fire and fever, and when the hot storm broke within her, she sobbed his name.

He covered her face with light, frantic kisses as he climaxed, his mouth on her eyelids, her cheeks, the underside of her chin. In those treacherous moments, Carly felt cherished as well as thoroughly mastered.

When it was over, he fell to her, taking solace in her softness in the age-old way of men. His breath came hard and his words, spoken against her cheek, were labored. "If this gets…any better… I'm going to need… respiratory therapy."

Carly laughed softly and laid her hands to either side of his face. "Look at me, Mark. I've got to tell you something before I lose my courage."

He raised his head, his brown eyes mischievous. "You used to be a man," he guessed.

Carly's delight erupted in another burst of amusement. "Wrong."

"You have a prison record."

She couldn't let the game go on any longer. "I read

your play, Mark," she blurted out. "I found it and I read it."

He studied her somberly for a long time, then thrust himself upward and reached for his clothes.

"Mark?"

"I heard you, Carly."

"I don't blame you for being angry—I shouldn't have snooped. But it was fabulous—really fabulous."

He got back into his jeans and stormed across the room to his desk.

Carly dressed awkwardly while he wrenched open the drawer, found the screenplay and flung it toward her, its fanfold pages spreading out over the floor. "Mark—"

"You like it?" he rasped. "It's yours. Take it. Line bird cages with it!"

"What is the matter with you?" Carly demanded, snapping her jeans. When he didn't answer, but just stood gazing out through the dark windows, she knelt and gently gathered the play up from the floor. She handled it like the broken pieces of something she'd cherished. "Do you know what I'd give to be able to write like this?"

He turned around then, and to Carly's relief he was much calmer. "You'd have had to feel the pain," he said. "Believe me, the price is too high."

She held the manuscript to her breast like a child as she stood. "I *did* feel the pain, Mark—that's what makes it such a wonderful piece of work—"

"Look," Mark interrupted sharply, "I don't give a damn that you read it, all right? But it represents another part of my life and I can't talk about it—I don't want to be reminded."

"I can keep it?" Carly ventured cautiously. "I can take it home?"

"Do whatever you want."

Carly was filled with sadness as she carried the play across the room and tucked it into her briefcase. She should have known Mark would be angry; she'd been trespassing in the deepest reaches of his soul.

"Carly?"

She felt his hands, strong and gentle, on her shoulders. "I'm sorry, Mark," she whispered.

He turned her to face him. "No," he said huskily. "I'm the one who was wrong. I apologize."

She managed a broken smile. "We both knew this wasn't going to work, didn't we?" she asked.

He gave her a slight shake. "Of course it's going to work," he argued. "It has to."

She prayed she wouldn't cry. "Why?"

"Because I need you, and I hope to God you need me, that's why. Because I think maybe I love you."

"You 'think maybe'?" Carly asked, hugging herself. She felt shaky and confused. "What the hell kind of statement is that?"

Mark caught her by the belt loops at the front of her jeans and hauled her toward him. "I'm doing the best I can here, Carly, so how about helping me out a little?" he said, his face very close to hers. "I don't *know* if this feeling is love—I don't even know if there's any such thing as romantic love—but damn it, I feel *something* for the first time in ten years and I don't want it to stop!"

Carly drew a deep, shaky breath. "You're probably just horny," she said in a tone of resignation.

Mark laughed like a comical maniac, hoisted her up

over one shoulder and gave her a sound swat on the bottom. "You may be right," he agreed.

"Put me down!" Carly gasped. "I'm about to throw up."

"I love these romantic moments," Mark answered, carrying her toward his bedroom in exactly the same position. "I feel like Errol Flynn."

"You're an idiot!"

He hauled her up the steps to his bed and flung her down on the mattress. "Will you lighten up, Scoop? Something poignant is happening here."

"Like what?"

Mark stretched out beside her. "Damned if I know, but like I said—I sure don't want it to end."

Carly didn't know whether she was happy or sad, whether she wanted to laugh or cry, but tears filled her eyes and she said, "Hold me."

The next morning, she was careful to go to work in her own car, hoping no one at the newspaper would guess what was going on between her and Mark. But that night she went back to his house, and he cooked spaghetti.

They laughed and talked and made love, but they didn't discuss Mark's play. Or the assignment they might be sharing.

Friday was hectic. The decision to end the advice column had been made, and Carly felt responsible for its demise to some degree. After all, there had been the "Frazzled in Farleyville" incident.

She still had her office, however, and Mr. Clark announced in a special staff meeting that she and Mark would be working together for the time being. Carly could not have been happier, but there was something disturbing about the remote look she saw in Mark's eyes when he looked at her.

"We'll start working on the story tonight," he announced peremptorily, when everyone else had left the conference room.

Carly swallowed. "I can't."

He raised his eyebrows. "You can't?" he echoed, with a maddeningly indulgent note in his voice. "Why not, pray tell?"

Carly dragged in a deep breath and let it out with a whoosh. "I've got a dinner date. Jim Benson, remember? Channel 37?"

Mark walked over to the door and calmly pushed it shut. "Break it," he said.

Hot pink indignation throbbed in Carly's cheeks. "I beg your pardon."

He was glaring at her. "You heard me, Carly."

Carly had no feelings for Jim Benson one way or the other. She just wanted to establish contacts, to "network" the way other people in the media did. She struggled to stay calm. "Look, it's no big deal. Besides, when I made this date, there was nothing going on between you and me."

"And now there is," Mark pointed out evenly.

Carly laid her hand on his arm. "It's only dinner," she said, and then she left the conference room.

Mark didn't follow.

Back at her apartment, as she showered and dressed, Carly decided it would probably be a good thing if she saw other men. After all, whatever it was that had flared up between her and Mark had come on fast, and she'd had little or no chance to distance herself from the situation.

The other side of that coin, of course, was that Mark would have just as much right to date other women. And the prospect didn't appeal to Carly at all.

Jim Benson arrived promptly at seven. He was tall and handsome, with dark hair and streaks of premature gray at his temples, and bright blue eyes. He took in Carly's soft yellow dress with obvious appreciation.

As she and Jim were leaving the apartment, they encountered Janet, who stood there in the hallway, clutching a grocery bag and staring at them with her mouth open.

Carly knew there would be a message on her answering machine when she got home. "My best friend, Janet McClain," she explained as she and Jim descended in the elevator.

Jim laughed. "When people gape like that, I get this overwhelming compulsion to see if my fly's open."

Jim's car, a sleek sports model, was waiting in the parking lot, and he chivalrously opened the door for her. He turned out to be a very nice guy, the kind of man Carly might have gotten serious about if she hadn't met Mark first.

When they'd reached the restaurant and were settled at their table, Jim said very companionably, "You must know Mark Holbrook, if you work at the *Times*."

Carly nodded thoughtfully. "Sometimes I wonder how well," she murmured.

"He and I have been good friends for a long time," Jim went on. "I hope you won't mind that I invited him and his date to join us for drinks later."

Carly had been sipping ice water, and she nearly choked at this announcement. "Tell me the truth," she said when she'd composed herself. "You didn't invite Mark—he invited himself."

Jim grinned. "Well…"

Carly had picked up her table napkin during her choking spell; now she tossed it down angrily. "Why, that sneaky—"

"Am I missing something here?" the newscaster asked politely.

Carly sighed. Jim was too nice; she wasn't going to play games with him. "The truth is, Mark and I have been seeing each other, and something's going on. I don't know whether it's love or not, but it's pretty heavy, and he was upset when I told him I was keeping my date with you."

A grin spread across Jim's face. "So he just wants to unsettle you?"

"I'm afraid so," Carly said with a nod and another sigh. "I'm sorry, Jim."

He shrugged. "No reason we can't be friends." He picked up his menu and opened it. "The shrimp scampi is good here."

Carly had no appetite at all now that she knew Mark was going to show up at any minute, but she ordered the shrimp and did her best to eat.

She and Jim were in the lounge, later, when he said, "Don't look now, but your partner just walked in. Let's dance and give him a thing or two to think about."

The idea sounded good to Carly. She smiled warmly and allowed Jim to lead her onto the small dance floor. Even though it nearly killed her, she didn't look to see who Mark was with.

"Is he watching?" she asked.

Jim chuckled and drew her closer. "Oh, yes. If that

expression in his eyes were a laser beam, he'd be doing surgery on me. The kind you don't recover from."

Carly laughed. "And the woman?"

"Weatherperson from Channel 18. Very cute."

Before Carly could maneuver into a position where she could get a look at Mark's date, he walked right onto the dance floor. Carly was pulled from Jim's arms into Mark's long before he took the trouble to grind out, "May I cut in?"

"No," Carly answered, but when she tried to pull away, he restrained her. "This is ridiculous."

He arched one eyebrow. "All right, I admit it—I'm jealous as hell."

Carly smiled acidly, her eyes widening in mock surprise. "No!"

He gave her a surreptitious pinch on the bottom, and she gasped and stiffened in response. "You've made your point, Barnett—I don't have any rights where you're concerned. But you're going to have to give up dating other guys, unless you want me tagging along."

"Why should I?" Carly asked. "Give up dating other guys, I mean."

"Because I l-like you."

"Well, I *l-like* you, too. Maybe I even love you. In spite of the fact that you're acting like a badly trained baboon tonight." The music stopped. "How about introducing me to your date, Mark?"

He cleared his throat, took her hand and started toward the table where Jim and the weatherperson were sitting, already deep in conversation. "I told you he was a lech," Mark whispered.

"And he told me you were his friend," Carly scolded.

"I was, until he made a move on you," Mark responded, still talking under his breath.

Jim stood when he saw Carly, and an unreadable look passed between the two men. Mark pulled out Carly's chair for her and, when she was seated, sat down beside the weatherperson.

"This is Margery Woods," he said. "Margery, Carly Barnett."

The young woman's brown eyes were round with admiration. "Miss United States—"

"Let's not talk about me," Carly broke in.

"But I saw your pageant—I recorded it. I record all the pageants."

Carly looked to both Mark and Jim for rescue, but neither of them offered it. In fact, they both looked amused, as though they'd set up some tacit conspiracy. "That's—that's nice," she said. "Have you been dating Mark long, Margery?"

That question wiped the complacent look from Mark's face.

"On and off for about six months," Margery responded with a philosophical sigh. Then she gave her date an affectionately suspicious glance. "But I've heard rumors that he's running around with some bimbo at the newspaper office."

Carly managed to swallow the sip of white wine she'd taken without choking on it, but just barely. She gave Mark a look that said, *just you wait, fella,* then changed the subject.

By the time Jim drove her home, she was exhausted. "I'm sorry," she said again at her door. "Tonight was probably a real drag for you."

He smiled and kissed her lightly on the forehead.

"Actually it was the most fun I've had in weeks. If it helps any, I can tell you that Mark's in love with you."

The words gave Carly a soft, melting feeling inside. "It helps," she said.

"That's what I was afraid of," Jim answered with a grin and a shrug. He kissed Carly again and walked away.

As soon as Carly was inside her apartment with the lights flipped on and the door locked behind her, she saw that she had messages. Kicking off her high-heeled shoes and pushing one hand through her hair, she played the first message.

"Who was that hunk?" Janet's voice demanded without so much as a hello. "I mean, I know who he is because I've seen him on television. What I meant was, what are you doing going out with him when you've got this hot thing going with Mark Holbrook? You'd better call me *tonight,* Carly Barnett, or our friendship is over!"

Carly grinned as she moved on to the next message.

"Carly, honey, this is your dad. I was just calling to see how you're doing. Give me a ring tomorrow sometime, if you have a chance—I'll be at the filling station."

Her throat thick, because she would have liked very much to talk with her father and maybe get some perspective on the situation with Mark, Carly sank into the desk chair to hear any further messages.

"Okay, I acted like a caveman," Mark's voice confessed. "It's pretty strange, Scoop—I'm sorry, and yet I know I'd do the same thing all over again. I'll pick you up in the morning for breakfast and we'll get started on the new project. Bye."

She wondered what her dad would think of Mark Holbrook and his high-handed but virtually irresistible methods. Her teeth sinking into her lower lip, Carly glanced at the clock on her desk and wished it wasn't so late in Kansas.

The sudden jangling of the telephone startled her so much that she nearly fell off her chair. Knowing the caller was probably either Mark or Janet, she answered with a somewhat snappish "Hello."

"Hi, baby," her father's voice said.

"Dad!" Carly looked at the clock again. "Is everything okay? Are you sick?"

He chuckled. "Do I have to be sick to call my little girl?"

Carly let out a long sigh. "I'm so glad you did," she said. "I really need to talk to you."

"I'm listening."

Carly's eyes stung with tears of love and homesickness. Her dad had always been willing to listen, and she was grateful. "I think I'm falling in love, Dad. His name is Mark Holbrook, and he's utterly obnoxious, but I can't stay away from him."

Her father laughed affectionately. "Did you think it would be bad news to me, your falling in love? I'm happy for you, honey."

"Didn't you hear me, Dad? I said he was obnoxious! And he is. He's got this Pulitzer Prize, and he's always making comments about my title—"

"There are worse problems."

"I think he's going to ask me to move in with him," Carly burst out.

Don Barnett was quiet for several moments. "If he does, what are you going to say?"

Carly swallowed hard. "Yes. I think."

If her father had made any private judgments, he

didn't voice them. "You're a big girl now, Carly. You have to make decisions like that for yourself."

Carly sighed. "Maybe I should hold out for white lace and promises," she mused.

Her dad chuckled at that. "Even when you've got those things, there aren't any guarantees. The name of the game is risk."

It seemed like a good time to change the subject. "Speaking of risk, Dad," Carly began with a smile in her voice, "are you still eating your meals over at Mad Bill's Café?"

He laughed. "Bill's going to be real hurt when I tell him you said that."

Five minutes later, an impatient knock at Carly's door terminated the conversation. She said goodbye to her father, went to the peephole and looked out.

Her arms folded, Janet was standing in the hallway, wearing her bathrobe.

Carly opened the door, and her friend swept into the room.

"You didn't call," Janet accused.

"I was talking with my dad," Carly answered, grinning as she went into the kitchen to put on the teakettle. A nice cup of chamomile would help her sleep.

Janet followed her into the kitchenette. "Well? What's going on? Is it over between you and Mark?"

Carly chuckled and shook her head. "No, but it sure is complicated. Jim is just an acquaintance, Janet—I want to make contacts."

There was a pause while Janet inspected her freshly polished fingernails and Carly got mugs down from the cupboard, along with a box of herbal tea bags. "Maybe you could fix me up with him," she finally said. "Jim, I mean."

Carly smiled. "Sure," she said gently. "I'll see what I can do."

"You're a true friend." Janet beamed. But then she glanced at her watch and frowned. "I'd better not stay for tea—I'm putting in some overtime tomorrow. Let me know when things are set."

"I will," Carly promised, following Janet to the door and closing and locking it behind her.

It was very late and Carly had to be up early the next morning herself, but even after drinking the chamomile tea, she couldn't go to sleep. She got Mark's play out, carried it to bed and began to read.

Again she was awed by the scope of the man's talent— and a little jealous, too. No matter how hard she worked, it would be years before she was even in the same ball-park. In fact, in her heart Carly knew she would never be the caliber of journalist Mark was, and she wondered if she would be able to live with that fact and accept it.

Long after she had set the play aside and turned out the light, Carly lay in the darkness, thinking about it, envisioning it produced on a stage or movie screen. It would be remarkable in either medium.

A wild idea she barely dared to entertain came to her. The temptation to send the work to an agent was almost overpowering. After all, Mark had said the play was hers, that she could do what she wanted to with it.

Carly sighed. He'd been upset at the time.

Finally, after much tossing and turning, she was able to go to sleep.

It seemed to Carly that no more than five minutes could have passed when her eyes were suddenly flooded with spring sunlight from the window facing her bed. At the same time, Mark—it had to be Mark—was leaning on the doorbell.

Grabbing for her robe, Carly shrugged into it and went grumpily to the door. Sure enough, the peephole revealed Mark standing in the hallway.

Carly let him in, prepared for a lecture.

"You're not ready," he pointed out. "What kind of reporter are you, Barnett? There's a whole world out there living, dying, loving and fighting. And here you are—" his eyes ran mischievously over her pink bathrobe "—standing around looking like a giant piece of cotton candy."

Carly retreated a step and cinched her belt tighter. She knew the perils of standing too close to Mark Holbrook in a bathrobe. "I'll be ready in ten minutes," she said.

"Make it five," Mark retorted, glancing pointedly at his watch. "We have a plane to catch."

Carly stared at him. "A plane?"

Mark nodded, his hands tucked into his hip pockets. "If we're going to write about fathers' rights, Scoop, you're going to have to do a little research on the subject. We'll start by introducing you to Nathan."

"But I can't just leave—"

"Why do you think Clark gave me this story?" Mark interrupted. "He knows I've got my guts invested in it. And you're my assistant. Therefore, where I go, you go. Now hurry up."

Carly hurried into the bathroom, showered, and hastily styled her hair and put on light makeup. After that, she pulled a suitcase out from under the bed.

"How long are we going to be gone?" she called out.

Mark appeared in her doorway. He was sipping a cup of coffee, and he looked impossibly attractive in his jeans and Irish cable-knit sweater. "Long enough for you to see that women aren't the only ones who sometimes have their rights trampled on," he responded.

Carly wasn't about to comment on that one—not before breakfast. She packed as sensibly as she could, tucking the play into her suitcase when Mark wasn't looking, and left a message for Janet saying she'd be away on business for a while. Finally she and Mark set out for the airport in his car.

After they'd bought their tickets and checked in their baggage, they went to a busy restaurant for breakfast. Carly left the table for a few minutes, and when she returned, there was a long velvet box beside her orange juice.

Her hand trembled a little as she reached for it and lifted the lid to find a bracelet of square gold links. She was unable to speak when she lifted her eyes to Mark's face.

He took the bracelet from the box and deftly clasped it around her wrist. "I can't pretend this trip is strictly business, Carly," he said, his eyes warm and serious. "I guess what it all boils down to is, I'm asking you to move in with me."

# CHAPTER SIX

"I NEED SOME time to think," Carly said softly, gazing down at the bracelet in stricken wonder. The words sounded odd even to her, especially in light of what she'd told her father the night before, about saying yes if Mark asked her to live with him. Being confronted with the reality was something quite different, though, and whatever it was that she and Mark had together was still fragile. She didn't want to ruin it.

She was trying to unfasten the bracelet when Mark's fingers stopped her.

"It's all right, Carly," he said quietly. "No matter what you decide, I want you to keep the bracelet."

They finished their breakfast in a silence that was at once awkward and cordial, then went to board their plane.

Once they were settled in their seats and their aircraft had taken off, Mark was all business. He pulled a notebook and a couple of pens from his briefcase and started outlining his basic ideas about the piece on fathers' rights. He listened to Carly's input thoughtfully and even condescended to use some of it.

By the time they landed in San Francisco, they had the basic structure of the article sketched in.

In the cab that brought them into the city, they argued. Mark naturally felt that fathers got a bad deal, as a general rule, when it came to questions like custody and visitation rights. Carly responded that he was prejudiced, that many fathers didn't care enough about their children to pay support, let alone visit or seek custody.

The taxi came to a stop in front of an elegant house overlooking the Bay, and Carly was surprised. She hadn't paid attention when Mark gave directions to the cabdriver.

"We're not staying in a hotel?"

Mark grinned as he held the car door open for her. "My parents would regard it as an insult," he answered.

Soon they were standing on the sidewalk with their luggage, the cab speeding away down the hill. And Carly was nervous.

"This isn't fair, Mark. You didn't warn me that I was going to be meeting your family."

"You didn't ask," he said as a plump woman in a maid's uniform opened the front door and came out onto the porch.

"They're here!" she called back over one shoulder.

Mark was holding Carly's suitcase, but she grabbed it. "How are you going to present me?" she whispered out of the side of her mouth. "As the woman you want to live with?"

"I detect hostility," Mark whispered back just as a tall, striking lady with white hair came out of the house, beaming with delight.

Carly knew immediately that this was Mark's mother, and she smiled nervously as Mrs. Holbrook kissed her son's cheek. "It's so good to see you again, darling."

"It's only been a few days, Mom," Mark pointed out, but the look in his eyes was affectionate. "This is Carly," he added, slipping his free arm around her waist.

Carly smiled and offered her hand. "Hello."

Mrs. Holbrook's grasp was firm and friendly. "Welcome, Carly. I'm very pleased to meet you." She turned resigned eyes to Mark. "There is a problem, though."

"What?" Mark asked, starting toward the door.

Mrs. Holbrook stopped him with two words. "Jeanine's here."

Carly felt a wild urge to turn and chase the taxi down the street.

Mark paused on the step, frowning down into his mother's concerned face. "What the—"

Before he could finish, a tall beauty with auburn hair and Irish green eyes appeared in the doorway. Her complexion was flawless, and her gaze moved over Mark in a proprietary way, then strayed to Carly.

"So," she said, her voice icy. "This is Mark's beauty queen."

Although the words had not been particularly inflammatory, Carly felt as though she'd been slapped. She lifted her chin and met Jeanine's gaze straight on, though she didn't speak.

Mrs. Holbrook linked her arm through Carly's and politely propelled her toward the door, forcing Jeanine to shrink back into the entryway. "Don't be rude, dear," she said evenly. "Carly is my guest."

The maid led the way up the stairs, depositing Carly in a lovely room decorated in muted mauve and ivory. There was an inner door that probably led to Mark's quarters.

Sure enough, he came through it five seconds after Carly had popped open her suitcase.

"I should have warned you," he said, giving her a light kiss on the mouth. "Here be dragons, milady."

"Thanks a lot," Carly said furiously. She was still smarting because Jeanine had called her a "beauty queen," and because she had a pretty good idea where the description had come from.

Mark's eyes were dancing as he shrugged and spread his hands. "Don't feel bad, Scoop—I didn't like her, either. That's why we are divorced."

"How did she know we were coming?" Carly demanded in a furious whisper.

Mark sighed and sat down on the edge of Carly's four-poster bed. "Mom probably told her."

"It must be nice to be let in on little things like that!" Carly spat, pacing. She had half a mind to call a cab and head straight for the airport. The trouble was, half a mind wasn't enough for the task.

Mark reached out and pulled her easily onto his lap. She struggled, he restrained her, and she gave up with an angry huff.

He unbuttoned her blouse far enough to kiss the cleft between her breasts, resting his hand lightly on her thigh.

Carly felt as though someone had doused her in kerosene, then touched a match to her. "Mark, not here. Not now."

"Umm-hmm," he agreed, pushing down her bra on one side and nonchalantly taking her nipple into his mouth.

She stiffened on his lap, unwilling to free herself from his spell even though she knew it was desperately important to do so. "Mark," she moaned in feeble protest.

He raised her linen skirt, and dipped his hand inside her panties. His lips never left her breast. "Umm," he said.

Carly swallowed a strangled cry of delighted protest as he found her secret and began to toy with it. "You—are—an absolute—*bastard*," she panted.

He chuckled and nuzzled her other breast, nipping at it through the thin, lacy fabric of her bra. "No question about it," he admitted. And he slid his fingers inside Carly and plied her with his thumb.

She clutched his shoulders, and a soft sob of rebellious submission escaped her as he worked his singular magic. She felt a fine mist of perspiration on her upper lip and between her breasts as he made her body respond to him. She let her head fall back in surrender. "So—arrogant—"

He slipped his tongue beneath the top of her bra to find her nipple. "You love it," he said when he paused to bare her for his leisurely enjoyment.

That was the worst part of it, Carly thought, writhing helplessly under Mark's attentions. She *did* love it.

Her climax was a noisy one, despite her efforts to swallow her cries of release, and Mark muffled it by covering her mouth with his own. When she sagged against him in a sated stupor, he withdrew his hand and calmly fastened her bra, buttoned her blouse and straightened her skirt.

When he set her on her feet, she swayed, and he steadied her by grasping her hips in his hands.

He stood, kissed her gently on the mouth, then disappeared into his room.

Mark hadn't been gone five minutes when a light knock sounded at the outer door. Carly had been sitting on the window seat, staring out at the Bay and wondering whether what she felt for Mark was love or obsession, and she was grateful for a distraction.

"Come in," she said quietly.

Mrs. Holbrook stepped into the room. "Lunch is nearly ready," she said with a smile. "I do hope you're hungry, my dear. Eleanor makes a very nice crab salad sandwich."

Carly smiled lamely and hoped her clothes weren't rumpled from those wild minutes on Mark's lap. "That sounds marvelous," she answered. She didn't have the courage to ask if Jeanine was still present and, fortunately, she didn't have to.

"Jeanine is gone, for the time being at least," Mrs. Holbrook volunteered. "I should have known better than to tell her I was expecting you and Mark."

Carly lowered her eyes for a moment. The phrase "beauty queen" was still lodged in her mind like a nettle, and she wondered why Mark hadn't spoken of her as a journalist, or even an assistant. It hurt to be defined with a long-defunct pageant title when she'd worked so hard to learn to write. "It's all right, Mrs. Holbrook," she said.

"Please," the woman said gently, holding out a hand to Carly. "Call me Helen. And what do you say we give Mark the slip and have our sandwiches in the garden? He's on the telephone with his father."

Carly smiled and nodded, and she and Helen went downstairs together.

The garden turned out to be a terrace lined with budding rosebushes and blooming pink azaleas. There was a glass-topped table with a pink-and-white umbrella and a splendid view of the Golden Gate. A salty breeze blew in from the water, rippling Carly's hair, and she had a strange sensation of returning home after a long, difficult journey.

"Did you know Mark wrote a play about his marriage and divorce?" she asked when the maid had brought their sandwiches, along with a bone-china tea service, and left again.

"I'm not surprised," Helen said, and there was a sad expression on her still-beautiful face. "He deals with most things by writing about them."

Carly had known Helen Holbrook for less than an hour, and yet she felt safe with her. "It's absolutely brilliant," she went on. Just recalling the powerful emotions the play had stirred in her almost brought tears to her eyes. "And he's not going to do anything with it."

Helen sighed. "Sometimes," she reflected, "I delude myself that I understand my son. Mostly, though, I accept the fact that he's a law unto himself."

Carly nodded. "He gave me the play," she said. "He told me I could do anything I wanted to with it—that it was mine."

Helen's gaze met Carly's, and in that instant the two women came to an understanding. "Then I guess you'd be within your rights if you took certain obvious steps," Helen said.

Before Carly could respond, Mark appeared in the gaping French doors that led from an old-fashioned, elegantly furnished parlor. He was carrying a sandwich and a tall glass of ice tea. He winked at Carly, in a tacit reminder of the episode upstairs, bringing a blush to her cheeks.

"Jeanine's bringing Nathan over in an hour," he said.

Carly felt like an intruder, but didn't move from her chair. And she knew then that they hadn't flown to San

Francisco to work on the article, but to come to terms with Mark's past.

Helen looked extremely uncomfortable. "Jeanine's been drinking more and more lately," she finally confided.

Carly was about to make an excuse and retreat to her room when Mark reached out and closed his hand over hers, indicating that he wanted her to stay. She felt a charge go through her that probably registered on the Richter scale.

"And she was drunk when she had the accident," Mark ventured.

His mother pressed her lips together in a thin line for a long moment, then said, "I think so, but she denies it, of course."

Mark slammed his fist down on the glass tabletop and bounded out of his chair to stand facing the Bay, his hands gripping the stone wall that bordered the garden. "One of these days she's going to kill him."

Carly longed to help, to change things somehow, but of course there was nothing she could do.

Mark finally came back to the table, but he was too restless to sit. He put one hand on Carly's shoulder and squeezed, and she pressed her fingers over his.

Helen's lovely blue eyes moved from Carly's face to her son's. With a perceptive smile, she rose from her chair. "I think I'll make myself scarce for a little while," she announced, and then she vanished.

Carly stood and slipped her arms around Mark's waist. "I like your mother," she said.

He kissed her briefly. "So do I, but I don't think she's the topic you really want to discuss."

Carly shook her head, resting her hands on the lapels

of his lightweight tweed jacket. "You're right. I want
to know how you met Jeanine, and what made you fall
in love with her."

"I didn't 'meet' Jeanine—I've known her all my life,"
Mark answered, and there was a hoarse note of resignation in his voice. "We were expected to get married,
and we didn't want to disappoint anybody, so we did."

"You must have loved her once."

Mark shook his head. "I didn't know what love was,"
he answered huskily. "Not until Nathan came along. As
soon as Jeanine realized how much I cared about our
son, she began using him against me."

*I know,* Carly wanted to say. *I read your play.* But she
only stood there, close to Mark, her head on his shoulder, her eyes fixed on the capricious Bay.

"I want him back, Carly," he went on. "Not just for
weekends, or holidays or summer vacations. For keeps."

She wasn't surprised. "From what you've said," she
answered softly, "the chances of that aren't too good."

"I can fight her. I can sue for custody."

Carly turned so that she could look up into Mark's
face. She saw determination there, and fury, and she
had a glimmer of what he'd meant when he'd spoken
so bitterly of fathers' rights. Her heart went out to him.
"You might lose," she said.

"Life is full of risks," he answered.

Carly and Mark were in the parlor when Jeanine returned, bringing Nathan with her.

He was a handsome, serious boy, so like his father
that Carly's heart lurched slightly when she saw him. He
was wearing jeans and a red-and-blue striped T-shirt, and
there was a cast on his left arm, covered with writing.

He beamed, showing a gap where his two front teeth had been. "Hi, Dad," he said a little shyly.

Carly noticed the tears in Jeanine's eyes as she stood behind her son, and felt a moment's pity for the woman. Perhaps Mark had been telling the truth when he said he'd never loved Jeanine, but Carly knew for certain that Jeanine had once loved him. Maybe she still did.

"Come here," Mark said huskily, and the child rushed into his arms.

"Have him back by nine o'clock," Jeanine said crisply, her chin high. "And don't give him sugar. It makes him hyper."

Mark ruffled his son's rich brown hair and nodded at Jeanine, and that was the extent of his civility. Carly was relieved when the other woman left the room.

"I want you to meet somebody," Mark told the boy, putting an arm around Nathan's shoulder and gently turning him toward Carly. "This is my—friend, Carly Barnett. Carly, this is Nathan."

Carly held out her hand in a businesslike way, and Nathan shook it, looking up at her with solemn, luminous eyes.

"Hello," he said.

Again Carly had that peculiar sensation of déjà vu that she'd had in the garden. She could have sworn she'd met Nathan before. "Hi," she replied, smiling.

He crinkled his nose. "Mom said you were a queen. I thought you'd be wearing a bathing suit and a crown," he informed her.

Carly laughed. "I'm a reporter," she said, spreading her hands. "No queens around here."

Once Mark had hustled them out the door, they drove to Fisherman's Wharf in Helen's sedate Mercedes and watched the street performers. There were mimes and banjo players and even acrobats, all combining to give the place the festive flavor of a medieval fair.

Carly busied herself exploring the little shops for an hour or so, while Mark and Nathan sat quietly on a bench, talking. Occasionally she checked on them, and it twisted her heart that the expressions on their faces were so serious.

Having no real idea what ten-year-old boys liked, Carly selected a deck of trick cards in a magic shop, along with a bottle of disappearing ink. When Mark and Nathan had had an hour to talk, she joined them.

To her relief, they looked delighted to see her.

"I'm hungry," Nathan announced.

Mark glanced at Carly in question, and she shook her head. She was still full from lunch.

He bought hot, spicy sausages for himself and Nathan, and they ate as they explored the waterfront. When the wind off the water became chilly, they went back to the car.

"I bought you something," Carly told Nathan a little shyly, holding the bag from the magic shop out to him.

He reached between the car seats to accept the gift. "Thank you," he said politely. The bag crackled as he opened it. "Wow! *Disappearing ink!*"

Mark was pulling the expensive car into traffic. "Just don't spill it. Your grandmother wouldn't appreciate that."

Nathan gave a peal of delighted laughter. "She'd never know, Dad—it would disappear!"

They went to an adventure movie after that, and then to dinner at a rustic place on the waterfront.

By the time the evening was over, Nathan was asleep

in the backseat of Helen's car, the deck of magic cards still clasped in his hand.

Just looking at him made Carly's heart swell inside her until it seemed to fill her whole chest.

Mark brought the car to a stop in front of a town house on a steep, winding street, and Jeanine appeared on the porch as he awakened his son. "Come on, Buddy," he said quietly. "It's time to hit the sack."

Nathan woke up slowly and gave Carly a sleepy grin. "Would you sign my cast? Please?"

Carly swallowed and nodded, rummaging through her purse until she found a pen. She wrote her name beneath Pauly Tosselli's, and drew a heart beside it.

"Thanks," Nathan said. "When you come back, I'll know a whole bunch of card tricks."

"Okay," Carly replied in a small voice.

She waited in the car while Nathan and Mark approached the house. When Mark returned, his expression was strained.

She laid a hand on his arm. "It's progress, Mark. A few weeks ago Jeanine wouldn't even let you see him."

"She smells like she spent the afternoon at the bottom of a bourbon bottle," he answered tightly.

They drove back through darkened, picturesque streets that could only have belonged to one city.

"You neglected to mention," Carly ventured teasingly, her hand caressing the leather-upholstered car seat, "that your parents are rolling in money."

Mark relaxed a little and flashed her a grin. "Darn. I was going to tell you I'd started as a lowly paperboy."

"Is this the old stuff, or are you *nouveau riche?*"

"It's been around a few generations—my great-great-grandfather was a forty-eighter."

"A what?"

"He got here a year before the other guys."

Carly laughed. "And more than a hundred years later you're still carrying on the tradition," she said.

Mark's grin broadened and took on a cocky air. "Yeah."

When they reached the Holbrooks' house, Mark's father was home. He was an imposing man with a full head of snow-white hair, a ready smile and a firm hand-shake.

"So this is the reporter I've heard so much about," he said, winning Carly's heart with a single sentence. "It's about time my son had a little competition."

The four of them had nightcaps together and talked, and then Carly excused herself, wanting to give Mark and his parents some private time.

She almost jumped out of her skin when she came out of the guest bathroom, freshly showered and dressed in an oversize T-shirt, to find Mark sitting cross-legged in the middle of her bed. He was wearing a pair of black-and-gray striped pajama bottoms and nothing else.

"Eleanor laid them out for me," he said a little defensively when Carly giggled. "The least I could do was wear them."

"Get off my bed, Mr. Holbrook."

He fell back against the pillows, pretending to pull at an arrow lodged in his chest, and when Carly bent over him to repeat her order, he grabbed her and flung her down on the mattress beside him.

Her squirming struggles ended, as usual, when he kissed her. She wrapped her arms around his neck and scooted close to him.

Presently he tore his mouth from hers, his eyes dancing. Rising off the bed, he pulled Carly with him and led her toward the inner door, one finger to his lips.

His room was shadowy, but she could make out pennants on the walls, and framed pictures of athletes. "Do you know how long I've fantasized about this?" he whispered.

"What?"

He set her down on the edge of the bed and bent to subdue her with another kiss. "This," he finally answered long moments later when she was rummy and disoriented. "Sneaking a girl into my room."

Carly giggled. "Come on. You don't expect me to believe you never tried that!"

"I tried, and my mother, Helen the Terrible, always caught me. She'd rap on the door and say, 'This is a raid.' It always threw cold water on the moment, if you know what I mean."

Despite their bantering, Carly was trembling with excitement. She sighed when Mark laid her back on the mattress and began raising the T-shirt. Finally he pulled it off over her head, and she lay before him, naked except for a mantle of shimmering moonlight. Her nipples tightened and flushed dark rose under his perusal.

"You're so beautiful, Carly," he said, his voice low and husky. His hand came to rest lightly on her belly. "So remarkably beautiful."

She reached up and clasped her hands behind his head. "Come here and kiss me," she said, and drew him down to her mouth.

He moved his hands in ever-broadening circles. With his fingers he explored her satiny thighs, then parted them to venture into the tangle of silk.

Carly tried to wriggle farther onto the mattress, but

Mark wouldn't let her. He kissed his way down her body until he was kneeling beside the bed, the undersides of her knees clasped gently in his hands.

"I can't be quiet," she choked out in a panic. "Not if you do that."

"Then don't be quiet," he answered, and Carly pressed the corner of a pillow against her mouth to stifle her involuntary cry when he took her into his mouth.

She tossed her head from side to side as he enjoyed her, and she bit down on her lower lip to keep the noise to a minimum.

Mark was ruthless. He brought Carly to an excruciating release that arched her back like a swan's neck, his hands fondling her breasts as she whimpered, swamped in pleasure, unable to stop the violent spasms of her body.

Finally she collapsed to the mattress, gasping for breath, her skin glistening with perspiration.

Mark wouldn't let her rest. Seated on the floor now, with his back to the bed, he made her stand over him while he teased and tempted her, always stopping just short of appeasing her.

When she pleaded in broken gasps, he laid her down and came into her in a long, gliding thrust. After a few measured strokes, Carly's feeble control snapped. She hurled her body upward to meet his as a resonant string was plucked deep inside her, its single note shuddering throughout her body.

But her greatest satisfaction was in hearing Mark groan as her flesh consumed his, drawing on him with primitive greed. He was made to give everything.

"Are you using anything?" he gasped a full fifteen

minutes later when they were both coming out of their dazes.

Carly laughed. "Now's a nice time to think about that, Holbrook. I love it when the man takes responsibility."

He lifted his head from her breast, and the moonlight caught something strange and somber in his eyes.

"It's okay," she said softly, entangling her fingers in his hair. "I bought something while we were out."

"Carly." The name came out as a rasp.

She stroked the sides of his face. Maybe he hadn't made up his mind what he felt, but she knew her side of things. She was desperately in love. "What?"

"If I asked you to, would you give me a baby?"

Carly gazed up at him for a long time before she answered. "That depends on whether you planned to walk off with the little dickens or let me have a hand in raising it."

"We'd raise it together."

She sighed. "How do we know we wouldn't want to break up in six months or six years?"

"How does anybody know that, Carly? If everybody had demanded a guarantee, the human race would have died out before the dinosaurs did."

"I'd need some promises from you, Mark. Some pretty heavy-duty ones."

He lowered his head to her breast and circled the nipple with his tongue, causing it to jut out in renewed response. "How's this one, Scoop? As long as you want me, I'll be around."

Carly's eyes were wet. "This is scary," she said. "A month ago I was minding my own business, getting ready to come out here and start a new job. I'd never met the man who could get past my defenses. Now all of a sudden I'm lying in bed with you and talking babies."

Mark raised himself to look into her face, and kissed away her tears. "I know what you mean," he said, his voice a gentle rasp. "It's kind of like being caught in an avalanche."

Carly's laughter caught on a sob. "Such tender, romantic words."

Just then there was a light knock at the door.

"It's a raid!" Mark whispered, and jerked the covers up over Carly's head.

"Good night, son," his father called from the hallway.

## CHAPTER SEVEN

THE HOLBROOKS HELD an impromptu brunch the next day, and Carly was surprised at the variety of people who attended on such short notice. Mark introduced her to a bank president, a congressman and a film agent before she'd even finished her orange juice.

When Jeanine arrived, he excused himself and approached his ex-wife. Carly knew he was going to ask for custody of Nathan, and she crossed her fingers for him and stepped out onto the terrace to look at the Bay. The fainter blue of the sky and the deep navy of the water blended into azure at the horizon, and Carly yearned to hide the sight in her heart and carry it away with her.

"Lovely, isn't it?"

Carly turned, a little startled, to see Edina Peters, the film agent. "Yes," she said. "I could look at it forever."

Ms. Peters, a petite, well-dressed woman in her mid-forties, smiled, the spring sun glinting in her bright brown hair. "Who knows? Maybe you lived here in another life and were very happy. That would account—at least in part—for that look of controlled sorrow I see in your face."

Pushing a lock of windblown hair back from her forehead, Carly changed the subject. "Have you known the Holbrooks long?"

"Yes," she answered simply.

Carly was never sure, when she looked back on that moment, what made her say what she did then. "Mark wrote a play, and it's fabulous."

Edina's interest was obviously piqued. "I'm not surprised. After all, he has achieved a certain amount of success. Did he ever tell you that he was writing potboilers for detective and science-fiction magazines before he was even out of high school?"

Carly smiled and shook her head. She could easily picture Mark in that room where he'd made love to her, hurriedly penning stories on a yellow legal pad. "He's remarkable."

"Is he going to show the play to anyone?" Edina asked carefully.

Still leaning against the terrace railing, Carly interlocked her fingers and sighed. "He gave it to me," she said.

"*Gave* it to you?"

Carly shrugged, drinking in the view, taking solace in it. "I wouldn't put my name on it, or anything like that."

"Of course not," agreed Edina, who had no way of knowing what Carly's scruples were.

"I'd like to show it to someone, just to find out whether or not my instincts are right. Would you be willing…?"

Except for a glint in Edina's eyes, there was no outward sign of her eagerness. "I'd be happy to. And, naturally, I wouldn't do anything without talking to you first."

Carly nodded, went upstairs by the back way and took the manuscript from her suitcase. Edina was waiting in the kitchen when she came down, and her slender white hand trembled slightly as she reached for the play.

"Now remember," Carly said firmly, "I'm only looking for your opinion. I don't have the authority to sell Mark's work."

Edina nodded, gave Carly her card and left the party five minutes later.

Carly returned to the brunch to find that Mark had finished his talk with Jeanine. She knew it hadn't gone well by the strained look in his eyes and the muscle that kept bunching along his jawline.

She slipped her arm through his and pulled him into an alcove. "Well?"

"She said no."

Carly reached up to still the angry muscle. "You didn't really expect her to say yes so easily, did you? Good heavens, Mark, Nathan is her *son*."

He let out a ragged sigh. "Jeanine's an alcoholic," he said.

"That doesn't mean she doesn't love her child," Carly reasoned. "What you're asking is the hardest thing in the world for a woman to do." She thought fleetingly of the play, and felt an ache inside—and an urge to run after Edina Peters and ask her to give the manuscript back.

Mark pushed back the sleeve of his forest-green sweater and checked his watch. "We've got to catch a plane in two hours, Scoop," he said in a lighter tone. "Maybe we'd better start inching toward the door."

Carly stood on her toes to kiss his cheek. "It's so nice of you to keep me advised of our schedule," she mocked with a twinkle in her eyes. "First you tell me we're coming down here because of the piece on fathers' rights, without giving me any idea of how long we're staying, then you present me to your family, then you calmly announce that we're leaving in two hours. Is there anything else I should know, Mr. Holbrook?"

He leaned toward her and grinned, lifting his eyebrows a degree. "Yeah. You should know that when we get back to Oregon, I'm going to take you to bed and make love to you until you collapse in exhaustion."

A blush colored Carly's cheeks, and she turned away, infuriated that he could arouse her so thoroughly in a room full of people, then leave her to wait hours for satisfaction.

Forty-five minutes later, after Mark had spent a little more time with Nathan, he and Carly said goodbye to his family, got into a cab and headed for the airport.

The fact that she'd given the play to an agent was preying on Carly's conscience by then, but she didn't have the courage to confide in Mark. She pushed the subject to the back of her mind and the two of them brainstormed the fathers' rights issue during the flight back to Oregon.

"Are you coming home with me?" Mark asked as they landed.

Carly twisted the exquisite gold bracelet on her wrist. "No," she said after nervously running the tip of her tongue over her lips. "I think we need some space."

He didn't comment on that until they were out of the plane and on the way to the baggage-claim area.

"What's going on, Carly?" he demanded as they rode the escalator. "I thought things were pretty good between us."

Carly felt sad. "They are," she answered. "But they're volatile, too. I don't want this relationship to go up like a bomb and crash to the ground in flaming pieces, and it could if we push too hard."

He gave her a weary grin. "I hate to admit it, Scoop, but you may be right. But *damn,* I really wanted to make love to you tonight."

Again Carly blushed. "Well—you could come to my apartment for dinner. It's just that I don't think we should live together. Not yet."

His brown eyes caressed her. "Fair enough, but what about that baby we talked about?"

Carly glanced anxiously around to see if anyone was eavesdropping on their conversation. "I think we should forget that, at least until after this thing about Nathan's custody is ironed out. Creating a child isn't something you do on impulse, Mark, and besides..." She paused, swallowed and averted her eyes for a few moments before going on. "You can't replace one child with another."

He sighed, slipped an arm around her waist and pulled her close against his side. "All right, Scoop, you win. But we can at least *practice,* so that when we do make a baby, we'll get it right."

Carly laughed, but inside her there was a great sadness. For all her sensible decisions, what she really wanted was to pack up everything she owned, move into Mark's house and start a baby right away.

What she *didn't* want was to end up divorced in a few years because they'd tried to do things too quickly.

After collecting their baggage, Carly and Mark drove to his place. Carly waited in the car while he collected his laptop and a change of clothes. They stopped briefly at a Chinese restaurant, then retreated to Carly's apartment.

The light on her answering machine was flickering, and Carly had already pushed the button and started to play the message before she realized there might be messages she didn't want Mark to hear.

Sure enough, Janet's voice filled the living room. "I'll bet you're off in some romantic hideaway with that fantastic man you're dating, you fink. Call me when you get back."

Mark, who was sitting on the couch, opening the bags from the Chinese place, paused long enough to polish his fingernails against his shirt and toss Carly a cocky grin.

Subtly she went back to the machine and pressed the Off button. Then she kicked off her shoes and curled up beside Mark on the cushions. They watched an old movie on TV while they ate casually from the cartons, occasionally feeding each other, and the progression to the bedroom was a natural one.

Carly went in to change her clothes, and in the ancient way of men, Mark followed her.

"Remember what I told you in San Francisco?" he teased, his voice a low, throaty rumble as he stood behind her, his lips moving against her nape.

In spite of herself, Carly trembled. His words hadn't been far out of her mind since he'd spoken them. "Yes," she managed as he lifted her tank top and closed his hands over the bare, full breasts beneath.

He nipped at her earlobe. "What did I say?"

Carly wondered if there were other women in the world who'd gone from virgin to vamp in one easy lesson. "Y-you said you were going to t-take me to bed and make love to me until I c-collapsed."

Mark turned her in his arms and pulled the tank top

off over her head. Her plump breasts bobbed with the motion, and two patches of color throbbed in her cheeks. He lifted her up, and she wrapped her legs around his waist, her arms encircling his neck.

He was kissing her collarbone, the warm, quivering tops of her breasts. He found her nipple and suckled, and she flung back her head in ecstatic surrender, pulling in her breath. His glossy brown hair was like silk between her fingers.

"Tell me what you want, Carly," he paused to mutter.

"You," Carly answered in a helpless whisper. "On top of me, inside me—part of me…"

Mark laid her down on the bed and pulled away the shorts and panties she'd just put on. His eyes glittered with desire as he entered her.

Their time together was everything it had ever been, and more. Carly thought, at times, that she could not endure the pleasure, that she would be unable to survive it. When the tumult had overtaken them, when glory had been reached and shared, they lay quietly for a long time, shadows slipping over them. And Carly wept.

"What?" Mark asked gruffly, brushing away her tears with his thumbs.

"I want this to work," Carly managed to respond, feeling silly and bereft. "I want so much for this to work."

Mark kissed her, not in a demanding way, but in a gentle, reassuring one. Then he got up and held out his hand to her. "That part of it is up to us, Scoop—it's not like we're at the mercy of a whimsical fate or anything."

He led her to the bathroom and they showered together, then Mark dried himself with a towel and began putting his clothes back on. Carly, wearing her pink robe, stood in the doorway, watching him, thinking what a marvel he was. His body was beautifully sculpted, like one of Michelangelo's statues come to life.

"You're leaving?" she asked softly.

He paused in the hunt for his other shoe long enough to plant a kiss on her forehead. "Yes. You're all done in, babe. You need some rest."

Carly swallowed. "I guess loving you is exhausting work," she said.

Mark stopped and recoiled comically, like a victim in one of the old Frankenstein movies. "Did I actually hear it? The L word?"

Carly nodded. It was so hard, taking the risk, laying all her feelings on the line when he might just walk out and never come back. "I love you, Mark."

He came to her, gripped her shoulders gently in his hands and searched her face. "Carly, I'm going to owe half of next year's income when I say this, because I bet all my friends I'd never let it happen, but I love you, too. And it's not like anything I've ever felt before."

She was too moved to speak, so she just nodded again, and he kissed her lightly and went back to the search for his shoe.

"Get some shut-eye, Scoop," he said. "Tomorrow we start working in earnest." After that, he kissed her once more and left.

Carly locked the apartment door after him and let her forehead rest against the wood.

Presently she turned around and made her way to the desk. She listened to a series of messages while she gathered up the cartons and bags left on the coffee table from their Chinese meal. Abruptly she stiffened when Edina's voice filled the room.

"Carly, you were right—this play is wonderful. I read it at one sitting. We've simply *got* to persuade Mark to let me market it. Call me back at the number I gave you on Monday morning, and we'll formulate a plan."

Carly's knees weakened as she imagined what would have happened if she hadn't stopped the machine after Janet's message played. She dropped the debris from dinner into the trash and made her way somewhat shakily to the telephone.

Janet answered on the third ring.

"It's me," Carly said, and then she began to cry.

Her friend was there in less than a minute. "What's wrong?" she asked, taking in Carly's mussed hair, bathrobe and tear-reddened eyes.

"I'm in love with Mark!" Carly wailed.

Janet smiled gently as she pressed her friend into a chair and then went to the kitchenette, talking loudly to be heard over the sound of water running into the teakettle. "Now there's stunning news," she called. "Nobody would have guessed you were crazy about the guy or anything."

Carly got out of the chair and followed her friend's voice, watching as Janet took mugs and tea bags from their respective places. "I've done something sneaky and underhanded," she went on, sniffling. "He's probably never going to forgive me."

Arms folded, Janet leaned against the kitchen counter to wait for the water to boil and sighed. "What could you have done that was so bad?" she asked skeptically.

Carly bit her lower lip for a long moment before answering. "I showed his play to an agent without telling him first."

Janet's pretty eyes went round. "You did what?"

"It seemed like a good idea at the time," Carly reasoned fitfully. "And I told the agent I didn't have the power to sell it. But she called back a little while ago—it was just lucky that Mark didn't hear the message—and I have an awful feeling she's not going to be able to control her enthusiasm."

The teakettle whistled, and Janet poured boiling water into the two mugs and carried them past Carly to the table, where they both sat down.

"You're right," Janet said. "I think you're in very big trouble."

Carly nodded miserably, her fingers curved around the steaming mug. "I thought it would be okay," she said. "I mean, he *said* I could do what I wanted to with it, and his mother and I tacitly agreed that somebody in the business ought to look at it. That might even have been why she invited Edina to the brunch."

Janet didn't pursue the subject of the Holbrooks' brunch. "You've got to tell Mark what you did before he hears it from somebody else," she said. "It's your only chance, Carly. If the agent calls him and starts raving about what a hit the movie's going to be, he'll be furious with you."

Carly's throat ached, and she was on the verge of tears again. "Do you suppose I did this on purpose, Janet? You know, to sabotage myself, to keep things from being too good?"

"You've been watching too much trash TV," Janet said, dismissing the idea with a wave of one hand. "You did it because you love the man, and you want to see him get the recognition he deserves. Thing is, your methods leave something to be desired, kid."

Mark's laptop was still sitting on the coffee table—

they'd never gotten around to actually using it—and the sight filled Carly with guilt. With shaking hands, she lifted the mug full of tea to her mouth.

"He'll probably be mad at first," Janet went on when Carly didn't speak. "But he'll see that you meant well when he calms down."

Remembering how Mark had exploded when she'd confessed that she'd *read* the play, Carly had her doubts about what his reactions would be when he learned she'd shown it to someone else. Now, she guessed, she'd see how much—or how little—Mark loved her. She grimaced.

"There's always the sneaky way out," Janet suggested. "You could call the agent, tell her to send back the play and never breathe a word about it to anybody— after which you conveniently forget to mention the blunder to Mark."

Carly dismissed the idea with a shake of her head and, "I'd never have a moment's peace for worrying that he'd find out."

Janet gestured toward the phone. "Call him. I'll be down the hall if you need me." With that she got out of her chair, carried her cup to the sink and then left the apartment.

Carly stared after her, her thumbnail caught between her front teeth, but she didn't make the call. No, she reasoned, she wouldn't do that until after she'd spoken to Edina in the morning and asked her to send the play back.

She made herself another cup of tea, selected a book from the shelves underneath the living room window and went to bed. It seemed lonely without Mark.

Fluffing her pillows behind her, Carly opened the

new adventure-espionage novel she'd bought at the grocery store and began to read. By the time she'd gone over the same paragraph for the third time, she gave up.

There were dark circles under her eyes when she got up the next morning, and no matter how skillful she was with her makeup, she couldn't hide them. She had tried Edina's office number twice, without success, when Mark showed up.

The moment he got a look at her face, he frowned and put a hand to her forehead. "You're not looking so good, Scoop. Are you sick?"

*Yes,* Carly thought miserably. "No," she said out loud.

He didn't look convinced. "I can start the interviews without you," he said. "And I'll bring my notes by later, so we can go over them."

"Mark, I'm new on this job. I don't want to mess up—"

"One day won't make a difference, Carly. And, like I said, I can get the legwork done without you."

Stubbornly Carly shook her head. She grabbed an orange while Mark reached for the laptop, and they set out to begin their day's work. It was ten o'clock before she got a chance to sneak out of Mark's office at the *Times,* where they'd been arranging interviews with divorced fathers, and put a call through to Edina.

"Did you talk to Mark?" the agent asked immediately.

Carly sat on the corner of her desk, the telephone receiver pressed to her ear. "No," she said. "I shouldn't have given you the play without talking to Mark first. I want you to send it back."

There was a short, stunned silence on the other end of the line. "Ms. Barnett, this is a very special property, and I could have half a dozen producers fighting over it by nightfall."

"I just wanted your opinion, remember?" Carly said, pulling her reading glasses off and setting them aside on the desk with a clatter. "Please. Just express it back to me—"

"I can't do that, I'm afraid. I'm going to call Mark myself. We're old friends—maybe he'll listen to reason."

Carly fairly leaped off the desk. "You can't do that," she cried in a frantic whisper. "He'll be furious—"

Edina sighed indulgently. "Mark is quick-tempered, I'll give you that. But once he's had time to think—"

*"Send back the manuscript!"* Carly broke in.

"If Mark asks me to—personally—I will."

Rage and panic filled Carly as the door of her office opened and Mark peered around it. "Ready to go out and talk to the man in the street?" he asked.

"Goodbye," Carly said into the receiver, and slammed it down.

Mark's eyebrows drew together in a frown. "Who was that?"

Carly tried to smile, and failed. She wanted to tell Mark the truth, but she was afraid.

They went back to work after that, and for the next three days, they were busy. By the time Mark was ready to draft the first version of the article, Carly was sure they'd talked to every divorced father in Portland.

Mark worked on the computer on his desk at home, and the keys clicked rapidly as his fingers raced to keep up with his thoughts. Carly stood behind him, one hand resting on his shoulder, reading the little words as fast as they appeared on the screen.

"Biased," she commented, when he finally reared back in his chair and pushed the Print button. "Some of these guys are card-carrying sewer rats and you know it. I could go to their wives and get an entirely different story!"

Mark turned far enough in his chair to give Carly a challenging look. "So do it," he said.

Carly pulled her notebook from her purse and reached for the phone. "Okay, I will," she replied, already punching out a number. She'd have to do some investigating to reach most of the ex-wives of the men she and Mark had interviewed, but she had information on a few.

When Carly arrived home late the following night, Janet brought her an express package that had been left with her by the building manager. Carly opened it right there in the hallway and found Mark's play inside.

Unconsciously she raised one hand to her heart in a gesture of relief.

Janet looked horrified. "You mean you haven't told him?"

"We've been so busy with the assignment—"

"Thin ice," Janet said as Carly left her to walk down the hallway to her own door. "You're walking on thin ice."

In the privacy of her own apartment, Carly stood holding the manuscript, her lower lip caught between her teeth. Despite everything she'd said about telling Mark, Edina had returned the play. That meant she'd changed her mind—didn't it?

She laid the play down on the table and went to the desk. As usual, she had several messages. Carly played them, steeling herself against an angry call from Mark or some kind of threat from Edina, but all the messages were from women she'd been trying to reach for interviews.

In calling them back and taking notes, Carly was able to forget her outstanding problem for a while. She wrote rapidly, nodding to herself as the divorced mothers told stories about the former husbands she and Mark had interviewed about fathers' rights.

Late that night when she'd roughed in the outline for the first draft of her article, Carly held Mark's play in both hands for a moment, then dropped it into her desk drawer. *Out of sight, out of mind,* she thought with a pang of guilt.

She spent the next day interviewing, and the day after that squirreled away in her office, writing. She had just turned the finished product, an article rebutting Mark's, in to Allison when she was called to Mr. Clark's office.

Filled with nervous excitement, Carly obeyed the summons.

After telling her to sit, Mr. Clark launched right into the assignment. There was a new shelter for battered women opening in the city, and the director had some innovative ideas. He wanted Carly to get an interview.

Carly fairly danced out of his office. Here was her chance to really show what she could do. *Carly Barnett, girl reporter,* she thought with a happy grin. She stopped by Emmeline's desk.

"Is Mark—Mr. Holbrook in yet?"

Emmeline shook her head, seemingly unconcerned. "His hours are flexible," she said. "He pretty much sets them himself."

Carly sighed and nodded, then vanished into her office. She had work to do.

MARK STOOD GRIPPING the telephone receiver, a glass of orange juice in his free hand, his body rigid with shock.

"So you see," Edina Peters finished up, "I really think it's time you stopped hiding this jewel of a play in your desk drawer and let me sell it. It could be adapted for the screen in five minutes, and we're talking major money here, Mark."

His muscles finally thawed, and he flung the orange juice at the fireplace. Glass shattered against brick. But his voice was deadly calm. "Carly showed you the play," he said like a robot, even though Edina had already told him that. He guessed he was hoping the agent would say no, she'd made a mistake, it had been someone else.

"She meant well," Edina said. "Afterwards she had an attack of conscience and begged me to send it back to her. I did—after making a few copies."

Mark closed his eyes tightly. His stomach twisted inside him, and an ache pounded at his nape. *Carly,* he thought, and the name splintered against his spirit the way the glass had against the fireplace.

"Mark?" Edina prompted.

He felt sick. He forced himself to speak evenly, to relax his grip on the receiver. "I'm here, Edina," he rasped.

"Will you let me sell it?"

*My guts are in that play,* he thought. *It's an open door to my soul.* "No," he answered.

"But—"

"The discussion is over," he broke in. And then he

hung up the telephone with only a moderate amount of force.

He'd planned to work at home that day on a human-interest piece he and Clark had been discussing, but now that he knew what Carly had done, he could only think of one thing—confronting her. Resolute, he strode into the bathroom, stripped off the shorts and T-shirt he'd worn for a late-morning run and showered.

He dressed hastily, and drove away from the house with his tires screeching on the asphalt. He shouldn't have trusted Carly, he thought as he sped down the freeway. He shouldn't have loved her.

He jammed one hand through his hair and cursed when he heard a siren behind him, then glanced into his rearview mirror. A silver-blue light whirled on top of the squad car—sure enough, he was the man the officer wanted to see.

Filled with quiet rage, Mark pulled over to the side of the road and waited.

# CHAPTER EIGHT

CARLY HAD BEEN down in the morgue in the basement of the newspaper building, reading up on past articles about shelters for battered women, and her heart did a little leap when the doors whisked open in the lobby to reveal Mark.

Her instant smile faded when their eyes linked, however, and she knew in that moment that she'd waited too long to tell him about the play. She wanted to explain, but when she tried to speak, no sound came out of her mouth.

Mark jabbed a button on the panel and the doors closed. The look in his eyes was cold and remote. "I guess I didn't lose those bets with my buddies after all," he said, his voice as rough as gravel in a rusty can. "I wasn't in love—just lust."

Carly sagged against the wall of the elevator, her hands gripping the stainless-steel railing. "That was cruel," she said. "I had a reason for what I did."

He struck another button, and the elevator stopped where it was. His hands came to rest against the wall on either side of Carly's head, and his eyes bored into hers. "Oh?" he rasped.

She swallowed, wanting to duck beneath his arm and start the elevator going again, but unable to move. She was like a sparrow gazing into the eyes of a cobra.

"I wanted a professional opinion," she managed to say. "I was h-hoping to persuade you to let *Broken Vows* be produced."

Mark ran the tip of one index finger down the V of her blouse in a impudent caress. "And make lots of money? The joke's on you, baby—I already have a fortune. And until an hour ago I would have given you anything you wanted."

Carly's eyes stung with tears of humiliation and frustration. "Will you stop being a melodramatic bastard and listen to me, please? I don't give a damn about your money—I never did! I wanted to see the play produced because something that good should be—"

"Shared with the world?" he interrupted acidly, arching one eyebrow. "Come on, Carly—that's a cliché."

"I'm not the one who said it," she pointed out, battling for composure. "You did."

He turned away, touched another button and set the elevator moving again. "Goodbye, Carly," he said. His broad shoulders barred her from him like a high, impenetrable wall, and when the doors opened on their floor, he stepped out.

Carly couldn't move, she was so filled with pain. And she let the elevator go all the way back to the lobby before she pressed the proper button. Reaching her floor, she hurried into her office, glancing neither right nor left, and closed the door.

She was sitting behind her desk, still trying to pull herself together, when Emmeline buzzed her and announced, with a question in her voice, that Helen Holbrook was on the line.

"Hello, Helen," Carly greeted Mark's mother sadly, not knowing what to expect. Despite their conversation in the garden that day in San Francisco, the woman was probably furious with her, and Carly steeled herself to be harangued.

"Edina told me about the play," Helen said, her voice calm. "She said Mark wasn't pleased that you'd shown it to her."

Recalling the way he'd looked at her in the elevator, the cold, bitter way he'd spoken, Carly was anguished. "I'd say that was an understatement," she got out. "He doesn't want to have anything to do with me now."

Helen sighed. "Mark can be positively insufferable. He's hardheaded, just like his father."

A despairing smile tugged at the corners of Carly's mouth. "You're being very kind," she said, "but there's something else you're trying to tell me, isn't there?"

"Yes," Helen confessed in a rush. "Carly, something has happened, and I don't want Mark to be told about it over the telephone. I must ask you to talk to him for me."

Images of another automobile accident, with Nathan seriously hurt, filled Carly's mind with garish sounds and colors. "What is it?" she whispered.

"Jeanine has crashed her car again," Helen said sadly. "Nathan wasn't with her, thank God, but naturally he's very upset."

Carly's forehead was resting in her hand. "And Jeanine?"

"She's in a coma, Carly, and not expected to live."

Carly squeezed her eyes closed, remembering the beautiful auburn-haired woman who had once been Mark's wife. "My God."

"Jeanine has her parents, but Nathan needs Mark. Carly, could you please go to him and tell him, as gently as you can, what's happened?"

After swallowing hard, she nodded and said, "Yes." Her heart twisted inside her to think how frightened Nathan must be. "Yes, Helen, I'll tell him."

"Thank you," Helen replied with tears in her voice. Then she added, "I'll try to reason with Mark while he's here. He loves you, and he's an idiot if he throws away what you've got together."

Carly thought of the look she'd seen in Mark's eyes and grieved. She knew that as far as he was concerned, their relationship was over. "Thanks," she said softly. Then the two women said their goodbyes and hung up.

Carly found Mark in his office, standing at the window and glaring out at the city. His name sounded hoarse when she said it.

He turned to glower at her.

"Mark, there's been an accident," she said in measured tones. She saw the fear leap in his eyes and added quickly, "Nathan wasn't hurt—it's Jeanine. She's—she's not expected to live."

The color drained out of Mark's face, and Carly longed to put her arms around him, but she didn't dare. In his mood, he would probably push her away, and she knew she couldn't bear that. "Dear God," he said, and turned around to punch out a number on his telephone.

Carly slipped out of the office and closed the door.

Mark left five minutes later without saying goodbye, and Carly went into the women's restroom and splashed cold water on her face until she was sure she wouldn't cry. Then she went back to work.

When quitting time came, the relief was almost overwhelming. She stuffed her files and notes into her briefcase, snatched up her purse and drove home in a daze. When she pulled into her parking space in the apartment lot, she was ashamed to realize the drive had passed without her noticing.

She went to her apartment without stopping for the mail or a word with Janet, dropped all her things just inside the door and then raced into her room, flung herself down on the bed and sobbed.

After a while, though, she began to think that if Mark was so easily angered, so lacking in understanding or compassion, she didn't want him anyway.

At least, that was what she told herself. Inside, she felt raw and broken, as though a part of her had been torn away. Carly showered, put on shorts and a summer top and went downstairs to exercise.

When she got back to her apartment, the phone was ringing. Carly made a lunge for it and gasped out an anxious hello, praying the caller was Mark. That he'd come to his senses.

She was both disappointed and relieved to hear her father's voice. "Hello, Carly."

Instantly Carly wanted to start blubbering again, but she held herself in check. Her dad was hundreds of miles away, and there was nothing to be gained by dragging him into her problems. "Hi, Dad. What's up?"

"I just thought I'd tell you that I liked that piece you sent me about the food contest. That was really good reporting."

In spite of everything, Carly had to smile. Don Barnett wasn't interested in soufflés and coffee cakes, she knew that. He called purely because he cared. "Thanks, Dad. I'm expecting a Pulitzer at the very least."

He chuckled. "I never was very good at coming up with excuses. I want to know what's the matter, and don't you dare say 'nothing.'"

Carly let out a ragged sigh. "I finally fell head over heels and it didn't work out."

"What do you mean, it didn't work out?" her dad demanded. "What kind of lamebrain would throw away a chance to make a life with you?"

"One named Mark Holbrook."

"Is there anything I can do?"

"Yeah," Carly answered, making a joke to keep from crying. "You can eat a banana split in my honor. I'd like to drown my sorrows in junk food, but if I do, none of my clothes will fit."

"Maybe you should just get on a plane and come back here, sweetheart. Ryerton may not be a metropolis, but we do have a newspaper."

Carly was already shaking her head. "No way, Dad—I'm standing my ground. I have as much right to live in Portland and work at the *Times* as Mark does."

"Okay, then I'll come out there. I'll black his eyes for him."

Carly smiled at the images that came to her mind, then remembered that Jeanine was lying in a hospital, near death, and was solemn again. "I'm okay," she insisted. "If you want to come out and visit, terrific. But you're not blacking anybody's eyes."

"Maybe I'll do that. Maybe I'll just get on an airplane and come out there."

"That would be great, Dad," Carly said, knowing her father wouldn't leave Kansas except under the most dire circumstances. He hadn't been on a plane in twenty years.

Five minutes later, when Carly hung up, she dialed the Holbrooks' number in San Francisco, and Mark's father answered.

"Hello," he said when she'd introduced herself, and there was a cool note in his voice.

Carly wondered what Mark had told him about her. "I'm sorry to bother you, but I wanted to know if there was any news about Jeanine."

Mr. Holbrook sighed. "She's taken a turn for the better," he said. "The doctors are pretty sure she'll survive, though how long it will take her to recover completely is anybody's guess." His voice was a degree or two warmer now. "Shall I ask Mark to call you when he comes in, Carly?"

She shook her head, forgetting for a moment that Mr. Holbrook couldn't see her. "No!" she said too quickly. She paused, cleared her throat and tried to speak in a more moderate tone. "Please don't mention me to Mark at all."

"But—"

"Please, Mr. Holbrook. It will only upset him, and he needs to be able to concentrate on helping Nathan right now."

Mark's father didn't agree or disagree; he simply asked Carly to take care of herself and said goodbye.

JEANINE WAS LYING in the intensive care unit, tubes running into her bruised and battered body, her head bandaged. She opened her eyes when Mark took her hand, and her fingers tightened around his.

"Nathan…?" she managed to rasp.

"He's safe, Jeanine."

Tears formed in the corners of her eyes. "Are you—taking him home?"

It wouldn't be a kindness to lie to her, Mark decided. Jeanine needed to know their son would be loved and taken care of. "Yes," he said, still holding her hand. He didn't love her—since his relationship with Carly he'd come to realize that he never had—but it hurt him to see her suffering.

"I was drinking," she said clearly, her eyes pleading with Mark to understand.

He nodded. "You need some help, Jeanine."

She tried to smile. "Maybe it's hopeless."

Mark shook his head. "You'll make it," he said hoarsely, even though he had no idea whether that was true or not. Jeanine was in serious trouble, and they both knew it.

"Take care of Nathan," she finished. And then her eyes drifted closed and she slept.

Mark went out into the hallway to find Jeanine's father and mother waiting. They both had deep shadows under their eyes.

"Was she upset that you're taking Nathan?" his former mother-in-law asked.

Mark shook his head. "She knows I love him," he said, pitying these people, wanting to ease their pain but not knowing how. "I'm sorry you have to go through this."

The Martins nodded in weary unison, and Mark left them to keep their vigil.

When he arrived at his parents' home, his mother was waiting up for him. She served him a cup of decaffeinated coffee and launched right into her lecture. "You're a fool, Mark Holbrook. An absolute idiot."

He sighed and rubbed his tired, burning eyes with a thumb and forefinger. "Mother, I'm not in the mood for this."

"I don't care what you're in the mood for," Helen

retorted. "Carly showed Edina that play because she hoped some professional feedback would convince you to let it be produced, and for no other reason."

Mark had been cherishing secret dreams of leaving the newspaper business to write plays for over a year, but he hadn't meant for *Broken Vows* to be seen by anyone. He'd written it in an attempt to clear his mind of the pain. "When I was married to Jeanine," he said slowly, "I didn't know where she was or what she was up to half the time. As you already know, I had some pretty unpleasant surprises. I don't want to live like that again."

"Carly is nothing like Jeanine, and in your heart, you know that. Besides, I believe you love her."

Mark sighed. He was tired, and he ached from the core of his spirit out. "Carly is more like Jeanine than you'd like to think, Mother," he said evenly, "and as for loving her—I'll get over it."

"Will you?" Helen challenged. "Don't be so sure of that, my dear. You can't turn love on and shut it off like a faucet, you know."

He thrust himself out of his chair and bent to kiss his mother's forehead. "Give it up," he said with quiet firmness. "It's over between Carly and me."

Upstairs, Mark carefully opened the guest-room door and stepped inside. Nathan lay sprawled on the bed, arms and legs askew, his eyelids flickering as he dreamed.

Gently Mark brushed his son's hair back from his forehead. *I wanted you to come and live with me, buddy,* he told Nathan silently, speaking from his heart, *but I didn't expect it to happen like this. Honest.*

The child stirred, then opened his eyes. "Dad?" he asked on a long yawn.

Mark sat down on the edge of the bed. "Sorry, big guy. I didn't mean to wake you up."

"Is Mom okay?"

"Yeah," Mark answered. "But she has to stay in the hospital for a while."

Nathan accepted that with the sometimes remarkable stoicism of a ten-year-old. "I can visit her, can't I?"

In that moment the decision was made. Mark would return to San Francisco, buy a town house and build a life for himself and his son. Maybe he would even write a play—one that didn't touch every raw nerve in his soul, one he could bear to show to an agent. "Sure you can visit her," he said. "Now get some sleep. You've got school tomorrow."

Nathan screwed up his face. "I have to go to *school?*"

Mark chuckled. "No," he teased. "Of course not. A fifth-grade education will take you a long way in the world." He started to rise off the bed, but Nathan stopped him with one anxious little hand.

"Dad, where's Carly? Is she going to live with us?"

Those two simple questions left Mark feeling as though he'd just stepped into the whirling blades of a giant fan. *Carly,* he thought, and the name was a lonely cry deep in his spirit. "Carly's in Portland, doing her job," he managed to say, after a moment or two of recovery. "And no, it's just going to be the two of us for a while, buddy."

For a moment Nathan looked as though he might cry. Mark could see that the kid had been spinning dreams of a real home and a regular family in his head, and seeing his disappointment was painful. "Mom said Carly probably had a baby growing inside her. Does she, Dad?"

Mark swallowed, and it felt like he'd gulped down a petrified grapefruit. *God, I hope not,* he thought. "No," he said forcefully, trying to convince himself as well as Nathan. "No, big guy, there isn't any baby."

EMMELINE LOOKED CONCERNED as she handed Carly her morning coffee. "I guess you know that Mr. Holbrook is leaving the paper and moving back to San Francisco," she said.

Carly felt as though Emmeline had just flung the scalding contents of the cup all over her. "N-no," she answered, avoiding the secretary's gaze and fumbling in the depths of her purse for her glasses. "No, I hadn't heard about that."

"Oh," said Emmeline, and her voice was small and confused. "I'm sorry if I said anything I shouldn't have."

Carly took her glasses from their case and poked them onto her face. "What Mr. Holbrook does is nothing to me," she lied, flipping on her computer. She'd been living at the battered women's shelter for three days, pretending to be hiding from a violent husband, and she was ready to write about the experiences of the people she'd met there.

Emmeline couldn't seem to let the subject drop. "His ex-wife was hurt in an accident, you know, and he's got custody of his son now. I guess he didn't want to uproot the kid and make it so he couldn't see his mother."

"You're probably right," Carly answered, deliberately sounding distracted and preoccupied.

Finally Emmeline took the hint. She slipped out of Carly's office with a muttered goodbye and closed the door behind her. The moment she was alone, Carly slammed one fist down on the desk and whispered, "Damn you, Holbrook. Damn you to hell."

Fortunately the article absorbed her attention for the rest of the day. As she was leaving that evening, she passed Mark's office and couldn't help noticing that Emmeline and several of the other assistants were inside hanging streamers.

"There'll be a going-away party tomorrow," Emmeline called to her.

Carly nodded and bit her lower lip. She hadn't had to say any goodbyes to Mark; he'd said them for her. She made up her mind to busy herself outside the office the next day.

She spent a miserable night, finally falling asleep in the wee hours of the morning, only to be awakened by a wave of nausea with the rising of the sun. One hand clasped over her mouth, she made a dash for the bathroom.

"Oh, great," she complained, staggering to the kitchen for a cup of chamomile tea, "now I've got the flu."

The tea settled her stomach, though, and after a shower Carly felt better. She also felt guilty about staying away from the office just because of Mark's going-away party.

Resolutely Carly put on one of her best outfits—a pink silk suit from Hong Kong—and took extra care with her hair and makeup. She walked into the newsroom half an hour later, a Miss United States smile on her face, her briefcase swinging jauntily at her side.

When she was sure no one was watching, she fairly dived into her office and leaned against the door, feeling as though she'd just picked her way through an emotional mine field.

She switched on her computer and opened her brief-case, planning to go over her notes for a proposed article and hide out until Mark had heard a round of for-he's-a-jolly-good-fellow and left. Then Mr. Clark called an unexpected meeting.

Carly felt like a martyr being summoned from the dungeon for execution. She stood, smoothed her skirt and checked her hair and lipstick in a small mirror pulled from her purse. Then she walked bravely down the hall to the conference room.

Thanks to some cruel fate, she was seated directly across from Mark, and he was making no effort at all to ignore her. His solemn brown eyes studied her thought-fully while he turned an unsharpened pencil end over end on the tabletop.

Carly willed him to look away, and he seemed to sense that, refusing to give in. Finally she dropped her eyes, her cheeks burning, and devoutly wished she'd fol-lowed her original instincts and called in sick that day.

Mr. Clark got up and made a speech about what an honor it had been to work with Mark Holbrook and how they were all going to miss him. Everyone tit-tered when he mentioned Mark's plans to write a play—everyone except Carly, that is. Her eyes shot to his face in angry question.

He responded with an infuriating grin.

After what seemed like a millennium, Mr. Clark finished raving about Mark's accomplishments and suggested that everyone take time for cake and punch. Carly slipped out of the conference room and hurried in the opposite direction.

Even in her office she could hear the laughter and the talk, and it made her heart turn over in her chest. Mark, gone. It was almost impossible to believe that after today she wouldn't so much as catch a glimpse of him or hear his voice in the hallway.

She hadn't had such a hard time holding back tears since the time she'd set the stage curtains on fire with one of her flaming batons during the Miss Feed and Grain pageant. She'd been fourteen then, and she felt younger than that now.

The only thing to do was work. That, her father had always told her, was the salve that healed every wound.

She turned to her computer and sat back in her chair when she saw the message that popped up on her screen.

Goodbye, Scoop. Better luck next time.

That did it. Carly's tears began to flow, and she couldn't stop them. She was standing at the window, gazing out at the city and frantically drying her cheeks with a wad of tissue, when she heard a gentle rap at the door.

She was afraid to turn around—afraid Mark would be standing there, afraid he wouldn't. "Yes?"

"The party's over, Carly," Emmeline's voice said quietly. "I'll cover for you if you want to go home."

Carly was a trouper, and she knew the show had to go on, no matter what kind of show it was. But the front she was hiding behind was teetering dangerously, and she needed to be alone. She nodded without looking at the assistant, grimly amused that she'd thought no one in the office knew about her affair with Mark.

*What a naive little idiot you were,* she scolded herself, gathering up her purse and turning off the computer. She left her briefcase behind, under no delusion that she would get any worthwhile work done that night.

When she arrived at her apartment, she stayed only long enough to exchange her silk suit for cut-off jeans and a turquoise T-shirt. She went to a matinee at the mall, where she cried silently all through a comedy, then had supper at a fast-food place. When she still couldn't face going home after that, she went to another movie.

She never remembered what that one was about.

In the morning Mr. Clark called her into his office and asked her if she was aware that she was covered by a company health plan. "You don't look well, Ms. Barnett," he finished.

*It's only a broken heart,* Carly wanted to reply. *In about sixty years it will probably heal.* "I guess I'm just a little tired," she said, hoping he wouldn't decide the job was too much for her. Being demoted or getting fired would be beyond bearing.

"I liked that piece you did on battered women. It was damn good."

Carly was reassured, if only slightly. "Thank you. I've been thinking about a piece on women entrepreneurs—"

Mr. Clark waved her into silence. "No, that's been done too much lately. There's a river rafting expedition leaving on Saturday—one of those things meant to give executives confidence in their inner strength. I'd like you to go along on that. It's going to last about three days."

Carly thought of pitching through rapids and spinning in whirlpools and felt her flu symptoms returning, but she managed a brilliant smile. "That sounds exciting," she said.

"Of course, we'll send a photographer along, too. That way, if one of you drowns, the other one can still bring back the story." Mr. Clark beamed at his joke, and Carly dutifully laughed.

Carly took down the information he gave her and left the office early. She had preparations to make, and she was going to need hiking boots, flannel shirts and a sleeping bag, among other things. She went shopping and bought more things than she could possibly have carried without help from the sales staff.

On the way home her car mysteriously headed toward Mark's house instead of the apartment building. She knew he wasn't there as soon as she reached the end of the driveway, but she didn't leave. She just sat, her eyes brimming with tears, remembering how she and Mark had talked and laughed and made love in that house. She'd given him her virginity there, and no matter how many men she might meet in the future, she would never forget that first night in Mark's arms.

She touched the gold bracelet he'd given her, then fumbled open the catch. Stepping up onto the porch, she dropped the glimmering chain through the mail slot. Then Carly hurried back to her car, started the ignition and left.

That night she slept, but it was only because of nervous exhaustion. And in the morning she was sick again. Evidently, she decided, she'd caught some kind of intermittent flu. She made herself a cup of herbal tea, forced it down and presently felt better.

She spent the day at a local high-school gymnasium, sitting on the bleachers with a lot of other potential adventurers, listening to the head river rafter explain what was involved in the expedition. He said the trip wasn't for weaklings, and anybody who couldn't stand three measly days grappling with the wilderness should just go home and forget the whole thing.

That option sounded good to Carly, but she had her job to think about, so she stayed. Besides, she needed to stay busy in order to keep herself from dwelling on Mark and all the things that could have been.

She drove home that night and found a message from Jim Benson, the anchorman, on her machine. He obviously knew that Mark had left town, and he wanted to know if Carly would have supper with him after the six o'clock newscast.

"What the hell?" Carly said to her empty apartment. Life was like a river, and she had to raft down it. She called Jim back and left a message with his assistant that she'd meet him at the station at seven o'clock.

## CHAPTER NINE

JIM'S GAZE WAS filled with gentle discernment as he joined Carly in his office after the newscast. "You're as gorgeous as ever," he said, "but you look as though somebody's been batting you around like a croquet ball."

Carly managed a smile. That 'somebody' was Mark Holbrook and they both knew it. "And this is a pity date, is that it?"

Jim chuckled and shook his head. "Nothing so magnanimous," he said. "I'm still nursing a vain hope that when you get over Mark, you'll begin to see that I'm a nice guy with prospects."

She slipped her arm through his. "I already know you're a nice guy. If you weren't, I wouldn't be here."

He escorted her out of the station by a back way, and opened the door of his fancy sports car for her. "I know of a great seafood place," he said. "Does that sound good?"

Thanks to the strange case of flu that had overtaken her in recent days, Carly didn't have much of an appetite for anything. But she smiled and tried to look enthusiastic as she nodded.

"I've got to ask you a question," she said when they were zipping along the freeway. "How did you know it was over between Mark and me?"

Jim gave her a sidelong look. "He told me. Like I said once, Carly, I've known Mark for a long time."

Carly bit down on her lower lip to keep from asking what Mark had said about her. Probably Jim was one of those buddies he'd talked about, the ones he'd bet that he'd never fall in love.

She didn't care, damn it. She *wouldn't* care.

"If you love Mark," Jim said reluctantly, "don't write him off just yet. Between getting custody of his son and what's happened to Jeanine, I don't guess he's thinking straight. He needs some time to adjust."

"He's planning to 'adjust' in San Francisco—or didn't he tell you that?"

"He told me."

Carly gazed out the window for a long time; there was an emotional storm gathering inside her and she didn't want Jim to see her face. "I love him," she said presently in a small, choked voice, "but it's probably better that we ended it when we did. Mark is temperamental—I would have spent the rest of my life walking on eggshells, worrying that I'd offended him somehow. Who needs it?"

Jim chuckled ruefully. "What am I doing? I should be trying to impress you with what a terrific guy I am." He paused to draw a deep breath, then let it out again. "Carly, Mark isn't a temperamental man—he's practical and pragmatic, like any good journalist. None of this stuff is typical of him."

Carly finally dared to look at Jim again. "What are you saying?"

"That meeting you caused some kind of upheaval in Mark's emotions. If I know him—and believe me, I do—he's still reeling from the shock. Given time and distance, he'll realize he's being a jerk."

Although she had no intention of waiting around for Mark to forgive her, Carly was comforted by Jim's words. They gave her hope that one day the hurting would stop and she could go on with her life without limping inwardly. "I have this friend who wants to go out with you," she said, remembering Janet's request to be "fixed up" with Jim.

He grinned. "The good-looking one with the grocery bag who was standing in the hall the first time we went out?"

Carly nodded, smiling. "That's Janet. She's a wonderful person."

Jim laughed. "We're a pair, you and I. Will somebody tell me why I'm sitting next to one of the most beautiful women in America, extolling the virtues of some other guy?"

"That's easy," Carly answered softly. "It's because you're a sensational person yourself. Watch out, Jim— I'm starting to get the idea that there might be a few nice men out there after all."

Dinner was enjoyable, though Carly wasn't able to eat much. After Jim brought her home, she took a bubble bath and went to bed with a book. And her thoughts strayed to Mark with every other word.

On Friday afternoon, her extra clothes and sleeping bag stuffed into a canvas backpack, Carly got into her car and drove southeast to the town of Bend, where the river expedition would begin. It was late when she finally found the riverside park where the others had camped, and she noticed first thing that the mosquitoes were out in force.

"Don't be a negative thinker," she muttered to herself, getting out her backpack and making her way toward the camp.

The others were gathered around a huge bonfire, and they all looked at home in their skins, as Carly's grandmother used to say. It was evident that river rafting was nothing new to most of them, but Carly already had motion sickness just thinking about it.

Wearing her trusty smile, along with jeans, hiking boots, a flannel shirt and a lightweight jacket, she joined the gathering.

THE HOUSE MARK selected was in a good part of San Francisco, just far enough from his parents' place to promote good relations. The windows in his den offered a view of the Bay, and Nathan wouldn't have to change schools in the fall.

To Mark's way of thinking, the place was perfect.

Except, of course, for the fact that Carly wasn't there.

He reached into the pocket of his sports jacket and touched the bracelet she'd dropped through the mail slot at the house in Portland. Sometimes he fancied that he could feel her warmth and incredible energy still vibrating through the metal.

With a sigh, Mark stepped closer to the windows and fixed his gaze on the Bay. The furniture wouldn't arrive for another week, so there was no place to sit.

Life without Carly was like running in a three-legged race, he reflected; what should have given him more mobility and freedom only made it more awkward to move. He thrust his hand through his hair.

"Dad?"

He turned to see Nathan standing uncertainly in the doorway. "Am I allowed in here?" he asked.

Mark frowned. "Why wouldn't you be?"

Nathan lifted one of his small shoulders in a shrug. "Mom didn't like me to go in her living room. She was afraid I'd spill something on the carpet."

With some effort, Mark kept himself from expressing his irritation. Being annoyed with Jeanine wouldn't do anyone any good. "Things are different here, big guy," he said as the boy came to stand beside him. "We're not going to worry much about the carpets."

Nathan looked up at him and flashed the gapped grin that always gave Mark's heart a little twist. "I used to have to go to bed at nine o'clock," he said, obviously hoping Mark would shoot another rule down in flames.

"You still do," Mark replied.

"Darn."

"Hello!" a feminine voice called suddenly in the distance. "Is anybody home?"

"Grandma," Mark and Nathan told each other in chorus, and left the room to go down the stairs and greet Helen.

"I've come bearing gifts," she said, indicating the bucket of take-out chicken she carried in one arm. "Am I invited to stay for dinner?"

Mark smiled at his mother, while Nathan rushed forward to collect the chicken.

"She can stay, can't she?" the boy asked, looking back over his shoulder.

"No," Mark teased. "We're going to hold her up for the chicken and then shove her out through the mail slot."

The three of them ate in the spacious, brightly lit

kitchen, at a card table borrowed from the elder Holbrooks. When the meal was over, Mark sent Nathan upstairs to take his bath.

"I still think both of you should be staying at our house," Helen fretted when she and Mark were alone.

Mark grinned and shook his head. "We're having a great time camping out in sleeping bags and living on fast food."

"If you're having such a 'great time,'" Helen ventured shrewdly, "then how do you account for that heartache I see in your eyes?"

Mark's grin faded. "It shows, huh?"

Helen nodded. "Yes. Mark, when are you going to admit you were wrong, fly up to Portland and ask that lovely young lady to forgive you?"

He sighed, glad his mother couldn't possibly know how many times he'd made plans to do just that, only to stop himself at the last second. Carly was just getting started on her career, and he had to make a solid home for Nathan. He told himself it would be better if they just went their separate ways.

"She's already dating Jim Benson," he said, hoping that would throw Helen off the subject for good. "I was a passing fancy."

"Nonsense. When the two of you were in a room together, the air crackled. I don't care if she's dating a movie star and an underwear model on alternate nights—Carly loves *you*."

Mark was fresh out of patience. "Well, I don't love her—okay?"

"Liar," Helen responded implacably. "Don't you think I can see what's happening to you? You're being eaten alive by the need to see her."

"You've been reading too many romance novels, Mother," Mark replied evenly. What she said was true, he reflected to himself, and he damned her for knowing it.

Helen got out of her chair with a long-suffering sigh and began gathering up the debris from their impromptu dinner, only to have Mark stop her and take over the task himself. He wasn't about to start depending on other people, even for little things.

When she was gone and Nathan was asleep in a down-filled bag on the floor of his bedroom upstairs, Mark got out his laptop, set it on the card table and switched it on. After a few minutes of thought, he poised his fingers over the keyboard.

"Carly," he typed without consciously planning to.

"Now that's brilliant, Holbrook," he said to himself. "Neil Simon is probably sweating blood."

He sat back in his chair, cupping his hands behind his head, and closed his eyes. In his mind he saw Carly dancing with Jim Benson that night when she'd insisted on keeping her date with the guy. And even though Benson was one of the best friends he'd ever had, his nerve endings jangled just to think of another man holding Carly, kissing her, taking her to bed.

He cursed. Carly wasn't going to go to bed with Jim or anyone else, not for a while, he told himself. She was too sensible for that.

Then he recalled the way she'd responded to him, the soft, greedy sounds she'd made as he pleasured her, the way she'd moved beneath him. His loins tightened painfully, and her name rose to his throat in an aching mass. She was a healthy, passionate woman and, in time, she would want the release a man's body could give her.

In anguish, Mark thrust himself out of his chair and stormed across the room to the telephone. He picked it up from the floor and punched out her number before he could stop himself, not knowing what he would say, needing to hear the sound of her voice.

Her machine picked up, and Mark leaned against the wall in mingled disappointment and relief. "Hi, this is Carly," the recorded announcement ran. "If you're a friend, I'm off braving the wilds of the Deschutes River, and I'll be back on Tuesday morning. If you're a potential burglar, I'm busy bathing my Doberman pinscher, Otto. Either way, leave a message after the beep. Bye."

Mark closed his eyes and swallowed, unable to speak even if he'd had words to say. He hadn't expected hearing her voice to hurt so much, or to flood his mind and spirit with so many memories.

He replaced the receiver gently and went back to his computer, but no words would come to him. Finally he turned the machine off and went upstairs, where he looked in on Nathan.

The boy was sleeping soundly, a stuffed bear he wouldn't have admitted to owning within easy reach. Mark smiled sadly, closed the door and went on to his own room.

It was more of a suite, actually, with its own sizable bathroom and a sitting area that had probably been a nursery at one time. The walls were papered in pink-and-white stripes, the floor was carpeted in pale rose, and the place had an air about it that brought whimsical things to mind—sugar and spice and everything nice.

He allowed himself another bleak smile, imagining a baby girl with Carly's big blue-green eyes and tousled blond hair. The knowledge that such a child might never exist practically tore him apart.

Resolutely Mark stepped out of the sitting room and closed the door behind him. In the morning, he told himself, he'd see about having it redone to suit a confirmed bachelor.

CARLY UNROLLED HER sleeping bag and spread it out on the ground near two other women who hadn't bothered to include her in their conversation. The photographer the newspaper had sent along was a man—a very uncommunicative man.

After removing her boots, she crawled into the bag in her jeans and shirt, listening to the hooting of an owl and the quiet, whispering rush of the river.

The sky was bejeweled with stars, and the tops of ponderosa pines swayed in the darkness. It was all poetically beautiful, and there was a rock poking against Carly's left buttock.

She got out of the bag with a sigh and moved it over slightly, but when she lay down again, the ground was still as hard and ungiving as ever. A desolate feeling overcame her; she was surrounded by strangers, and Mark didn't love her anymore.

She began to cry, her body shaking with sobs she silenced by pressing the top of the sleeping bag against her mouth. It wasn't fair. Nothing in the whole damn world was fair.

After a long time Carly fell into a fitful, exhausted sleep, and she awakened with a start, what seemed like only minutes later, to find the gung-ho leader crouching beside her.

He was handsome, if you liked the Rambo type,

but Carly wasn't charmed by his indulgent grin or his words. "Wake up, Girl Scout," he said. "Everybody else is practically ready to jump into the rafts."

Horrified, Carly bolted upright, squirmed out of the sleeping bag and was instantly awash in nausea. She ran for the log shower rooms.

When she came out feeling pale and shaky and having done what absolutions she could manage, an attractive dark-haired woman wearing khaki shorts and a plaid cotton blouse was waiting. There was a camera looped around her neck.

"Feeling better?" she asked, offering a smile and a handshake. "My name is Hope McCleary, and I didn't come on this trip willingly."

Carly swallowed, glad to see a friendly face. "Carly Barnett," she answered. "And I was sort of shanghaied myself—I'm doing a piece for a newspaper."

Hope grinned. "With me it's a magazine. I work for a regional publication in California."

Carly felt a little better now that she'd found a buddy.

The two women walked back to the campsite together, and Hope helped Carly roll up her sleeping bag and stow it, with her backpack, in one of the rafts. The stuff was carefully covered with a rubber tarp.

Rambo sauntered over and looked Carly up and down with disapproving eyes. "You missed breakfast," he said.

Carly felt her stomach quiver.

"Maybe she wasn't hungry, all right?" Hope snapped, putting her hands on her hips and glaring at him. "Give her a break!"

Rambo backed off, and Carly looked at Hope with undisguised admiration. "Admit it—you're really an angel sent to convince me that life is worth living after all."

Hope grinned and shook her head. "I'm no angel, honey, but you're right about part of it—life is *definitely* worth living." She paused to pull in a breath. "Like I said, I'm just a humble magazine editor from San Francisco. Where do you live, Carly, and what newspaper do you write for?"

A pang went through Carly at the mention of the city that had charmed her so much. She might have visited it often if things had worked out between her and Mark. "I'm from Portland—my managing editor wants the scoop on adventure among executives. I guess I'm lucky he didn't want me to run with the bulls in Palermo."

Hope laughed and laid a hand on Carly's shoulder. "A woman called Intrepid," she said. "But you are a little green around the gills. Are you sure you wouldn't prefer to stay here and just question everybody when we get back?"

Carly would have given her rhinestone tiara for a room at the Best Western down the highway, but she wasn't about to let the weak side of her nature win out. "I'm going on this trip," she said firmly.

Soon they were seated in one of the rafts, wearing damp, musty-smelling orange life preservers and listening to Rambo's final speech of the morning. Everybody, he said, was responsible for doing their share of paddling. His eyes strayed to Carly when he added that one slacker could send a raft spinning into the rocks.

She sat determinedly on the wet bench, her jeans already soaked with river water, staring Rambo in the eye and silently praying that she wouldn't throw up.

Soon they were off, skimming down the river between mountains fringed with ponderosas and jack pines. The dirt on the banks had a red cast to it, and here and there the color had seeped into the trunks of trees. Carly got over being scared and was soon paddling for all she was worth.

Diamond-clear water sprayed her, and her morning tea rose to her throat a couple of times, but all in all the experience was exhilarating.

The convoy of three large rafts traveled until noon, then Rambo led them ashore for lunch. Shivering with cold and with the delight of finding a new area where she was competent, Carly drank tea and cheerfully chatted with the others.

After thirty minutes Rambo herded them all back into the boats again and they were off.

Several breathless hours later they stopped for the night, making camp in a glade where a stone circle marked the site of the last bonfire.

Carly plundered through her backpack for dry clothes, then went into the woods to change. When she returned, there was a fire blazing and food was being brought out of the boats in large, lightweight coolers.

Reminding herself that a Girl Scout always plans ahead, Carly hung her wet jeans and shirt on a bush, with the underwear secreted behind them.

She jumped when she turned and came face-to-face with Rambo. He was grinning down at her as though she'd just greased herself with chicken fat and entered a body-building competition.

"What was your name again?" he asked. Apparently, now that he'd decided Carly had a right to live, he was going to be chummy.

She barely stopped herself from answering, *Call me Intrepid.* "It's Carly," she said aloud. "Carly Barnett. And you're...?"

His dark brows drew together in a frown. "Weren't you listening during orientation?" he demanded. "It's John. John Walters. Remember that." Displeased again, he turned and stormed away.

Carly raised one hand to her forehead in a crisp salute.

Hope came to her, laughing. "Come on, Carly—let's go gather some wood before he decides you're plotting a mutiny."

"I just can't seem to please that guy," Carly told her friend, following Hope into the woods.

"Do you want to?" Hope asked over one shoulder.

Carly chuckled. She was feeling stronger by the minute. It was nice to know she was a survivor, that she wasn't going to die just because Mark had left her without so much as a backward look. "No, actually. There's bad karma between Rambo and me."

They found enough dry wood to fill their arms and returned to camp.

"Have you ever thought about writing for a magazine?" Hope asked as they dropped the firewood beside the blaze in the middle of the clearing.

Carly shrugged. "No, but that doesn't mean I wouldn't like to try it. Why?"

"You're obviously a very special lady, Carly, and I'm looking for someone to replace a staff writer at the end of the month. Could you send me some clips as soon as you get back to Portland?"

Carly was intrigued. Mentally she sorted through the pieces she'd done for the *Times*—the inside view of the shelter for battered women, the rebuttal to Mark's article on fathers' rights, the coverage of the food contest. "I don't have much, I'm afraid," she said finally. "I haven't been working for the paper all that long."

Hope shrugged. "Just send me what you can," she said.

That night was pleasant in a bittersweet sort of way. Everyone sat around the camp fire, full of roasted hot dogs and potato salad, and sang to the accompaniment of John Walters's guitar. The pungent perfume of the pines filled the air, and the river sang a mystical song begun when the Ice Age ended.

And Carly's heart ached fit to break because Mark wasn't there beside her calling her Scoop. She wondered now why she'd been so insulted at his jibes over her title; it seemed clear, in retrospect, that he'd only been teasing.

"Who was he?" Hope asked as they rolled their sleeping bags out, side by side, within six feet of the fire. Some of the other people had small tents, but most were stretching out under the stars.

"Who?" Carly countered, hedging. She didn't know whether talking about Mark would ease her heartache or get her started on another crying jag.

"The guy who left you with that puppy-loose-on-a-freeway look in your eyes, that's who."

Carly sat down and squirmed into her bag. "Just somebody I used to work with," she said. *And sleep with,* added a voice in her mind. *And love.*

Hope was looking up at the splendor of the night sky, her hands cupped behind her head. Her voice was too low to carry any farther than Carly's ears. "You're going to have his baby, aren't you?"

For a moment the ground seemed to rock beneath Carly's sleeping bag. Her hands moved frantically to her flat abdomen, and her mind raced through the pages of a mental calendar.

"Oh, my God," she whispered, squeezing her eyes shut.

"Sorry," Hope said sincerely. "I thought you'd already figured it out."

Carly sank her teeth into her lower lip. The nausea, the volatile emotions—she should have known.

"What are you going to do?" Hope asked.

"I have no idea," Carly managed to say. But there were things she did know. She was going to have the baby, and she was going to raise it herself. Beyond that, she couldn't think.

"You should tell him, whoever he is," Hope said.

"Yeah," Carly agreed halfheartedly. Mark had a right to know he was going to have another child, but she wasn't sure she had the courage to tell him. He might think she was trying to rope him into a relationship he didn't want, or he could hire lawyers and take the child away from her. After all, he'd planned to sue Jeanine for custody of Nathan.

Hope was quiet after that, and Carly lay huddled in her sleeping bag, imagining the ordeals of labor and birth with no one to lend moral support. After a long time she fell asleep.

She woke with the birds, went off to the woods to be sick and began another day.

That morning her raft overturned, and she and Hope and eight other people were dumped into the icy river. As Carly fought the current, her mouth and nose filled with water, her eyes blinded by the spray, she prayed. *Please, God, don't let anything happen to my baby.*

She made it to shore, half-drowned and gasping for breath, and so did everyone else who'd been spilled out of the raft, but their sleeping bags and backpacks were gone.

A camaraderie had formed between the travelers, though, and the others pooled their extra clothes to help those who'd lost their packs. Rambo had spare blankets in the lead raft.

"This is going to make one hell of a story," Hope said as she stood on the shore beside Carly, soaking wet, snapping pictures as the overturned raft was hauled toward the bank.

Carly could only nod. When she got back to the office, she was going to ask Mr. Clark for a nice, easy assignment—something like skydiving, or jumping over nineteen cars on a motorcycle.

For all of it, she was sorry the next afternoon when the trip ended and pickup trucks hauled the exhausted, exhilarated rafters back to the original camp.

Since Carly had lost everything but the clothes she'd been wearing when the raft tipped over the day before, she was spared the task of packing her gear. She and Hope stood by her car, talking.

"Be sure you send me those clippings, now," Hope said as the two women hugged in farewell.

Carly smiled and nodded. She was never going to forget what a good friend Hope had been to her on this crazy trip. "Take care," she said, slipping behind the wheel of her car.

That day's spate of morning sickness had already passed, and Carly was possessed of a craving for something sweet. She stopped at a doughnut shop and bought two maple bars that were sagging under the weight of their frosting.

"Here's to surviving," she said, taking a bite.

The drive back to Portland was long and uneventful. When Carly arrived, she staggered into the bathroom, without bothering to look through her mail or play her telephone messages, and took a long, steaming-hot shower.

When she'd washed away the lingering chill of the river and the aches and pains inherent in sleeping on the ground, she ate another maple bar, brushed her teeth and collapsed into bed.

Arriving at the paper the next morning, she immediately shut herself up with her computer and started outlining her article. She barely raised her eyes when Mike Fisher, the photographer who'd been sent on the trip with her but kept mostly to himself, brought in the prints.

Carly flipped through them, smiling. Her favorite showed her crawling out of the river with her hair hanging in her face in dripping tendrils and every line in her body straining for breath. *And for her talent, ladies and gentlemen,* she thought whimsically, *Miss United States will nearly drown.*

She made a mental note to ask for a copy of the photograph, then went back to work. Almost as an afterthought, she asked Emmeline to send her clippings to Hope in San Francisco.

A full week went by before Carly allowed herself to dream of moving to California and joining the staff of one of the most successful magazines published on the

West Coast. When Hope called and offered her a job at an impressive salary, Carly accepted without hesitation.

Maybe she couldn't have Mark Holbrook, but nobody was going to take San Francisco away from her.

# CHAPTER TEN

JANET GAVE CARLY a tearful hug in the parking lot behind their building. "Be happy, okay?" she said.

Carly nodded. Happiness was a knack she hadn't quite mastered yet, but she had the baby to look forward to and the challenge of another new job in another new city. "You, too," she replied. Janet was dating Jim Benson regularly, and things looked promising for them.

The two women parted, and Carly got behind the wheel of her car and began the drive to San Francisco. She would live in a hotel until she found an apartment, and her dad was breaking all precedent to fly out for a short visit.

Carly wanted to tell him about the baby in person.

As she wended her way out of Portland, she considered his possible reactions. After all, in Don Barnett's day women just didn't have babies and raise them alone—they married the father, preferably before but sometimes after conception.

Mentally Carly began to rehearse what she would say. By the time she drove into San Francisco two days later, she had her story down pat.

When Carly checked in at the St. Dominique Hotel, she was told that her father had arrived and wanted her to call his room immediately.

He met her in the hotel lobby, looking like a real-

estate agent in his black slacks, white shirt and blue
polyester sports jacket. His graying brown hair was
still thick, and his skin was tanned. Carly was pleased
to realize he'd been spending a reasonable amount of
time out of doors, away from the filling station.

She hugged him. "Hi, Dad."

Don kissed her lightly on the forehead. "Hello, doll,"
he answered, and his voice was gruff with emotion.

Carly was tired from her trip, and she wanted to have
something light to eat and lie down for a while, but she
knew her dad had been eagerly awaiting her arrival.
She couldn't let him down. "How was the flight out?"
she asked as she dropped her room key into her purse.

He grinned broadly. "Wasn't bad at all. In fact, there
was this cute little stewardess passing out juice—"

Carly laughed. "They call them 'flight attendants'
now, Dad. But I can see that you're up-to-date on your
flirting."

He smiled at that, but there was a look in his eyes
that Carly found disturbing. "For all this success you're
having," he said as they gravitated toward one of the
hotel's restaurants, "there's something really wrong.
What is it, button?"

Tears were never very far from the surface during
these hectic days, and Carly had to blink them back.
She waited until they'd been seated in a quiet corner of
the restaurant before answering. "Dad, I hate to be so
blunt, but it wouldn't be fair to beat around the bush.
I'm pregnant, and there's no prospect of a wedding."

Don was quiet for a long moment, his expression unreadable. But then he reached out and closed a strong,
work-callused hand over Carly's. "That character with

the Pulitzer Prize?" he asked. "I knew I should have blacked his eyes."

Carly couldn't help smiling at her dad's phrasing. "That's him," she said. Her eyes filled, and this time there was nothing she could do about it.

"Does he know?"

"Not yet. I'll send him a registered letter after I'm settled."

Her father looked nonplussed. "That's what I like to see—the warm, human touch."

Carly averted her eyes. "It's the best I can do for now. I'm taking things one minute at a time."

"You in love with him?"

Carly sighed. "Yeah," she admitted after a long moment. "But I'll make it through this, Dad." She paused, thinking of that photograph of her crawling out of the Deschutes River. "I'm a survivor."

"There's more to life than just surviving, Carly. You shouldn't be hurting like this—you deserve the best of everything."

"You're prejudiced," Carly informed him as a waiter brought menus and water.

Don studied his choices and chose a clubhouse sandwich while Carly selected a salad. During the meal they discussed the latest gossip in Ryerton and Carly's prospects of finding an apartment at a rent she could afford.

"You need money?" her dad asked when they'd finished eating and were riding up in the elevator.

Carly shook her head. "There's still some from the endorsements I did," she answered.

"But a baby costs a lot," Don argued.

She waggled a finger at him. "I'll handle it, Dad," she said.

At the door of her room, he kissed her forehead. "You go on in and take a nap," he ordered. "As for me, I'm headed over to take the tour at the chocolate factory."

Carly touched his face. "We have a date for dinner, handsome—don't you dare stand me up."

"Wouldn't think of it," he answered. "It isn't every day a fella gets to go out on the town with a former Miss United States on his arm."

With a laugh and a shake of her head, Carly ducked inside her room and closed the door.

There were a dozen yellow rosebuds waiting in a vase on the desk. The card read, *Welcome aboard, Carly. I'm looking forward to working with you. Hope.*

Carly drew in the luscious scent of the roses and made a mental note to call Hope and thank her as soon as she'd had a shower and a brief nap. When she awakened, though, it was late, and she had to rush to dress and get her makeup done.

Wearing a pink-and-white floral skirt and blouse, Carly met her father in the lobby, bringing along one of the rosebuds for his lapel. They had dinner at a place on the Wharf, then took in a new adventure movie.

The next morning Carly called Hope first thing, thanked her for the flowers and made arrangements to meet for lunch. Hope said she'd had her assistant working on finding an apartment for Carly, and there were several good prospects for her to look at.

"You're spoiling me," Carly protested.

"Nothing is too good for you, kid. Besides, I want to hook you before you find out what a slave driver I am."

Carly laughed, and the two women rang off. Three hours later they met at one of the thousand-and-one fish places on the Wharf for lunch.

"I can see where Carly gets her good looks," Hope said to Don when the two had been introduced.

Don blushed with pleasure, and Carly reminded herself that he was still a young man. Half the single women in Ryerton were probably chasing him.

Lunch was pleasant, but it ended quickly, since Hope had a busy schedule back at the magazine's offices. Carly promised to report for duty at nine sharp the following Monday, then accepted the list of apartments Hope's assistant had checked out for her.

She and her father spent the afternoon taxiing from one place to another, and the last address on the list met Carly's requirements. It was a large studio with a partial view of the water, and it cost more to lease for six months than her dad had paid to buy his first house outright.

Carly left a deposit with the resident manager, then she and Don went back to the hotel.

She was exhausted, and after calling the moving company in Portland to give them her new address, she ordered a room-service dinner for herself and Don. They had a good time together seated at the standard round table beside the window, watching a movie on TV while they ate.

"You going to be okay if I go back home tomorrow?" Don asked when the movie was over and room service had collected the debris from their meal. "I hate to leave you way out here all by yourself. It's not like you couldn't find somebody in Ryerton who'd be proud to be your husband—"

Carly laid her index finger to his lips. "Not another word, Gramps. San Francisco is my town—I know it in my bones—and I'm going to stay here and make a life for myself and my baby."

Respect glimmered in her father's ice-blue eyes. "Maybe you could come home for Christmas," he said.

"Maybe," Carly answered, her throat thick.

Her dad left then, and Carly took a brief bath, then crawled into bed and fell asleep. She didn't open her eyes again until the reception desk gave her a wake-up call.

Carly and Don had breakfast together, then he kissed her goodbye and set out for the airport in a cab. Even though he'd obviously been reluctant to leave her, he'd been eager, too. The filling station was the center of his life, and he wanted to get back to it.

At loose ends, Carly went to the offices of *Californian Viewpoint* to tell Hope she'd found an apartment.

Hope was obviously rushed, but she took the time to show Carly the office assigned to her.

"You didn't forget," Carly began worriedly, "that I'm pregnant?"

Hope shook her head, and her expression was kind and watchful. "I didn't forget, Barnett. And your dad told me who the father is—I must say, I'm impressed. With genes like yours and Holbrook's, that kid of yours is going to have it all."

Carly laid her hands to her stomach and swallowed. "I should skin Dad for spilling the beans like that. When, pray tell, did he manage to work *that* little tidbit into the conversation?"

Hope smiled. "When we were having lunch and you went to the restroom. Does Mark know you're here in San Francisco, Carly?"

"No," Carly said quickly. Guiltily. "And he doesn't

know I'm pregnant yet, either, so if this is one of those small-world things and he's a friend of yours, kindly don't tell him."

Cocking her head to one side and folding her arms, Hope replied, "It is a small world, Carly. I went to college with Mark."

Carly sighed. "I suppose that means I'm going to be running into him a lot," she said.

Hope was on her way to the door. "Worse," she said, tossing the word back over one shoulder. "I want you to interview him about his new play." With that, Carly's new boss disappeared, giving her employee no chance to protest.

There was no escape, and Carly knew it. She'd signed a lease on an expensive apartment and she needed her job. She was going to have to face Mark Holbrook, in person, and tell him she was carrying his child.

All through the weekend she practiced what she would say and how she'd say it. She'd be cool, dignified, poised. Mark could have visitation rights if he wanted them, she would tell him. If he offered to pay child support, she would thank him politely and accept.

Despite two solid days of rehearsal, though, Carly was not prepared when she rang the doorbell at Mark's town house at ten-thirty Monday morning.

Nathan answered, and his freckled face lit up when he saw who'd come to call. "Carly!" he cried.

She smiled at him, near tears again. "Yeah," she answered. "Learn any good card tricks lately?"

The child nodded importantly and stepped back to admit her. "You're here to see my dad, aren't you?" he asked, his voice and expression hopeful. "He's really going to be surprised—he was expecting a reporter."

*He's going to be more surprised than you'd ever guess,* Carly thought, but she smiled at Nathan and nodded. "Where is he?"

"I'll get him," Nathan offered eagerly.

Carly shook her head. "I'd rather not be announced, if that's okay with you."

The boy looked puzzled. "All right. Dad's in his office—it's up those stairs."

Carly drew a deep breath, muttered a prayer and marched up the stairway and along the hall.

Mark was sitting at his computer, his back to her, his hands cupped behind his head.

Carly felt a pang that nearly stopped her heartbeat. "Hello, Mark," she said when she could trust herself to talk.

He swiveled in his chair and then launched himself from it, his face a study in surprise.

All weekend Carly had been hoping that when she actually saw Mark, she'd find herself unmoved. The reality was quite the opposite; if anything, she loved him more than she had before.

His expressive brown eyes moved over her, pausing ever so briefly, it seemed to Carly, at her expanding waistline. "What are you doing here?" he asked, his tone lacking both unkindness and warmth.

Carly shrugged. "I'm supposed to interview you for *Californian Viewpoint.*"

"What?"

"I work there," she explained, wondering how she could speak so airily when her knees were about to give out.

"You've living in San Francisco?"

She nodded.

"Oh." Mark looked distracted for a moment, then said abruptly, "Sit down. Please."

Gratefully Carly took a seat in a comfortable leather chair. Her hands trembled as she pulled her notebook out of her oversize handbag, along with a pencil. "Hope tells me you're writing a new play."

Mark looked confused. "Hope?"

"McCleary. Editor of *Californian Viewpoint* and your friend from college."

"Oh, yeah," Mark replied, and his gaze dropped to Carly's stomach again. Was the man psychic?

Carly crossed her legs at the knee and smoothed her soft cotton skirt. "A photographer will be along in a few minutes," she said. "Before we get started, how's Jeanine doing?"

Although Mark still looked a little off balance, he was obviously recovering. The ghost of a grin tugged at one corner of his mouth. "She's out of the hospital and attending regular AA meetings," he answered.

"Obviously Nathan is still with you."

Mark nodded. "He's had a lot of upheaval in his life during the past few years. Jeanine and I agreed not to jerk him back and forth between her place and mine."

In the distance the doorbell chimed, and Mark frowned at the sound.

"My photographer," Carly said brightly, though she begrudged the precious few moments she'd had with Mark and didn't want to share him.

"Great," Mark said, and the word was raspy.

Carly had been introduced to Allen Wright, the photographer, that morning in Hope's office. Besides his talent with a camera, she'd learned, he was a computer whiz.

True to form, Allen barely greeted Carly and Mark before zeroing in on Mark's computer and looking it over. A handsome young man with brown hair and blue eyes, he turned to grin at the master of the house. "Nice piece of equipment," he remarked.

Mark was looking at Carly; she could feel the heat and weight of his eyes. That extraordinary brain of his was probably developing one-second X rays of her uterus. "Yeah," he said pensively. "Great equipment."

Carly urged Allen to take the candidly posed photos needed for the layout and then shuffled him out the door.

When he was gone, she turned to Mark, her eyes feeling big, her teeth sunk into her lower lip. She was going to have to tell him now but, God help her, she couldn't find the words.

He made it all unnecessary. "My baby?" he asked in a husky voice, his gaze dropping again to Carly's stomach.

Her face flushed with color. "Who told you?" she demanded. "My dad? Hope?"

"Nobody had to tell me," Mark said, shoving splayed fingers through his hair.

Carly picked up her notebook again. "Let's just get the interview out of the way, okay? Then we can go our separate ways."

Mark shocked her by wrenching the notebook from her hand and flinging it across the room. "How the hell can you be so calm about this?" he demanded. He was gripping her upper arms now, forcing her to look at him. "Did you think I was just going to say, 'Oh, that's nice,' and read off my entry in *Who's Who* for your damned article?"

Carly pulled free. "I told you about the baby, Mark. That's the end of my obligation."

"The hell it is," he grated.

Carly's old fear that Mark might want to take her child from her when it was born resurfaced in a painful surge. "I'd better send someone else to do the interview," she said stiffly.

With a harsh sigh, he turned away from her. "I'd rather just get it over with, if it's all the same to you."

Legs trembling, Carly made her way back to her chair and sank gratefully into it. Mark picked up her notebook and brought it back to her.

"I want a place in this baby's life, Carly," he said.

She nodded briskly, unable to look at his face, composed herself and asked, "How's the new play going?"

"Well enough," Mark answered, falling into his own chair. "But I think I prefer nonfiction."

It was a relief to have things on a professional level again. "Does that mean you'll be going back into the newspaper business?"

He considered the question for a long moment, then shook his head. "I think I'd like to do books," he responded finally.

"Starting with?"

"One about what's happening in China, I think. I'd like to write about how the cultural and political conflicts interweave."

"Doesn't the prospect of danger bother you?" Carly asked, only marginally aware that *she* was the one troubled by the idea of Mark risking life and limb.

He lifted one shoulder in a shrug. "There are a lot of hazards in everyday life," he reasoned. "I can't hide in a closet, hoping the sky won't fall on my head."

Carly lowered her eyes for a moment, then shifted the conversation back to the craft of writing plays. "How about your *Broken Vows?*" she asked moderately. "Whatever became of that?"

Mark smiled sadly. "Not a subtle question, Scoop, but I'll answer it anyway. Edina sold it to a movie producer, and it's being filmed in Mendocino even as we speak."

Shock and fury flowed through Carly's veins like venom, and she scooted forward in her chair. "After all you put me through, Mark Holbrook, you went ahead and *sold* that play?"

He nodded. "I read it and decided I'd been a jerk about the whole thing."

Carly recalled Jim Benson saying that Mark would eventually come to exactly that realization. It was too bad, she reflected to herself, that he hadn't felt any compunction to tell *her* about his change of heart.

She supposed there was someone else in his life now, and the thought filled her with pain.

"Well," she said, standing. "I'd better get back to the magazine and start writing." She offered her hand. "Thanks for the interview."

THE MOMENT CARLY was gone, Mark raced up the stairs, down the hallway and into his bedroom suite. In the nursery a painter's helper was just getting ready to strip the pink-and-white striped paper from the walls.

"Stop!" Mark yelled, making the guy jump in surprise.

He didn't stay to explain, however. He ran back downstairs to his office and flipped through the phone book until he found the number for *Californian View-point.*

When the receptionist answered, he identified himself and asked for Hope.

CARLY SAT AT the computer in her office, her fingers making the keys click with a steady rhythm as she worked on the draft of her article about Mark. A rap at her door interrupted her concentration, and she raised her eyes to see Hope standing in the chasm.

She pulled off her glasses and set them aside on the desk. "I told him," she said.

Hope nodded, her eyes eager. "And what did he say?"

"Not much, actually. He wants to be part of the baby's life."

Hope closed the door. "Didn't he—well—ask you to dinner or anything?"

Carly gave her boss a wry look. "No, Yenta, he didn't," she answered. And then she sighed and sat back in her chair. "This is going to be an odd situation, I can see that right now. It'll be like being divorced from a man I was never married to in the first place."

"There isn't any hope that the two of you might get back together?" The editor looked disappointed, like a kid who'd expected a pony for Christmas and gotten a stick horse instead.

"Even if Mark Holbrook came to me on bended knee," Carly said with lofty resolution, "I wouldn't take him back. He was absolutely impossible when I showed that agent his play—there was no reasoning with him. If you think I want a whole lifetime of *that,* you're a candidate for group therapy."

Hope had drawn up a chair, and she leaned forward

in it, looking at Carly in amazement. "You gave some-one his play, without even *asking* him about it?"

Carly swallowed. "I know it sounds bad, but you have to consider my motives—"

"What would *you* do if you'd written a play and somebody snitched it and passed it on to an agent?"

"I'd have a fit," Carly answered defensively. "But I'd also forgive that person, especially if I happened to love him."

Hope let out a sigh that made her dark brown bangs rise from her forehead. By tacit agreement the two women dropped the subject of love. "How did the in-terview go?"

"It was great," Carly answered, her gaze drifting toward the window. She could see a bright red trolley car speeding down a hill, looking for all the world as though it would plunge into the Bay. She swallowed hard. "After all of it, he's letting them produce the play. It's being made into a movie in Mendocino."

"So in a way you won," Hope reasoned, spreading her hands.

"Right," Carly answered forlornly. "I won."

At the end of the day Carly went home to her apart-ment, where she'd been roughing it, waiting for her fur-niture to arrive. Her new kitten, Zizi, greeted her at the door with a mewling squeak.

Whisking the little bundle of white fur to her face, Carly nuzzled the cat and laughed. There was some-thing about a baby—no matter what species it was—that always lifted her spirits.

She fed Zizi the nutritious dry food the pet store had recommended, then changed her cotton skirt and blouse

for cut-off jeans and tank top. She was just opening a
can of diet cola when the telephone rang.

*He won't call,* Carly lectured herself as she struggled
not to lunge for the phone. *So don't get your hopes up.*

For all her preparations, her voice was eager when
she lifted the receiver and said, "Hello?"

"Hi, Carly," Janet greeted her. "I'm calling with big
news."

Carly closed her eyes for a moment, knowing perfectly well what her friend's announcement would be.
She was happy for Janet, of course, but she felt a little
left out, too.

"Jim and I are getting married!" Janet bubbled.

Carly smiled. "That's great," she said, and she meant
it.

"I want you to be my maid of honor, of course."

*Always a bridesmaid,* Carly thought. She knew she
was feeling sorry for herself, but she couldn't seem to
help it. She generated enthusiasm befitting the situation. "What colors are you going to use?"

"Pink and burgundy," Janet answered without hesitation.

Carly remembered when she'd first arrived in Portland, and Janet had been talking about getting married.
At that time her ideas about the institution had been
practical, but hardly romantic. "Have you decided that
love isn't a myth after all?" she asked.

Janet laughed. "Have I ever. Jim's my man and I'm
nuts about him." She paused. "Speaking of nuts, have
you and Mark been able to touch base or anything?"

Carly sighed. "I interviewed him this morning," she
said sadly. "And I told him about the baby."

All the humor was gone from Janet's voice. "Don't tell me he didn't ask you to marry him on the spot?"

"Of course he didn't," Carly replied breezily. "It's over between Mark and me—has been for a long time."

"Right," Janet replied, sounding patently unconvinced. "Now that the two of you are in the same city again, the earthquake people had better keep an eye on the Richter scale."

Carly shook her head. "It's really over, Janet," she insisted. Her words had put a definitive damper on the conversation, and it ended about five minutes later.

Zizi came to amble up Carly's bare legs and sit down on her stomach. "Reooow," she said sympathetically.

"Ain't it the truth?" Carly sighed, sweeping the kitten into one hand as she got back to her feet. She cuddled Zizi for a few moments, then put her down again. There was no sense in moping around the apartment, waiting for a call that was never going to come. She'd go down to the market and pick out some fresh vegetables and fish for supper.

After finding her purse, she left the apartment. She walked to the market, since it was a warm August evening and the sun was still blazing in the sky.

She chose cauliflower, and broccoli and crisp asparagus, then purchased a pound of fresh cod. As she climbed back up the hill to her building, she was filled with a sort of lonely contentment. Maybe her life wasn't perfect—whose was? But she lived in a city she was growing to love, worked at a job that excited her and, come winter, she would be a card-carrying mother.

Those things were enough. They had to be.

Carly didn't know whether to be alarmed or encouraged when she saw Mark's car parked in front of her building. When she went inside, she found him sitting on the bottom step, a big bouquet of pink daisies in his hand.

Her traitorous heart skipped over one beat as he stood, a smile lighting his eyes. He took her grocery bag from her and handed over the flowers.

Carly looked at him with wide, worried eyes. "What do you want?"

"Now there's a cordial greeting," he observed, putting a hand to the small of Carly's back and propelling her gently up the stairs. "I guess I should be grateful you aren't shooting at me from the roof."

"If this is about the baby…" Carly began as she stopped in front of her door and rummaged in her purse for the key.

"It's about you and me," he said in a husky voice. "Carly, I came here to ask you to marry me."

She'd forgotten how old-fashioned Mark could be. Obviously he meant to do his grim duty, however distasteful he might find it.

She stepped into the apartment, snatched her groceries from Mark's arms and shoved the riotously pink daisies at him. "Don't trouble yourself," she snapped, and slammed the door in his face.

## CHAPTER ELEVEN

CARLY CLOSED HER eyes and leaned against the door, Mark's knock causing the wood to vibrate.

"I'm not leaving until you hear me out, Carly," he called. "And I'm as stubborn as you are—I can keep this up all night, if necessary!"

"Go away!" Carly cried as the kitten, Zizi, brushed her ankles with its fluffy, weightless body.

"I'm not going anywhere," Mark retorted. "Damn it, let me in—I have things to say to you."

Carly shook her head, even though there was no one to see the gesture. "Give me one good reason why I should listen to anything you have to tell me."

He was silent for a moment, and the knocking stopped. "Because inquiring minds want to know," he finally responded.

Carly's lips curved into an involuntary smile. She crossed the room to set her grocery bag and purse on the counter by the stove.

The knocking started again. "Carly!"

She sighed. At this rate the neighbors would be summoning the police any second. "All right, all right," she muttered, returning to the door and sliding the bolt. "Come in!"

Mark stepped inside the spacious studio, looking irritated. He fairly shoved the pink daisies at her. "Here," he snapped.

"Thanks," Carly retorted just as shortly, but there was a softening process going on inside. Mark was getting to her in spite of her efforts to keep him at a distance.

She found a cut-glass vase in one of the cupboards and put the flowers into it with water. Then she set them on the sunny windowsill above the sink.

She stiffened when she felt Mark's hands come to rest, ever so gently, on her shoulders. He said her name hoarsely, and turned her to face him.

"I was wrong."

Carly jutted out her chin. "You can say that again."

The merest hint of a smile flickered in his eyes. "But I won't," he answered. "Carly, I love you. And I need you."

"Why?" she asked in an ironic singsong voice. "You've got everything—a son, money, a career anyone would envy—why do you want me?"

"Why do I want you?" He arched one eyebrow, and his voice was gruff. "Because you gave my life a dimension and a perspective it's never had before or since. With you I was one hundred percent alive, Carly."

She touched her upper lip with the tip of her tongue, watching Mark with wide eyes. "I know what you mean," she admitted softly, reluctantly. "I've got a great job, and I've proven to myself that I can make it on my own. And for all that, something vital is missing."

Mark's dark gaze caressed her. "Please," he said, "give me a chance to prove to you that I'm nothing like that jerk who threw such a fit over a play."

Without moving at all, he had pulled her to him. She

came to rest against his strong chest, her body trembling, and he moved his hands over her back, soothing her. She slipped her arms around his waist, telling him physically what she could not say in words.

His lips moved, warm, against her hair. "I know now that I was scared of what I felt for you, Carly—and then there was getting Nathan back and Jeanine's accident. I distanced myself from you, thinking that would keep us both from getting hurt, but it didn't work." He paused to draw in a deep, ragged breath. "I promise I'll never do that again, sweetheart. When we have problems in the future, we'll stand toe-to-toe until they're worked out—agreed?"

Carly lifted her head and nodded. "Agreed."

He curved a finger under her chin. "I love you," he said, and then he lowered his mouth to hers.

Carly gave a little whimper as he kissed her, and her arms went around his neck. The feel of his hard frame against her set her flesh to quivering beneath her clothes.

He rested one of his hands, fingers splayed, against her belly. The muscles there leaped against his palm in response, and Carly smiled as she drew back from the kiss. In a few months he would be able to lay his hand there and feel the movements of their child.

"Marry me," he said, kissing her neck. He unsnapped her jeans and slid his fingers down over the warm flesh of her abdomen to find the swirl of silk.

Carly's head was light, and her eyes weren't focusing properly. She gave a little moan as Mark toyed with her. "Yes," she whispered, "oh, yes…"

He chuckled as he spread his left hand over her bottom, pushing her into the fiery attendance of his right. "It would be convenient if you had a bed, Scoop."

"Oooooh," Carly groaned, closing her eyes and letting her head fall back. During those moments, her every emotion and sense seemed to center on the motion of Mark's fingers.

He left her swaying and dazed in the middle of the room, while he gathered the three large and colorful floor pillows she'd bought in an import shop and arranged them on the floor.

It never occurred to Carly to protest when he came back to her and spread her gently on the pillows, a prize to be examined and savored. He stripped her methodically, kissing her insteps when he'd tossed aside her shoes, nibbling at the undersides of her knees when he'd taken away her cut-off jeans. He removed her T-shirt next, and then, with excruciating slowness, her bra.

Carly cupped her hands beneath her breasts, lifting them to him, offering them. He shed his jacket and shirt and flung them aside before bending, with a low groan of pleasure, to catch one pink gumdrop of a nipple between his teeth.

Carly writhed on the soft pillows, her heels wedged against the hardwood floor, while Mark suckled her. Then he hooked a thumb under the waistband of her panties, her last remaining garment, and drew them down.

She wriggled out of them, kicked them away, and Mark stayed with her breast, as greedy as a thirsty man just then allowed to drink. Desperate, she found his hand and pressed it to the warm, moist delta between her legs.

He chuckled against her nipple and began moving his

palm in a slow, titillating circle. Carly's body followed
him obediently, yearning for his attentions.

He left her breast to kiss his way down over her belly,
and Carly clutched at the floor in anticipation though, of
course, the waxed wood would grant her no purchase.

She felt his lips on her still-flat abdomen. "I'm going
to make your mom really happy," he promised the little
person inside.

A great shudder shook Carly; she knew what Mark
was going to do to her, that he would make her perform
a physical and spiritual opera before he let her up off
those pillows, and she couldn't wait another moment.

"Oh, God, Mark," she whispered, "now—please,
now."

He parted her with his fingers, gave her a single flick
with his tongue.

Carly cried out in lusty delight, not caring who heard,
and sank her teeth into her lower lip when she felt Mark
position himself between her knees. She covered her
breasts with her hands, not because she wanted to hide
them, but because she could not lie still. Mark made
her show herself again.

"I want to see them," he said, his voice low and rumbling. Then he went back to the taut little nubbin of flesh
that awaited him so eagerly.

He was greedy, and Carly clamped a hand over her
mouth to stifle her cries of pleasure. Immediately,
firmly, he removed it, and the gesture told Carly that
he would demand an unrestrained response from her.
He would hear every sound, see every inch of her flesh.

She gave a series of choked gasps as he took hold of
the undersides of her knees, lifting and parting them

so she was totally vulnerable to him. And then, having conquered her completely, he was ruthless.

He brought her to a thunderous crescendo that had her writhing beneath his mouth, and the sounds of her triumphant submission echoed off the walls and the ceiling.

She had known he wouldn't permit her to reach only one climax, no matter how soul shattering it might be. His own pleasure was in direct proportion to the heights Carly reached. Still, knowing these things, she pleaded with him.

He only chuckled, nibbling at the inside of her thigh while she came down, trembling and moist with exertion, from the top of a geyser. "We haven't even begun," he said.

Soon she was bobbing on the crest of an invisible spray of energy again, her back arched, her eyes dazed and sightless, her hair clinging to her cheeks and forehead. And Mark was already arousing her anew long before she'd recovered.

The instinct for power gave her the strength to open his jeans and reach inside, pressing her palm against his magnificence, closing her fingers around it.

He groaned, and his wonderful eyes rolled closed. "Oh, Carly..." he grated out. "Carly."

She caressed him until he was muttering in delirium, then maneuvered him so that he was lying sprawled on the pillows, as helpless as Carly had been earlier. She finished stripping him, bold as the queen of some primitive tribe, and bent to touch him lightly with her tongue.

He gave a guttural cry, and Carly felt a sweep of loving triumph. She had Mark where she wanted him, and she wasn't going to let him go until she'd enjoyed him thoroughly, because she had won the battle and he was the spoils.

His submission was glorious, full of honor, and Carly loved him with a sweet and tender violence.

Finally, though, he stopped her, his hands clenched on either side of her head. She watched his powerful chest rise and fall as he struggled for the breath to speak. "Inside you," he managed after a long time. "I want to be inside you."

Carly would not give up her position of dominance—this time it would be Mark who lay beneath the pleasure, drowning in its splendor.

She placed a knee on either side of his hips and guided him to her portal with one hand, smiling when he buckled beneath her in a desperate search.

Splaying her hands over his heaving chest, feeling his nipples tighten under her palms, she allowed him only a little solace. He tossed his head from side to side, half-blinded with the need of her, and Carly loved him all the more for his ability to surrender so completely.

"More?" she teased.

"More," he pleaded.

She was generous, giving him another inch of sanction. His skin was moist beneath her hands, and she could feel an underlying quiver in his muscles as he struggled for control.

He arched his neck, his eyes closed, and Carly bent forward to kiss and nibble the underside of his chin. Then she felt him clasp her hips, and she knew the game was almost over.

Sure enough, he pressed her down onto him in a strong stroke that immediately set her afire. She groaned as he raised his fingers to her nipples and rolled them into tight little buttons.

He made another pass into her, and the tiny muscles where the magic lay went into wild spasms, making Carly toss back her head and cry out over and over again in satisfaction. When she finally went limp, Mark shifted her so that she lay beneath him, and took her in earnest.

At peace, she watched in love and wonder as pleasure moved in his eyes. She spread one hand over his muscular buttocks as he strained to give himself up to her, while the other traced the outline of his lips.

His teeth clamped lightly on her finger when he stiffened suddenly, emptying himself into her. And this time the cry that filled the shadowy room was Mark's, not Carly's.

He fell onto the pillows beside her when it was over, curving an arm around her waist and holding her close against his chest. They lay in silence for a long time, but even then there was some kind of dynamics going on between them.

It was a mystical mating process, fusing their two spirits together at an invisible place. Carly's eyes filled with tears as one indefinable emotion after another swept over her.

She was Mark's, and he was hers, and not just until the next time they disagreed over something, either. By a process she could not begin to understand, an age-old link between them had been reinforced.

Carly kissed Mark's shoulder and closed her eyes.

BEYOND THE FENCED boundaries of the little churchyard, Kansas stretched in every direction. Plump matrons

in colorful dresses chattered, while men smoked and
talked about their crops and "them politicians back in
Washington," whom they held in a healthy and typically
American contempt. Children zigzagged throughout,
filled with exuberance because the ripe summer was
still with them and because there would be cake and
punch aplenty at the reception.

Clad in her mother's gossamer wedding dress, her
arm linked with Mark's, Carly stood a little closer to
her husband. The limo he'd hired to drive them from
the church to the reception at the Grange Hall glistened
like a sleek silver ghost at the curb.

Carly smiled at the stir it caused.

"Came all the way from Topeka," she heard someone say.

Mark broke off the conversation he'd been having
with Carly's father and his own, and grinned down at
her. Something unspoken passed between them, and
then they were getting into the plush car, Carly grappling with her rustling voluminous skirts of lace and
satin. Her bouquet of pink daisies and white rosebuds
lay fragrant in her lap.

She gave a happy sigh.

Mark chuckled and leaned over to kiss her cheek. "I
love you, Mrs. Holbrook," he said.

She beamed at him, answering with her eyes.

The driver obligingly turned on the stereo, filling the
car with soft, romantic music. It was his way of telling
the newlyweds, Carly figured, that he wasn't listening
in on their conversation.

They talked with their foreheads touching about their
brief upcoming honeymoon in Paris. After that, Carly
would be returning to San Francisco and Nathan and the

magazine, while Mark jetted to the Far East to gather material for his book on China.

Whether or not he would get into the country remained to be seen. Carly suspected he had contacts who would be willing to smuggle him over the border, but she didn't allow herself to think about the possible ramifications of *that,* because she wasn't about to spoil the happiest day of her life.

When the limo pulled up in front of the ramshackle Grange Hall, which had never been painted, there were already a number of wedding guests waiting, and country-and-western music vibrated in the hot August sunshine.

Mark and Carly went inside, and Mark immediately pulled her into his arms for a dance. This delighted the onlookers, who loved a wedding almost as much as a rousing cattle auction.

Playfully Mark touched his lips to hers, and everyone clapped and cheered with delight.

"Show-off," Carly said, one hand resting lightly on his nape.

He laughed. "Me? Tell me, Mrs. Holbrook—was *I* the one who put on a sparkly outfit and twirled flaming batons in front of a whole nation?"

Carly's cheeks warmed. "You're still going to be teasing me about that in fifty years, aren't you?"

Mark pulled her a little closer. "Yup," he said.

After that, Carly danced with her father, then with Mark's father, then with Nathan.

"You look real pretty in that dress," her stepson said.

Carly smiled. "Thanks—you're looking pretty handsome yourself." She wanted to touch his hair, but she held back, unwilling to embarrass him. "You don't mind

about my taking your dad away to Paris for a week?"
she asked.

Solemnly Nathan shook his head. "And you don't
need to worry when he goes to China, either. I'm pretty
tough, and I won't let anybody hurt you."

Carly's heart swelled with love. "Okay," she said. "I
won't give it a thought."

Toward the end of the song, Mark tapped his son
on the shoulder to cut in. "Judging from the look on
your face, I've got some pretty strong competition in
that kid."

She smiled, glad to be close to her husband again.
"He's one terrific guy," she agreed. "He just told me not
to be afraid when you go to China, because he's tough
and he can take care of me."

Mark searched her face. "*Are* you worried about me
going to China, Scoop?"

"Of course I am," Carly answered. "What kind of
wife would I be if I didn't consider the dangers? But
I'm determined not to stand in your way where your
career is concerned, and I expect the same courtesy
from you."

It was time for more photographs and for the cutting
of the giant cake decorated with white sugar doves and
scallops of pink frosting.

They posed and exchanged sticky, crumbling bites
of cake, and a collective sigh of approval arose from the
guests when Mark took Carly into his arms and gave
her a sound kiss.

"For better or for worse, Mrs. Holbrook," he said,
his voice a hoarse whisper, "and for always, I love you."

Happy tears sprang into her eyes for the hundredth
time that day. "Could I say something to you?"

He smiled. "Anything, as long as you never say goodbye."

"I'm so glad I met you," Carly told him. "And so glad I'm a survivor."

He kissed her. "So am I, Scoop. So am I."

She gazed up at him with loving eyes. "One more dance before we go?"

Mark nodded.

They whirled around the dance floor, unaware now of the guests, and the teetering cake, and the mountains of beautifully wrapped presents. Mr. and Mrs. Mark Holbrook were, for those precious moments, aware only of each other.

*San Francisco*
*One year later...*

Carly wore jeans and a blue T-shirt, and the baseball cap Nathan had given her on Mother's Day sat firmly on her head, the brim covering her nape. Riding on her back, papoose style, was Molly, who watched her father approach with solemn aquamarine eyes.

Out on the diamond, Nathan was speeding between third base and home. The ball came in from left field; the pitcher caught it and hurled it to the catcher.

Nathan dived, sliding into home plate on his belly, his hands outstretched.

"Safe!" yelled the umpire, who was, like everybody else on both teams, a kid from the neighborhood.

Reaching the place where his wife and daughter stood, Carly still unaware of his approach, Mark leaned over to give Molly a light kiss on the forehead.

She rewarded him with a gurgling chortle and a, "Da-da!"

Carly spun around at that, her eyes big in her dusty, gamine's face. Her baseball cap fell off onto the ground when she flung her arms around Mark's neck.

He kissed her soundly, even though he knew he'd hear about it from Nathan. In his son's world, a guy just didn't kiss a woman in front of everybody in the neighborhood like that.

"How was China?" Carly asked. Her voice was throaty and low, and her eyes were filled with a blue-green come-hither look.

"Same as always," Mark answered gruffly. He'd made two trips since he and Carly were married. "Big. Isolated. Awesomely beautiful."

"I think we should go home and discuss this," Carly crooned.

He bent to pick up her fallen baseball cap and put it back on her head. This time the brim stuck out to the side, giving her a jaunty, Our Gang kind of look. "You're absolutely right, Mrs. Holbrook," he responded, his body tightening at the luscious prospect of being alone with her in the shadowy privacy of their bedroom. "But what about the short person here?"

Carly grinned. "Molly's due for a nap," she replied, "and Nathan will be out here playing baseball until you come back and drag him home for supper."

He lifted his brown-haired daughter out of the back sling and kissed her glossy curls. "You do look tired, kid," he told the child, his expression serious.

Molly's lower lip curled outward as though he'd insulted her, then she tossed back her head and wailed.

Twenty minutes later, when her mother had washed

her face and hands and given her a bottle, Molly closed her enormous Carly eyes and went immediately to sleep.

Mark led his wife out of the nursery and into their bedroom, taking off her baseball cap and tossing it aside. "As for you, Mrs. Holbrook," he said, "you're about to spend some quality time with your husband."

He saw the tremor of pleasure go through her, watched as her cheeks turned a delicious apricot pink. And he knew he loved her as desperately as he ever had.

"Mark," she began shyly, "I need a shower...."

He nodded. "So do I," he answered, catching hold of her T-shirt and lifting it off over her head.

Her breasts, full ever since she'd given birth to Molly, seemed to burgeon over the tops of her lace bra, and the sight of them filled Mark with a grinding ache that would take a long time to satisfy. He anticipated the feeling of a nipple tightening in his mouth, the arch of Carly's body against him, the little purring groans that would escape her throat.

He brought down one side of the bra and bent to taste her.

They undressed each other in a slow, romantic dance they'd learned together, and when they were naked, Carly led Mark into the bathroom. He adjusted the spigots in the double-size shower and drew her underneath the spray of the water with him.

Taking up the soap, Carly turned it beneath her hands, making a lather. Then she began to wash her husband, to prepare him for a sweet sacrifice that would be offered on their bed.

His muscles quivered beneath his flesh as she soaped him all over, gently washing away the loneliness, the grit, the frustration of being parted from her. She was kneeling before him, washing his feet, when she looked up at him through the spray and ran one slippery hand up the inside of his thigh.

He felt his Adam's apple bob in his throat as he swallowed. "Carly," he managed to grind out just as she closed her mouth over him.

He entangled his fingers in her dripping hair and let the crown of his head rest against the shower wall, and he tasted warm water when he opened his mouth to moan in helpless pleasure. She gripped his tensed buttocks then, as though she feared that he would leave her.

His knees weakened as she continued to pleasure him, and he wondered how long he could stand before her. He was on the verge of slipping to the floor of the shower as it was.

"Carly," he choked out, and he tried to lift her head from him, but she would not be deterred.

Only seconds later his raw cry of surrender echoed in the shower stall, stifled by the sound of the water.

THEY LAY NAKED in the middle of the bed, arms around each other, legs entwined. Carly's head rested on Mark's shoulder.

"That was your last trip to China," she said, hardly able to believe he'd really said he wouldn't be leaving her again for a long time.

With his hand he cupped her breast possessively. "I'll be underfoot from now on," he said. "Even though I'll be writing a book, your friends will all think I'm a house husband."

Carly laughed, but the sound caught in her throat as Mark's thumb moved back and forth across her nipple. She purred as warm pleasure uncurled within her. "We could use one around here," she said, stretching as Mark continued to stroke her. "You see, the Holbrook family is about to get bigger again."

He reared up on one elbow to search her face with those wonderful, luminous brown eyes of his. "We're having another baby?" he asked hopefully, as though such a thing could happen only once in an aeon.

Carly held up two fingers. "It's a double play, Mr. Holbrook," she answered, her throat thick with emotion, "and our team is about to score."

Mark laughed for joy, and there were tears glistening in his brown eyes, but his body was conducting an independent celebration all its own. He parted Carly's legs and lay between them, letting her feel his heat and his power and his vast love for her.

His face somber again, he slipped his hands under her bottom and lifted, then went into her in one unbroken stroke. And Carly welcomed him with her whole soul.

Mark Holbrook was home to stay.

* * * * *

Dear Reader,

Thank you for traveling with me to Safe Haven! I've always liked the idea of picking up and moving somewhere entirely new—preferably somewhere warm with a beach. I adore the South, from North Carolina to Florida, and I have a particular fascination with the Low Country. The salt marshes, the gumbo and hoppin' John, the gorgeous small towns rich with complicated history... It's fabulous fuel for a writer's imagination. Doing the research for the Safe Haven series has been a joy.

As far as the darker side of the story, centered on the shelter, is concerned, we've all heard the statistics: one in three women suffers violence from an intimate partner in her lifetime, and one in fifteen children witnesses it. This breaks my heart. Just before I started writing *Low Country Hero*, I ended a relationship that had become controlling and possessive. I'm thankful I was able to get out before things ever got violent, but that scared, vulnerable feeling caused me some sleepless nights...and during one of them, the idea for this story pushed its way into my mind and wouldn't leave until I wrote it down.

Women who face domestic violence often display tremendous courage as they work to rebuild their lives. If you'd like to help, please consider donating to a shelter in your community. Or visit my website, www.leetobinmcclain.com, for ideas about how and where you can help.

I hope you found the community of Safe Haven to be a warm, welcoming place to spend a few hours. And I hope you'll come back this summer and again this fall, when Liam's and then Cash's stories hit the shelves.

Be safe,

*Lee*

# LOW COUNTRY HERO

## Acknowledgments

It truly took a village to bring this book into being. On the professional side, I am enormously grateful to my agent, Karen Solem, and my Love Inspired editor, Shana Asaro, who first saw the potential in *Low Country Hero*. Thanks are due to everyone at HQN Books, from Susan Swinwood and the editorial staff, who have been so supportive every step of the way, to the art department, who created the cover that makes everyone who sees it want to abandon their responsibilities and visit, to the marketing folks, who've given me amazing opportunities to reach readers. Special thanks to Michele Bidelspach, whose insights on character and emotion helped to make *Low Country Hero* the very best it could be. I'm also thankful to the staff of Waterfront Books in Georgetown, South Carolina, for all their help with local resources, and to my Wednesday-morning critique group, especially Kathy Ayres, for reading and critiquing the project with keen perception and good humor.

On the personal side: Bill, thank you for being an extroverted, fun-loving, upbeat travel companion and for making such an effort to understand and support your introverted writer-girlfriend. And Grace: thank you for being my inspiration, my motivation and my daily delight.

# *PROLOGUE*

*Twenty Years Ago*

WALKING FROM THE small-town grocery store back toward their new home at the Safe Haven Women's Shelter, Rita O'Dwyer felt her shoulders start to relax. Maybe this was going to be okay. For her boys, and even, maybe, for her.

They passed a little tourist stand, full of South Carolina beach trinkets and toys.

"Mom, can we go in?" her middle boy, Cash, pleaded. "Please? I want to see what they've got." He was the most driven of her three sons, and she always joked that he'd become a billionaire, but his strong focus worried her a little. Today, like any other kid, he just wanted to see the toys.

She paused. Even her oldest, Sean, leaned past his brothers to look in the little shop, and of course her baby, Liam, joined in the begging. "Please, Mommy? There's swords and stuff!"

They sounded like normal kids. Normal, wonderfully whiny kids, and she couldn't resist their request.

She ached with the desire to give her boys a carefree childhood.

While the boys looked at the beachy souvenirs, Rita fingered a little five-dollar necklace, with a sea turtle, a shark's tooth and a palm tree. If she could spare the money, she'd buy it for herself. A symbol of her new life, away from Alabama and Orin.

She gave her head a little shake and bent down to look at the candy. After the long hours in the car and the strangeness of setting up housekeeping in a women's shelter, they all needed a treat. And candy was cheap.

"You don't want that ordinary stuff, ma'am," said the tall, stoop-shouldered clerk. "You'll want some real Carolina pralines for your boys." As he spoke, he slid three caramel-colored candies into a bag. "And for you…" He plucked the necklace she'd been studying from the stand and held it out to her.

"Oh no! We can't afford all that!" What was *this* guy's agenda?

He smiled with an expression of wisdom and sympathy older than his years. "Just consider it a little Southern hospitality. Y'all look like you need a lift."

For some reason, she trusted him. Again, hope rose in her. Maybe this was all going to work out. "Thank you. You're very kind."

She'd just taken the bag and turned to locate the boys when she felt something poke into her side. A familiar, sickeningly strong cologne assaulted her.

Orin.

Silent terror exploded inside her, making her head spin and her stomach heave with nausea. She looked around frantically. There were Liam and Cash, fingering the crocodile heads on sticks. But where was Sean? He had to get the other boys to safety, now.

How had Orin found them so quickly? And what new punishment would he inflict on her and, worse, on the boys?

"You're not leaving me." Orin's voice was a quiet snarl.

"Everything okay, miss?" the clerk asked from behind her.

"You tell him it's fine and come with me," Orin said into her ear, "or I'll kill him, and then those worthless boys, and then you."

She nodded back to the clerk, forcing a sick smile across her face. "I'm fine." Her chest seemed to crumple inward, as if all the backbone she'd tried to build in herself, all her bones, turned to jelly.

Her dreams and plans to save her children faded, then disappeared.

Orin pulled her along like they were normal people in a hurry, jamming the gun into her side. As he reached the pickup and opened the door to shove her inside, she saw Sean, squatting on the sidewalk, caught up in his favorite battered military novel, one of the few possessions he'd insisted on bringing along when they'd fled Alabama.

There were people out on the street, shopping and chatting. Should she scream? Or would that incite Orin even further? He was shaking, his face red with fury. She'd never seen him this bad. Her head spun; her heart thudded.

*Think.* No. She couldn't expect help from strangers— not without endangering them and the kids, too—but she had to get Sean's attention. "Oh, Orin, you don't have to be in such a hurry!" she cried in a loud, fake voice.

Sean looked up, and their eyes met, and then his gaze turned to his father. Bleak understanding darkened his eyes. Always protective, he scrambled to his feet and started to come toward her and Orin, but she gave a sideways jerk of her head, indicating that he should go to his brothers, help them first, as she'd drilled into him on the ride up from Alabama.

He looked back, biting his lip, and every tendon sung with the need to go to him, to hold him and tell him not to worry, she'd take care of it. As a mother should.

But she couldn't take care of this. He was only thirteen, but today, he had to be a man and protect his brothers from their father. Her stomach ached like dull knives were stabbing it. She'd failed.

Sean squared his thin shoulders and headed toward the other two boys, who were play-fighting inside the store, now armed with toy swords. Tears filled her eyes to witness their last minute of carefree childhood.

Then she was shoved headfirst into the pickup truck and the door closed behind her.

THREE HOURS LATER, sore in every public and private part of her body, she fell from the truck to the side of the road, limp as a rag doll, barely feeling the gravel dig into her elbow and cheek.

"You wanted to live here, you can die here." Orin's voice was dim, and then the truck door slammed. There was a roar and the truck drove away.

Her consciousness was fading, her vision blurring.

She tried to move. Couldn't.

Tractor trailers roared past on the highway, but none of them stopped. Maybe no one could see her. It was getting dark.

Liam was scared of the dark. Who would he turn to when he had a nightmare? Who would teach Cash the right values, how to be more generous? How would Sean have a childhood now?

Her thoughts circled, becoming more distant. Something burned her eyes, and she realized, vaguely, that she was crying. Crying for all the mothering she wouldn't get to give to her sons.

A vehicle was coming, a truck. She clawed at the gravel and managed to heave herself closer to the pavement. Another claw to the gravel, another heave. She had to get help, had to get to her boys. She pushed herself up on one bloody elbow, tried to lift a hand to wave to the truck as its headlights beamed so bright that she reeled backward. Pain made her stomach roil, and blackness dimmed the edges of her vision.

She pushed herself up higher. "Hey!" she tried to call out.

The truck thundered on past her and she collapsed down again.

Her head hurt like the worst headache she'd ever had, times ten.

She hadn't wanted it to end this way, but somehow, she'd always known it would.

# CHAPTER ONE

To make an end is to make a beginning.

T. S. Eliot

*Present Day*

SEAN O'DWYER LOOKED around the lived-in bayou cottage where he'd spent his teenage years, rubbed the back of his neck and dug deep for patience. Nothing like your childhood home to make you feel like a rebellious teenager.

He hadn't been eager to return to the town where he and his brothers had a history that made people pity them. But Safe Haven was known as the place where you could lick your wounds in peace, and while that primarily applied to women, a handful of men had gotten their footing here, too.

Maybe he'd be one of them. He had nothing left to lose.

"Living by yourself out there in the salt marshes isn't going to make you feel any better." Ma Dixie, the woman who'd taken him in when he was an angry thirteen-year-old and raised him to be a decent man, glanced over from clearing the lunch dishes, her broad face wrinkled with concern. "You could just as well plan the renovation staying right here with me."

Liam, who at twenty-eight was the youngest of Sean's motley crew of adopted and biological brothers, leaned back against Ma's kitchen counter and sipped sweet tea. "Your ex-wife was worried you'd do something rash."

Sean blinked. "You talked to Gabby? You *listened* to her?"

Liam spread his hands and shrugged. "She was concerned."

"Concerned enough to dump me for our marriage counselor," Sean muttered, and then was sorry he had. He didn't need their pity. He and Gabby had grown apart after his two tours in Afghanistan, so her sudden turnaround on their agreement about not having children had broken what was left of their marriage. That, he couldn't compromise on. He knew himself and his history too well.

He didn't even miss her, not really. He just missed the hope he'd felt, getting married. That an O'Dwyer could overcome his past, be a happy husband who treated his wife well and was loved in return. His throat tightened and he shoved aside that stupid dream. "I'm caretaking the place, too, that's why I have to live there. Eldora was afraid kids or vandals would break into the cottages."

Liam studied him steadily. "When I heard you were coming home, I thought you'd find a way to help the shelter. It's not doing so well."

"That's your department." Liam was a police officer and lived smack in the middle of Safe Haven.

"Your brother's got his hands full. Looking at a promotion to chief." Ma smiled at Liam with fond pride. She hadn't raised him or their brother Cash when their family had fallen apart. Her small bayou house had only had room for Sean, but her heart had always been big enough to consider both of Sean's natural brothers as kin. And although Liam and Cash had landed in different local families, both of them looked at Ma Dixie's cabin as a second home.

Sean lifted an eyebrow. "Congratulations. Never thought my little brother would end up the top guy."

His brother punched his arm, none too lightly. "Thanks for the vote of confidence. Where's Cash, Ma? I thought he was supposed to help us talk sense into Stupid, here."

"Sean's not stupid. And Cash called. Some high-flying deal, so he's stuck in Atlanta." Ma Dixie pulled the shades to block the afternoon sun, then put her hands on ample hips. "I agree with Liam. You ought to stay in town, figure out a way to help the shelter, not go off and lick your wounds alone. Eldora can find another caretaker."

Sean ignored the wounds part. "I'm no use to the shelter." Just like the shelter had been no use to their mother. "Do I look like the kind of guy a woman in trouble would trust?"

"You could clean yourself up." Ma pinched his bristly cheek. "Shave. Cut your hair."

"Lighten up on the steroids," Liam joked, then raised a hand when Sean bristled. "I know, you wouldn't. But you're huge! You must've been working out 24/7."

Sean didn't bother to correct his brother. The truth was, he'd been doing hard physical labor back in Knoxville, working construction alongside his team. Partly to pay for the divorce, and partly to keep his mind off things.

But the noise and chatter had gotten to him. It was getting to him now, making him think too much. Ma and Liam both had his best interests at heart, but they were overly optimistic about healing wounds and moving on and being happy. He stood. "If the intervention's over," he said, softening his words with a smile, "I've got a job to do."

"You'll come for Friday-night suppers, now that you're back in the area?"

"Sure, Ma." He put an arm around the woman and squeezed her shoulders. He owed her his life and would lay it on the line for her or any one of his brothers. Outsiders, not so much. "Don't worry about me. I'm going to be fine. I just need a little peace and quiet."

ANNA GEORGE STOPPED her car in front of a pair of padlocked gates and stared at the sign.

*Sea Pine Cottages: Closed for Summer Renovations.*

Letting her forehead rest briefly on the steering wheel, she took a deep breath. What was she going to do now?

This whole mad, cross-country trek had been a terrible mistake.

"Mommy? Are we there yet?" Hayley's voice piped up from the back seat.

Uh-oh. When one twin woke up, so did the other, and patience wasn't a virtue most five-year-olds possessed. Anna needed a plan, fast.

She knew no one in South Carolina—which was the point—but as she and the twins had fled the cold mountains of Montana, she'd told them all about the low country's cute, friendly little towns, salt marshes and warm, welcoming beaches. Right now, though, the closed gates in front of them blocked the first step of her plan.

"Mommy?" Hope was awake now, too, and her voice sounded anxious. "Where are we?"

"Let me think a minute." Anna reached a hand to the back seat and gave each girl a reassuring leg pat. After what they'd seen and heard, they needed to know that they were safe, and that she was safe, and that she had a plan.

There were nice hotels, farther down the coast, but prices were too high. And the kind of small motels she could afford didn't offer the protection and privacy she and her daughters needed.

Her stomach twisted and turned, but she didn't dare panic. She wiped wet palms down the sides of her shorts and studied the sign again. If the place was closed for renovations, they had to be renovating *something*. Ideally, the cabins she remembered from her sole, idyllic childhood vacation—the same cabins that were supposed to house them now. And, God willing, the renovations wouldn't have started yet and would happen at a slow Southern pace. Or maybe never; sometimes places put up an optimistic Reopening Soon! sign when it was doubtful they'd ever do business again.

The girls were murmuring in their abbreviated secret twin language, and they apparently reached a conclusion. "We want *out* of the car!"

"Okay. One minute." She put the car in Reverse, backed up and pulled off to the side of the gates, where shiny azalea bushes grew thick and high. She eased deep into a hollow section, well sheltered from the road and entrance. Grabbed a couple of tools from the glove box.

*You can do this, Anna. You don't have a choice.*

"Come on, girls," she said, forcing cheer into her voice. "Let's go exploring!"

Fifteen minutes later, they'd ascertained that there were no construction machines and no signs of workers. The place was deserted, which suited Anna just fine. From the road, they scouted the row of tumbledown cabins and selected a sturdy-looking one.

"Come on. It's going to be an adventure!" She pushed sweaty hair out of her eyes and urged the girls up the overgrown path toward the cabin. This had to work.

"I don't like bugs!" Hope, always more fearful and fretful, waved away a cloud of tiny sand flies and leaned into Anna's leg, making it hard to walk.

"I'm first!" Hayley, as usual, ran ahead, reaching the door of the shuttered cabin and turning the handle. "It's locked, Mom," she said, tossing back her blond ringlets. "Where's the key?"

"That's the adventure part." Tugging Hope along, Anna reached the door and knelt to study the lock, putting an arm around both girls. She'd hoped for an old-fashioned bolt she could just slide a screwdriver under, but this lock was modern and tight.

That would be better in the long run, safer. She swallowed a lump in her throat.

Who'd have thought that law-abiding, rule-following Anna George would calmly break and enter? She shoved aside her good-girl fear of what would happen if they got caught. She had no other choice. No way would she be a lawbreaker long term, but for now, she'd do whatever was necessary to keep them safe.

Around them, birds had resumed their chirping and cawing. The salt air blew warm, bringing the fragrance of the sea, just beyond the dunes, if her childhood memories served. In fact, if she closed her eyes, she imagined she could hear it: the rhythmic pounding of waves against the sand.

"Mommy? What're we going to do?" Hope's voice trembled.

"I'm hungry," Hayley complained.

But at least they were speaking. And Anna meant to make sure that continued, that their voices weren't silenced as they'd been in the past.

She stood, stepped back. "Let's take a walk around the cabin."

"Yeah!" Hayley started to rush off.

"Wait. What's the rule?"

Her impulsive daughter stopped. "Stay together," she said reluctantly.

"That's right—good job," Anna said to Hayley, and then looked down at Hope's anxious face. Though her twins were identical physically, their personalities were nearly opposite. "Want a ride on my back, kiddo?"

"Okay."

Anna knelt. "Jump up." When Hope did, Anna staggered to her feet. Blackness started to close her vision, but she grabbed the trunk of a live oak tree and steadied herself, took a couple of deep breaths. No sleep and a boatload of worries were wearing her down, but she'd gotten this far. She could do this.

She looked up at the cloud-mottled sky. "Okay, let's take a look."

They made their way around the small cabin. Up close, she could see that time and neglect had taken their toll. Part of the screen that sheltered the porch was ripped, and white siding curved away from the cabin, warped by weather. She let Hayley slip through the torn screen to test the cabin's back door, but it was locked, too.

They continued on around. Mushrooms, bold red and yellow, sprouted in the sandy soil near the small picnic table. No footprints, no trash, no abandoned beach toys.

The loneliness unnerved her a little, but it was what she and the girls needed, at least for now. And the cabin's basic structure seemed sound. "Peek inside," she urged Hope, moving closer to a promising window.

Hope hesitated, then leaned from her perch on Anna's back to peer into the window. "It's got a kitchen table! And a sofa and chairs."

Perfect. As long as the furniture hadn't become a nest for rodents or bugs, but she'd keep that fear to herself.

On the third side of the cabin, Anna found what she was searching for: a low window that looked loose in its frame. Just the entrance she needed. "Slide down, sweetie. I want you and Hayley to walk out to the road and back. Count the steps."

"But what if it's more than a hundred?" Hope asked. That was as high as the twins could count.

"Then we'll start over." Hayley grabbed her twin's hand and tugged. "Come on!"

As the girls headed toward the road, squabbling, Anna watched them until she was sure they couldn't see her, and then pulled a screwdriver out of her back pocket and eased it between the sill and the window edge. Working quickly, she jiggled the window open enough to get leverage, and then wedged the screwdriver in. The wood was swollen and tight, but she manhandled it upward with brute strength she hadn't known she had.

If she didn't find shelter for the night, and longer, she feared what harm might come to her children. It was bad enough, sleeping in the car and tangling with the drifters who hung around roadside rest areas and truck stops, but even worse was the ultimate fear: that Beau would find them.

The window broke free in a rush and sped upward, splintering the sill. A long needle of painted wood dug into her hand. She pulled it out, wincing, and leaned into the room.

Musty, but that could be fixed with open windows, as long as the slight breeze kept up. She heard skittering feet, saw a shadow race across the floor. Small and compact: probably a mouse. Mice she could handle. She just prayed there were no snakes.

Most important, she didn't see any signs of human habitation: no stacks of clothes, no dishes on the little kitchen counter. She didn't want to disturb another squatter. Didn't trust such a person, even though she was about to become one herself.

She couldn't believe that protecting her children had come to this.

For the thousandth time on their three-day pilgrimage, she questioned whether she'd made the right decisions. Leaving Beau, yes. And her job, telemarketing from home, hadn't been a reason to stay in Montana. But heading to the South Carolina coast, based on a town's name and some hazy childhood memories? That had been impulsive.

On the other hand, where else could she have gone? Her father didn't have a lick of spare energy for her problems, and she wasn't blessed with a big, close extended family.

"Mom! It was seventy-eight steps!"

"No, eighty!"

The twins rushed to her, red faced and bedraggled, and she knelt and hugged them fiercely, one in each arm, inhaling their sweaty-kid scent. They needed baths, or at least a swim, soon. She was just thankful that they were safe and with her.

"Whatcha doing with that window?" Hayley asked.

"Are we allowed to open it?" Hope looked worried.

"It'll be fine," she said to Hope. "You'll see what I'm doing in a minute. But for now, I want you to go stand on the front porch, and close your eyes, and count to…"

"Fifty!"

"A hundred!"

"Seventy-five," Anna said. "Go on. Scoot." It was a good thing they'd reached their destination, because she was running out of creative games to keep the girls entertained.

Hoisting herself up, she flung a leg through the waist-high window and eased through the casement, scraping her thigh on the rough wood. Blood beaded bright against her fading yellow-green bruises.

She was in. She dusted her hands together, did a quick inspection to assure herself that the place was solid and safe, and threw the front door open just as the girls shouted "seventy-five" together. "Come see our new vacation home!" she said, smiling at them.

They walked in, wide-eyed but accepting, and the three of them explored the small cabin. Faded, vinyl-covered camp mattresses remained on rusty cots, a single in one bedroom and a double in another. The living room was fully, if only basically, furnished, and the pine paneling on the walls gave the place a cozy, old-fashioned feel.

"Where's the stove?" Hayley asked.

"And the fridge?" Hope added.

Anna came into the kitchen area and looked around, putting her hands on her hips. "They were taken out because people don't live here anymore. But we'll be fine. We have our cooler, and we can cook things on our camp stove."

"Or just eat cereal," Hope added helpfully.

Anna blew out a breath. "No. We're going to start having real meals again, just as soon as we can go to the grocery store." If memory served, there was a small one in the coastal village of Safe Haven, just a few miles down the road. For more supplies, they'd take the highway to Myrtle Beach.

"Hey, the lights don't work!" Hayley stood flicking the light switch in the kitchen. Hope ran to check the one in the living room, and then the girls ran from switch to switch, testing each one and getting the same result.

Anna tried the faucet: no water. Of course. It made sense given that the rustic little resort wasn't open for business. Electricity they could do without, but they needed water.

She let the twins run as she looked around, planning. A worried glance out the window showed a low-hanging sun, so she had to get moving. They'd bring in what they needed, light the lantern, get out dinner. Probably peanut-butter sandwiches, but she'd fix the girls some fruit at least. She'd locate a flashlight and go hunting for the main water valve, set the girls to work wiping down mattresses. They'd find a broom and sweep up the dust and litter on the floor. For tonight, they'd be okay.

Tomorrow, she'd deal with the fact that she was in a strange state where she knew no one, with two little girls to support on very limited funds. She'd figure out their next step.

She was just so grateful that they'd found refuge. They were beginning a new life without Beau, and for now at least, they were safe. That was all that mattered.

AFTER LOADING UP his truck with supplies from the hardware store—and a six-pack of beer to wash away the taste of his family's annoying interference—Sean O'Dwyer pulled up to the closed gates of the Sea Pine Cottages, rolled down his window and just sat for a minute, enjoying the moonlight.

The vibrating hum of cicadas rose and fell, and in the distance, waves pounded. The Southern breeze that cooled his face felt like home, as did the looming cedar and live oak trees draped spookily with Spanish moss. Marshy salt smells reminded him of long days spent canoeing through the area's black water rivers.

The low country would heal him. It always did.

And living here, alone, would be enough for him.

He got out of his car, keyed open the padlock and unwound the chain. He was pushing the squeaky, rusty gate open when the hair on the back of his neck rose.

Something was out of place.

His heart rate accelerated as he stepped back to his truck to retrieve his pistol, then did a deliberately slow three-sixty. His intuition for danger had been honed on the streets of Kabul and he knew better than to ignore it, even in these much-more-peaceful surroundings.

There. A flash.

He walked quietly toward it and realized there was a car parked behind the bushes that framed the gate. Decently hidden, but not to someone with his experience. A small Hyundai sedan that had seen better days. Hand on his weapon, he approached it.

Most cars held some evidence of their owners—a potato chip bag, kid toys, a spare jacket or sweater. This one was completely clean. Almost as if its owner didn't want it to reveal anything.

It was too dinged up to be a rental, and it had Montana plates. Whoever owned the car was far from home.

He felt the hood. Cold.

He got back in his truck and let it roll silently down toward the cabin he'd been working on and living in, already mostly renovated. As he rode, he scanned the darkness.

There. A light. Bobbing up and down inside Cabin Three, just two doors down from the beachfront one he'd selected for himself. Somebody must think they could get a vacation for free. Either that or they were up to something illegal. Between Kabul and Knoxville, he'd learned to trust no one.

He coasted past, parked the truck and headed back toward the cabin with the bobbing light. He'd figured some locals would disregard the Keep Out signs, but he would've expected partying teenagers. A single flashlight suggested someone with more nefarious aims.

He approached the cabin slowly, watching, listening.

The light was off now; either that or it had moved to another room.

He shuffled through nettles and hackberry, glad for his work boots, looking in the windows. There was stuff that shouldn't be there, barely visible in the moonlight. A carton of food in the kitchen, a cooler, a couple of suitcases. Someone was intending to settle in.

But that wasn't happening, not on his watch. He came around to the back porch of the cabin and lifted aside a broken section of the screen. Used his knife to slit it the rest of the way open. Stepped cautiously through.

The slight, silent figure that rose in front of him gave him two seconds of warning, and he ducked, but not soon enough.

Fire stung his eyes and he staggered backward, his skin burning. He grabbed his assailant's wrist, realized with shock that it belonged to a petite woman, lost his balance and pulled her down with him.

# CHAPTER TWO

WITH HER FREE HAND, Anna pummeled the giant who'd latched on to her wrist like a tiger on prey. Her heart pounded and sweat poured down her sides as she tried desperately to twist out of his grasp.

*It's happening again. I can't let it happen again.*

His chest was a wall of muscle, his hands enormous. Panting, she tried to knee him, but he blocked her with a twist of a solid thigh, trapping her.

She was breathing loudly and at first that was all she heard, until his big, choking breaths invaded her consciousness, too. His eyes were closed and tears ran freely down his face. He lifted a hand and rubbed his eyes, grimacing.

The pepper spray had fallen out of her hand when he'd grabbed her wrist, but it had obviously done its job.

The thought of her girls inside the cabin made her start kicking again, and hitting, and he grabbed her other hand and kept her legs trapped between his. "Be still, will you? It's okay."

She didn't have much choice about being still, and irrational rage bloomed inside her. Why were men blessed with superior strength? Why were women always the victims?

At least he wasn't hitting her. He wasn't moving at

all, until, warily, he let go of her hands. "I'm not going to hurt you," he said.

She kicked free of his legs and he let her, and she crab walked backward until a wicker chair stood between them. She spotted the pepper spray, grabbed it and got to her feet. "Stay over there. Don't move or I'll spray you again."

"Please don't." He used the backs of his hands to wipe his eyes. "Do you have a towel?"

"I'm not helping you. Why should I? You were breaking into my place."

"Common kindness?" he gritted out. "And it's not your place."

She studied the man narrowly, but he seemed in genuine pain, his eyes rapidly swelling. She felt a moment's guilt. But he'd broken in, and what kind of intentions could he have? "Stay there," she repeated. "I'll be right back."

She glanced in at the twins, and her tight shoulders relaxed: they were sleeping peacefully in the double bed. But she couldn't let down her guard. She grabbed a kitchen towel and took it out onto the screened porch, pulling the door to the cabin closed behind her. "Here," she said, handing it to him. She was still shaking a little and hoped he couldn't see well enough to notice. Showing weakness to a man was like feeding blood to a shark.

As he wiped his eyes, still kneeling, she spotted one of Hope's little dolls and jammed it behind a pillow. No way was she letting this behemoth know that the girls were inside.

When she looked up, he was squinting at her, frowning.

Had he seen the toy? Who was he and what did he want? He couldn't be up to any good, out here in the middle of the night. And she and the girls had few weapons at their disposal, but she'd fight to the death for them. She wiped a sweaty hand on her shorts and then clutched the canister of pepper spray tighter.

He seemed to notice the motion. "Look, lady, I don't know who you are, but you have no right to be here, let alone to attack someone who's not doing anything to you."

"You were trying to break into this cabin."

"I have permission to be here and you don't."

She swept her eyes over him, taking in his shaggy hair, military-style tattoos and flannel shirt with ripped-off sleeves. Plus the fact that he badly needed a shave. "Really?"

He wiped the dish towel across his face. "Not that it's any of your business, but I'm the contractor for the renovation. I have a legitimate reason to be here. Which is more than I can say for you."

Oh. Her face went hot and her stomach twisted.

Now that her breathing had quieted down, she heard the rise and fall of a chorus of frogs. An owl hooted from one of the tall trees, and another responded.

The lonely sounds reminded her of how rural and deserted this place was. Just her and this man and the frogs. And her girls. A tremor started at the base of her back and rose up her spine. "You're the contractor, and you're staying here?" she said to distract herself from her fear. "Sounds like the old boys' network is alive and well in these parts."

He made a sound in his throat, draped the towel on

the wicker chair and rose to his feet with a dancer's grace, despite his alarming size. "I'm also the muscle watching over the place. Come on. You're going to need to get out. I'll help you carry your stuff to your car."

Anna's thoughts raced, testing excuses and discarding them. *My car's broken down. I'm sick. I'm scared of the dark, can't drive at night.* But the behemoth seemed sharp, and she doubted she could convince him with any standard lie.

She *could* leave, pack them up and drive somewhere else, except she didn't trust any man around her girls, even briefly. Their safety and sense of security was paramount. And they'd had enough trauma this week. Uprooting them again, making them move in the middle of the night—no. "I can't leave tonight," she said firmly.

"What's your business here, anyway?" he asked. "Are you alone?"

"Of course," she lied without a second's hesitation. "I just need a place to stay for a little while."

"There are hotels for that."

"Not in my price range. But I'll definitely look for a cheap place as soon as I get my bearings. Look, just give me a week. Ignore me for a week. You won't even notice I'm here." Even as she said it, her heart sank. Antsy five-year-olds were hard to miss.

"Why should I?" He swiped the towel across his face again, and though his eyes were bloodshot, she still recognized their hooded mistrust.

"Want me to get you some wet cloths for your eyes?" she asked desperately.

"Trying to earn points? It won't work." He crossed his arms over his chest. "And if you're looking for chivalry, it's dead."

She snorted out a laugh. "Believe me, I'm not looking for that. Just maybe a little— What did you call it? Common kindness."

He turned his head, looking out into the moon-dappled darkness, seeming to consider her words. In the distance, she heard the faint sound of waves, pounding. A roselike, sweet fragrance drifted in on the warm breeze, and she summoned up the name from childhood. Oleander flowers. Beautiful, but she seemed to remember the plant was poisonous.

A faint sound from inside the house made her snap to attention, every muscle tightening. *Don't wake up, don't wake up*, she tried to communicate telepathically to whichever of her girls was stirring.

The man had heard the sound, too. Either that or he noticed her reaction. "I thought you said you were alone." His hand went to his pocket and rested there.

Anna's stomach tightened and sweat dripped down between her breasts. Of course he was packing. Why wouldn't he be?

She stood to make a barrier between him and the door of the house.

The door opened. "Mommy? There are noises."

Anna flew to Hope as the sleepy child stepped out onto the porch, trying to block her view of the man. Trying to block his view, too.

But Hope, hypervigilant as she'd become lately, had seen, and she clapped a hand to her mouth, her eyes wide. She grabbed Anna's leg with a grip of steel.

"Go inside and get back in bed with Hayley." She forced a smile onto her face and pressed her sweating palms against her sides. "Everything's okay."

Hope clung tighter.

Anna looked at the man. Her heart pounded like a drum, but she kept her face impassive.

"You said you were alone." His mouth twisted a little as he looked from her to Hope.

"Please, mister. Just go away. Leave us be for the night."

Hope's back convulsed and she buried her face against Anna's hip. The poor kid had thought they were safe, thought they were having a beach vacation away from the miseries of life with their father in Montana. But now here was another big, scary man, ready to force them to run again.

Or maybe worse.

"You mentioned Hayley. So you have another child inside?" Something tense and angry flashed over the man's face.

Why, oh why, had she let Hayley's name slip out? She hesitated, then nodded. What was the use of lying now?

He made a frustrated sound and turned toward the door. "All right. You can stay the night, but that's all. I want you out of here tomorrow."

Hope's sobs got louder and she tried to muffle them against Anna's leg.

Anna drew herself up to her full five foot four and squared her shoulders in an effort to put herself on more of an equal footing, for Hope's sake if not for her own. She lifted her chin to project a confidence she didn't possess. "Fine. We'll talk tomorrow."

THE NEXT MORNING, Sean stood in the thick bushes by the squatter's car, watching as the woman and her two girls approached. Unexpected warmth spread behind his breastbone.

She was gorgeous in a different kind of way. Short, messy brown hair, full lips, big green eyes. Today she wore jeans and long sleeves, but her modest clothes couldn't conceal her knockout figure.

The little blondes, identically cute, were chattering excitedly. The woman listened and laughed, paying real attention. A rare quality in a time when so many parents tripped over their kids because they were glued to their cell phones. His own mom had been stressed, she'd had her issues, but she'd done her best to give him, Liam and Cash that kind of full attention, too. At least, when they were small and their father was away. Before she'd disappeared and their family had been blown apart.

He walked out into view as they reached the car, and the woman exclaimed and stepped back, pulling the girls closer to her sides. "What are you doing here?" she asked. She was trying for aggression, but he could hear the fear underneath.

Maybe he *should* clean himself up a little, at least enough so he didn't terrorize women and children.

"We planned to talk," he said, "but besides that, there's a problem."

"I've got a bucketload of problems, mister, but what now?"

He pointed at her tires, two of them flattened.

She gasped and bent to look. "Who did this?" The little girls looked, too, and then pressed closer to their mom.

LEE TOBIN McCLAIN 227

"Just a bunch of construction nails. You happened to park right by the trash pickup." He felt bad—if he'd been neater, maybe her tires would've survived the proximity to the trash—but then again, she'd pulled entirely off the road. She was the one trespassing.

Sweat beaded on the woman's forehead and she couldn't conceal the fact that she was shaking. Obviously, she didn't believe the pierced tires were an accident.

He swallowed the knot that rose in his throat. What had she been dealing with, and what dangers did she face now, to make her so suspicious? "Hey," he said, walking closer to pat her shoulder awkwardly, "are you okay?"

She cringed, so he stepped away and let her get her bearings. She leaned against the car, closed her eyes and drew in deep breaths.

After a minute, she opened her eyes and bent to look at the tires again. "I guess we're not going anywhere."

Which was exactly what she'd wanted last night. Suspicion nudged at him. Had she punctured the tires herself, to get insurance money or an excuse to stay here?

But no; her fear had been real.

The little blondes came out from behind her, foreheads wrinkled, tears staining both pairs of cheeks. She cuddled them to her sides and squatted down. "It's okay. It's no big deal. We're fine."

One of the girls pointed at the tires and shook her head, her lower lip jutting out.

"Okay, not fine exactly, but we're safe." She looked up at Sean. "We were planning to go to the grocery."

"Settling in?"

She glared at him. "Feeding my children."

When she put it like that, he felt like a heel. "Come on. I'll give you a ride into town. I was headed there myself." He indicated his truck, pulled off to the outside of the gates he'd opened.

"Oh, I don't think…"

Her two girls looked up at her, with identical puppy dog eyes. Man, were they cute.

And it made all the sense in the world that she didn't want them getting in a truck with a stranger. "I can show you my military ID," he offered. "Or my badge from my last construction site. Or give you my mom's phone number." Not his real mom's, Ma Dixie's, but close enough.

She studied him, and then looked at his truck.

He found himself hoping she'd say yes, mostly for the sake of those little girls. Their innocent eyes made him want to be the kind of guy who reached out to others and helped them.

She swallowed hard. "We do need groceries. All right. And thank you."

He let out the breath he'd been holding. "No problem. Maybe we'll get a chance to have our little talk." He held out a hand. "I'm Sean O'Dwyer, by the way."

She swallowed, the muscles working in her throat. "Anna George," she said, and then bit her lip, as if she wished she hadn't given him her name. "And these are my daughters, Hayley and Hope."

She got booster seats out of the trunk of her car and put them in the narrow back seat of his truck, then settled the twins there. "It's a truck like Grandpa used to have, remember?"

One of the twins nodded vigorously. The other looked sad.

Where was their grandpa now that he wasn't helping them out? Was that another loss they'd faced?

They rode a couple of miles in silence, passing the occasional small house and, as they got closer to town, the little AME Church and Mr. Nathan's Carryout and a roadside stand featuring fresh shrimp and boiled peanuts and vine-ripe tomatoes. He was debating what to pick up for his own dinner, later, when Anna pointed at the picture hanging from his key chain. "Who's that?"

He glanced down at the faded photo. He'd grabbed it out of his wallet and stuck it in the holder when he'd removed Gabby's picture, just to remind himself of what was important and who you could trust.

"Me and my brothers." He didn't expand on it.

She nodded and stayed quiet until they reached Safe Haven's small downtown, bustling on a Saturday morning.

"It's a cute place," she said, and turned back to face the girls. "Didn't I tell you we were coming to a real nice town?"

No answer from the back seat. He wondered if the girls were hearing impaired. But no, when he glanced in the mirror he saw they both looked animated. And then he remembered that the one had come out last night because she'd heard a noise.

"It's quaint," she added, looking back at him. "Different from...where we're from."

"Montana?" he asked, and he felt her tense beside him. "Your plates."

"Oh of course. Yes."

Since she was so obviously nervous, he looked away to give her space and gazed around town. Was Safe Haven cute and quaint? Well, sure, there were benches and flowers in window boxes in front of little brick shops. Jarvon Davis tapped his horn and waved, his pickup laden down with produce for the Saturday-morning farmers' market. Laraba Brown made her slow way across the street, and Sean lifted a hand in response to her wide smile.

Maybe it was quaint to others—and a safe haven, its name arising out of the town's history—but to him it was just home. Home, no matter where else he traveled or lived. Home, where the community had embraced him and his brothers with few questions asked. Home, for better or worse.

He pulled up in front of the corner market. "I'll meet you here in half an hour. Is that enough time?"

"It is." She met his eyes directly and smiled. "Thank you for being so kind."

A cold place in his heart warmed a little, just from the sunshine of that smile. "Sure. No problem."

She jumped down and helped the girls out of the back. "We appreciate your help. Right, girls?"

They both nodded and the bolder one gave him a smile that lit up her face, the same smile as her mother's.

Sean's heart pretty much melted.

He watched the trio walk into the store, the girls bouncing with excitement. They'd obviously been through a lot, but they were resilient. Able to play and have fun even in the worst of circumstances. He glanced down at the photo of him and his brothers. They'd done the same, as kids.

Things were a lot more complicated now. He drove

the several blocks to his brother's apartment building. Tony wasn't his biological brother, but one of Ma Dixie's many foster kids. He and Tony had been inseparable throughout most of their teen years, and that was why Sean wanted to help him in his current trouble.

He trotted up the stairs and knocked on the door of the ivy-clad but modest second-floor apartment. No answer.

The next apartment over, a neighbor came out onto the shared wrought-iron balcony, a potbellied man Sean knew slightly. "He ain't around, but he sure enough was last night."

A cold hand squeezed Sean's heart. "Trouble?"

"Nah. Just drinkin' and partyin' noise, but it don't bother me." He pointed at his behind-the-ear hearing aid. "I just take these things out and go to sleep."

That was a relief. With Tony, you never knew. "Thanks, man. I'll catch him later."

He still had some time after parking near the market, so he strolled to the hardware store to pick up some mulch and a drill bit. After putting his purchases in his truck, he walked toward the market.

From the bakery's open door, a buttery cinnamon smell wafted out. He bet Anna's twins would love some of Jean Carol's cinnamon rolls.

*Don't do it.* He didn't need to be getting close to this little family, didn't need to make those little girls think he'd be a positive force in their lives. Best not to raise any hopes or confuse things.

He forced himself to walk right on past.

In the store, he grabbed a bunch of bananas and a carton of milk and got in line. Up ahead, Anna and the twins were checking out. He noticed the generic cereal and the sale sticker on the meat.

He should have bought the cinnamon rolls for the girls.

"Is that you, Sean O'Dwyer?"

The melodious voice behind him took him straight back to the past. "Hey, Miss Vi!" He turned and gave the dark-skinned, gray-haired woman a hug. "What've you been doing? Still running the library?"

"I'll be there until they push me out the door. Which you would know, if you ever stopped in to check out a book."

"I should, now that I'm back in town." Sean read a lot, but these days, he mostly bought books for his e-reader. It suited him to travel light.

He really ought to stop into the library, though, just to see Miss Vi. She'd been a rock in the lives of Sean and his brothers after they'd lost their mom. She'd encouraged and scolded and spoken up for them, even, he suspected, had played a role in getting each of them the foster placement that would work best.

A loud voice turned their attention to the front of the line. The cashier, big and blonde, had stepped out from behind the cash register to set a bag of groceries in Anna's cart. "And what are your names?" she asked the twins.

The twins pushed into Anna's side, not speaking.

"Are you shy? Huh?"

The bolder of the twins put a hand on her hip and shook her head, frowning.

Anna offered an apologetic smile to the cashier. "They aren't big talkers."

"Aw, that's not going to get y'all anywhere! Come on, ladies. Tell Miss Claire your names."

Both twins clamped their jaws shut and backed up, glancing at each other.

"Do you know that family?" Miss Violet asked behind him, her voice quiet.

"Not well. I think they're just passing through."

"I've seen that behavior before. She may need some help with it." Miss Violet plunked her purchases on the belt as Anna and the girls paused in front of the cash register to rearrange their cartful of grocery bags. "I'll pay for these later, Claire," Miss Vi said. Then she walked purposefully over to the small family.

Sean paid for his own items, one ear cocked toward the conversation. "It's a nice program and there's no obligation," Miss Vi was saying in her quiet-but-insistent voice, the one that had kept Sean and his brothers sitting still and reading in the library years ago.

"That's very kind, but we won't be able to," Anna said.

Identical sulky expressions appeared on the twins' faces.

"Books are very important to little girls, and our after-school program is free." Miss Vi smiled at Anna. "If you're in town Monday, stop by for our Spring Party."

Anna's forehead wrinkled and she worried her lower lip as she looked at the girls.

"There's entertainment for the kids," Miss Vi went on, "and prizes, and the best pecan pie bars you ever tasted."

The twins tugged on Anna's arms. No way was she going to withstand those cute, pleading expressions.

Anna opened her mouth, and Sean's heart lifted. Good. She was going to do something fun with her girls.

But then a cloud crossed Anna's face, and she shook her head. "I know books are important," she said. "But we probably won't be here long enough to stop by for a visit."

She pushed up her sleeves and put a hand on the cart, obviously trying to speed their departure.

And Sean saw what it had been too dark to notice last night. Fading bruises. All up and down her arms.

## CHAPTER THREE

ONCE THEY'D GOTTEN back in the truck, Anna felt her shoulders relax. Of course she and the twins had to interact with other people, for things like getting groceries, but she wanted to keep to themselves as much as possible. Not forever, but for now.

They cruised down the town's main street, where clusters of people chatted outside pretty little mom-and-pop storefronts. A man with an enormous Saint Bernard–type dog stopped to greet a woman with a Chihuahua, and the two dogs sniffed each other like old friends.

*Someday, maybe the twins and I can have a dog, too. And friends.*

Another block down, and there were two dark-haired women, obviously mother and daughter, pushing a stroller and chatting nonstop.

She watched, and swallowed a golf-ball-sized lump in her throat. Three generations. A blessing and a safety net she'd never have. The mother Anna only dimly remembered would have loved her girls, and would have provided refuge when things got bad for them and Anna.

Sean turned, and turned again. This didn't seem like the way back to the Sea Pine Cottages.

Alarm squeezed Anna's chest. "Where are you taking us?"

"Right here." He pulled up to a white clapboard church, parallel parked the truck in front of it and turned off the engine.

The girls squealed to see a small, old-fashioned playground beside the place, complete with wooden teeter-totters and a merry-go-round. They wouldn't speak, of course, not in front of Sean, but they unbuckled their seat belts and leaned forward, tapping her arm and pointing.

A smile quirked the corner of Sean's mouth as he watched them, and that involuntary response eased Anna's tension. He had been awfully kind so far. She needed to remember that not every man was out to get her.

The girls tugged at her more insistently. They'd been troupers about the long days in the car, and they hadn't been having much fun lately. And the playground was safely fenced and carpeted with thick, soft grass. "All right. You can play for a few minutes." She opened the truck door and let them run through the gate to the play equipment.

She could watch over them easily from the parking area, so she turned toward Sean, who'd also gotten out of the truck. "Are you trying to evangelize us, bringing us to a church?"

"No. Just come inside a minute."

She crossed her arms. "I can't leave the girls out here alone. And I don't want to get mixed up with church people."

That made him study her with curiosity. "It's not church people I want you to meet."

"Then who?"

Instead of answering, he watched a car pull into the

small parking lot beside the church. A woman who looked to be in her late twenties got out and trotted up the church's front steps.

"We'll be in," Sean called to her.

The woman looked a little more closely at Anna, then gave Sean a thumbs-up. "Anytime."

Anna narrowed her eyes at Sean. "What's this about?"

"It's a women's center. For domestic violence." He paused, and then, when she opened her mouth to protest, he said, "I saw your bruises."

Heat rose up her neck and into her face and she crossed her arms, trying to hide them with her hands. How had she, the scruffy tomboy kickball queen, become an adult woman who let a man hit her, leaving bruises all the world could see? She tugged down her rolled-up sleeves. "That's not your business."

His eyes were steady on hers, holding a depth of what? Wisdom? Compassion? Something kind, anyway. "You made it my business," he said, "when you holed up at a place I'm responsible for."

"I'm taking care of it myself." She said the words firmly, trying to convince herself as well as him.

"Are you?" His gray eyes were clear and steady. "Those bruises tell a different story. How do you know he hasn't followed you here?"

"He hasn't." From the market, she'd texted her friend Sheila and learned that Beau had been seen back home in Montana last night. In their small community, it was easy to check on people.

Though no one had checked on her and her girls, much, during the months that Beau had constricted their lives more and more until he had them in a stranglehold. Maybe it was Western independence. People might know a little bit of your business, back home, might even ask a kindly question or two, but they didn't persist. Nobody wanted to be nosy or interfere.

And Beau had been careful never to hit her in the face.

"Look," Sean said, "just get some brochures and say hello."

"No."

He did a palms up. "If that's how you want to live your life. I tried." He looked away, and then focused on another man, headed up the stairs of a small apartment building down the street. "Hang on a minute. I have to talk to someone."

She perched on a low concrete wall beside the playground. The girls ran from one piece of play equipment to the next, talking their twin language, their voices low, but excited. It was good to see them having fun.

She glanced down the street to where Sean and the other man now stood talking. The other guy was handsome, too, though in a different way than Sean, not as huge.

If she could appreciate a couple of handsome guys—at least from a distance—she must be doing better.

Was that wrong? She was still married to Beau.

Or actually, not.

Anxiety tugged at her gut, making her stomach roil and churn, but she pushed the feelings away. Instead, she focused on the Saturday-morning world around her: the sound of birds singing, of kids riding bicycles down the street, shouting. From the open window of a nearby house, she heard a squeaky sound. Someone playing a scale on a violin, badly. Probably a kid's music lesson.

Behind her, she heard the door of the church open, and the lady they'd seen before came out. *Great*.

"Hey, I'm Yasmin." She sat down on the ledge a couple of feet away from Anna and pulled a bagel out of a paper bag. "Breakfast. I like to eat it outside. Cute girls," she added, gesturing toward the playground with the bagel.

Anna nodded, not wanting to get into a conversation where she had to reveal things about herself.

"I haven't seen you around before. Anything I can help you with?"

"No. We're fine." Anna fumbled to button her shirt higher and softened her abrupt words with a smile. "He thinks we're not," she said, waving a hand toward Sean, "but we are."

"Sure thing," Yasmin said easily. "I can take off my professional hat, then. I'm not in the business of forcing people to use our services."

"Thanks." The complete lack of pressure in Yasmin's voice was refreshing. She looked over at the woman in time to see her frown at Sean and the other man.

"What's wrong?" she asked.

"Men." Yasmin's voice was disgusted.

"What?" Then Anna was distracted by Hope, who'd run over to the fence and was waving to get Anna's attention. "What's wrong, honey?"

Hope pointed to where Hayley stood balancing on the middle of a teeter-totter, arms spread wide, tilting to make the ends clank to the ground.

"Hayley! That's for sitting." Anna stood and waited, and Hayley jumped off. "Why don't you go teeter-totter with her?" she said to Hope. "You sit on the other end and go up and down. Show Hayley how."

Hope smiled and ran toward her sister.

Pitiful that her girls had never been on a teeter-totter before. "Take it slow, Hayley, okay?" Anna called.

Hayley nodded reluctantly and raised her end of the teeter-totter so Hope could climb onto the other end. Soon they were going up and down, laughing.

Like normal kids. Her throat tightened and she looked upward to keep the tears from forming and falling. The sight of the clear blue sky reminded her to say a quick prayer of thanks.

Yasmin was watching Sean and his friend, and that made Anna curious. "So what's the scoop on those two guys?"

Yasmin blew out a breath. "Not my circus, not my monkeys."

"But it's kinda my circus, since I'm staying near him and letting my girls ride in his truck."

"You're Sean's friend?"

"I just met him yesterday. I wouldn't call us friends— I'm not attached to him or anything." *But I'd like to know a little more about him.*

Yasmin hesitated, then shook her head and bit her lip. "Okay, I know they're foster brothers, but I have some reservations about that man."

"Why? What's the problem?"

Yasmin crossed her arms. "His name's Tony, and he and his wife used to have terrible fights. She even pressed charges against him, although she dropped them pretty quickly."

Indignation burned in Anna's chest. "Why'd she drop them? Did he threaten her?"

"No, no, she's gotten in a lot of legal trouble herself, and all her lawsuits against other people were just

making her look bad, like she was spoiling for a fight."
Yasmin shrugged. "I'm usually on the woman's side,
but this time I'm just not sure."

Anna's heart had started thumping as the other
woman talked, and now it settled into a steady, uncomfortable rhythm. *She* was sure, and she didn't even
know the two people involved.

"He does seem to be making changes in his life,"
Yasmin continued, "but I wouldn't necessarily put a
lot of trust in him. Sean has, though—he's given Tony
all kinds of help."

Of course he had. Men stuck together in this type
of situation.

"For Sean, family is everything, I get that." Yasmin
stood. "Tony might be innocent, but then again…" She
spread her hands, shrugged. "I'd better stop gossiping
and get to work. Let me know if I can do anything for
you, okay? It was nice to meet you."

Anna stood, too, her hands clenching into tight fists.
The twins had moved to the swings, and as she watched
them dangle and twist on their tummies, kicking the
dirt, she fumed inside.

She'd forgotten, for a minute, just how cautious she
needed to be.

She'd accepted a ride from Sean. That smacked of
dependence, something she'd vowed to avoid.

She knew, from Beau and his friends, how closely
men could stick together. Beau's friends had a disregard
for women, didn't even really think of them as people,
but rather as lower beings designed to serve as cooks,
sex workers and punching bags.

Even though Sean O'Dwyer had been really nice to

them, she couldn't depend on him. She needed to stand on her own two feet. Starting now.

SEAN FIST-BUMPED his foster brother Tony, older than he was by a couple of years but still, in some ways, trying to find his way in life. "Come look the site over whenever you want. I'll get you a key."

"Can't tell you how much I appreciate this," Tony said. "I'll work hard. I just want to pay you back and put this behind me."

"We'll figure it out." Sean was glad he could help his foster brother, who'd done so much for him when he was a hurting young teenager. "Just, you know, stay away from her."

"Believe me, I plan to. See you later."

As he made a quick detour to the bakery and then headed back toward the church, Sean thought about Tony. If there had been even the slightest chance that he'd beat up on his wife, Sean would never have given him a helping hand.

But Brandi, Tony's wife, was a notorious liar. Besides, Sean knew Tony, knew his values. Tony had a few issues, but he was the type who'd pick up a spider and take it outside rather than kill it. Hitting a woman was out of the question.

Back at the church playground, Sean looked around for Anna and the girls, but they weren't there. Had they gone inside? Or had something happened to them?

Worry hammered his chest, and he barged into the church too forcefully. Yasmin raised an eyebrow. "You done aiding and abetting?"

"Brandi dropped the charges and changed her story. Now she's saying Tony is a wuss who can't stand up for himself. Which isn't true, but I know it's not in his nature to hurt his wife."

Yasmin sighed. "You're probably right, but considering what I see every day here at the women's center, you'll have to forgive me if I'm a little skeptical."

He had no time to argue with Yasmin, to tell her that he'd have Tony's hide if the man had laid a finger on a lady. "Did you see that woman I was with? The one with the blonde twins?"

She took her time straightening the paper clips on her desk. "What are your intentions toward that mother and her twins?"

"I don't have any. I was just planning to give her a ride back to the cabins where she's staying—temporarily. If you have a better offer for her, I hope you'll make it. Seems like she could use a hand up."

She studied him skeptically, but seemed finally to see something honest in his eyes. "They're at Shorty's."

Shorty's car repair. Okay. At least they were safe. He strode across the street and down a block in the other direction, only to find Anna filling out paperwork while the twins sat in adjoining chairs in the waiting room, avoiding the friendly townspeople's attempts to speak to them.

In the adjacent auto bay, a couple of Shorty's uniformed workers looked at Anna with open appreciation. Without thinking twice, Sean stepped closer to block their view.

"All right, we'll be out tomorrow morning and do the repair right there," Shorty was saying to Anna as she signed a paper and counted out cash.

He saw the tense line of her shoulders and guessed

that the price of new tires hurt. "You might be able to get insurance to pay for it," he suggested.

She turned toward him, her face closed down. "It's all figured out."

Over in the waiting area, one of the twins got up, marched to a chair across the room and sat down, crossing her arms, lower lip out in a pout.

"You ready to go?" he asked Anna.

"Shorty said he could give the twins and me a ride."

Sean frowned, wondering why she was being so curt.

"But you'd have to wait awhile, ma'am," Shorty said. "We're understaffed. If he can give you a lift…"

She frowned. "No, it's okay."

What had happened while they'd been apart, that she didn't want anything to do with him now? Sean skimmed back over the last half hour and realized: Yasmin. The shelter director must have said something about Tony's supposed crime and his connection to Sean.

Which was fine. In Yasmin's line of work, she saw the bad side of men, and it seemed like Anna had reason to share those views.

So maybe Yasmin had talked some trash about him, but he didn't feel right leaving Anna here to deal with Shorty and his men, alone. "Come on. I'll take you back. It's no problem."

"I don't…"

A sob and the sound of ripping paper came from the waiting area, and they both looked over to see one of the twins holding a magazine away from the other, who was grabbing for it. Tears ran down both faces.

The girls had to be tired and hungry. "Your groceries are in my truck," he said. "And their booster seats."

She blew out a sigh. "True. Fine. Thank you."

He held out the little bag he'd been carrying. "Okay if I give them each a cinnamon roll? Might cheer them up for the ride home."

Her eyebrows came together as she studied him, and he could read the questions in her eyes. She was wondering what his game was, and understandably so.

He opened the bag and held it out, waving it a little. "Local specialty. We're all addicted. I got you one, too."

She inhaled, and her eyes widened. "Wow."

"Sean O'Dwyer. Did you go to Jean Carol's and forget to bring me something?" Shorty's receptionist leaned out from behind her computer and threw up her hands. "Where is the justice around here?"

"Sorry, Maria. Next time." He was still holding the bag out toward Anna.

"You better grab 'em while you can," Shorty advised Anna. "People have committed larceny for Jean Carol's rolls."

The twins came over and pressed against Anna's legs, watching the adult banter, wide-eyed.

Anna put a hand on each blond head. "Mr. Sean has a treat for you girls. But you can only have it if you use your good manners and don't fight."

They both nodded rapidly.

Anna turned to answer a question from Shorty, so Sean knelt to get down at the girls' level. "These are the best cinnamon rolls on this side of the Mississippi River," he said gravely. "There's one for each of you, and one for your mom. I already ate mine."

Timidly, they each took a roll from the bag he held out to them. The bolder one, Hayley, took a big bite. Hope nibbled at hers.

Identical expressions of childhood ecstasy appeared on their faces. Sean got a warm feeling right at the center of his chest.

Apparently, Shorty did, too, because he leaned over the counter, smiling. "Welcome to Safe Haven, little ladies," he said.

"It's nice to share," Maria added in a joking voice.

Hope glanced at Hayley and then walked over, holding out the rest of her bitten cinnamon roll to Maria. Hayley quickly took a couple more bites and then did the same with her considerably smaller piece.

"Oh no, sweeties, I was kidding. But aren't you dolls for being willing to share." Maria looked over at Anna, who was signing paperwork. "You've raised up some lovely little girls."

"Thank you." Anna's quick gaze at her daughters was full of motherly pride.

In the truck on the way home, the girls fell instantly asleep. Once Sean saw that, he spoke quietly to Anna. "What happened, that you didn't want to ride with me?"

"I… Never mind," she said, and turned to look out the window, and then her phone buzzed. She looked at it, frowned. "Hello?" she said, and then, "Yes, that's me."

There was a lot of talking on the other end. Anna's fingers gripped the edge of her shirt tighter and tighter. "It was for their safety!" she said finally.

Sean kept driving, glancing over at her from time to time.

"It turns out we weren't married, although he defrauded me into thinking so."

*Not good.* Sean kept his eyes on the road.

She went on talking into the phone. "Being married

to two women at once is illegal. And I don't see how he has any claim on my children."

Sean's head jerked to stare at her for a split second. *Bigamy? Really?*

She listened some more. Frowned and glanced over at Sean. "How about if I can prove abuse?" she asked quietly.

There was a long period where Anna didn't talk. Then: "He's not a safe man, Mr. Rubin, and if you've gotten to know him at all you'd realize that. If not, I'm happy to provide physical evidence. All you need is a subpoena." She clicked off the phone and stared out the window.

Whatever problems she had must have just gotten worse. He looked over at her, and when she brushed the back of her hand over her cheek with an angry gesture, he realized she was crying.

Oh man. Crying women turned him to mush. "Where will you go when you get your car fixed?"

She cleared her throat. "That's the million-dollar question."

"You know," he said, against his better judgment, "there are worse places to be than Safe Haven. There are good people here, and Yasmin runs a decent women's shelter. Tourist season's heating up, so there are jobs."

She didn't answer, but her stillness told him she was listening.

"Look, I don't have the right to offer you shelter at the cottages myself, but I can check with management and see if we can let you slide by for a while. Maybe in exchange for some work."

She sniffled and blew her nose, not answering.

What was he doing? He needed to be kicking her out, not inviting her to stay.

It was the wretched tears, plus the fact that her situation mirrored what he'd gone through as a kid a little too closely for comfort. Women in trouble, especially those with kids, tugged at his heart extra hard.

He pulled up to the gate, got out and unlocked it. When he came back toward the truck, he realized that one of the twins had woken up and was talking. "Can we go to the library like that lady said, Mommy?" Sean heard her say.

Now that he'd realized she didn't like to talk in front of people, he paid attention. Her voice sounded sweet through the open truck window, and she was perfectly articulate. No speech impediment, no vocabulary problem.

"I don't know, honey."

"I want to go, Mommy! I want to stay here and go to the library and play on that playground." The voice was getting sulky now. "And have friends. And not have to stay in the house all the time. And Hope does, too."

Sean blew out a breath, watching as Anna closed her eyes for a second, like she was gathering her strength. He wondered about her past, what she'd lived with, what the girls had lived with.

Protective urges surged inside him, but he had to be careful. He'd had the same feelings toward Gabby. He'd been so protective that, one day when she wasn't feeling well, he'd gone back home midday to check on her.

And he'd gotten an eyeful that he dearly wished to forget.

Anna's plight got to him, which was natural given his

own history. But trusting her—trusting any woman—was a risk he wasn't quite ready to take.

Knowing what he did about his own father, he'd made the decision early on that he wouldn't have children himself. The bad blood he carried would stop with him. And that meant he needed to steer clear of a woman like Anna, whose very identity centered around her kids.

Because the tug he felt toward her and her girls wasn't just the ordinary kindness you'd show any person in need. Anna and her girls touched his heart, and that was dangerous.

So he'd check with Eldora about whether she could stay on awhile, even do some work around the place, but if Eldora said yes, Sean would keep his emotional distance from Anna.

The whole thing was a confusing mess, just what he'd come out to the marshes to avoid. He got back in the truck and heard the tail end of a word. Then the twin who'd been talking clamped her mouth shut.

He frowned, concerned against his own will. The twins' talking issue needed fixing. And he had the feeling that Miss Violet, or Yasmin, would have some good ideas about how.

When he dropped them off at Cabin Three, she told the girls to run ahead and then turned back to him. "Look, I appreciate your help with the groceries. And if you can talk to the people who own this place about my staying in exchange for work, I would be grateful." She paused, her hand clenching on the doorjamb of the truck.

"But…" he prompted, and watched her fish for words. Even in the bright afternoon sun, her skin shone flawless—except for faint dark circles under those big green eyes. She glanced toward the cabin, gave an encouraging smile and a thumbs-up to Hope, who sat on the little porch step, watching them.

Anna was so young to have so much on her shoulders. His heart seemed to expand, wanting to reach out toward her.

"Look," she said, "I'm going to get the girls settled and fix them some food. But there's something—someone—I need to discuss with you before we could even consider the possibility of staying. Can we talk later today?" When he nodded, she spun and marched toward the cottage and her girls, her back very straight.

He should be glad to hear that she had reservations about staying, because he sure had his share of reservations about getting more involved with her.

*CHAPTER FOUR*

ON SATURDAY AFTERNOON at exactly three o'clock, Rita Tomlinson brushed her hands down the sides of her best black skirt and pulled open the door of the Southern Comfort Café.

She *really* wanted this job.

The fragrances—pies baking, burgers frying and coffee brewing—filled her senses and calmed her down. The bang and clatter of dishes and soft Southern accents somehow sounded like home, even though this *wasn't* her home.

"Rita?" A man her age, maybe a little older but surely not sixty with those muscles, held out a hand. He wore an open-collar dress shirt and dark pants, typical restaurant manager attire, but his shaved head and the tattoo peeking out from rolled-up sleeves suggested another side to him. "Jimmy Cooper. Come on back where it's quiet."

The café was about half-full, a mix of young and old, black and white, some late lunchers and some who'd clearly stopped in for an afternoon snack or coffee. The decor was classic: chrome and vinyl chairs surrounding aluminum-edged tables, retro pictures and record album covers on the walls, a row of stools at a long lunch counter.

Jimmy—or should she call him Mr. Cooper?—

indicated the back booth on one side of the café, and as she slid in, she noticed his subtle once-over. She was old enough not to mind. Her looks had held up okay, but at fifty-six, the attention she'd gotten twenty years ago was a thing of the past.

And who knew: maybe she'd been a real looker back in her teens. The thought bounced into her mind and knocked at her confidence, and she lobbed it away. Years of experience had taught her it was best to avoid thinking about the missing part of her past.

They made a little small talk and then she handed him her résumé, which he took the time to scan.

"Good experience," he said when he looked up. "You've waitressed mostly in truck stops, though. Our clientele is a little more…" He trailed off.

"Refined? I can clean up my grammar."

That made him laugh. "Believe me, yours is better than most I interview. And our clientele is mixed. We've got everything from local homeless to rich tourists looking for an authentic Southern breakfast."

"How are the tips here? And the food?" Of course he wouldn't talk down his own restaurant, but she needed to know she could speak her mind, that he wasn't expecting her to act like she didn't know which end was up.

"Most people tip well. Food is excellent. Our cooks are experienced, mostly been here quite a while." He went back to studying her résumé.

She hoped the cooks hadn't been here for twenty years or longer. All the reconstructive plastic surgery had changed her, but she didn't know how much. She didn't need to get recognized before she figured things out.

He looked up and tapped the résumé. "So, Maine? That's a far cry from South Carolina."

"I'm ready for a change. I still need to work, but I'm gonna play like I'm retired in my off hours, and I'd rather do it on the beach than the ski slopes."

"Found a place to live yet?" He looked a little skeptical, and she could understand why. People just passing through tended to apply for jobs like these.

"Just signed my lease yesterday," she said. "I'm living in a little rental a couple blocks over. Magnolia Manor apartments? I can walk to work." Which was one reason she'd chosen the place and why she wanted this job. "But I do have a car," she added quickly, to show that she was stable and dependable.

He looked down at her résumé again, and she took the opportunity to scope out the restaurant. The two waitresses she could see—one behind the counter and one carrying a tray to a table—were hustling, busy, but she noticed they stopped to chat with the customers. Nice. For some people, their meal out was the only social contact they had all day, and Rita liked to take the time to joke around with them, give them a laugh or a boost.

"Any arrests?" Jimmy looked at her hard.

"No, sir. And I never took a penny from a cash register. Good with math, too, not like the kids. I don't need the calculator on my phone to count change."

He smiled, and a little zing of recognition passed between them, making Rita's pulse rate speed up a little. It might be fun to work here in ways she hadn't anticipated.

"Do you need benefits, or are you on your husband's plan?"

Oldest way in the world to find out marital status. She wondered whether it was because Jimmy preferred married waitresses for stability or because he preferred her single for other reasons. "No husband," she said, "and, yes, benefits would be a help. I'm surprised you offer them."

"I like to do the right thing by my employees. In return, I hope they won't dump me for the first fancy seafood restaurant that offers them a job." His brown eyes were still studying her in that thoughtful way that made her glad she wasn't a liar or trying to cover something up.

Well, in a way she wasn't.

"I'm not a fancy person," she said truthfully. "This is my kind of place."

They talked through more of the details, uniforms, paperwork and mandatory drug testing, and she realized halfway through the conversation that she had the job. He confirmed it by asking, "When can you start?"

"Tomorrow, if you'd like. Or do we have to wait for uniforms and test results?"

"Just wear a white shirt and black pants. I'll get you a couple of aprons in back."

"Great. Glad you don't do the old-fashioned diner uniforms."

He chuckled. "You'd look good in one, but no. Pants are more practical and more comfortable." Then he smacked his forehead. "Not supposed to make any personal comments about an employee. Forget I said that."

"If that's the worst you say, I'm fine." Like her, Jimmy was old enough to have grown up before political correctness. And while she welcomed all the improvements for working women, she wasn't one to turn away a kindly-meant compliment.

He led her back into the kitchen, and again, it was a familiar world. Huge pots simmered on the stove, and she peeked into a couple, spotting collard greens and bean soup. She inhaled the smells and appreciated the laughing and joking, and the fact that the fun didn't stop when Jimmy came around. Meant he probably wasn't a jerk as a boss.

He introduced her to the two younger cooks and then to a tall, white-haired, stoop-shouldered African American man. "This is Abel. He's been here longer than I have and knows everything."

The man laughed quietly. "Not the case, but I've fried a few eggs in my day." He leaned down to look at Rita more closely. "Seems like I've met you before."

Rita's heart pounded, both with fear and hope that he might know something about her past. But she shook her head. She didn't recognize him. "I doubt it."

He cocked his head to one side. "Really?" And then he seemed to read something in her eyes. "Beg your pardon, ma'am. I must be thinking of somebody else."

As they said their goodbyes and Rita walked out of her new place of employment, she fingered her necklace, the sea turtle, palm tree and shark's tooth that she'd been wearing when T-Bone had found her. She didn't know much. But she did know she'd had to come back here if she was to ever recover that part of her life.

She just hoped she liked what she discovered.

SATURDAY AFTERNOON, ANNA cleaned up the cabin and fixed the girls real homemade mac and cheese from the groceries they'd bought. The domestic activities soothed her. She could arrange the little cottage the way she wanted to. Didn't have to worry about whether the dinner would be to Beau's liking, and what would happen if it wasn't. Could wear her old clothes and forget about makeup.

She could *almost* forget about the possibility of Beau tracking them down.

After dinner, she gave in to the twins' begging about going down to the beach. It wasn't a hardship. As a child, on that one family vacation, she'd fallen in love with the ocean. When she'd gotten back home, she'd bought beach posters and worn beach perfume, all of which seemed outlandish in Montana, but she'd always dreamed of coming back.

Just not under these circumstances.

Anna's heart almost burst when she saw the sea, foamy waves crashing rhythmically to a white sand beach. Beside her, the girls went still, their eyes wide.

This was the scene she'd dreamed of, locked inside the house in frigid Montana. Warm sand under her feet, sea breeze in her hair and the delight of the girls' faces as they took in the ocean for the first time.

"It's big!" Hope said finally.

"What's that noise?" Hayley asked.

"It's the waves," Anna explained. "Come on. Take off your shoes. It's too cold to swim, but we can wade in the water."

Hayley kicked off her sneakers and sprinted toward the ocean, and Anna called her back and gave both girls a serious safety lecture. Jellyfish stings were nothing to laugh about, and riptides could sweep away a grown person, let alone a five-year-old.

Once they'd given her a solemn promise to stay together and at the very edge of the water, not in deep, she hugged them and shooed them off. "Go have fun. Careful fun."

Then she watched as they ran ahead of her, holding hands. She blinked back surprising tears and looked up at the sky, going golden as the sun sank lower. If only they could have come here without all the trauma beforehand, for a vacation.

But being here with Beau would have been no vacation at all.

Shaking off that thought, she followed the girls and waded in, relishing the cold water around her ankles, the sand squishing up under her feet. Hayley was already ankle deep, jumping and splashing and squealing, but Hope hung back.

"Just stand a little closer and the water will come to you," she encouraged her shy one, and Hope inched forward. When water washed over her toes, she giggled and took another small step.

"I'm not afraid like she is," Hayley boasted. But when a big wave came in, wetting her up to her knees, she leaped back into Anna's arms.

They played and ran and laughed until the western sky turned a gorgeous shade of orange-pink. Not wanting to leave the beach quite yet, Anna pulled spoons and cups—makeshift beach toys—from the bag she'd brought, and showed the girls how to build a sandcastle.

They got engrossed, and Anna stood and stretched her back.

When she looked toward the dunes, there was Sean, headed their way. He'd kicked his shoes off, too. Wearing loose beach shorts and an old T-shirt, he looked like something out of a surfer magazine.

For giants. Anna swallowed.

"Having fun?" he asked, smiling toward the twins, who were too caught up in their castle building to notice him.

"Yeah. It's their first time at the beach." Then, because she was so tempted to relax and enjoy his company, she got right to business. "What's up? Did you talk to the cottages' owner?"

"Yes, and she okayed your staying here for a week or two, more if it works out," he said. "She has a soft spot in her heart for women and children in need."

"How much did you tell her?" Anna asked, feeling uneasy. The more people who knew about her and the girls, the more chance Beau would find them.

"Just enough. As long as your references check out and you do a good job, you can stay as long as the work lasts. You have references?"

"A couple." Her friend Sheila and a long-ago pastor. She hoped it was enough.

"It's mostly physical labor, cleaning and landscaping." He studied her, curiosity darkening his eyes. "Don't know if you'd be interested. It's not exactly glamorous."

Anna lifted her chin. "Physical labor is fine with me."

"Mommy!" Hope shouted, then clapped a hand over her mouth when she realized Sean was there. She hunched and turned back to the sandcastle, blocking the adults out.

"Are they scared of me? Is that why they don't talk?" Sean asked quietly.

"They talk just fine!" She hated when people assumed that just because they didn't talk, they couldn't. Her girls were perfectly bright.

"I know—I heard them," Sean said equably, "but it seems like they won't talk in front of strangers. Are they just shy?"

All her anger whooshed out of her, replaced by her constant, nagging concern for her girls. "It's a condition called selective mutism." She sighed. "And, yes, I'm worried about it, especially since they're getting old enough for school."

"They haven't been to preschool?"

"No." *Beau wouldn't let me enroll them.*

"Hmmm," he said, and she read the judgment in his eyes. No school, no beach—what a limited life they'd had. And it was true. She'd done her best to keep their world open, taking them to museums and parks when Beau was at work, but it hadn't been enough. The worst of it was that there hadn't been much room for friends.

For Anna, either. She was out of practice with people.

As they'd talked, she and Sean had started strolling slowly, reaching a spot where the dunes dipped down toward the beach. Sea oats blew and rustled, and among them, she spotted small white flowers and knelt to smell them. "White freesia. So beautiful."

"You know the plants here?"

"I read a lot about plants." She'd been perusing South Carolina guidebooks at the public library for months, and she was naturally drawn toward the nature parts.

"Think you could figure out some sturdy ones to plant around the cabins?"

She looked back toward the cabins. Landscaping around them would be a blast.

And the girls… Their faces were relaxed and peaceful, soothed by the fresh air and sound of the waves. Her heart warmed and opened as she watched them dig in the sand.

She made a quick decision. "I'll stay the week and help you with landscaping as much as I can. After that, we'll see."

"What about your girls?"

"I'd have them with me. Would that be a problem?"

He shook his head. "Not a problem for me if it's not for you. But there are day cares and sitters in the area if you'd like to give them that."

Day cares she couldn't afford, and besides, with their speaking problems and anxiety issues, spending days with strangers wouldn't be right for them now. "No, I'll keep them here. Maybe take them to that after-school library thing the woman was telling us about this morning."

"That's great." Sean seemed to mean it. "We'll figure out the details Monday morning, but meanwhile, let me know if you have any questions about the job."

She looked up at him, feeling uneasy. *Speak up. You have to learn to speak up to protect yourself and your girls.* She swallowed and put a hand over her twisting stomach. "I'm just… Look. Is that guy, Tony, going to be around? Yasmin said he was your brother. But she also told me about the trouble with his ex."

Sean hesitated. "Actually…"

At the sound of a shout, they both turned. There was a man coming over the dunes toward them, too far away to see clearly, and Anna instinctively stepped toward her children. "Who's that?"

"It's Tony. He's going to be working with me."

Alarm bells went off in Anna's head. "I changed my mind. I can't stay here. *We* can't stay here." She crossed her arms and squared her shoulders.

He tilted his head to one side. "So you heard one person mention a connection to abuse and you're assuming the worst about him?"

"I heard his ex pressed charges," she corrected. "It sure didn't sound like empty gossip. Was it?"

Sean blew out a sigh. "No. No, but the charges were dropped."

The man in question reached them. "Hey," he said, smiling at Anna, letting his gaze sweep over to the twins. "Thought you were alone out here, buddy."

"This is Anna George. She may be doing some work for us." Sean's voice was completely emotionless.

"Sounds good. Place could use a woman's touch." Tony held out a hand to shake.

Anna stared down at the sand, pretended she didn't see it.

There was a beat of silence. Anna looked up and saw both men looking at her.

*He's an abuser. You don't have to be nice to him.* She clamped her mouth shut and let the images she usually tried to avoid crash into her mind.

Beau throwing a steak against the wall because it wasn't cooked to his liking. Beau putting a hand to her throat and squeezing, just enough so she could feel how strong he was, so she'd know what he could do if he wanted to.

Beau yelling at her in front of the girls, terrifying them. And that last time, Beau knocking her to the floor, kicking her with his big pointed cowboy boots while she tried to crawl away, to get to her sobbing girls hiding in the front closet.

All the shame and anger and fear washed over her, loud and overwhelming as waves in a storm. Nausea churned her stomach, and she clenched her jaw and raised her eyes to look from Sean to the man who'd apparently done something similar to his wife.

After a couple of beats of silence, Tony spoke. "There's some damage up at Cabin Three."

Her cabin. Immediately, her mind switched from past troubles to present dangers.

"What damage?" Sean asked. "It was fine last night."

Anna's heart thudded a heavy, anxious rhythm. "It was fine just an hour ago."

"Paint on the outside of the cabin. Didn't look like anyone had broken in. I checked the locks."

The thought of this Tony guy creeping around her cabin made her skin crawl. As did the thought of someone defacing the place she and the girls were calling home, however temporarily. Could Beau have found them?

Tony's phone buzzed, but he ignored it.

If Beau had somehow gotten here and found them, she needed to collect the girls and leave ASAP.

"That's your cabin." Sean frowned at her. "Do you have a history in the area you didn't tell me about? Enemies, old boyfriends?"

"No! I don't know anyone here!"

Tony's phone buzzed again, and he looked at it, groaned and stepped away from them to answer.

Anna looked up at Sean to find him scrutinizing her. "Are you telling the truth?"

The nerve! Hands on hips, she faced him. "Of course

I am! I don't know anyone here, let alone anyone who'd do something to try to upset me." She pushed down her uneasiness. She *was* worried about Beau finding them, but she was *almost* certain Beau was still back in Montana.

Sean continued studying her for a full thirty seconds, and she met him, glare for glare.

"Okay," he said finally. Then he gave a sideways nod toward Tony, now engaged in a conversation that looked heated. "So you're entitled to the benefit of the doubt, but he isn't?"

"I didn't… Oh." She guessed she *was* condemning Tony without knowing the whole situation. "You really think he's a safe person for my girls to be around?" she asked skeptically.

"I know it. I've known him for twenty years. He's not perfect, but he would never hurt anyone."

Well. Sean seemed sincere, which counted for something. Not everything, but something. Anna brushed back strands of hair that were blowing in her eyes. She looked at her happy girls and thought about the difficulties of moving again, versus staying here and earning some money, outdoors, with her twins beside her. "He's not staying out here?"

"No. He has a place in town."

She could keep her girls away from Tony. And Sean seemed convinced that his foster brother posed no risk.

Tony clicked off the phone and came back, looking frazzled. "She won't leave me alone. Anyway, if you want, I can get rid of that paint tomorrow. It's not exactly the kind of thing you want to see on a place you're staying. Or that you want those girls to see."

"Why? What does it say?" Anna asked, forgetting to be hostile toward him.

"A couple of swear words—insults—in big red letters," he said.

Anna's heart gave a great thud and then raced, making it hard to breathe. It had to be Beau. Who else could it be?

## CHAPTER FIVE

THE NEXT MORNING, Sean slid into the familiar aqua-blue booth of the Southern Comfort Café, greeting his brother Liam, who was already there in full uniform.

Before Sean could lift a hand to beg for coffee, the bells on the door jingled and Tony walked in.

Sean let out a breath and felt his shoulders relax. It was good to be around family again.

The waitress, with her long red hair tied back and a few wrinkles, held up the coffeepot with a friendly smile. When they all nodded, she poured three coffees and spun onto the next table.

"You should do AA—you look like crap," Sean said to Tony, softening the remark with a smile to hide his concern. He'd thought Tony had cut down on drinking. That phone conversation with his ex must have gotten to him.

And since Tony would be working in the vicinity of Anna and her kids, he needed to make sure he was sober, at least out at the cottages.

Tony blew on his coffee, gulped and then spoke. "You're no day at the beach."

Sean inhaled the smell of frying onions and potatoes, sipped his own strong coffee. Coming back to Safe Haven had seemed like the best step to take—a job offer, the chance to get away from Gabby and her new boyfriend, time with his brothers and Ma Dixie.

But this place also held memories of the worst days of his life. He looked out the window toward the street where his mother had disappeared, and his stomach churned. He closed that door and focused on now.

Same as always, the diner gave off a mixed vibe of tourist-tacky and down-home Southern charm. The background music caught his attention: blues, not fifties pop. So that was different. The place must've changed hands.

"Sorry, boys. It's my first day. Take your order?"

Something about the husky voice beside and behind him sent Sean even further into the past, but when he looked up, it was just the redheaded waitress, now poised with her order pad and a friendly, professional smile.

"You may as well learn my usual," Liam said. "Two eggs over easy, grits, bacon extra crispy."

She scribbled. "You got it."

"Tomato juice and wheat toast. Thanks, hon." Tony leaned his head back and closed his eyes.

The waitress lifted an eyebrow, a smile tugging at the corner of her mouth. "Health nut or hangover?"

"Hangover," Sean and Liam said in unison.

Sean ordered the special with extra sausage. He planned to work hard today and needed the energy. It would save him fixing himself a big lunch.

In the corner, the same booth full of senior gentlemen that had always gathered waved coffee cups. They looked older but acted the same, like they owned the place. Sean scanned the group. "Where's Mr. Jefferson?" he asked Liam. The old man had been a favorite, letting Sean and his brothers ride along in his fishing boat when they'd needed to escape their problems for a little while.

"He passed. Bugs Bohnefeld, too." Liam raised an eyebrow at him. "You've been away too long. You planning on staying awhile this time?"

The question was casual, but Sean knew his little brother well enough to hear the seriousness of it. Their brother Cash lived in Atlanta, and up until now, Sean had been away, too.

Liam, though, had never wanted to leave Safe Haven. He was dedicated to protecting it, making it a better place.

But it was a family town. Everyone had aunts and uncles and great-grandparents right down the street. For the first time, it struck Sean that being here alone must have been hard for Liam. There'd been women, including Yasmin, who ran the shelter; in fact, that relationship had seemed pretty serious for a while, but nothing had come of it.

Another reason for Sean to stick around awhile. Keep his little brother company.

Tony came back to life as a tall glass of tomato juice appeared in front of him. He took a long pull on it. "You tell him what happened out at the cottages?"

"Yeah," Liam said before Sean could answer. "Not that there's anything to investigate, seeing as how you scrubbed away the paint before I could take a look."

Tony lifted a shoulder. "Didn't want the little kids to see it."

Liam turned to Sean. "Yeah, and how about those

little kids? What's the story with the lady staying out there? I thought the place was closed."

"I shouldn't have hired her," Sean admitted. "It's just…those little girls. And she's bruised up."

Liam met his eyes. "Bad?"

"She's moving okay." Even though Liam was five years younger, Sean knew he could remember their mom limping or wearing an arm sling. Couldn't be much of a memory, though.

And why was Sean thinking about the past so much? That was what he hated about coming home. It made him crazy.

"Pretty lady," Tony contributed. "Cute kids."

"Stay away from her." Sean wasn't sure, exactly, why he felt so strongly about that. But it was enough that Anna didn't feel comfortable with Tony. "She's skittish from something that happened to her and her girls. You're both working for me, but there's no reason you need to work together."

Tony snorted. "I'm staying away from anything female. Believe me, I learned my lesson."

Their breakfasts arrived and they spent a few minutes digging in. The food was solid, a little extra spice in the eggs like Sean remembered, pancakes light as clouds. Which meant old Abel must still be running the kitchen.

When the waitress returned to check on them, Sean asked her.

"Tall black guy? He's there," she said.

"Tell him Sean O'Dwyer's back in town," Liam said. "He better start ordering more food."

"You boys grow up here?" She leaned a hip against the side of their booth.

Tony gestured toward the wall of newspaper clippings, framed and yellowed. "We're somewhere over there. Him and me—" he pointed at Sean "—we were on a state championship team."

"Before you got kicked off," Liam reminded them.

"I'll take a look when things slow down. Enjoy your food, gentlemen." She refilled their coffee cups and headed for the kitchen.

Sean watched her go. "She looks kinda familiar," he said.

Liam shrugged, and Tony didn't respond. He must be mistaken.

Once they'd finished, Liam waved for his check. "I've got a clock to punch, unlike you guys."

"Hold on." Sean didn't know exactly how to put what he had to say. "Listen, about Anna and her twins, out at the cabins…"

Tony lifted an eyebrow and Liam stopped digging for cash.

"I got a feeling she's hiding from somebody. Look into it?" That was directed to Liam.

His little brother frowned. "Chief's a good man, but he's by the book. Doesn't want us misusing the system."

"Yeah, and he's looking at a promotion, which would open up a spot for you." Tony hooked a thumb toward Liam. "Don't get yourself in trouble. It'd be nice to have a police chief in the family."

"Sure would." Sean socked Liam in the arm, lightly. Thought about telling Liam how proud he was, decided not to be a sentimental idiot. "Don't take a risk."

Liam stood. "Don't need you fools to tell me that. But if I get a chance...what's her last name?"

"George. Anna George. From Montana."

"And if I do manage to check her out, you can pay me back by doing some work at the women's center. Place is falling down around Yasmin."

Being anywhere near the women's center always depressed Sean, but he respected the work they did. "See what I can do."

After Liam left, Sean and Tony finished up. As they stood, Sean bumped Tony's shoulder. "Keep an eye out yourself," he said. "I got a bad feeling about whoever's chasing Anna."

Tony nodded.

"And no drinking on the job."

"I know that." Tony tossed a ten on the table and walked out.

Sean blew out a breath. It was one thing being crew boss for a bunch of strangers up in Knoxville. Different to be hiring on his foster brother. He hoped he hadn't made a mistake with Tony.

"That his, or did he leave you to pick up the check?" the waitress asked, nodding at the bill on the table.

"It's his. I hurt his feelings."

A smile tweaked the corner of her mouth. "Poor baby."

Sean decided he liked her. "See you again soon," he said, and left a bigger-than-normal tip.

THAT AFTERNOON, ANNA drove her newly repaired car toward the library in Safe Haven, her stomach jumping and churning. She took deep breaths. Anxiety was her constant companion these days, but she'd like to lose it.

The graffiti on the cabin last night had spooked her. Even though it didn't seem possible for Beau to have found them so quickly, who else could have done it? In light of that, was she making a mistake in staying?

The girls chattered sleepily in the back seat. *They* seemed relaxed, at least. They'd probably doze off just as they reached the library.

The library. It seemed to symbolize getting into a routine and building a life and settling down. Something she wanted, and the girls needed; but something that could make them sitting ducks for Beau.

Walking around the Sea Pine Cottages with Sean today, thinking about what the job there would entail, had made her realize that she needed something special for her girls to do, to make up for the fact that they'd have to behave and entertain themselves while she was working. And the only thing that came to mind was the after-school library program she'd heard about at the grocery that first morning in town. So she'd decided to sign them up, even if they were here for only a short time. Libraries were good places and she wanted her girls to grow up smart, to be readers.

She also needed to do something for herself, and the library just might be the place to do it.

Being around Sean had been weird. The way he'd studied her, as if he liked what he saw, had made her feel way too warm inside, and that feeling had disconcerted her. And maybe she was wrong about what his appraisal had meant.

Was he going to report her to his police officer

brother, get her car traced somehow? Do something that could broadcast their whereabouts to Beau?

And there had been that moment when she'd looked back at him, right in the eyes, and felt a connection that warmed her whole body.

Was she *attracted* to the big man?

Not that she'd do anything about it. Relationships were not for her. Maybe, one day, when she'd done a bunch of therapy and the girls were grown up, but not anytime this decade.

That little burst of attraction, or interest, or whatever it was, had made her uncomfortable enough that she'd decided to look for other jobs in the area.

She'd looked online a little, hindered by the rustic resort's spotty cell reception, and she'd discovered what she'd known back in Montana: she was basically qualified for nothing except the type of telemarketing she'd done, and disliked, since the girls had been born.

So, she had her own goal at the library today, if she was able to get the girls settled.

As she approached the little town, she glanced up in the rearview mirror and saw that the girls had fallen asleep in the back seat. No surprise; they'd always been car sleepers. She slowed down and took the long way to the library, observing the streets of the little town.

This took her back, too. Where most places changed and modernized over the years, Safe Haven hadn't really. Which meant that she'd walked these streets as a little girl, most likely. Her dim memories of that vacation didn't include much except several trips to an ice-cream store.

What she hadn't remembered was how pretty the streets were, overarched with live oaks. Two-story houses with big wraparound porches mingled with smaller, cottage-type homes. It could've been a small-Southern-town movie set, except for the touches of realism: a raggedy-clothed man with a grizzled beard, riding an old bike, his fishing poles lashed across the back. A discordant pink-and-purple house, its yard strewn with kids' toys and lawn ornaments. The faint sulfur smell of the paper mill drifting in on the warm breeze.

It was a real place, not a rich-and-famous beach community, and she liked it the better for that.

She saw the library up ahead. "Wake up, sleepyheads," she said quietly as she turned in and parked the car.

She got out and opened the back door. Hayley climbed out, rubbing her eyes.

Hope stayed inside, burying her face in her frog lovey.

"Come on, honey," she said, undoing Hope's seat buckle. "Let's go see the books!"

"I'm scared."

"Come *on*," Hayley said. She took a few steps toward the library.

"Parking lot," Anna reminded her. "Stay close."

"Come on," Hayley said again. "It's not gonna be scary."

"We're just trying it to see if you like it," Anna reminded Hope. "Get a move on, now. Out you come." She gave Hope's arm a little tug and the child climbed reluctantly out.

Inside, before they could ask for directions, they saw another mother and daughter headed for the stairwell. Following them, Anna saw the AFTER-SCHOOL PROGRAM, ELEMENTARY sign.

When they reached the children's area, Hayley practically leaped for joy and Anna's heart leaped, too. Colorful carpet squares on the floor, a table with craft supplies along one wall, and rows and rows of books.

There were seven or eight other kids there, including a couple of girls near the twins' age. The noise level was about what you'd expect from kids, which was nice—it meant those who ran the program had realistic expectations. They weren't trying to keep the little ones quiet because they were in a library.

Not that being loud was a problem for Hayley and Hope.

Miss Vi, the woman they'd met in the grocery store on that first morning, came over. She was an indeterminate age, straight-backed and gray-haired. She smiled at the twins and gestured toward the carpet squares.

"We start with a story time, as soon as Miss Reba gets here. You may each pick out a book to look at while you wait, and quiet talking only, please."

The twins nodded, big eyed, and then hurried over to a shelf of children's books.

Miss Vi approached Anna. "I'm glad you decided to come," she said, her voice warm.

"They need a kids' program, especially since I have to work all day," she said, feeling apologetic. "I… Is there a cost?"

"Never." Miss Vi smiled at her. "That's the beauty of libraries, my friend."

"My girls don't talk much," Anna said, twisting her hands as she looked from Miss Vi to the girls and back again. "At all. They don't talk at all, to strangers. But they're real smart. They'll take everything in."

"They seem to be doing all right." Miss Vi waved a hand toward them. They stood listening to a little girl who was enthusiastically explaining something to them. "Little Mindy doesn't ever *stop* talking, so she'll welcome them as an audience, as long as they put up with her. Excuse me," she added, and bustled across the room to stop a pair of boys from climbing on the shelves.

Anna wandered around the children's room, wanting to keep an eye on the twins for a few minutes. She was the only parent there, and she didn't want to make them feel bad by babying them, so she stayed in the background, strolling the perimeter of the room.

A book propped open on a shelf made her pause. *Put Me in the Zoo.*

Her throat caught. How did she know that book?

Hands shaking, she took it off the shelf, the colorful, spotted creature on the cover whooshing her back to the past.

She paged through it and suddenly she was a little kid on her mom's lap, her mom who had smelled like flowers, counting the dots and laughing together.

She'd been so young when her mom died that she didn't have many clear memories. But this was a warm and vivid one. Made her feel more normal, made her remember she'd had a mom who loved her, even if for too short a time.

After making sure Hope and Hayley were engrossed by the storyteller, Anna slipped down the stairs to the adult section. It didn't take long to find the big display of books she was seeking.

She pulled out three thick volumes and carried them up the stairs, finding a desk with an ancient-looking desktop computer in the back of the children's section, just out of sight of the kids' program. She could study the books while still keeping an ear open for any upset from the twins.

She sat down and opened one of the books, but her mind drifted to the place she'd tried to keep it from all day.

Who had painted things on her cabin? Who had slashed her tires?

Her friend back in Montana had told her that Beau's car was in front of his apartment, but had he left it there and flown here? He wasn't much for airplanes. Anna shouldn't talk—she'd never been on one herself, but for her, it was the lack of opportunity. For Beau, it was an unwillingness to give up control. He had to be the driver.

And that wasn't the only thing he wanted to control. She'd never gotten her high school diploma because Beau had strongly encouraged her to drop out. He hadn't liked her being around all those other boys. He'd promised to take care of her, insisted she come live with him, even married her in what she now knew was a fraudulent ceremony.

"You know, we have more comfortable seating downstairs in the adult section."

Miss Vi's voice jolted Anna and she looked up. How had the woman approached without Anna hearing a thing? She had to be more observant. "Thanks, but it's okay. I like to keep an eye on the girls."

"Um-hmmm," Miss Vi said in a neutral voice.

The way the older woman just stood there, looking at her, made Anna self-conscious. No other parents were hiding out watching their kids.

But no other parents were in her situation, either.

"You know," the older woman said, "there's a GED class that meets here, twice a week."

Only then did Anna realize that Miss Vi was looking at the books she'd selected. She turned the top one over to cover the title, heat rushing into her face. "No, no, thanks. It's okay." Man, was Miss Vi nosy or what?

The librarian nodded toward the thick books. "That's a lot of material to get through on your own."

*I'm uneducated, not stupid.* "I'm more of a do-it-yourself type," Anna said, hearing the stiffness in her own voice. It was just so ridiculous of her never to have finished high school. Now, *that* had been stupid of her.

"I understand. I've got that independent gene myself." Miss Vi smiled at her. "But there's also something to be said for asking for help." She turned and disappeared, her steps soundless in black orthopedic shoes.

Anna watched her go, and then, maybe to defy the woman's doubts, she started looking into the first thick GED guide.

In the background, she heard the children singing a song, something about letters and numbers. The surrounding shelves held mostly old books, and their musty smell made her strangely happy.

From the guides, she learned that there was a website giving the latest information on GED exams. She fired up the old desktop computer to look up the nearest one. Hmm, there was a test date next month, in a nearby town she vaguely remembered passing on the way to the Sea Pine Cottages. Could she do it? How hard would it be?

She dug into the review guide with new purpose, and sounds of the children, playing freely now, blurred into cheerful background noise.

Sometime later, with the fine-tuned radar of a mother, she heard a young boy's voice raised to a taunt. "You can't talk. What are y'all, babies?"

She thrust the book away and stood. Nobody was going to make fun of her girls. She headed for the children, who all seemed to be putting things away and collecting their belongings.

Miss Vi appeared in her path, and when Anna tried to pass her, she didn't step aside.

"My girls are being teased." Anna stood on her tiptoes, looking over the older woman's shoulder, trying to see Hope and Hayley.

"I noticed." The librarian tilted her head to one side, studying Anna. "They seemed to be handling it, though. Children often do better working things out for themselves."

Anna bit back a sharp retort out of respect for the woman's age and apparent status here at the library. "Listen, I appreciate your concern, but—"

"But you're overprotective." She patted Anna's arm. "Ah, well, some have reason to be."

*Way* too nosy. And wasn't it amazing how many people were experts on other people's child-rearing skills? "Excuse me," she said, and sidled past the woman.

Anna made her way over to the twins, who didn't

seem at all upset with the mild teasing they'd faced. Hope tugged at her arm and held out a lopsided flower made of pipe cleaners. Hayley pushed in front and held up hers, too, and Anna took them both and admired them. Then both girls led her to a display of books about flowers and plants, and again Anna saw one she remembered: *The Carrot Seed.*

Her father had never taken her to the library, so this must be another book her mom had read to her.

Anna had always loved to read. She'd gone through the few stories she owned as a child over and over again, had always checked out the maximum number from school on library days. During her marriage, she'd stocked up during rare trips to the used-book store, and occasionally, she'd even spent some grocery money on brand-new novels.

Romances and mysteries. She liked the ones where everything turned out right in the end.

It had never occurred to her to wonder where her reading habit had gotten started, but seeing these old children's books made her realize: it was from her mother.

Her mom would have loved reading to the girls. Anna bit her lip and looked upward, toward the heaven where her loving mother surely resided. *I'll make sure they have plenty of books.*

So when Hope held up a copy of *The Very Hungry Caterpillar,* her eyes pleading, Anna made a quick decision. "Let me find out if we can get a library card. Maybe we can borrow a couple."

Ten minutes later, they left the library, each twin clutching three picture books.

They sat on the library's stone steps to examine their loot. In between exclaiming over the books, Anna breathed in the warm, salt-scented air. The garden area beside the library sported a stone fountain, and the sound of its waters soothed Anna's weary heart.

Just as she stood, ready to encourage the girls to get going, there was a shout from the downtown side of the block. A tiny woman seemed to be in a shoving match with a much-larger man, and their angry shouts included language that made Anna want to cover her girls' ears.

Both girls shrank behind her, clutching her legs. Anna's own heart pounded with a mix of anger and remembered fear. She looked around, hoping someone could help the woman, because she didn't dare take the twins any closer. They were already upset. Hope was gasping, her face buried in the side of Anna's long shorts, shoulders shaking. Even Hayley was pressed close, uncharacteristically quiet.

She'd give anything if she could erase what they'd seen back home. But she couldn't. Anna clamped her jaw. She'd make sure nothing like that ever happened in their little family again.

Something about the man looked familiar. Anna squinted to see.

"Hey, is everything okay?" The voice beside her belonged to Yasmin, the woman from the shelter.

"It's that guy you were talking about, Tony. He's beating up on a woman. Why don't you do something?" Anna heard the shrillness in her own voice as both girls clutched her tighter, obviously upset by their mother's display of emotion. She knelt and put an arm around each girl. "Shhh. We're safe."

"I'm not sure he's the one doing the beating up." Yasmin crossed her arms and nodded toward the couple.

Anna looked. The man and woman stood a few yards apart now, still yelling. Then the tiny woman ran at the man and head butted him in the gut, knocking him to the ground.

Anna glanced up at Yasmin, eyebrows raised. "Wow."

They all watched as the woman stalked down the street toward them, her occasional stumbles suggesting that she'd been drinking.

"What're you looking at?" she burst out as she passed their small group. She nearly tripped, caught herself on the railing that skirted the library's little lawn and glowered.

The girls outright hid behind Anna. Now they were both crying.

"Get on home, Brandi," Yasmin said. "You need to chill."

"I wish I could." The woman took a quick glance down the sidewalk. Anna did, too, and saw that Tony was talking to another man, their angry voices audible, though not their words.

Anna did a double take when she saw that the man was Sean.

Why should that be a surprise? Men stuck together.

"You! Hey, you, new girl. Keep your hands off Tony." The woman who'd shoved Tony stood with hands on hips now, glaring at Anna. "I saw you looking at him. He's *mine*."

Anna straightened and glared right back. "Believe me, lady, men are the last thing I have an interest in."

She glanced at Yasmin, then back to the woman on the street. "I'm better off on my own."

But she was all too aware that she *wasn't* on her own; she was starting work with Sean the next morning.

# CHAPTER SIX

THE NEXT MORNING, Sean marched out of his cabin and batted away a hunk of Spanish moss that had blown down onto the railing beside his door.

It was Anna's official start day and he was pretty sure he was making a big mistake. He should have stuck with family. Not an outsider with secrets.

He stood a minute, looked at the oaks making a tunnel back toward the bayou, shadowy even in the early morning light. As always, the place soothed him and he felt his breathing calm, his heart rate slow to bayou pace.

Anna's cabin door opened and she came out, her twins close beside her. She knelt beside the shy one, spoke quietly, gave her a hug, her darker hair merging with the little girl's blond curls while the other stood, hands on hips, obviously impatient to start the day.

Once, he'd wanted that for himself: a pretty woman's love, family to cheer up the morning and remind him that each day held excitement and that life was meaningful.

But all that wasn't for him.

She looked up, saw him and rose gracefully. She took a hand of each girl and they walked toward him. As the girls approached, their chatter ceased.

"Morning," she said.

"Like I texted you, I got the go-ahead for you to work on a contract basis. We start now." He glanced at the girls, who were looking up at him, eyes wide.

He looked away from their winning cuteness and met Anna's eyes. "What's your plan for them?"

"I have one." She knelt between them, a hand on each girl's back. "Remember what we talked about. Mom's working, so no silly bothering."

"But we can come if there's a 'mergency," the quiet one said.

Anna squeezed her shoulders. "Of course. Right away." She stood and gave them a tiny shove. "Now, go play. But stay where you can see me, and not in any water or jungly stuff."

"C'mon!" The more aggressive one grabbed her twin's hand and they ran for an old playground, a little overgrown, but still featuring a couple of rubber riding horses and an old jungle gym.

She looked back at him and straightened her back. "Where do we start?"

"You're confident they'll behave?"

"Yes." She met his eyes for a long few seconds.

He didn't drop his gaze.

She sighed, looking over at the girls. "We can hope. They're kids."

As if to prove her point, Hayley nudged Hope off one of the rubber horses. Hope got right up in her twin's face and scolded, pointing back at Anna.

Anna's teeth worried her lip as she looked from the girls to him and back again.

Hayley rode the faded horse hard for a few seconds, then slid off and walked over to the other horse, slumping and huffing with an attitude evident even from this distance.

Sean chuckled. "They did pretty well. My brothers and I would have been rolling around on the ground punching each other."

Her tight shoulders relaxed a little. "Just tell me what you want me to work on."

He gestured toward the cabin before them. "We'll start with this one. You clear brush—tools are in my truck—and I'll fix the porch railing and then work on gutters. We'll do this for each cabin and see how it goes, what's next."

She hustled over to his truck and pulled out a shovel and rake.

"Grab some work gloves, too," he said. "In the toolbox."

She hesitated, then did as he'd suggested.

She surveyed the area and started in while he took his time getting out boards and a saw and nails. Watching her, wanting to see how she worked but also curious about her.

Some people would have dithered, trying to figure out what brush to clear and what to leave. But she just studied the way the plants grew, glanced at the cabin for perspective and then started in clearing.

He liked that, someone who could work without a lot of direction.

Once, she glanced over and caught him looking. Straightened, and met his eyes with a cool gaze. "I saw you with your friend Tony by the library."

"Yeah?" He measured a board, marked it and set it on the sawhorse.

"My girls saw it, too." A muscle jumped in the side of her face and her eyebrows drew together.

She didn't want her girls to see people fighting. He couldn't blame her for that. Kids should be spared from grown-up misbehavior. They should be free to play, like Hope and Hayley were doing now.

Still, he didn't want her to get the wrong impression of Tony. He picked up his saw. "Don't make assumptions. It's not always the man's fault."

"Right." She turned back to her work, digging the rake into a heap of leaves and branches. "He only has a hundred or so pounds on her," she threw over her shoulder.

*Don't get mad. This isn't about Tony.* Sean shook it off and got back to work, not answering, not keeping the argument going.

She looked out toward the little playground. "Excuse me a minute. I need to check on the girls. I'll take any time I spend doing that off my hours." She strode over toward the girls, back straight. Knelt and talked with them for a couple of minutes, and then walked them over to a puddled area just off the road. For the first time, he noticed she had a backpack with her, and from it, she pulled a couple of plastic bowls and cups and some big spoons. She showed them how to dig in the dirt, and both girls smiled and started in.

Pretty smart as a mom, finding ways to keep them occupied. Reminded him of how Ma Dixie had entertained the foster toddlers she'd had in the house when he'd lived there. Most evenings, while she cooked, kids were banging lids together and beating spoons on pots. The loud chaos had driven Sean and the other older boys crazy. But it had been heaven for the little kids.

Anna was a throwback, not having any fancy electronic toys for her kids. Of course, she probably couldn't afford them. But she was making the best of it, like Ma Dixie had.

He inhaled the rich, tangy smell of the salt marsh and listened to the semiquiet world around him, punctuated by birdcalls and chittering squirrels, the rhythmic pounding of the surf audible even here, if you listened hard.

It sure beat the sirens and traffic noise of Knoxville.

He sawed his boards, soothed by the rhythmic motion, and tried not to pay attention to the sight of Anna, back working now, bending over to rake under a line of bushes.

She didn't dress to flaunt her figure—the opposite, in fact—but she was a knockout. Pretty enough to be a Victoria's Secret model, except she was petite. So it was only natural he'd notice, any man would. He just wasn't going to act on it.

Anna moved over to the area surrounding the cabin, putting her in voice proximity, but she didn't talk.

He liked the silence, and then felt compelled to break it. "You know," he said, "you might be able to get benefits, health insurance and such, if you did a full application. Otherwise, it's just contract work."

She didn't look at him. "Contract work is fine."

Having run his own construction company since returning from overseas, he knew what *that* meant. "Avoiding something?" He didn't know why he wanted to needle her.

She looked over at him and lifted her chin. "I haven't worked much before."

He frowned, puzzled by that. Especially since she

seemed confident and self-assured in what she was doing now. How had she gotten by?

"I became a stay-at-home mom pretty young," she added, pulling a tangle of wire out from beneath a juniper bush and adding it to the trash pile.

"How old are you?" It wasn't apparent, because she had a young face and figure, but old eyes.

"Twenty-three."

His eyebrows lifted. She'd said the twins were five, so she must've had them at eighteen.

He bet there was a story there.

She was raking vigorously now, pulling out piles of debris from behind the bush, her face flushed with the exertion. When she turned to start on another section, she caught him looking at her. Again.

"You sure you didn't work before?"

"I earned my keep," she said, lifting her chin. "I did telemarketing and surveys from home. Stuff I could do with the girls around."

"Makes sense."

"Look," she said, "is there a problem? Do you want to withdraw the offer?"

"Nope." He gestured toward the pile she'd created. "I'm not judging." Just curious. "You're working hard. You're allowed to take a break, you know."

She looked at her rake as if she didn't want to put it down, but then, to his surprise, she dropped it and perched on an old dried-out stump. She wiped her forehead on her sleeve.

Flushed and sweaty, she looked even more appealing. And in a way that made his imagination go wild, but he reined it in.

Anna obviously had a lot of issues on her plate right now. She didn't need to add a man like him to the list.

As the oldest brother, he'd been close with his mom, her protector, her confidant. And then he'd watched his father shove her into his truck and take her away.

His biggest, deepest fear was that he was more like his dad than he wanted to be. And he never wanted other kids to suffer what he and his brother had suffered.

He'd tried to make a go of marriage with Gabby. When she'd changed her mind about having kids, he'd agreed to go to marriage counseling with her, had talked some about his feelings, figured some stuff out.

But when Gabby had admitted that her relationship with the marriage counselor had changed, that she'd fallen in love with him... Well, any insights Sean had gotten during their counseling sessions were questionable to say the least.

Best to just remind himself that it was safer, all around, for him to be alone, to avoid any situation where his resemblance to his father might come out.

He ripped a rotting board away from the cottage's foundation. Then another, shoving away the emotions that wanted to rise up when he remembered his foolish hopes of a happy marriage, a little house he'd build. Now he limited himself to women who wanted a good time, nothing serious. Women who helped him meet his physical needs because they had needs of their own. Women who didn't kick up all his longings for things that, ultimately, he wasn't likely to have.

A vulnerable woman on the run, with two cute special-needs kids under her wing—a woman who was superhot but didn't show it off—that kind of woman was totally off-limits for him.

Way too appealing, but he wasn't going to let himself be that vulnerable, ever again.

He looked over from his ruminations to find her looking at him, and hoped his thoughts hadn't shown on his face.

"Is it the same kind of work for all of the cabins?" she asked.

He nodded. "They're a mess. The owner wants to bring them back to life, but I have my doubts."

"They used to be real nice." She snapped her mouth shut and looked away.

A clue into her past. "You've been here before?"

She shrugged. "Long time ago." Then she got up and got real busy with raking all her separate waste stacks into a pile. "Where do you want me to haul this stuff when I'm done piling it?"

"I'll haul it." He was curious about her reticence, but it wasn't his business to know everything about her past, was it?

They'd both just turned back to their work when a familiar loud, croaking sound cut the silence.

The twins shrieked and ran from where they'd been playing into the little cabin's yard and slammed into Anna, their faces frightened.

"What was that?" Anna sounded alarmed, too, kneeling to hold and comfort both girls.

"Nothing to be afraid of," he said, trying to hold back laughter. "It's just egrets. Type of waterbird." He located the source of the sound, then went over to the trio, squatted down beside them and pointed through the trees and growth.

When the girls saw the stately white birds, they gasped.

"They're so pretty!" Anna said, and the girls nodded, wide-eyed.

"Pretty?" Sean chuckled. "Nobody from around here would get excited about an egret, nor think it's especially pretty." But as he watched another one land beside the first, white wings spread wide as it skidded into the shallow water, he realized that there was beauty there. He'd just not noticed it before.

That was what kids did for you: made you see the world through their fresh, innocent eyes. A fist of longing clutched inside his chest.

The twins were tugging at Anna's shirt now, trying to get her to take them over toward the birds. "You may go look as long as you can see me," she said, "but take careful steps by the water." She took the bolder twin's face in her hands. "The water's not deep, but I still don't want you to wade in. Do you understand?"

Both little girls nodded vigorously.

They ran off and she watched for a few seconds, then turned back to her work with a barely audible sigh.

"Go take a look with them," he urged her. "It's not every day kids see an egret for the first time."

"You're sure?"

"Go on." He watched her run like a kid over to her girls. And then he couldn't resist walking a few steps closer and watching them, shielded by the trees and brush.

The twins were so excited that they weren't remembering to be quiet. "It caught a *fish*!" the one was crowing, pointing at the bird, which, indeed, held a squirming fish in its mouth.

"That one's neck is like an *S*!" The quieter twin squatted down, rapt.

Anna eased down onto the sandy beach, obviously unworried about her or the girls getting wet or dirty, laughing and talking to them and sharing their excitement.

The sight of it gave him a melancholy twinge. His own mom had been a nature lover. She'd taken him and his brothers fishing, visited a nature reserve a few times, back in Alabama, where they'd lived before coming here.

*Get to work.* He set up an old ladder and climbed up to clear the cabin's gutters.

"You need me to hold that ladder?" Anna asked a little later, her voice newly relaxed. "Looks kind of rickety."

"I'm fine. I'll be careful." But when he reached over to tug out a broken piece of screening, the ladder lurched.

"I'm holding it," she said firmly, and came to stand below him.

"If you want." He started to climb down when a rung splintered under his foot.

He pulled back and jumped the few feet to the ground, unhurt, but knocking into Anna a little. She flinched and jerked away and started to fall, and instinctively he grabbed her shoulders to steady her.

Even through her T-shirt, she felt alive beneath his hands, warm and muscular. Which fit what he knew about her. She *was* warmhearted. And she was strong.

He should let go of her, and he did, after he was sure she was steady. But in the process his hand glided down her arm, over skin as soft as the petals of a peach blossom. Attraction stirred, deeper than what he'd felt in a long time.

*Whoa. Cool it.* He drew in a breath, going for calm, and smelled a fruity shampoo at odds with her no-nonsense attitude.

He fought the entirely inappropriate need to wrap his arms around her, to bury his face in that soft, fragrant hair.

She was looking up at him, her eyes wide, but not with fear. With something else, far more womanly and aware.

He liked that expression on her. He didn't want to look away. Their gazes locked together, tangled, and then her eyes flicked down to his lips.

Oh, if things were different, he'd run with this, see where it led.

His hands tightened a little on her shoulders. But she twisted away from him, shaking her head like she was waking up from a dream. "I guess you *can* handle it yourself," she said with a little laugh. "I'll head over to start on the next cabin down."

Before he could catch his breath and answer, she was gone.

He threw his energy into ripping off screens and hauling them to his truck. Working with Anna was going to be tough. He definitely needed to focus on the cottages and not on his coworker. No more touching, not even the accidental kind. Because even that felt sweet and hot and dangerous.

THEY KNOCKED OFF work for a long lunchtime, and Anna was glad. One, because it gave her time to fix the girls a real lunch and give them real attention. And two, because it got her away from Sean.

That moment when he'd jostled into her had been

weird. She was jumpy around men—that was inevitable after Beau and didn't surprise her.

What did surprise her was that, after the initial jolt, she'd actually liked being close to him. She'd felt safe, somehow. The man was just so big and muscular. And even falling off a ladder, he'd been careful not to hurt her, had steadied her and made sure she didn't fall.

And he'd done so with a gentleness that made her feel protected, held by his strength and heat, supported.

The odd thing was, she'd gotten the feeling that he wanted to know her better, too. His eyes had held hers a little too long. His touch on her shoulders had lingered just a few seconds after she was steady on her feet.

It was a zing, an electricity, stronger than what she'd felt as a young girl flattered by Beau's attention. It was a feeling that wanted to settle around her heart and mind, something more than just physical.

She blew out a sigh and focused on washing lunch dishes, scrubbing hard at the mac and cheese pan. No way, no way did she need to be imagining getting closer to Sean. It was a ridiculous thought when what she actually needed to do, when what she could handle, was to steer completely clear of men. Her experience with Beau had taught her that men were not for her. Some women had grown up seeing how adults navigated relationships and how good marriages looked; she hadn't.

"Are we gonna go play, Mom?" Hayley's voice rang above the beeps and bells of her handheld game.

"In a little bit," Anna said. Truthfully, she wouldn't have minded taking a little break, after a morning of physical work and anticipating a physical afternoon.

But she'd be fine. Getting tired would help her sleep

better tonight. And what a blessing to be able to have her girls nearby while she worked, to actually have a job and a place to stay.

Her escape from Montana and Beau had turned out far, far better than she'd hoped. She knocked on wood, because she didn't want to jinx it, and then sent a prayer of thanks upward.

There was a rhythmic knock on the door, and Hayley jumped up and ran toward it.

"Wait." Anna said the word sharply and Hayley stopped. Then she turned and trudged back to the couch.

Anna looked at her daughter's slumped shoulders, and her whole chest ached. If only she could have protected them better, let them think that the world was a safe place for kids.

Hayley had understood exactly why Anna was stopping her. Doors were dangerous. Their father might be on the other side, in a rage.

*Was* it Beau? Her heart picked up its pace. She'd been working hard enough to push her fears and the vandalism out of her mind, but now all of it came back to her in full force. Could he have found them? Was he here to try to take the girls from her?

She eased to the window and looked out.

Then let her breath out in a relieved sigh. Sean.

Relief made her trot happily over to the door and open it. "Hey," she said, unable to restrain a smile.

He looked a little surprised, and then smiled back, and the transformation in his features shocked her.

Beneath the scowls and the scruff and the attitude, he was a really handsome guy.

They spent a second too long just staring at each other. Warmth heated Anna's midsection and spread outward, making her tingle and bringing an involuntary smile to her face.

He was the first to look away, laughing a little. "Hey, I... There's something your girls might like to see."

Hayley and Hope ran over to her, pushing into her sides.

"What is it?" she asked.

"I don't know if I can explain it. It's down by the beach. Have them wear old clothes or swimsuits, if they have them."

"It won't... It's okay to take the time off work?"

"I'm the boss," he said with a wink that transformed his face from handsome to devilish.

*Oh my.* "Run and change into your swimsuits, girls," she said.

"You could do that, too," he said, his voice playful. "Cool off, have some fun with your girls."

He wanted her to put on a swimsuit? No way. But the comment, however he'd meant it, brought her back to reality. Reminded her of the quick hookups most men wanted from women, at least women like her, and she wasn't up for that.

No matter how attractive Sean was.

She straightened. "I don't think so. We'll be right out."

Ten minutes later, the four of them approached a shallow tide pool rimmed by a small bridge of sand. "We don't get real tide pools," he explained, "but every now and then we get a temporary one. And even more rarely, one that's deep enough to have animals in it."

Hope and Hayley stopped dead, stared at Sean with wide eyes and then ran to the edge of the pool.

She chuckled. "They think you mean dogs and squirrels and such."

"You pretty much read their minds, don't you?" He was studying her, a curious smile softening the sharp planes of his face.

Heat rose in her cheeks. She wasn't sure whether to be proud or ashamed of that ability, born of necessity. "Kind of."

He walked forward, slowly, and knelt between the girls. Not close, and when he spoke, his voice was quiet. "See the starfish?" he asked, and pointed.

Anna's heart melted a little. Such a big man, yet so sensitive to the anxiety of a couple of little girls.

A small fish jumped, and Hayley let out a squeal, then clapped her hands over her mouth. Hope giggled, then nudged Sean's arm and pointed at a crab that had climbed out of the water and was waving its claws.

"They're all stuck here by the tide," Sean explained. "When the tide comes back in—when the water gets deep here again—they'll swim back out to sea." He leaned forward and scooped something up. Then he sat back between Hope and Hayley. "This guy is a hermit crab," he explained. "See his legs and antennae sticking out of his little house?"

Hayley squinted at the crab, then turned her puzzled face to Sean. She wanted to ask what he meant by "house."

Did she want to know badly enough to speak in front of him?

Sean smiled at her. "He lives in a shell, see? Like a turtle. He takes his house with him wherever he goes."

By now, both twins were staring alternately at the crab and then at Sean, eyes wide.

"Touch it," he encouraged, and Hayley did, with one finger.

Anna stayed several feet behind them, listening as Sean explained more features of the tide pool and identified whelks and snails and various types of fish.

Hayley stuck her bare foot in the pool, then looked up at Anna, eyebrows raised.

"Is it safe for them to put their feet in?"

"Uh-huh. If they actually stepped on a crab, they might get a tiny pinch, but nothing that would really hurt."

Hayley immediately plunked her other foot in and started wading, while Hope tested the water with one hesitant toe.

Sean rose to his feet, unfolding gracefully for such a large man, and stepped back to stand beside Anna. "My brothers and I always used to get excited when a good deep tide pool formed," he explained. "When I saw this one, I figured your girls would feel the same."

"They do." She gestured at where they were both squatting down in the water, studying some small creature. "Thank you," she added, looking up at him. "They haven't...well, they haven't seen much of the world. This is so good for them."

"I figured."

"It's that obvious?" She'd hoped all the things she'd done to compensate for their limited opportunities—reading aloud, singing, watching public television—had worked.

He shrugged. "Being three boys, we probably had a little more freedom. But our young childhood was restricted, too. Maybe for the same reason."

Anna cocked her head and stared at him. "What do you mean?"

He looked out across the water. "We didn't always live in Safe Haven. We moved here, or tried to, with our mom, when I was thirteen."

*Tried to.* "You must have succeeded," she said, "if you're here now. Right?"

"We three boys succeeded."

His flat words pressed down on Anna. "What about your mom?" Then she flushed. If he wanted her to know, he'd have told her. "I'm sorry. Your history is none of my business."

He blew out a breath, still looking out to sea, like he was trying to figure out how to answer. "We don't know what happened to her. All I know is, our dad... got to her." There was the slightest catch to his voice. Not noticeable unless you were paying close attention.

But Anna heard it. And she saw the muscle that jumped in his cheek. She put a hand on his arm, her whole chest aching. "Were you staying with family? Did she just not come back or something?"

He turned his head and looked at her, his eyes dark pools of unreadable emotion. "We were staying at the Safe Haven Women's Center. It was a residential shelter back then." He paused, looked away. "I saw my father shove Mom into his truck and drive off. But I couldn't..." He broke off, shook his head, spread his hands and then stuffed them into his pockets. He was still gazing out toward the ocean.

Anna put a hand over her mouth, staring at him. Every motherly atom in her body throbbed with the ache of what that kind of loss and uncertainty would mean for a child. "You never saw her again?"

He shook his head. "The people who ran the women's shelter back then, they did everything they could to locate her. But I was the only witness to him pushing her into his truck, and I was thirteen." He lifted a shoulder in an elaborate shrug. "I tried when I was older, and my brother Liam—he's a cop—he *really* tried, but she disappeared. So did our dad."

"Wow." Anna's throat tightened on the word, and she swallowed, looking up at him. "That must be so hard, not knowing."

"Uh-huh." His lips clamped shut.

Anna's heart broke for him. All of his tough attitude, the parts of him that seemed closed off—the puzzle of Sean snapped together in a different way. How did you get over your father actually, probably, killing your mother?

And yet he *had* gotten over it, enough to be kind and well liked, hardworking, gentle with the twins.

She put a hand on his arm, gave it a brief stroke. She wanted to hold him, comfort him. Wanted to tell him she admired the man he'd become despite all the pain he'd faced in the past.

But he took a couple of steps forward, knelt down and splashed a little water onto Hope, who squealed and splashed back, and the moment was over.

They spent another half hour playing with the girls, Anna snapping photos on her phone, and then she checked the time and gasped. "I'm so sorry we spent all this time. I'll work extra."

"It's fine. I'm glad they had fun."

"But you didn't have to—"

"Anna." He put a finger to his lips and shook his head. "Let someone do something nice for you."

His kindness made tears spring to her eyes, made her throat tighten. The implication was that she deserved nice treatment. But she *didn't* deserve it, or at least, she'd never thought she did. She'd never gotten it, especially from men. What she'd gotten was neglect from her dad and abuse from Beau.

Beau had told her no one else would ever want her, that he was doing her a favor by being with her. She no longer believed that—at least, about the favor he was supposedly doing her—but she'd internalized his idea that no better man would want her, that no man would value her enough to treat her well.

Sean O'Dwyer was making her question that notion for the first time.

They gathered the girls and walked back toward the house. Both girls were yawning now, and Anna decided she'd get them to lie down on a blanket near where they were working this afternoon. With any luck, they'd have a nice nap and she could focus on work.

They reached the little path to Anna's cottage and she glanced over, expecting Sean to head for his place. Instead, he walked along with her. She opened her mouth to protest, and then closed it again.

What had he said? *Let someone do something nice for you.*

Okay. She would.

Besides, walking in step with him was lovely.

Suddenly, he stepped in front of her, nudging her back. It was so graceless, so unlike him, that she was startled.

He put out an arm. "Stay back."

She did, and she stopped the girls, too, but she

looked. And her jaw dropped as hurt and fear rushed back in, pushing away the day's happy feelings.

Across her car, spray painted in enormous letters, was one of Beau's favorite names for her: *slut*.

## CHAPTER SEVEN

As RITA TOMLINSON left her apartment that evening, she felt the tiniest prickling of unease in the back of her neck.

There was no reason for it. It was a beautiful day, a low bank of clouds to the west, sun sinking into them, blue skies overhead. The air felt soft, enveloping her in a gentle warmth worlds away from her busy, hardworking life in Maine.

But she knew why she felt strange: Would this be the day that her past bubbled up to find her? And would that be a good thing or a bad one?

*Don't dwell on it.* She walked briskly toward a residential section of town. Her workout tights were feeling just that, tight. She did her best to keep her figure as good as it could be at her age, without stressing about it, which meant that exercise was imperative. Anyway, walking was fun, not a chore to her—she'd always loved it for the way it cleared her head.

But the memories she'd hoped to rediscover here were nowhere to be found.

When T-Bone had told her, on his deathbed, that he'd lied about finding her in the middle of nowhere, that he'd actually found her outside of a town called Safe Haven in South Carolina, he was too sick and near gone for her to stay mad at him for long. He'd saved her life all those years ago, and caring for him, forgiving him, as his own life ended had been the right thing to do.

And then, after he'd passed, there'd been the details: selling his truck and the house they'd lived in, getting all the paperwork in order. They made their common-law marriage official toward the end, thanks to the black market ID one of T-Bone's friends had found for her, so she inherited everything. But there wasn't much once the bills had been paid off.

She'd had friends in Maine, a life, but she'd had to quit her job to take care of T-Bone. And when the money had gotten low and she'd needed to get back to work, she'd felt a pull toward South Carolina.

It was time to figure out what had happened between her dim inklings of a childhood, a courtship and an abusive marriage in the deep South, and waking up in Maine with a big, gentle trucker who'd taken her into his home and nursed her back to health.

Figuring it out had meant selling off a lot of her things, packing up her car and moving. Here, for now; who knew where she'd end up later.

Now that she was in Safe Haven, she liked the place. Just a couple of days in, she was pleased with the job and the town. It wouldn't be a bad place to build a future.

Unfortunately, though, there were no glimmerings of her past.

"Hey, girl!"

The friendly greeting surprised her, since she was new in town. But when she turned, she vaguely recognized the young blonde woman with the big smile and wide hips. "Hey, yourself. You work at the grocery, right?"

The younger woman nodded. "Yes, ma'am. I'm Claire. I've seen you around and heard you work over at the Southern Comfort."

"That's right."

Claire fell into step beside her. "Sorry. If you're not from a small town you might not know how in each other's pockets we live around here. Everybody knows everything."

"I kinda figured. Where are you headed?"

Claire grinned. "I try to take my evening walk at the same time the men's rec league plays down at the park. Want to join me?"

"I'll walk a ways with you, sure. I'm just looking to get some exercise and get to know the town."

"Great." Claire was breathing hard. "Man, I'm out of shape. I've got to take off some pounds."

"Noticed my leggings were a little tight, myself. That's why I pushed myself to get out even though I was on my feet all morning."

"You and me both." Claire looked sideways at her, assessing. "You look great, girl. I don't see an extra ounce on you."

"The ounces just shift downward when you get to be my age." Rita chuckled as they crossed the street. "I guess we all want what we don't have. Look at you, with your hourglass figure and your smooth skin and pretty hair. I had some of that, when I was younger, but I didn't appreciate it."

They passed a row of brick buildings housing the *Safe Haven Gazette* and the Rice-and-Indigo Museum, and Rita was tempted to stop and read a couple of plaques that told about the town. But the walk was for exercise. She settled for asking Claire. "Lots of history here, looks like."

Claire smiled. "Oh yeah, and there's plenty of people will bend your ear about it."

They reached the park and Claire gestured toward its center. "You're interested in history, check out The Tree. It's supposed to be anywhere from five hundred to a thousand years old, depending on who you ask."

Rita studied the enormous trunk surrounded by stone benches that seemed to be the park's focal point. Its gnarled branches reaching out in every direction, some so low they nearly touched the ground. "Beautiful."

"Sure is, but there's some even-finer scenery over this way." Claire picked up the pace, gesturing toward the basketball court, active with players.

Rita chuffed out a laugh and followed along. Claire was a hoot. She hadn't expected to make a friend this fast, but she loved it. When they reached the court, she recognized one of the cooks from the diner. There were other men, ranging in age from thirty to gray-haired.

A man came out from behind another, side-arcing a perfect basket, and she actually stopped to watch because it was Jimmy. He was probably the oldest man there but he looked fitter than most.

"I love it when they do shirts and skins," Claire said fervently beside her, fanning herself as she looked wide-eyed at the players, her enjoyment obvious.

Rita smiled her agreement. Jimmy wore a shirt, but it was a tight white T-shirt that showed his muscles and tattoos. *Mercy.*

Coincidentally, or maybe not, the men took a water break. Jimmy drank deeply and then jogged over. "Hey, how's my new employee enjoying the town?"

"I like it." She lifted an eyebrow. "Lots to look at."

He grinned. "To my mind, the scenery got better about two days ago."

"Aw, you're just saying that." What was she doing flirting with Jimmy? He was her boss in a job she liked. Not only that, but she was here for a reason: to figure out who she was. And who she was might be a good person or a bad person; she might have things to hide. She wasn't going to play around with a guy until she knew more about herself and her past. She looked over at Claire. "I'm going to head out, get another half hour in before it rains," she said.

Jimmy heeded a shout from his friends and turned, gave them a quick "see ya" and jogged back into the game.

"He's *built* for an old guy," Claire volunteered.

Rita had to laugh at that. "Yes, he is. Is he a local, born here? For that matter, are you?"

"Me, yes, I've lived my whole life on this little stretch of coast. Jimmy took over the café three or four years ago when his aunt and uncle wanted to retire. Moved here from somewhere north. After a divorce, maybe? Looking for a new start, I guess, like a lot of people around here."

"I thought this was a tourist town, but it seems like people come here and stay. Right?" As they walked, she was looking around, paying attention with half her mind to whether anything seemed familiar. But so far, nothing.

Claire shrugged. "It's a mix. Lots of us grew up here, but the beaches bring in tourists and retirees and some of 'em stay." She glanced sideways at Rita. "What brought you here?"

Rita shrugged. "Needed more sunshine in my golden years." She wasn't going to admit to more details. She liked Claire, but the woman was a talker—that was already clear.

Claire sighed. "I'd like to get away, do some traveling. Everyone in town knows me as the plump gal who's worked at the grocery forever. They think they've got me pegged."

"Why don't you move? Something keeping you here?"

"My folks." Claire gestured toward the south. "Their health isn't great. They couldn't do too well without me."

"Then it's good of you to stay." Rita felt a qualm about her own family of origin. Had her parents passed on? Did she have siblings? She had a few dim memories of watching television with other kids and of swimming in a pool. That was all she remembered of her childhood.

"Hey, lady!" Claire called out a greeting and stopped to wave at a woman on the steps of a church. "Come on over and meet my new friend."

Obviously, walking with Claire was going to have a lot of stops and starts, but Rita didn't mind. She wanted to get to know the town, and that included the people in it. And she was flattered that a young woman like Claire already considered her a friend.

The woman approached, a pretty, copper-skinned woman with beaded braids. She held out her hand. "I'm Yasmin."

Rita took it, smiling. "Rita Tomlinson. Good to meet you."

"Yasmin runs the women's program here," Claire

explained. "Helping women who've been battered or abused. This town is kind of known for that, and these days, it's all on Yasmin's shoulders."

"You're always talking me up bigger than I am. How's your mama?"

As the two women talked, Rita zoned out of the conversation and paid attention to a couple of scraps of memory floating in her head. This street, this place, seemed more familiar than anywhere else she'd been in Safe Haven.

But along with the surprising familiarity came feelings of fear and distress, vague but so unpleasant that she wrapped her arms around her stomach. Part of her didn't want to feel this, didn't want to remember. Deliberately, she focused on the clouds gathering darker overhead, the sun sinking down behind a bank of them to the west. A breeze whipped up, and although she was sweating from their exercise, goose bumps rose on Rita's arms.

"I know, it's practically falling down around me," Yasmin was saying when Rita tuned back in to the conversation. "If we don't raise some money soon, we may just have to shut down."

"That would be a shame," Claire said. "It'd be nice if it could go back to actually being a shelter, you know? So women in trouble could stay here."

Something deep inside Rita clicked into place.

It had been a shelter. Had she been one of those women in trouble? Had she stayed here?

She looked at Yasmin, opened her mouth to ask if they had old records and then snapped it shut.

It was a story line that would make sense, given that

T-Bone had found her beaten senseless on the edge of the highway.

A wisp of pain and heartache rose inside her, but she shook it off. At least for today, her mind veered hard away from the truth. She really didn't want to remember how she'd gotten that way.

LATE THAT NIGHT, Sean lost the battle with himself and headed over to Anna's cabin. He'd just do the little fix he'd jerry-rigged for the spray painting on her car, until they could figure out a real solution, and then hustle right back to his own place. A couple of beers and a hockey game would be fine entertainment for a loner.

Except her light was on.

He couldn't see inside the cabin. She'd closed the shades, which was smart. But if she were jumpy, and he was out here messing with her car, he was likely to get pepper sprayed. Again.

The thought of that first night made him grin a little, now. Although Anna was a sweet, quiet woman, she was fierce when it came to keeping her girls safe.

Beneath the toughness, though, was another layer of vulnerability. She was on her own, doing her best, but she was young and without a lot of resources.

He couldn't stand to see a woman in trouble. Couldn't let her suffer alone when he could find a way to help.

After a moment's consideration, he climbed the steps and tapped on the door. "Hey, Anna," he called quietly through the slightly open window. "It's me, Sean."

After a moment, she unlocked the door and opened it, and he swallowed.

She wore short, frayed cutoffs and a thin T-shirt. No bra, if he wasn't mistaken.

Which was *not* his business. He kept his eyes pinned to her face, refusing to let them stray lower. "I, uh, I have a temporary fix for your car." He held up the car magnets he'd dug out of storage. "It's not perfect, but it'll cover up most of the, well, the writing. Until you can get it fixed. Okay if I put 'em on there?"

"Um, sure. Thank you." She looked blankly at the rectangles. "Bayou Brothers Construction? Is that your company?"

"Was." He lifted a shoulder in a shrug. "Tony and I tried to start a company just out of high school. Things didn't work out, but we still have some of the promo stuff."

"Oh. Well, thank you." She looked past him toward the car, worry crossing her face. "I don't want the girls to see it and start asking what that word means. Or remember that's what their daddy used to call me," she added bitterly.

Sean had to work to keep his fists from clenching. He didn't want to scare her, but the idea that any man would call her that name... He swallowed. "Do you think it's him who did it?"

"I don't know. I feel like it must be, since nobody around here even knows me, so why would they do this? But my friend swears he's still back in Montana." Her shoulders sagged.

"This friend," he said. "Did he—or she—help you get away?"

She shook her head. "We weren't close that way. Somehow, I ended up without a lot of friends back there. But she was a neighbor, and we helped each other out every now and then."

*She didn't notice him hitting you? Some friend.*

"I'm kind of at my wit's end. I appreciate your kind-ness." She glanced back into the cabin, then shut the door behind her. "I'll come out and help. The girls are sound asleep."

He didn't need the help, but it seemed like she needed the company, so he stepped down and moved toward her car to make room for her to follow. "So…you're pretty sure your ex is behind this? I thought he was working through a lawyer."

"I imagine he had a falling-out with his lawyer," she said. "He usually does. And he probably doesn't have money to pay the guy. So it's possible he's gone rogue." Her recitation held dreary certainty.

He knelt beside her car, handed her one of the car magnets and fitted the other to the door. "There. That's a part of it. Let me see the other magnet." He fitted it over the rest of the word.

A few drips of spray paint still showed, but at least the word itself was hidden. "What were you doing with a guy this classless?" he asked before he could think better of it. But it just didn't make sense. She seemed to have it together, especially considering how young she was.

Her sigh broke into his thoughts. "I was immature," she said. "Leave it at that. Can I get you something to drink? I have Kool-Aid and water." She wrinkled her nose and she did look young. Young, and impossibly cute.

"I'm picky about my Kool-Aid. Is it cherry?"

"Of course. Though I could mix up some grape if you'd prefer it." She arched an eyebrow like she was offering him the finest wine, then spoiled the effect with a giggle.

"Cherry's fine," he said. *And please don't get cuter than you already are.*

She went inside and came back out a minute later with two plastic cups. "Sorry," she said, "I'm limited in glassware."

He saluted her with his cartoon-character mug. "I love Scooby-Doo." He waved a hand toward the cabin. "You said the girls are sacked out?"

She nodded. "They had fun today. But, Sean, I don't expect you to entertain them every day like you did today. And honestly... I'm not sure how well it's going to work for me to have them with me while I work. They'll do it, they're used to holding back and behaving, but I want better for them."

He nodded, inhaling deeply of the warm ocean air. At night, the sound of the waves traveled better, and he could dimly hear the rhythmic sound of the surf. They were in a world of their own.

She was looking out into the trees, and the moon cast a silvery light on her face. As he watched her in profile, an overwhelming urge to protect came over him, along with a familiar ache. His mother had wanted to protect Sean and his brothers; she'd spent their drive from one home to the next talking to him about it. She'd wanted better for her boys.

He guessed, in a way, she'd found it. Except he'd never have gone for it at the expense of her life.

He shook away that memory and focused on Anna. Her short-chopped hair and big eyes, her flawless skin kissed with a few freckles, her lush lips... She took his breath away. But he shouldn't be focusing on her beauty, not when she needed his help.

She glanced over and caught his eyes on her. He

expected her to freak out or criticize, but instead, she met his eyes in a speculative way. Was she thinking the same thing about him that he was thinking about her?

He grabbed for some businesslike thread of conversation. "There are some day cares in town you might check out, if you don't want to enroll them in kindergarten. But kindergarten would be free."

She sighed, the breath making her bangs fly up. "I know. And even though the pay you're offering is more than generous, I can't afford much. It's just..." She broke off, picked up a stick and started tracing patterns in the sandy soil.

"What?"

"They haven't spent much time with other kids. And they've had so much change lately, I hate to add a big classroom situation to it." She looked over at him, her expression vulnerable. "Do you think I'm making a mistake?"

He let out a chuckle. "You're asking the wrong guy. I have zero experience with kids."

"Really? You did well with them today. I thought maybe you were somebody's favorite uncle, at least."

"Nope." None of his brothers had kids yet, at least not Liam or Cash. He guessed they'd all struggled with relationships, given how they'd grown up. Although both of his younger brothers had sowed more wild oats than he had.

"Well, anyway. Because they don't talk, I'm afraid they'll struggle. Get teased."

"All kids get teased." Still, he hated to think of that happening to Hope and Hayley.

"Yeah. Believe me, I know. But it's just...when it's your own kids, and you haven't been able to provide them with the life you wanted to…" She crossed her arms and leaned forward on the porch step, kind of hugging herself.

The glimmerings of a possible solution came to him. "Are they able to be away from you? Did they ever stay at a babysitter's house, say?"

"We had a neighbor back in Montana. An older lady who took care of her grandson. In a pinch, I could leave the twins with her. In fact, they loved going over there because she had a dog, and parakeets, and more toys than we had."

Perfect. "I have an idea."

"Yeah?" She looked over at him, her eyes hopeful.

"Yeah." Then he nearly forgot it, looking at her face. He had the most ridiculous desire to put his arms around her and tell her everything would be all right. To take care of her and help her carry her burdens.

He shook it off. "Look, I'll follow you to town when you drive the twins to their after-school program tomorrow. We can take your car to the garage, at least get an estimate on fixing the paint job. And later this week… Well. I'll take you and the girls somewhere that might solve your problem."

She lifted an eyebrow. "You expect me to just trust you?"

*Yeah, I was hoping…* "I think you'll have fun. You'll get a good low country dinner, anyway. And maybe, a babysitter."

She tilted her head to one side, studying him. Her stormy eyes seemed to ask whether she could take him at his word.

As for him, he couldn't believe he was offering to

do what he'd only ever done with Gabby: taking her home to Ma Dixie.

Ma was special. She'd been his port in the storm of his adolescence, and her bayou home had been the place he and his brothers were able to hang out together and be themselves.

No casual dates and precious few friends ever got invited. He just liked to keep the place private, for family.

Plus, the one woman he'd taken to Ma's, Gabby, had hated it. Too humble, too down-home, full of fattening food and unsophisticated conversation.

But that was Gabby. He couldn't imagine Anna having the same snobbish reaction.

As if to prove him right, she smiled and shrugged. "As long as my girls will be safe, and not scared by whatever you have in store…sure, okay."

"Great. We're on." But uneasiness nipped at Sean's gut.

Bringing Anna home to Ma's place meant something, in his world. It brought her into his life and made him vulnerable in a way he wasn't sure he was ready for.

# CHAPTER EIGHT

"WHERE, EXACTLY, ARE you taking us?" From the passenger side of Sean's truck, Anna took in the vegetation on either side of the road, thick as a jungle. The trees met overhead, dripping with Spanish moss. She couldn't keep the nerves out of her voice, but at least she'd pitched it low, so the girls couldn't hear her anxiety from the back seat.

"You'll see." Sean guided the truck onto an even-narrower gravel-and-mud road.

She checked the back seat. Hope was asleep, and Hayley was playing some kind of finger game, singing to herself. Good.

"It's dark here. Spooky."

"You're safer here than in a city or even a town. And I won't let any harm come to you or your girls."

His confident words warmed her, soothed a hollow, lonely place inside. Sean was strong and capable and protective. She knew he'd keep her safe.

They drove on, bumping over an increasingly uneven road, and Anna clutched the truck's door handle. She was starting to trust Sean, and that was even more dangerous than the swampy bayou around them.

Yes, he was kind. But *why* was he being kind? And encouraging her to feel at home in the community, when odds were that they'd just have to leave?

"Here we are." He pulled into a sort of driveway, and suddenly the jungle opened up to reveal a ramshackle cabin on stilts, surrounded by several vehicles, some ancient, some newer, and one a downright luxurious Lexus.

Sean parked and, without being asked, guided Hayley out of the back seat, leaving Anna to wake up Hope. To Anna's complete shock, by the time she got Hope out and standing, Hayley was on Sean's shoulders, giggling at the unaccustomed high perch.

The smell of grilling meats filled the air, and voices rang from the screened porch. A couple of kids ran up, looked curiously at Hope and Hayley, and then rushed back down to a creek.

Warm, damp air brushed Anna's face, seeming to come straight from the fertile swampland surrounding the cabin.

"Come meet Ma." Sean put a hand on Anna's back to usher her in. He seemed looser, more mellow all of a sudden; the shadows that normally haunted his eyes absent.

They walked into a low-ceilinged, hot kitchen, Sean swinging Hayley down to the ground next to Hope. The smell of something baking made Anna's mouth water.

Sean's hand touched her back now, lightly, in a way that felt just a little bit possessive. But strangely enough, she didn't mind. In fact, his touch made her warm all over.

A short, round-faced woman was removing a big pan of corn bread from the oven. Aha, the source of the scent. She had curly white hair and coppery skin, and when she smiled, her face creased into a thousand wrinkles.

"There's my boy," she said, lifting her cheek for a kiss, which Sean delivered, bending down.

Hayley giggled and pointed at Sean, obviously amused at the notion of a big grown-up being a boy.

"Now, who's this?" The woman knelt with some difficulty, holding on to the back of a kitchen chair and looking expectantly at the twins.

"This is Hayley—" Sean touched Hayley's head lightly "—and that's Hope." He pointed in Hope's direction.

"Welcome, ladies." She looked into both faces, giving the impression that she could read behind the twins' wide eyes. "You're right pretty, and I'll bet you're smart, too." Then she looked up at Anna. "You must be Mama, and I want to meet you. But it's kids first around here."

Anna laughed, already liking her. "Of course! I agree with that philosophy."

Ma straightened, moved to the window and called outside. "Toby, come on in and show these girls your frog." She turned back to the twins. "You're not afraid of frogs, are you?"

They both shook their heads, although Hope's wrinkled forehead indicated she wasn't so sure of her answer.

Ma came to stand between them and ran a gentle finger over each blond head. "If you want to grow up tough, you gotta learn to play boys' games, too. Not just dolls and books."

A little boy came running inside, one of the ones who'd looked at them before, maybe a year older than the twins. He was holding a squat, wide-mouthed jar. Inside it were some weeds, some water—and, yes, a frog, big and green with lazy red eyes.

The twins might not be afraid of frogs, but Anna could do without them. She took a step backward and Sean caught her by the elbows, keeping her from running right into him.

Ma was back at the stove, speaking to the children over her shoulder. "Toby, you know you've got to let that creature go in…" She looked shrewdly at the boy. "How much time did we say?"

The boy studied the clock. "When the big hand is on the twelve and the little hand's on the seven?"

"That's right. Now, you kids sit over there on the floor where I can see you, and, Toby, you keep the frog in the jar."

"I will! C'mon!"

The twins looked a little overwhelmed, but they followed Toby to a corner of the kitchen and sat down to examine the jar he thrust at them.

Ma dredged tomato slices in flour, then egg, then some other kind of crumbs. "I don't believe in digital time-telling," she explained. "Nor in letting a kid like Toby too far out of my sight. He's a handful. You gonna introduce me to your friend?" The last comment was directed at Sean.

"If I can get a word in." He urged Anna forward, again with a hand on the small of her back, again making her feel even warmer than the hot kitchen warranted. "Ma, this is Anna George. Anna, Ma Dixie. Ma pretty much deserves canonization for raising me from thirteen."

"You weren't the worst I've raised," Ma said, patting Sean's arm with a hand covered in flour. The look she gave him was pure motherly love. And then she looked thoughtfully at Anna. "Anyone Sean brings here, I'm pleased to meet."

The door from outside opened, and a man in a designer suit strode in and wrapped Ma Dixie in a big hug. Anna took one look at his face and knew he was related to Sean. He and Ma began talking rapidly, their Southern accents thick and dotted with words she didn't know.

Anna turned to check on the girls. They were helping Toby build a complicated block structure for the frog. Another boy was there, too, and Toby was pointing to him. "He can't hear," he explained to the twins. "He's deaf."

The boy signed with rapid hands, and Toby signed back.

The twins stared, fascinated.

When Anna turned back to the adults, the man in the suit raised an eyebrow and held out a hand. "And who are you?" he asked, his Southern accent almost unnoticeable now.

Sean stepped closer to Anna. "Friend of mine, staying out at the Sea Pine Cottages," he said.

Anna lifted her chin and extended her hand. "Anna George. I'm doing some contract work there, and my girls and I are staying in one of the cabins."

"Cash O'Dwyer." The man wrapped a big hand around hers. "Pleased to make your acquaintance. Hope you're keeping your distance from my brother." He nodded toward Sean, softening his words with a grin.

Sean opened his mouth as if to respond, and then settled for giving his brother a light punch on the arm.

Anna decided she'd leave the brothers to bond in

their own guy way. "Ma, is there something I can do to help?"

"Darlin', if you'd chop about five of those onions I'd be obliged. And you boys better get busy shucking shrimp for my shrimp and grits." She thrust a big, fishy-smelling plastic bag toward Cash.

"Watch the suit!" Cash stepped back, took off his suit jacket and hung it on a hook, then rolled up his sleeves.

"Wuss." Sean gave him another friendly punch on the arm as he took the bag from Ma. "You okay here for a bit?" he asked Anna.

"I am," she said, and surprisingly, it was true.

The door opened to admit a couple bearing a baking dish, and then two young women and a little boy, carrying soda and chips. Everyone loaded their offerings onto the small kitchen table, kissed Ma and then drifted out onto the porch.

"Those boys," Ma said, looking fondly out onto the porch. "Sean was almost the death of me, but he's the most loyal of all my kids."

"Cash seems like a different kind of person," Anna said, chopping.

"He sure is. If they didn't look practically identical, you wouldn't know they were brothers."

"Did you raise Cash, too?"

"No, Cash went to a family out to Tugger Island. Rich folks. Suited him fine." She shook her head. "That boy is aptly named. Everything he touches turns to gold."

"Does he come here to see Sean?"

Ma laughed. "Those two are oil and water, but yeah. Some. Honey, everybody comes to my place on Friday nights."

As if to prove her point, another man walked in who looked related to Sean and Cash. He'd barely put down the watermelon he was carrying when voices called him from the porch. He gave an apologetic wave to Ma. "Be back in a sec," he said, and went out onto the porch.

"That's Liam, the youngest of the three. He was raised in town and lives there still. Police officer, looking at a promotion to chief even though he's not yet thirty." Ma's eyes were fond and proud. "If those boys had to get left somewhere, Safe Haven's the right place. We all took 'em in and helped raise them, same as we'd do with anyone in need. You done with those onions?"

Anna carried them over and watched, amazed, as Ma scooped up a big spoonful of lard and dropped it into an already-hot cast-iron skillet. The onions followed, then the raw bacon Ma had been cutting with a big cleaver. "Now, once I get these greens going—could you wash them, hon?—we'll be ready to put the shrimp on."

Things got hectic then, as Cash brought in the shrimp and others started carrying dishes outside. Anna helped as best she could, but everyone seemed to have a role and a job, so once she'd delivered the washed collard greens to Ma, she stood with her back against the wall, near the twins, and just watched.

Sean came to stand beside her. "You overwhelmed yet?"

"Kind of." She smiled up at him. "But in a good way."

"Really?" He tilted his head and smiled at her. "Ma's the salt of the earth."

"I like her."

"Good." He nodded thoughtfully. "If the girls like

her, too…she might be willing to care for them a few days a week."

"Oh, I don't think…" Anna trailed off. She couldn't trust a stranger with her girls. Only Ma seemed to be the type of person who didn't let anyone remain a stranger. Anna already felt like part of the family.

And the girls seemed fascinated with the other kids, Toby's frog and another boy's harmonica, and when "Come and get it!" was bellowed through the property, they raced outside to the long plank table along with everyone else.

Anna followed, and was getting ready to sit beside them when Cash called her name. "Pretty Anna," he said, "that's the kids' end of the table. Come on up here to the grown-ups' end."

Sean said something sharp to Cash, leading Cash to lift his hands, palms out, chuckling. Anna's cheeks heated and she leaned down between the girls. "I can sit right across from you if you want," she said, gesturing to the other side of the table, "or I can be up at the other end with the grown-ups." She already knew their answer. They always, always wanted her close.

Toby and the boy with the hearing impairment slid into chairs across from the girls.

"You can go to the other end," Hayley said into Anna's ear.

Anna stared at her. "Really? Oh, uh…great!" She turned to Hope. "Okay with you if I sit with the grown-ups?"

Hope shrugged and nodded.

A giant weight she'd been carrying on her shoulders lifted, leaving her almost giddy as she walked to the other end of the table.

Her girls could grow up, grow away from her. They could be like other kids. She blinked back tears as she looked around the loud, friendly gathering. These people had made that happen.

For so long, her focus had only been on her girls, and on how to survive. If they became more independent, she'd be overjoyed. But her own life would take a different turn. A more complicated one.

Like, where did she sit at dinner?

"Over here, Anna," Cash called with a wink at Ma Dixie.

Sean stood. "You'll be more comfortable by me."

Well, that was true. Cash seemed nice but he was a stranger.

She sat by Sean, marveling at how she felt so comfortable around him. It was worlds apart from the way she'd felt around Beau, always on edge, afraid of what he might think, how he might take a comment, what he'd do if he got angry. Sean, although he was big and tough looking, made her feel safe.

Heat seemed to radiate from the side of his leg, of necessity tucked close to hers at the crowded table. His arm brushed hers as he lifted a pitcher to pour her tea.

Maybe being close to him didn't feel *entirely* safe.

She drew in a breath and let it out slowly and tried to focus on the food, a mouthwatering blur of okra soup, greens and a peas-and-rice dish called hopping john. There were spicy sausages from the grill and tender shrimp on top of buttery, cheesy grits. Anna made a couple of trips down the table to help her kids pick out foods they'd like. Turned out the baked macaroni and cheese was the hands-down favorite on the kids' end of the table, so much so that the big dish was settled there, with firm instructions to a couple of older kids to help the little ones dish it out.

As big brownies and slices of pecan pie were passed around, Anna reflected that two things made her comfortable. First, no one was drinking, which severely differentiated this gathering from those she'd attended with Beau and his friends. And second, no one was calling attention to the fact that her girls didn't talk. They seemed to fit in just fine.

After dinner, a third refreshing thing happened: the men shooed Anna and Ma Dixie out of the kitchen so that they could clean up. They even brought tall glasses of sweet tea out to the front porch, where a breeze off the bayou was cooling everything down.

Men serving women? That was a first in Anna's experience.

Ma settled down with a heavy sigh, looking out into the swamp where a couple of white birds waded for fish. "Nice evening. Come summer, we'll have to break out the window AC, but I prefer real air."

"It's nice." Anna lifted her face to feel the soft wind on it, and listened to the gentle music of frogs and crickets and lapping water.

"Sean tells me your girls might need taking care of during the day."

Anna sucked in a breath. She didn't need for him to arrange her life!

"Now, don't be mad at the boy. He's a leader, always has been. He protects his own."

Anna tried to loosen her clenched muscles. "We're not his own."

"True enough," Ma said amicably. "All the same, he's taken an interest in you and your girls. They're welcome to join the menagerie if you'd like. I only have two young fosters right now. Used to have a whole bunch, but since I hit seventy-five, I've been cutting back."

"You're seventy-five?" Anna would have guessed ten years younger, or more.

"Yes, and I like the little kids, but these days it's considered best to place those with parents who can adopt them if they come available. I'm too old to adopt." She turned to Anna, her face breaking into a million wrinkles as she smiled. "The point is, though, that I've got room in my heart for more kids. And plenty of toys and things to do. Up to you, though."

"Thank you for the offer." Anna hesitated, not wanting to offend the older woman. "My girls have some special needs."

"Most of mine do, too," Ma said.

"And they've seen some bad stuff in their young lives. It can make them needy."

"Yep. True of most foster kids. There's a reason they're in the system." Ma lifted her hands, palms up. "I like working with the tough cases. Though your girls don't seem real tough. Don't hold a candle to Sean and his foster brother Tony, way back when."

Anna blew out a breath as more of her doubts were demolished. She plowed on, wanting to make sure she was completely honest with Ma. "Their father…he's not a good man." She hated to admit it to Ma, since it reflected so poorly on her, but honesty compelled it. "I think he's still out West, but there have been some signs he's around here." That could be a deal breaker for Ma, and understandably so.

Ma looked over at her and held out a flat hand. "Look

at that. Steady as a twenty-year-old." She grinned. "But I'm a better shot."

Anna's eyes widened. "You…"

"Honey, I live out here in the middle of nowhere with kids from all kind of messed-up families. You think I haven't seen an angry or violent dad before?"

Around the corner of the house, two little boys ran and flung themselves into Ma's lap. "Me!" pleaded one.

"No, let *me* in your lap!"

She chuckled and held them both tight, then winked over at Anna. "That's the thing, fellas. I have a big lap for a reason. There's room for everybody."

Clearly, there was room for her girls, both physically and in Ma's big heart. If they could come here for babysitting, it would allow Anna to work more and better, even to study for her GED. "I don't know if I could afford you," she said as her own girls appeared and pressed against her legs. "But a few days a week…"

"We'll work something out," Ma said.

And Anna held her girls as her heart alternately cramped with worry and loosened with hope. This was a good place, a loving place. But if she was starting to get attached, the girls must be, too.

If only they could stay here in Safe Haven, put down roots. If only the girls could grow up in a safe, loving, caring community.

If only she didn't have this nagging worry that Beau was on their trail.

AFTER THEY'D HELPED Sean do the dishes, Liam and Cash started toward the side yard. Ma's longtime friend, Pudge LeFrost, was playing banjo while his son plucked along on a lap harp and the kids caught crawdads in coffee cans.

"Not so fast." Sean beat his brothers to the back door and stepped in front of it, blocking their way. "Need your help with a project."

They glanced at each other, and Liam frowned. "Thought we'd get away without fixing something around here for once. What is it now?" His complaint was good-natured, as was Cash's eye roll. They both loved Ma. And they knew that Pudge, at over three hundred pounds and with diabetes-related leg problems, wasn't able to help Ma around the house a whole lot.

"Won't take long," Sean reassured them. "It's just hauling and carrying. Back bedroom is packed so full I can't get in to fix the floor. We're gonna load up my pickup and I'll take it to the dump tomorrow."

Cash grabbed three beers from the cooler beside Pudge, slid a twenty out of his wallet and tucked it in the cooler pocket despite Pudge's dismissive arm wave and grin, and then came back into the house. He handed a beer to each of them. They headed to the back of the low-slung house, and Liam, who was the organized sort, groaned when he saw the piles of boxes, clothes and old magazines.

"Ma going to let you throw this stuff away?" Cash asked.

"Uh-huh. She pulled out a few things. Says the rest of it can go."

"All right, then." Liam grabbed a couple of boxes and turned toward the hallway, then paused beside a couple of fist-sized holes in the wall. "Hey, wasn't this your room?"

"Mine and Tony's." Sean hadn't been back here much

since those teenage days. "And yeah, I'll fix the wall, too."

"That'd be nice," Liam said. "You caused Ma a lot of grief."

Sean couldn't deny it. "We used to sneak out," he said, pointing to a high window. "Trick was, you had to swing along the gutter until you got to the side of the house, or you'd fall right in the swamp."

Once Liam had disappeared, Sean took a closer look at Cash. He was dressed better than Sean would ever have cause to be, but his face was lined, and... "Hey, you're going gray," he said, ruffling Cash's hair just because he knew his brother hated it.

Cash shoved his hand away. "One strand. I look better than you, ya hulk." Cash grabbed a stack of magazines and headed out.

"Don't strain yourself," Sean called after him, and made sure his own stack of junk was twice as large.

As they worked, Liam talked about police business and the politics of becoming chief when city council was full of blue blood types who didn't approve of Liam's background. Cash talked about deals he was working on.

On about the eighth trip, Cash wiped his forehead on his rolled-up shirtsleeve. "I feel like I'm breathing water. Don't know how you lived here without air-conditioning."

"Because I wasn't a wuss." Sean looked out over the bayou, at the last shimmer of evening light reflected in the low river. Water lapped gently against the shore, and crickets and frogs chirped their rhythmic backup to Pudge's banjo playing.

"Heard you're gonna help out at the women's center," Liam said.

"Yeah." Sean had mixed feelings about the place, but they definitely needed the kind of help he could offer. The church's roof was leaking, putting their office at risk.

"It's a good place," Cash said unexpectedly. "It helped us."

"I don't recall it helping Mom." Sean knelt and picked up newspapers and old plastic fast-food toys that had decorated the floor, probably for years.

"Dude." Liam leaned back against the doorjamb and spread his hands. "Nobody could've helped Mom."

Sean tried to focus on a big box labeled Baby Clothes, opening and looking inside to make sure it could be tossed. But all he could think about was that no matter what anyone said, *he* should have helped their mother. He'd been the oldest. He'd seen their father push her into his old truck and drive away.

That had been the end of it. They'd never seen her again. And most of the time, knowing how dedicated she'd been as a mom, how much she'd loved them, he figured she hadn't made it. Most of the time, he believed that if she'd been alive, she'd have found a way to come back and get them.

Most of the time, he felt guilty. If only he'd gone after his dad instead of gathering his brothers, she might have survived. They could have stayed a family.

In his angry moments, he thought maybe she'd dumped them on purpose. Why else hadn't she screamed her lungs out when their father had dragged her toward his truck?

"Hey, check this out." Liam had opened a box and

was pulling out an old backpack, camo, with Sean O'Dwyer written on the back in permanent marker, their mother's neat hand. "Here's that book you were always reading."

*Rogues of War.* Seeing it twisted his heart, because he'd been reading it on the day when their father had taken their mother.

And afterward, when the dark despair had come on, when even the good people of Safe Haven couldn't love away his pain, he'd buried himself in that book, read it again and again. It seemed to bring his mother closer, since she'd read it, too, and they'd talked about it.

Probably, that book and others in the series were why he'd joined up as soon as he was old enough. That, and some survival instinct that warned him if he didn't change something about his life, get some discipline, he'd end up dead or in prison.

Liam dug farther into the box and pulled out a framed photo of the three of them, elementary school age. "Jeez, when was that taken?"

"Dorks," Cash said, leaning over Liam's shoulder to look more closely at the photo. His throat sounded tight, though.

Their mother wasn't in the picture, but Sean remembered the day she'd taken it. Back in Alabama, by the river. A happy, carefree day that had sent their father into a rage.

It wasn't very often that he remembered they'd had good days, too. That their mom had tried hard to give them a good childhood.

Liam cleared his throat. "I'll hold on to this one," he said.

Cash pulled out his wallet again, extracted a couple

of hundreds. "I can't help at the shelter, gotta get back to Atlanta and I suck at repairs, anyway. But give 'em a donation to buy what they need, okay?"

"Thanks, man." Liam pocketed the money as Cash picked up a couple of the remaining boxes and headed out to the truck.

"How you gonna get that money to Yasmin?" Sean asked, knowing that Yasmin and Liam had complicated feelings for each other. Their breakup hadn't been an easy one.

Liam had located a broom and was sweeping the now-almost-clear floor. "Anonymous drop-off?"

"Might work." Sean picked up the box with the mementos and headed outside. Pudge and his son were packing up their instruments, and Anna, at a nod from Sean, guided the sleepy twins into the truck.

Liam left and then Cash. Sean hugged Ma goodbye, and then headed toward his truck, where Anna and the girls were waiting.

Halfway there, he realized he still had that box of things from the old days under his arm.

Bitterness, dark as the black water in the swamp around them, rose up in his chest.

Being here at Ma's, bringing Anna and the girls here, made that old longing tug at him again. He clenched his teeth and stiffened his spine against it. A family just wasn't in the cards for Sean. There was a hole in his heart from when his mother disappeared, and his father's tainted blood ran through his veins. His brothers understood everything he'd been through, but he couldn't expect anyone else to understand it. To put up with it.

The box he was carrying suddenly seemed to weigh

five hundred pounds. He didn't want anything to do with the memories it represented. In fact, he didn't want this box anywhere near him for a minute more.

He walked over to Ma's incinerator box and hurled it in, ignoring the pain that stabbed his heart.

# CHAPTER NINE

FIVE DAYS LATER, Anna rubbed sweaty hands down the sides of her shorts and took deep breaths to calm the too-fast pace of her heart. If she had to sit in this truck, alone with Sean for a whole hour, waiting for the twins to emerge from the library program for the evening, she'd explode.

He'd been kind to offer transportation while her car was being repainted; she could hardly complain that he needed to come to town an hour before the twins' program ended. And Tony, who was growing on her despite his questionable past, had insisted on doing the paint job himself since her insurance coverage was minimal, and she didn't want to risk alerting Beau to where she was by filing a claim, anyway.

Ma Dixie, wonderful Ma Dixie, was caring for the girls three days per week. After their first day, Monday, they'd been counting the hours until they could go back. Today, Wednesday, was their second day, and they'd jumped out of Sean's truck and run inside this morning without a glance behind them.

And to top it off, Pudge had kindly offered to drive the girls from Ma's place to the library program, since the timing was right, or so he said; he visited his ninety-something mother at the personal care home in Safe Haven at about that time each day.

Everyone in Safe Haven was so helpful, Sean chief among them. It was scaring her to death.

If she dared to let herself and her girls get attached to this town, these people, this strong, protective man beside her, what would happen if—*when*—it all blew up in their faces?

"I'm going to take a walk," she said to Sean. Then that felt rude, so she said, "Want to come?"

"I wouldn't mind stretching my legs," he said to her surprise.

*Oh no...don't do this to me. Please?*

Between working at the cabins and now driving, they spent most of each day together. And it was both easy and hard. Easy, because they liked the same music and worked at the same quick pace; because they both talked a little, but not a lot, and they shared the same sense of humor.

Hard, because all those similarities—not to mention how good-looking he was, in a bad boy way—made him way too appealing.

And now she was taking an evening stroll with him.

They walked from the library parking lot, through the town, toward the water. She thought again about being dependent on everyone, about how dependency had been her mistake before, with Beau. And speaking of Beau, he was supposedly acting weird back in Montana—because, yes, he'd been spotted there again, thank heavens. Talking to her friend Sheila and to people at his work about how much he missed them and wanted to be with them. It was good he wasn't on her trail, but the sweet talk didn't sound like Beau.

The uncertainty of what was going on dug at her. Maybe Beau had hired someone to scare her with the graffiti on her cabin and car. If so, maybe he'd soon follow up himself, in person.

If he came after them, then what might happen to all of the nice people offering kind help and making her and the girls feel at home? What if she just had to disrupt it all again, uproot the girls and move on?

"Slow down," Sean said from a few paces behind her. "You're in the South."

His rumbly low voice sent tingles up and down her spine. Not scared tingles, good tingles.

"Sorry," she said. "My thoughts got ahead of me."

"Thinking too much can get you in trouble, especially on a warm Wednesday evening." He took her hand and placed it in the crook of his arm. "Let me show you the right pace for a stroll."

Up ahead, at the Methodist church, a few people were emerging from the side door.

"Is that Tony?" she asked, squinting. "He must be pretty religious, going to services in the middle of the week."

Sean chuckled. "Not so's you'd notice," he said. "But if I'm not mistaken, there's an AA meeting at that church."

"Oooohh." She drew out the word as a few things she'd noticed came into clearer focus.

"Yes, he has a problem. And he's working on it." He slowed and put out a hand to stop her from walking forward. "Hold up. He'll like it better if we don't see him."

"Sure." She looked up at Sean. "You care about him like a brother, but he's not really your brother, right?"

"In every way that matters, he is. He helped me through a lot of stuff in my teens. Probably kept me from going off the deep end, getting arrested. Now it's my turn."

She wasn't sure she trusted Tony, but she admired Sean's loyalty.

Minutes later they turned onto the boardwalk that ran on the edge of town, where the bay and the river converged on their way out to sea. The saltwater smell, always in the background in Safe Haven, intensified. A pelican sailed above the water's surface, then dived down for a fish.

Small tables with red-checked tablecloths filled a small patio just off the boardwalk, and a few pairs and trios of people sat, talking and eating and sipping drinks. Hanging baskets overflowed with flowers, red and white and pink.

Anna slowed her pace more, enchanted. "I'd never have believed in any of this, living in Montana," she said, waving her arm to indicate the whole scene.

"Would you like a drink?"

"Oh…no. That's okay." *That would be way too intimate.*

He raised an eyebrow, almost as if he could read her mind, and heat rose to her face. Would he call her on it?

But he lifted a shoulder in a shrug, and they walked on.

"Speaking of back in Montana, how did you get involved with your ex?" Sean asked the question but didn't look at her, instead staring off into the distance, seeming to watch the clouds rolling in.

Anna blew out a sigh, wondering how much to tell him.

"I mean, he sounds like a jerk. And you're a good person."

He seemed to mean it, and that warmed her heart. Of course, he didn't know her well enough to make an assessment, but she still appreciated his vote of confidence. "When I was a teenager, hanging around outside the roller-skating rink, Beau seemed like the most sophisticated guy I'd ever seen. Lots of girls wanted to take a ride on his Harley."

"And he chose you?"

She nodded, remembering her own surprise and pleasure. "He chose me."

"What did your parents think of him?"

A smile quirked the corner of her mouth at the thought of her father. "Dad could barely keep track of himself. That was my biggest issue, when I ended up with Beau—wondering how my dad would get by without me." A blanket of sadness settled on her heart. For all his shortcomings, for all his neglect, she still loved him. Maybe, once she was more settled, she could get him to visit, try to mend their relationship.

"Your mom?"

"She died when I was eight." She kept her voice matter-of-fact, knowing from experience that most people didn't like to hear sad things.

"I'm sorry." He looked down at her then. "Rough to grow up without a mother." He paused. "Your husband, or ex, or whatever. Is domestic abuse his only crime?"

That made her stop and stare at him. "His only... No. No, he's gotten in trouble for selling stolen cars. And drugs." Just saying that gave Anna a sense of shame. "I shouldn't have been involved with him at all, and I knew that almost from the beginning. When I found out I was pregnant, I was even ready to go it on my own, but when the sonogram picked up twins..." She looked out across the water. "It was too much. I needed, *we* needed, a place to stay and food to eat."

"Your dad wouldn't help you?"

"By then he'd…" She thought of her father's bad times, which had started soon after Anna had moved out. She'd realized then that, however ineffectively, he'd tried to hold it together while he had a child to parent. Luckily, he now did janitorial work at the shelter in exchange for a room to live in. "Let's just say he was never in a position to help us." She looked out at the water and felt the wind pick up. In the distance was the faint sound of thunder. "Hey, why are we talking about the past? Let's appreciate the day. I can't remember the last time I had time to myself."

"I'm glad you're enjoying it," he said, and they walked on down the boardwalk, past the fishing pier to the edge of town.

A sign with an arrow indicated the location of the shrimp dock. A red-and-white boat sailed toward it, nets gathered in. Sean called a greeting, and the trio of men aboard waved back.

Beyond the dock, the natural world took over, with dunes and beach grasses and water as far as could be seen.

Anna felt water on her face and looked up to see that the sky had darkened. She felt another drop, then another.

"Come on!" Sean tugged at her hand and they ran down the pier's steps to shelter under it as the skies opened.

The water had turned gray-green, cloudy with rain. There were a few voices above them, then none; everyone else had hurried inside.

It was just her and Sean alone under the dock. And maybe it was the lightning that crashed on the edge of the sky that filled the air with electricity, but Anna felt close to him.

She'd never told anyone about Beau. She had assumed there would be embarrassment and judgment for all the bad choices she'd made. And she did feel embarrassed, talking about it now, but she didn't sense judgment from Sean. More like anger on her behalf.

The neglected little girl inside her, the vulnerable young woman who'd fallen for Beau and lived to regret it—they were still a part of her. Now she'd revealed them to Sean. And instead of ignoring or scorning them, Sean treated them with care and respect and sympathy, just as warmly as he treated Hope and Hayley.

Lightning struck closer, too close, and she shrank back, and then Sean's arms were around her from behind. "Come on. Back up away from the water." He tugged her with him, and she walked back, his body warming hers.

He pulled her closer, sheltering her, and she felt safe, protected, maybe for the first time in her life. It felt so unfamiliar that it scared her.

With all her responsibilities, the last thing she should be doing was cozying up to Sean under a dock. But she was always doing everything for the kids, had ever since the pregnancy test had shown two little lines instead of one. Right now, just for this moment, she kind of wanted to do something for herself.

She leaned back into his strength and was rewarded with him tightening his arms around her.

She tried to relax. Except that his hard chest was not

just protective, but exciting, and she really wanted to turn around in his arms, face him, touch him.

Kiss him.

The heat inside shook her, shocked her, because it was new. She leaned her head back against his shoulder, and then she could feel his breath against her ear.

Could hear it, getting a little faster. Just like her own breathing.

Her insides seemed to melt, and she wanted to just give in to the heavy, warm feeling. Right now, she could turn around in his arms, put her own arms around his neck and...

His arms tightened, and she knew he was sensing what she felt.

Possibilities sparked in the electrified air around them.

She ached to be close to him, to let herself go, to press into his arms and rest her head against his chest. To relax into his strong, protective arms.

But that would be a huge mistake. She struggled free. "The girls will be scared. I'd better get to the library."

"Not in the midst of a lightning storm." He put a hand on her arm. "The folks running the program will keep them safe inside."

She shook off his hand. "I'll meet you by the truck later."

"Anna—"

"Later." She waved—and ran for her life, or what felt like it.

THAT FRIDAY NIGHT, Rita walked into the Palmetto Pig a few minutes before seven. A glance around told her that her new friend Claire wasn't here yet, and that the place was a typical small-town dive: lit-up beer signs, a thick, scarred mahogany bar, air heavy with a greasy smell from the onion rings, fried fish and hush puppies that dominated the chalkboard menu.

She sat on a stool and ordered a draft. When Claire had suggested meeting for a drink, Rita had chosen the town-side bar purposely, wanting to be a part of the local scene, not the upscale tourist sites near the water.

But when two bearded, camo-clad men sat down on either side of her, she wondered if she'd made a mistake.

"Y'all is new in town," one of them said.

"Look lonely," added the other in an identical accent.

They were huge, and younger than she was, forty at the most.

"Just waiting for my friend," she said. Where *was* Claire?

The two men exchanged glances over her head, seeming to communicate without words, and shifted subtly closer to her.

Dark fear rose inside of her. She hated looming and physical pushing from men. That seemed normal—most women probably felt the same—but her own visceral reaction of sweating terror had always felt extreme.

It also seemed like a clue to her past, but one she had never wanted to explore too deeply.

She drew in a breath, held it and then let it out slowly. "Look, fellas. I just want to enjoy my drink in peace." Funny, in daylight, working as a waitress, she was known for being able to handle the toughest tableful of drunk jerks.

As a civilian, in a strange place—that was different.

She looked around, taking in more details of the place: the televisions on either side of the bar, tuned to hockey; the oversize beer mugs hanging on hooks with people's names on them, all male; the small groups of men talking loudly to each other.

She was definitely out of place.

The two guys had slumped into inaction, staring at the television broadcasting a hockey game. They were still sitting too close, but they hadn't touched her.

Her purse buzzed, and she pulled out her phone and studied the lock screen. Claire. She had a flat.

Want me to come help you fix it?

She'd love the excuse to get away from Mutt and Jeff, here.

A pause, during which the two guys appeared to get interested in her again.

Then: Tony just stopped, says he can change it.

There's two big dudes with beards and camo kinda bugging me here.

Do they look alike?

She took a furtive glance from one to the other.

Yes. One's skinnier.

Mahoney brothers. Ugh. Be there soon.

There were a few more people in the bar now, talking and partying, but no one she knew. Music was playing, loud enough to conceal anything anyone said.

"Hey," the one on her right said, "she's a MILF."

"What's that?"

Rita's insides recoiled, because she knew.

"Mom I'd like to f—"

"Boys," came a deep voice from behind her. "I need to talk to Rita. Why don't you take off." It wasn't said as a question.

Jimmy. Thank goodness.

The two men grumbled and looked at Jimmy, then her, probably deciding whether she was worth fighting for.

They slid off their bar stools. One bumped into Jimmy and one into her.

"Mind your manners," Jimmy said, but mildly, like he knew he'd won.

The two men sneered and left.

Relief washed over Rita, followed quickly by annoyance at herself. Why did she need a man to rescue her, in a public place? "Thanks," she said to Jimmy, who meant well and had definitely gotten her out of a sticky situation.

"The Mahoney brothers are known for causing trouble. They're not the sharpest, but they're big." He cocked his head to one side and concern crossed his face. "Hey, you're shaking. I'm sorry that happened. That's not what this town is about. You could've asked anyone in here for help and they'd have given it." He paused, reached out and squeezed her hand briefly, looking into her eyes. "I'm glad I was the first responder, though."

"Me, too." His warm brown eyes had little circles of amber right around the pupils. She bit her lip and he glanced down at her mouth, just for an instant.

She took a deep breath, let it out slowly. *Calm down.*

"They gave me the creeps. Big guys looming over me... never have liked it."

If only she knew why, what it evoked at that gut-deep level inside her.

"Makes sense." He sat down beside her. Not too close, like those brothers, but still, she could feel the heat from his thigh.

He turned his head to look at her again. "I've been wanting to talk to you."

Nerves tightened her stomach. "Is my work okay?"

"It's stellar. Everyone loves you." He raised a hand to get a drink, and when the young bartender came over, Jimmy looked over at Rita. "Buy you another beer?"

"Thanks. Still working on this one." She'd definitely lost her taste for a night of drinking.

Once he had his beer in front of him, Jimmy looked over at her. "Look," he said, "I like you. I'm single, you're single. I'd like to ask you out, but with you working for me, it's awkward."

Heat rose from her chest to her face. She'd been alone a good while, especially since T-Bone had been sick the last two years of his life. Their relationship had turned into more of a caregiver-patient one than husband and wife.

Jimmy was watching her intently as if trying to figure out how she was reacting to his words. "Not trying to be one of those creepy bosses. If you're not interested, no harm, no foul. Your job's safe and I won't pout."

Rita stared at her nearly empty beer glass, her face still hot. Inside, she admitted it: she *was* interested.

Jimmy seemed like a good, protective man, just as

T-Bone had been. She was drawn to that kind of guy at a deep level.

She'd never regretted the opportunity to take care of T-Bone, repay him for some of what he'd done for her. But he'd been gone two years now. And looking over at Jimmy's muscular arms, she couldn't help imagining how it would feel to have them around her.

But how could she let that happen when she didn't know who she was?

She was opening her mouth to regretfully decline his offer when the bar door opened. Claire came in, with a good-looking, dark-haired young guy behind her. "Rita!" Claire said, approaching the bar. "I'm *so* sorry to leave you stuck here alone." She looked past Rita to Jimmy. "Although it looks like you found some higher-quality male company. What happened to the Mahoney brothers?"

Rita looked sideways toward Jimmy. "He had a word with them and they decided to leave. For which I'm very grateful," she added.

"The pleasure was mine." He held her gaze.

Warmth started deep in Rita's belly and radiated outward, climbing her neck, heating her face. She couldn't look away.

"Rita. Rita!" Claire tugged at her arm, oblivious. "This is Tony. He was my knight in shining armor tonight. That's why I'm buying him a drink." She fumbled in her purse and pulled out a twenty.

"Put your money away," Tony said. "We'll have a... What do you like, draft or bottle?"

"Yes, sir," Claire said promptly, pocketing her money.

"Long as you're paying, I'll have a glass of wine. Dry and white, if they've got it. Should we get a bottle?"

"Nah. I'm drinking Coke."

Tony's words made both Claire and Jimmy stare. Jimmy caught himself first. "Good man." He pounded Tony on the back.

Tony's face colored. "What? Can't a man order a soda without people making a federal case of it?"

"You do what you have to do." Claire patted his arm. "That's just fine. I'm awful grateful you drove by when you did."

"Looks like we've got trouble." Jimmy pitched his voice low and directed the comment to Tony. He nodded toward the door and lifted a hand. "Hey, Brandi," he said, louder.

"I'll g-g-get Eldora," the young bartender said, and fled.

Brandi marched toward Tony. "What are you doing with that ugly thing?" she fumed, pointing at Claire, and then grabbing Tony's shoulder and spinning him around on the bar stool.

An older couple had gotten up from their table the moment Brandi came in, and now they came over to the bar. The woman spoke in a soothing voice to Brandi, putting an arm around her, while the man urged Tony away from the pair.

Claire's face turned red and her fists clenched, but two men from the bar, close to her age, came right over, one begging her to join him on the dance floor, the other waving a dismissive hand at Brandi and putting an arm around Claire.

Rita was impressed; the whole town, it seemed, knew

when emergency management was needed. She'd never been in a moment's danger from those Mahoney brothers. Something tight and nervous inside her loosened.

She glanced over at Jimmy, who'd stayed at her side, watching. "His ex-girlfriend?" she asked quietly.

"Ex-wife."

Brandi broke away from the woman who'd been talking to her and rushed at Tony again. He put out an arm, stiff, and held Brandi back as she struggled to get at him.

From the back of the bar, a woman emerged, long haired, sturdy and tall, about Rita's age. The way she carried herself made it obvious that she was at least the bar manager, probably the owner. She put a hand on the young bartender's arm. "Bring out a pitcher of sweet tea, honey," she said. Then she walked around the bar to step between Tony and the angry woman. "There'll be no fighting in this bar. One or both of you needs to leave."

Brandi started cursing at the bar owner.

"Okay, how 'bout we make it you." She took the woman's arm and started moving her toward the door, seemingly oblivious to her screeches and flailing fists.

Around the bar, people started to clap. "We love you, Eldora!" someone called.

The angry woman cursed, then shoved her way out the door.

"Show's over, people," Eldora said. "Eat, drink and be merry."

Somehow, during the argument, Rita had backed closer to Jimmy, and she now found herself standing pressed to his side, his protective arm around her.

Which felt good. Way too good. He was strong, broad chested and just tall enough that he could tuck her beneath his arm. She felt safe. Just the way she had with T-Bone, maybe more.

His hand played a little with her hair, and it made her yearn for closeness, as if her whole body wanted to lean in.

But it wasn't right. Not until she knew who she was. Gently, she extracted herself from Jimmy's grasp under the guise of going to Claire. "Come on. Let's sit down and get us some good greasy food," she suggested, and nodded toward the table Jimmy had grabbed for them.

Eldora poured a glass of sweet tea for herself and one for Tony. She clinked his glass with hers.

Tony downed his entire glass of sweet tea in one gulp, and then talked quietly to the bar owner.

"Never a dull moment," Claire said with a sigh as she followed Rita toward the corner booth. "Brandi and I used to be friends, when we were small, but in middle school she dumped me for the cool girls."

"She seems volatile," Rita said.

"She has a drinking problem, and when she's drunk, it's best to stay out of her line of sight. Guess I'm in it now."

"Jealous lady," Jimmy commented, letting both of them slide into the booth, and then sliding in himself, beside Rita.

As Tony came over, slid into the booth and started apologizing to Claire, Jimmy leaned close enough to speak in Rita's ear, his warm breath sending a bolt of awareness through her body. "We never finished that conversation," he said. "I'm not letting this go."

Rita closed her eyes for a brief moment, trying to gather the strength to slide out of the booth and go home.

When the truth was, she'd far rather stay here and melt into Jimmy's arms.

## CHAPTER TEN

ANNA WAS TALKING to the GED instructor at the library when she looked up to see Sean striding toward them.

Feelings rushed through her like a movie on fast forward. Simple happiness to see him, so broad shouldered and caring. Worry, because with her past, she knew better than to let down her guard.

And, oh no, he was going to find out why she was here. She stepped away from the Never too late to get your high school diploma! sign, heat suffusing her face. She'd thought she was safe from detection, safe from anyone she knew finding out her embarrassing secret.

It was one thing to talk to the GED teacher. He was accustomed to adult learners, and for him to know that she'd never finished high school was fine.

For Sean to figure it out was simply mortifying. "What are you doing here?" she asked as he approached.

"Tony had a setback, so I offered to pick you up. Did I interrupt something?" His tone was speculative as he looked from Anna to Rafael, the instructor.

But no time to figure it out. More important to hide the mortifying truth. She half turned away from Sean and stuffed her GED study guide into her backpack.

"Not at all," Rafael said affably. "Can I help you?"

"What's your business with Anna?"

Anna stopped what she was doing, staring up at him. "Sean, why in the world would you ask that question?"

Color climbed his face. "I get the feeling you're hiding something from me, and I just want to know what's going on," he said, half apologetically, half not. "Make sure you're safe."

"We're talking about a class I teach." Rafael gestured toward the sign and then looked over at Anna, his expression concerned.

"GED classes?" Sean looked from Rafael to Anna, and his eyes fell to the guide she hadn't succeeded in stuffing completely into her pack.

"Anna," Rafael said, "are you okay here? Do you want me to call someone or stick around?"

"No. No, thank you. I'm fine." She smiled at Rafael and then glared at Sean.

"All right. It was nice to meet you. Hope we'll see you in a class soon." Rafael headed toward the exit.

Eyes down, Anna tried again to zip her backpack. She couldn't look at Sean.

His hand came over hers, stopping her movements. "Anna."

She didn't answer, but she went still as a difficult part of her past came rushing back at her. Young, pregnant and uneducated—she remembered all too well the looks her classmates had given her, the principal who'd refused her request for extra time on assignments when her morning sickness had gotten so bad, the teacher who'd lectured her on the importance of self-control. Dropping out had been a relief. And a huge mistake.

Being here with Sean, having him know that she didn't have a degree, brought that helpless sense of failure back.

"You didn't graduate?" he asked quietly.

She looked away. "No."

He touched her chin, forcing her to face him. "Why not?"

"Because of the twins," she said, gesturing in the direction of the children's program.

"You love your girls and you're trying your best to care for them," he said. "What's more, I admire that you're working toward your GED now."

She took a quick look at his face then, wondering if he was telling the truth. How could going to a GED class be admirable?

"Sometimes we can't help what happens to us," he said, "but we can choose how to deal with it. You're choosing to improve your life."

His gaze *was* approving, warm, caring. It felt like a healing balm.

Sean jerked his head sideways, in the direction Rafael had disappeared. "Sorry to act like a jerk around your teacher," he said. "I thought he was bothering you."

She shook her head. "No, he was helping me."

He drew in a breath and let it out slowly, audibly. "Good. I got a little...jealous."

She tilted her head to one side, surprised at the admission. "But you don't... You're not..."

"I don't have any claim on you. But still." He hadn't taken his eyes off hers.

Anna sucked in her breath as every cell inside her came alive. He was being vulnerable. Almost admitting he cared.

The sound of children's voices and feet tramping down the stairs indicated that their moment together

was over. The twins ran to her, flinging their arms
around her. Having Sean here didn't seem to faze them.

They waved their craft of the day, paper bag puppets
with googly eyes that made Anna laugh. Sean knelt to
look, too, and Hayley boldly made her puppet grab his
arm. He played along, feigning fear, making the girls
giggle.

"Mr. Sean's going to take us home, because our car
isn't ready yet," she explained. Even as she said it, she
thought about how the little cabin had become home
so quickly.

The girls whispered in the back seat while they
drove, the radio playing softly.

"Have dinner plans?" Sean asked.

She frowned. "Um…not sure. We might have sandwiches, fruit. I don't feel like cooking." Was he hint-
ing for an invite?

"I have an idea." He pulled over in front of a dilapi-
dated wooden building with several hand-painted signs
posted: Boiled Peanuts and Fresh Shrimp and Strawberries caught her eye.

A black man with white hair emerged behind another customer who was loaded with bags. When Sean
jumped out of the truck, the man's face broke into a
wide smile. "You come for my fishies?"

"Depends if you'll give me a fair price, old man."
Sean grinned. "I have some girls need to try boiled peanuts for the first time."

"Bring 'em on, bring 'em on."

Anna expected the girls to hang back, but they were
both unfastening their seat belts. Moments later, they
were in the fish shack, watching Sean pick out large
fresh shrimp and lush strawberries. Once Sean had

several big bags, the old man—Ernest—fished some boiled peanuts out of a bin and showed the girls how to open them.

Hayley boldly took a bite and smiled, and then Hope did the same, more hesitantly. They both held out their hands for seconds.

Anna glanced over at Sean and caught him smiling just as she was. She felt a tug in her gut. This was so *normal*: a woman and a man, smiling over the cuteness of two great kids.

She looked down at the twins and saw that they were about to beg for more. "Goodness, we'd better get a big bag of them," Anna decided, and moments later they were back on the road, crunching on the salty, delicious snacks.

A few minutes later, from the back seat, Hayley's high, clear voice spoke up: "These are so good!"

She'd spoken in front of Sean. Joy exploded inside Anna, so intense that she didn't dare express it. She just gripped the seat tighter and looked over her shoulder in time to see Hope nudge Hayley's arm and point to Sean.

Hayley shrugged. "I don't care. Can I have some strawberries, too, Mom?"

It hadn't been just a fluke. Anna's heart pounded. Hayley had spoken in front of Sean, and it wasn't an accident, and she'd done it again. Now it was full-on fireworks inside.

And he'd noticed, because he was glancing over at her, one eyebrow lifted.

She was fumbling for strawberries—good heavens, whatever the child wanted—when Hope spoke up. "Can I have some, too, Mommy?"

Her throat tightened and tears pressed the backs

of her eyes. Sweeter sounds she'd never heard. "Of course," she choked out, and handed the whole box back to the twins.

She reached for Sean's hand, and he turned it over to clasp hers, the corners of his mouth turning up in a smile.

She was unprepared for the strength of his grasp, the size of his hand, the joy still dancing inside her. Her girls had spoken in front of a nonfamily member. That said such good things about Sean. They'd come to trust him.

It also said that their stress level was coming down.

Clearly, her girls were healing. She *had* to make it work here in Safe Haven.

SEAN HAD TO hand it to himself. He'd pulled off something nice for Anna and her girls.

Their dinner had been simple, just shrimp cooked over a fire on the beach.

But it was good to see the lines of tension fade from Anna's face, replaced by laughter. And to hear those sweet little-girl voices. He felt touched and honored that the twins had spoken, quite a bit, in front of him.

It was easy to make the little family happy. Seemed like no one had ever really tried. So when the air got cool, on a run up to the cabins for blankets and sweaters, he got an idea: s'mores. He dug around and found the supplies—Lord knew why he had chocolate bars and marshmallows in his cupboards, probably stuff Ma Dixie had bagged up to send home with him the last time they'd had a bonfire at her place. In Anna's cupboards, he found graham crackers to complete the snack.

As he approached them on the dark beach, three faces looked up at him, illuminated in the fire's golden light. Longing tugged painfully inside his chest. *I want this.*

He'd known this little family only a couple of weeks, but they'd become so quickly intertwined in his life, his thoughts, his heart.

"Mr. Sean!" Hayley jumped up and ran to him, hugging his leg, and the strings around his heart wrapped tighter.

"Hayley," Anna called. "Let go of Mr. Sean so he can walk."

The sweet child let loose of his leg and looked up at him, her little forehead wrinkled. "I'm sorry."

It still felt like a miracle to hear her voice. He drew a ragged breath. "It's okay, honey," he managed to say. "Carry the marshmallows for me?"

"Marshmallows!" she squealed. She grabbed the bag he put into her hand and ran to Hope.

"Maybe we can toast them like in the campout book," Hope said, and they both turned to look at Anna and Sean.

"If it's okay with your mom, we can. We can even make something called s'mores."

"S'mores! S'mores!" They shrieked and giggled and dug through the bag he set down beside them.

He knelt beside Anna, and she put a hand on his arm. "Thank you," she whispered.

Her lips were full and pretty. It was hard to stop looking at them. But he reined himself in and nodded. "Hope you don't mind. I'm a sucker for s'mores."

They taught the girls to roast marshmallows, comforted Hope when she dropped one into the fire, and helped them put the graham crackers, chocolate and toasted marshmallows together. Seeing their faces when they tasted the gooey treats tugged hard at his heart. So did the look on Anna's face.

When the twins got sleepy, Anna had them lie down on one blanket and covered them with the other. Then she sang to them, her voice low and sweet. When she got to "Ash Grove," he couldn't resist joining in.

By the end of the song, the girls were out.

Anna scooted quietly back toward the fire, and he followed her like she was a flower and he was the bee.

"This might have been a mistake," she said, wrinkling her nose at him. "Carrying them up to the cabins won't be easy. I just couldn't resist this chance to sit awhile longer and look at the waves."

"We'll work it out. I'll help you carry them." He stuck a marshmallow on a stick and handed it to her, making another one for himself.

"Wait—we're eating more?"

"We're eating grown-up s'mores."

"Oh really?" She looked sideways at him, something speculative in her eyes. She was young, and mostly seemed innocent, but clearly she wasn't unaware of vibrations between a man and a woman.

"Really." His body stirred. Awareness of her flowed and crashed through him like the rhythmic waves of the Atlantic. He busied himself pulling out dark chocolate and thin, crisp cookies while he tried to get a grip on his own desires.

Anna needed a strong, steady man who would be the perfect father for her daughters. But what did he know about how to be a good father? His own dad had abused his mother and that same blood ran through his veins. How could he take the risk?

Yet Anna and her twins made him feel like king of the world. They seemed to think he was something special.

And Anna, with her soft hair and shy, wise eyes, the little tilt in her nose saving her from model-like perfection, made him feel protective. And, yeah, turned him on, too. She was a real beauty. Man, when he'd seen her in the library talking to that guy—he still wasn't convinced the teacher didn't have designs on her—he'd felt a primitive urge to claim her as his own.

"It's on fire!" Anna whisked her marshmallow out of the fire and blew it out, and he could barely take his eyes off her lips. "What's next?" she asked.

*What's next is that I kiss you senseless.* He drew in a calming breath. "Next, you pop it right here with the good chocolate and a cookie—and we smash another cookie on top of that. Now taste it."

She opened her mouth and took a big bite. Her eyes closed as she savored it. Her tongue flicked out to grab a little bit that was on the corner of her mouth.

And he was a goner.

She opened her eyes and caught him looking at her. Lifted an eyebrow. "Are you going to join in, or just watch?"

"I didn't make one yet," he said.

"I'll share." She held out her s'more, smiling.

He took a bite and she seemed to be watching him with the same kind of intensity he'd felt watching her.

They finished the s'more and he held up the bag of marshmallows. "Another?"

"No." She shook her head, a dimple appearing in her cheek. "That was so good. Nothing else could be that good."

Sean could think of something that would be even better.

But he didn't say it, because he wanted to treat her well. She hadn't been treated well enough.

He wanted to lean over and kiss her. With any of his good-time dates, he'd have done just that.

But Anna was different. He didn't want to spook her. He needed to take it slow, nice and slow.

Anna was special. She was a loving mother, committed to her girls through the most difficult of obstacles, and that meant more to him than it probably would to most people, given his background. She had courage. And he admired the way she was trying to lift herself up. How many people would be working on their GED in the midst of escaping an abusive husband?

He wasn't going to add to the pressures on her. Nor destroy the infinitesimal chance that something might, just maybe, be able to grow between them.

He pulled out the final blanket from his bag and spread it beside the fire. "Are you a stargazer?"

She shrugged. "Never had much of a chance, but... every now and then, in Montana, you'd see something amazing."

He gestured to the blanket. "Lie down, and you can see some nice stars. I'll let you have the side close to the fire."

She bit her lip, studied him. Finally, she spoke. "This blanket, the stars...some guys might think it's headed toward something more. But it doesn't mean that for me, okay?"

She watched him steadily and he felt like a dog for the ideas he'd been having. Of course he knew what she meant; he'd thought that very thing.

But he wasn't going to act on it, and that was what was important. "You're a beautiful woman. And a complicated one, with a complicated life. I won't add to that, I promise."

She studied his face for a moment longer, eyes narrowing, then seemed to make a decision. She moved to lie down on the blanket. He lay down beside her, keeping a good six inches of distance between them.

"Do you have a favorite star?" he asked.

She moved a little, looking at the inverted bowl of the sky. Their hands touched, and it seemed sweet and natural to let their fingers intertwine in a quick squeeze.

She drew in an audible breath. "I don't know the constellations, not really. I mean, we learned some in school, but I never put it together with the real world."

He pointed out a couple, the Big Dipper and Orion. "He's supposed to be a mighty warrior. Do you see it?"

"Nope, not at all. That's clearly a ballet dancer."

"No way! If anything, it's a football player."

She snorted. "Spoken like a man. Did you play, back in school?"

"Yeah, just for a little while. Did you take ballet?"

"No. But I got a book from the school library about it, and spent hours in my room practicing. I can do the five positions to perfection, or so I thought." She paused, then turned to look at him. "How come you only played for a little while?"

"Kicked off the team. I was a bad kid." He'd said it often enough that he could make it sound like a joke, but this time, he felt a qualm. He didn't want to be a bad kid around Anna, didn't want her to think of him that way.

She turned her head, studying him. "That's hard to believe."

"Well… I *could* be bad. I scared you the first time we met."

Her mouth curved into a smile. "Yeah, to the point that I sprayed you with pepper spray."

"Don't remind me." He flashed back to that first night, his own suspicions, her actions and obvious fears. They'd come a long way since then.

"I'm sorry." She reached out and gripped his hand again, lightly, and the sensation strummed along his nerve endings until she pulled her hand away. "I don't know if I ever told you that, but I am. You've been more than kind to us."

He shrugged. "Case of mistaken identities, or expectations, or something." He looked up at the sky. "Kids like us—me, Liam and Cash—nobody expected us to accomplish anything. Just staying out of jail was doing better than we were supposed to do."

"I know what you mean," she said, low. "But you've accomplished a lot. You own your own business, you served overseas…"

He crossed his arms, a way to keep his hands to himself. "It was more than anyone expected of an O'Dwyer. And then look at my brothers. Cash makes a stupid amount of money, and Liam's up for police chief. I'm proud of them."

"You should be. You should be proud of yourself, too."

*Not hardly.* He lifted himself on one elbow to look at her. "How come you didn't get ballet lessons, if you were so good at it?"

She wrinkled her nose. "After my mom died, my dad wasn't really…" She shrugged. "He just wasn't really there. He didn't know anything about girls, and he was scrambling to make a living and keep himself together. I was just kind of in the background, you know?"

He risked putting a hand out to cup her chin, lightly. "You shouldn't be in the background, Anna George. You should be center stage, and someday, you will be." He let his finger push a strand of hair away from her face.

She searched his eyes as if she wasn't sure whether to believe him, as if she were thinking about what he'd said, weighing it. "I don't want center stage," she said finally. "But I want my girls to have the chance at it, if they like." She sat up. "I want to stay here, Sean. They're doing well, and it's a good town, and…" She looked down at him. "You've been so kind. To them, and to me."

Their eyes locked, and for a crazy moment he thought she was going to lean down and kiss him.

But she just turned and stared out to sea and he could see that the problems of their lives, of her family, had descended back onto her shoulders.

He wanted to give her a few more minutes of respite. "Show me the positions," he said.

"What?" She looked back at him, wide-eyed.

"The ballet positions. Show me."

A smile tugged at her lips. "I can't do that."

"Why not?"

"I'm embarrassed!"

He stood, reached down and pulled her to her feet. "Teach them to me, then. That ought to be good for a laugh."

She held on to his hands, and they were just inches apart, and he almost ditched the whole ballet idea. He'd rather just hold her.

But she was nervous, looking up at him, then looking away. He didn't want to scare her, so he dropped her hands. "I'm ready. What's first?"

"Really?"

"Really."

"Okay. First position, you put your heels together and point your toes out, like this." She demonstrated.

Sean did the same thing, less flexible than she was. "Like that?"

"Um, yeah." She fought a smile. "Then for second position, you just keep your feet at the same angle and move them apart."

"Easy. I could be on the stage," he joked. "Do I do anything with my arms?"

"You think you can learn the arms, too?"

"No problem," he boasted. "Bring it."

So she showed him how to hold his arms low in first, and out in second. Then they moved on to third position, which was a little harder to balance, and then fourth, which left him feeling foolish, one arm up.

"Now, fifth position is the hardest," she said, giggling. "Your arms go up like this." She demonstrated, and then he tried to duplicate her efforts. She moved around him, adjusting his arms.

Every time she touched him, his body registered the fact with extreme interest.

"Okay, now your legs go like this." She put her feet next to each other, one in front and one in back.

Sean tried to do the same and nearly lost his balance. "My feet don't go that way."

"Try again," she said with mock sternness, and when he did, she knelt in front of him. "That's good! Now straighten your knees. Especially this one. It's way bent." She touched his front leg.

Whoa. If she didn't know what her closeness and touch were doing to his body, she was blind.

He stepped back, thinking this had been a really terrible idea, and then he looked at her face, tilted up at him, laughing. It was the most lighthearted he'd seen her. For once, she wasn't thinking about her girls or her responsibilities. She was just having fun.

He put his hands down to pull her to her feet, but she surprised him, tugging him down, off balance. "Hey!" he said as he landed beside her.

"Hey, what?" She looked at him, her hand brushing back her hair in an unconsciously provocative gesture.

Or *was* it unconscious? Maybe she knew exactly what she was doing to him.

He ought to get up right now, load all their supplies into his pack and carry the girls to bed. Some good physical exertion was what his body needed. Physical exertion that *didn't* involve being inches away from this beautiful, mysterious woman.

That was what he ought to do. But when did an O'Dwyer ever do what he ought to do?

He reached out, touched her cheek and let his thumb play along her lower lip. "That was fun."

She laughed, shakily. "Yeah. Silly, but fun."

"You know what else would be fun?" He tugged her just a little closer.

"What?" She whispered the word.

"This." He closed the distance between them and lowered his lips to hers.

# CHAPTER ELEVEN

ANNA MOVED CLOSER to Sean as his arms encircled her. Was she making the best decision of her life, or the biggest mistake?

Or was it even a decision when she felt so melted, soft and warm, like she had no bones, no tension, no life before or after this moment? This tender kiss?

She lifted her hand to Sean's cheek as his mouth moved over hers, running her knuckles over the stubble of his heavy beard. Through her breathing, a little too fast, she smelled his woodsy, spicy aftershave.

The waves pounded in time with his movements as he pulled her closer and deepened the kiss.

She'd felt nothing like this before. In her marriage, in her few other dates, kissing had felt perfunctory. She'd never felt she deserved the kind of tender treatment women got in romantic movies or books.

But Sean made the kiss feel special in itself. Like he had all the time in the world, and like he wanted to give rather than take. Full of promise, as if the ocean, and Sean, were washing her past away.

Sean made *her* feel special.

Her heart pounded harder as his lips grazed hers, then tasted again more deeply. A blossom inside her unfolded, fragile and soft and new. It could be so easily crushed, but his tenderness nurtured it instead, brought it carefully to life. She was swept into a whole different world. Losing control, with no idea where she was going.

But she couldn't lose control! She jerked back and he let her go immediately, an expression of concern coming onto his face. "What's wrong?"

"I can't... I don't want to..."

"Shhh, it's fine," he said, and ran a gentle hand down her arm, shoulder to wrist. "There's no pressure. I just really enjoyed that."

She had, too. And this wasn't Beau—it was Sean, and though he was new to her and more an acquaintance than a friend, he seemed to care about her.

There was a murmur from the blanket a few feet away, where the girls were sleeping, and she welcomed the chance to check on them. Hayley turned and snuggled closer to her twin, and Anna adjusted the blanket, taking deep breaths, trying to regain control of herself.

That had been the most amazing kiss. She'd never felt so entranced, so cherished, so *melting*.

"Are they okay?" Sean's voice was a low rumble.

"They're fine. We should take them up to the cabin soon, though. It's getting chilly." Though chilly here was nothing like the harshness of Montana, but rather just a quickening in the air.

"Come here a minute." He slid onto the blanket and pulled it half up. "Let me hold you and talk to you just a minute, first."

An irresistible offer when her whole self yearned for more of him. "Okay, for a minute."

He pulled her close to his side and wrapped the top half of the blanket around her shoulders, and she felt the warmth radiating from his big body. Heavenly caring and safety and security.

"What made you so tense?" he asked.

Was he deriding her, scorning her for not falling into his arms, making love on the beach with her girls just feet away? "I…" She shrugged, gestured toward the girls. "Getting carried away is scary. I can't let it happen."

"If I promised that I won't get carried away, and I won't let you, either, would you let me hold you?"

"Oh, Sean…" She turned her face away, but didn't pull away, sort of leaned into him.

He stroked her cheek as gently as you'd stroke a tiny kitten. "You might find this hard to believe," he said, "but I don't want to get carried away, either. This isn't the time or the place, not with your girls right there."

Her tense muscles relaxed as she heard what he said and processed the sincerity in his voice.

"See? This is nice, too." He wrapped his arms loosely around her and pulled her back against his chest. Then he just stroked her arms and hair.

It felt so good to be held. Like nothing she'd ever experienced before. She sighed and relaxed into him.

But after a few minutes, it wasn't enough. She half turned and kissed him lightly.

He drew in a breath and touched her chin, and then he was kissing her more deeply. She could barely breathe. But who wanted to breathe?

He tugged her closer, and for a moment she had a vision of what it would be to make love with him. He was being gentle now, restraining himself, but he wouldn't hold back in the end. She felt the passion that was an inherent part of him. It wasn't far beneath the surface.

*Wow.*

And yet he wasn't putting his hands where they shouldn't be, wasn't trying to propel her into intimacy. He focused all his passion into kissing her and she felt like there was nothing in the world but the place where their mouths met and moved together.

He lifted his head and she opened her eyes to find him smiling at her. "You're an amazing woman," he said, then touched his mouth to hers again.

"You're...pretty amazing, too." She drew in a ragged breath.

The waves pounded on. In the distance, there was the sound of a car motor.

He brushed his lips over hers again. "I could do this all night."

That made her stiffen. "I don't... I can't."

He put a finger to her lips. "Shhh. I didn't mean anything by that. Just telling you how much I liked this. In case you didn't know yet." His voice was low, sexy.

"I could tell." Her voice shook and she knew she needed to back away from him or risk losing logic entirely. She forced herself to pull away, to put inches of cool, safe space between their overheated bodies.

He accepted her withdrawal without protest, and that made her appreciate him all the more. "Should we head back?" he asked.

"We should." And try to figure out how to deal with what had just happened, which would take a steadier state of mind than what she possessed right now.

"If you can carry one of the girls, I can get the other

and all our gear," he said. "Just let me make sure the fire's out."

So he used a cup to get seawater to douse the few remaining embers of the fire while she jammed supplies into the large bag he'd brought. He hoisted the bag onto his back and then knelt to pick up Hayley.

Even that was thoughtful. He could tell that Hayley was more likely to be okay with him carrying her than Hope was.

True sensitivity lurked in this giant man.

She picked up Hope, staggering a little under the weight of her, and Sean was strong enough to steady her, then to kneel and pick up the blanket they'd been lying on and drape it around Hope. He put the other blanket around Hayley, and the girls barely noticed being moved.

Minutes later, they'd laid the girls down in their bed in the cabin. When they slipped out into the front room, she shut the bedroom door behind them and then looked at Sean, her heart rate rising again. Would he kiss her good-night?

She hadn't had a regular dating life. She had no idea how to handle a normal, healthy, developing relationship.

But he didn't look in a kissing mood, not exactly. "This was on the porch," he said, holding up a package. "Looks like it was delivered UPS. Thought I heard a vehicle up here a while back."

She took the package, looked at it. It was addressed to Anna, Hayley and Hope George, and her heart gave a thud, then started to race. Who knew they were here? If Beau had found them…

But when she studied the package more closely, relief washed over her. "It's from my friend Sheila, back in Montana," she said, tapping the return address. "I didn't want her to send anything unless she picked up important mail or something," she said, looking for a knife to open it. "But she wouldn't have addressed it to me and the girls if it were something like that. Wonder if she sent me a present?" It wouldn't be unlike Sheila, who, beneath her issues and swagger, had a heart of gold.

She slid a knife through the package tape and then looked up at Sean. "I'm sorry. You're my guest and here I'm acting like this package is more important than you are. I hadn't realized I was a little homesick until just this minute. Would you like some tea, a soda?"

He smiled. "No. I'm headed home to bed. Except now you've got me curious about your package." He said it lightly, but there was something underneath his words.

She shrugged internally and went back to cutting open the package. Inside were two teddy bears, one pink and one purple. Not pastel, but garishly bright. Anna grinned. That was just like Sheila.

There was another little package, too, gift wrapped, with "Anna" written on it in Sheila's loopy handwriting. She ripped it open.

A heart-shaped metal container was inside, along with a small envelope. The "For My Anna" on the front *wasn't* in Sheila's handwriting. Her heart stuttered.

She slid open the envelope, her hands shaking a little.

The card inside was from Beau.

SEAN WATCHED ANNA drop the card with a gasp. Immediately, he put a steadying hand on her shoulder and sat down beside her. "What's wrong?"

"This card is from my ex." She shoved it away as if it were poison.

"The guy who hurt you?"

Anna nodded, her forehead wrinkled, mouth tight.

Sean glanced into the box, then did a double take. "Did you check these stuffed animals? This…" *Whoa.* There was a heart-shaped container inside the box, made of something that looked like hammered bronze.

Was her ex trying to win her back, her and the girls? Or could there be something dangerous hidden in the animals or the box?

He examined the bears, top to toe, but could find no resewn spots or suspicious lumps. Maybe they were just what they seemed, dollar-store toys.

Anna picked up the card and read it, her lip curling. "He says he's sorry about everything."

"You believe him?"

"No!" She put the card on the end table and shifted it farther from her, a convincing display.

But she didn't shove away the gift.

"You going to open the box?" He wanted to know how she felt about getting a gift from the man. "See what's inside?"

She looked over at him quickly. "What, you think I shouldn't?"

He lifted his hands, palms up. "Your call."

She put the big box down, lifted out the metal heart-shaped box and looked at it for a minute, forehead crinkled, biting her lip.

Then she lifted the lid by one edge as if whatever was inside might jump out and bite her.

She looked. Opened the box wider and looked closer.

He started to lean closer to look.

Anna slammed it shut. "The nerve of him! I can't even believe this." She set the box on the floor and kicked it away from her, arms crossed. "Give me those bears. I'm burning the whole box."

"What was in the heart?"

She opened her mouth and then closed it, caution coming into her eyes. "Just…something he knew would get to me."

Okay, he was officially very curious now. "Is it dangerous?"

"No." She looked away.

His bad gut feeling was getting worse.

His insides twisted as he remembered something he usually tried not to think about: the way his mom had gone back to their father, several times, and always because of things like this: flowers, gifts for the kids, apologies, promises of better future behavior.

As the oldest boy, he'd seen through the gifts starting about age nine. He'd known he didn't want to go back to his dad, definitely didn't want his mom or brothers to go. Had sensed that the gifts were a fake and that their father would end up beating her up again.

She'd seen through the gifts, too, sometimes. But their father had been persistent, and in the end, several times, he'd convinced her. Which had made Sean furious.

Of course, Sean hadn't been looking through the eyes of love the way his mother had. Plus, she'd had three boys to raise on no money, since their father hadn't let her work.

Their father had used material things to get to her. Not that she'd been materialistic, but she wanted food in her kids' stomachs and a roof over their heads, obviously.

His father had always promised them a better life, talked about how he'd take them camping and fishing, teach them to be men. The whole male role model thing.

He hadn't delivered, but he'd promised. His mom seemed to believe his promises to help her kids, at least for a while. She'd been dedicated, trying hard to do the right thing for her boys.

Anna was, likewise, a dedicated mother, raising a couple of kids on very little money.

He wanted to help her, but that was a heartbreak game if she was still attached to her abuser. Worse, if she was still attached, she was very much at risk, and so were her girls. "You know," he said, "sometimes men—abusive ones—use gifts to try to get back on your good side."

She dipped her chin and lifted her eyebrows. "No kidding."

"So just be careful, okay? You don't know what he wants." He was fumbling here; he didn't know quite what to say. He only knew it was important to warn her.

"I have a pretty good idea of his intentions." Her voice had gone cool.

He was making it worse.

The kissing had been awesome, the holding had felt like it could lead somewhere. His heart had gone into stupid mode where he'd basically do anything for the woman he'd given it to.

He wasn't logical and suspicious, like Liam. Wasn't cool and calculating behind a boatload of charm, like Cash.

No, he was a complete marshmallow inside, which was why he'd crafted an image that included excessive muscles and a macho attitude.

If Anna went back to her abuser and took those sweet twins with her... The very thought made his stomach churn.

The same thing could happen to them that had happened to his own family.

His heart rate amped up until his chest felt ready to burst. No way, no way could he let that happen.

Yet he had no control over it, no way to keep her safe if she chose to return.

Thinking about her ex made dangerous rage fire up inside him. He drew deep breaths to get control. His anger was a monster he didn't dare release.

"Look, I can tell you don't want me here, giving you all kinds of advice," he said. "I'll go. But only if you let me call Liam. If he's not on duty, he'll send someone out to patrol here." He tried to smile reassuringly. "Perks of having a cop brother."

She was gnawing on her lip, her eyes filled with confusion, her fingers tapping on the table in a staccato rhythm. What was going on in her head?

She straightened her shoulders, drew in a big breath and let it out with a whoosh. Then she stood up, the clear indication it was time for her guest to leave. "No. No, it's fine. The package spooked me a little, but it was sent through my friend Sheila, so we should be safe from Beau."

Should be safe. He blew out a breath. He wanted her for-sure safe. He was going to insist that Liam keep up a constant patrol here.

"Listen," she said. "I don't want you to feel like you're responsible for me just because of…" She waved a hand toward the beach, her face coloring. "Because of what happened down there. We'll be fine."

He set aside her offhand dismissal of their closeness—it hurt, but he was a grown-up and could deal with it—and made one last attempt. "Listen, I was planning to go scope out some materials at a lumber yard in Columbia for the next few days. But I can postpone the trip if you're nervous. If you think he—" He gestured toward the package, not wanting to dignify the jerk with a name. "If you think he might show up."

Some emotion flashed across her face and then was gone. "No, don't postpone your trip. We'll be just fine."

He opened his mouth to protest.

"Really, Sean. We're fine." She walked over to the door and held it open.

She was impossibly beautiful and vulnerable looking, standing there so upright, chin lifted, eyes firm. If he didn't get out of here *now* he was going to drag her back into his arms.

She lifted an eyebrow, waiting.

"Okay, then," he said. "You have my cell number if you need anything, and I think Tony was going to deliver your car tomorrow morning, right?"

"Right," she said. She tilted her head and gave him an exasperated look. "Sean, we're fine."

"I'll see you in a few days," he said. Forced himself

to turn around and head out of her cabin. Put one leg in front of the other, walking away.

In his mind one question persisted: What had changed her response to him so drastically?

## CHAPTER TWELVE

RITA WIPED THE café's already-clean counter and straight-ened already-organized napkins and silverware as she waited for her friend Norma's arrival. She loved the woman, no question, and they'd been strong supports to each other in Maine. Her visit would probably be great.

It was just that Norma knew why Rita had come to Safe Haven, and she would realize, instantly, that Rita was doing nothing to pursue her goals. No way could Rita distract her for the entire week of her visit.

Thing was, the bad possibilities had gotten more vivid to Rita since she'd moved here. What if her child had been taken away from her by social services? What if she'd been an unfit mom, even a criminal?

But ambivalence wouldn't wash with Norma. She was direct and blunt and sure of herself, and she'd push Rita further than she necessarily wanted to go.

Still, when she looked out the window and saw Norma's aqua-blue vintage Plymouth Falcon, top down, her friend grinning and waving from the driver's seat, she couldn't restrain her own big smile.

Leaving your home behind, everything and every-one you'd known for twenty years, was exciting, and it was working out well. But there was a lot of loss, too.

She ran out into the parking lot and caught Norma

just as she was getting out of her car. "You came! I didn't know if you really would!"

Norma hugged her close, then put hands on her shoulders to hold her at arm's length. "Let me look at you." She cocked her head to one side, swooped her eyes down Rita from head to toe, then back up. And then she smiled. "This place agrees with you," she said. "Must be all the sunshine. I want me some of that."

"Come in. I'm working until six." She slung an arm around Norma, escorted her inside and sat her down at the counter next to Pudge LeFrost and his son. "I'll bring you a milkshake. You've lost weight." She studied her friend. "You're okay?"

"I'm fine. Just skinny." Of course, there was a lot Norma wasn't saying, a lot they had to catch up on. Norma had been diagnosed with stage three breast cancer a couple of years ago, and the treatments had been rough. Hopefully, though, her remission would last.

Rita hurried around to her tables, taking care of everyone, explaining about her best friend, and soon lots of people were talking to Norma. Which was good. Rita was hoping that, once Norma saw what it was like here, she might move down. Not much keeping her up North at this point.

Claire sat at the counter, too, eating salad, so Rita leaned over to her. "Make sure Norma is okay," she said, knowing Claire liked to make herself useful and had never met a stranger.

"Yes, ma'am. We're walking tomorrow, right?"

"Wouldn't miss it. As long as I can bring Norma along."

"I don't have the wind I used to," Norma admitted.

"Quitting smoking would help."

LOW COUNTRY HERO

Norma stuck out her tongue. "Know-it-all."

Next, Jimmy came out of the kitchen and Rita introduced him, hoping her face didn't color up too much. She focused on Norma. "She's a therapist who took early retirement," she explained. "Hoping she might see fit to move down here."

Jimmy smiled at her, raising a "hang on" hand to someone calling him from the kitchen. "It's a good place for a new beginning. Nice to meet you."

As soon as Jimmy went back behind the counter, Norma tugged Rita closer and whispered in her ear. "'Bout time you found a man your own age." She was grinning broadly.

"I didn't find him and he's not my man," Rita said, keeping her voice low.

Norma just laughed. "Don't forget, I'm trained to see past all those defenses. We'll talk."

And they did, as soon as Rita's shift ended and she was free to ride back to her apartment with Norma.

"Your new friends seem nice," Norma said. "That Claire, she's a talker, but sweet. Pretty, too. Just needs someone to tell her not to wear those flowered leggings. Skintight patterns aren't a good look on anyone."

"I don't understand half of what young women wear these days," Rita admitted.

"No kidding," Norma said bluntly. "You're on the opposite end of the scale. You're too pretty to dress as old as you do."

She guessed Norma had earned the right to give her advice, since she'd been the one to counsel Rita through the early days of her amnesia. Norma could have made the big bucks in private practice, but she'd chosen to be the psychologist for a low-income health center. After their clinical relationship was over, they'd become good friends.

Rita led the way to her apartment and ushered Norma in, setting the woman's small suitcase in the guest room, and then she came back out. "Listen to yourself," she said. "You've got criticism for what Claire wears and what I wear. While you..." She gestured at Norma's plain shirt and shapeless jeans. "You're not one to talk, you know?"

"I'm not looking to attract a man," Norma said bluntly. "That's all over for me."

"We've talked about that. It doesn't have to be. A good man will look past your cancer scars."

"I'll believe it when I see it. Anyway, this talk isn't about me—it's about you. What's going on between you and your hot boss?"

"Nothing."

"Really?" Norma raised a questioning eyebrow.

"Well, not *nothing*," Rita amended, her face warming. "I just... I'm not ready." She opened her fridge and pulled out a beer and a pitcher of sweet tea. "Drink?"

"I'll take tea, and you're changing the subject."

"Maybe I am."

Norma took the cold glass of tea and sat down at Rita's little kitchen table. "I'm glad to see you all set up here. Place came furnished, did it?"

"Yep. The decor's not half-bad, and the furniture's comfortable. That's all I need."

Norma looked around thoughtfully. "It's as nice as what you had with T-Bone."

"Which wasn't really me, either." She'd cleaned up the place from T-Bone's bachelor days, but had never put her own decorating stamp on it.

Hard to do when she didn't really know her own style, nor anything else about her past.

"Anyway, about you and men," Norma continued, "what you had with T-Bone wasn't really a marriage, not at the end. You were his nurse."

Rita didn't deny it. "I was his wife. That's what you do. Caring for him when he's sick is part of it."

"Yeah," Norma said, "except you *weren't* his regular wife, just common law, until the very end. Yet you did more for him than a lot of wives would do. Kept him at home when everyone was telling you to put him in a convalescent center."

Rita pulled out a chair and leaned forward, elbows on the table. "You know why. T-Bone saved me from dying. Nursed me around the clock when I was completely out of my mind with that head injury. Changed my bandages and carried me to the bathroom and spooned chicken broth and Jell-O into my mouth. You don't think I should have taken care of him when he got sick?"

Norma took a pack of cigarettes out of her pocket.

Rita glared at her.

"I know, not in here."

"Not *anywhere*! You're a cancer survivor."

"I know, I know. I'm trying to quit."

Rita rolled her eyes.

"Anyway, yes, T-Bone did a lot for you, but he got plenty out of it. He wasn't the sharpest tool in the shed, and he wasn't exactly a looker. When he found you on the side of that road, he knew it was the best he'd ever get."

"Norma! T-Bone had plenty of smarts. He could fix anything with a motor, and he could grow anything, nurse any dead plant back to life. It doesn't matter he wasn't handsome."

"Maybe not, but looks were sure important to *him*. Your looks, I mean. He loved that you were pretty. Bragged about you all the time."

"He had the right. He helped to make me that way, all those plastic surgeries to fix my face. That's half the reason he didn't have money. He spent it on me." She looked down at the table. "I miss the man, even though I know he's in a better place."

Norma snorted. "Saint Peter had to order him a supersized robe and pair of wings. But that's not the point."

"What exactly *is* the point?"

"Point is you haven't ever had a real, good-looking man you chose yourself. So grab on to this Jimmy while you can, girl!"

"I don't know that I never had a handsome man before. I don't know *what* I had before." Rita sighed. "When you and I worked together, I got to the place where it didn't matter. And then T-Bone told me he'd actually found me here. Not on a deserted stretch of highway like he'd always said."

"Which is why I can't swear that he had a good heart. Who keeps the facts from someone with amnesia?"

"He said he knew I'd come back," she said, staring down at the table. "Because I'd wonder about my child."

"Of course you would! And rightly so."

*But what kind of mother doesn't remember her own child?*

"He was afraid I'd be killed if I came back. That my abuser would find me again. That's what he told me."

"Here's what I think," Norma said. "I think he was afraid he'd lose the best thing that ever happened to him. T-Bone took care of T-Bone. And that's why I'll be really happy when you jump into an affair with Mr. Tatted Restaurant Manager. It would do you good."

"We'll see." There was a part of Rita that felt the same way, but another part couldn't stomach the notion. T-Bone and her closest friends in Maine had known about her condition. People here didn't. An amnesiac was a freak. And if she got into a dating relationship, where you talked about your life and your history, the awful gaps in her self-knowledge would have to come out. Wouldn't they?

"So tell me what you've done to find out the truth, since you've been here."

Rita pulled cheese out of the fridge, crackers from a cupboard. "I'm scoping things out. Getting the vibe of the place."

Norma raised an eyebrow. "Vibes. What does that mean?"

"I walk around town and there are spots that seem more familiar. Spots that make me feel upset, actually." She poured more tea for Norma.

"Thanks. What kind of spots are bringing up your memories?"

"The women's shelter, couple of shops on the main street."

Norma leaned forward. "That's interesting. Have you talked to the people at those places? Does anyone remember you?"

Rita shook her head. "Twenty years later, the same people aren't going to be working there."

"But they might know who came before them. They could have records. And that shelter…" Norma narrowed her eyes. "Condition you were in when T-Bone found you, it would make sense if you'd turned to them."

"I know." Rita took a sip of tea and then shoved it

aside, opened the refrigerator door and pulled out a beer. She opened it up and took a long pull.

"Or how about the local library?" Norma persisted. "Do they have information from back then? Old newspapers stored digitally? And your Jimmy might know some old-timers who remember those days."

This was why she didn't really want Norma here. Norma was sharp, brilliant actually, and persistent. But almost as soon as Rita had arrived in Safe Haven, she'd realized that she didn't want to think about her past. Didn't want to know the truth.

And that in itself could be a key, right? Deep inside, she might know something horrible about herself.

Chiefly, that she'd had a child, but that child hadn't been with her when T-Bone had found her.

And although over the years she'd asked him to give her a specific location for where she was found, he hadn't done it. Had waved a hand and told her it was out in the country, away from any town.

Only when he was dying had he revealed that he'd found her just outside Safe Haven.

Having Norma here might force her to bring things to a head. Which was good, but not good, when you were this afraid of what you might find.

AFTER THE SCARE of receiving the bears and too-intimate gift from Beau, Anna had to make sure she and her girls were safe.

And she couldn't involve Sean. The note that had been on top of the lingerie in the heart-shaped box had made that clear: "Remember, you're mine, all mine."

She'd unintentionally pricked Beau's jealousy before, and the results had been ugly. Now that she'd upped the ante by leaving him—no. She couldn't put Sean at risk by getting him involved in her messed-up life.

The first step was to get the offending package out of the cabin, which she did as soon as she'd gotten back from dropping off the girls at Ma Dixie's. She'd had a moment's qualm about throwing away the teddy bears, since the girls had so few toys here. But she couldn't risk Beau somehow getting to them. What if he'd drugged the bears? Her heart raced, faster and faster. What if he'd put a camera or GPS in them, as she'd once seen done on a television show?

And if none of those rather outlandish things had happened, she still couldn't risk the girls starting to miss Beau and have warm feelings toward him. She wouldn't directly bad-mouth him, since he was their father, but she wasn't going to facilitate any kind of closeness.

She didn't even take a second look at the lacy lingerie Beau had sent her. The very notion of wearing it made her cringe inside.

There was some brush that needed to be burned. She started the fire, and when it was going strong, she threw the bears, then the lingerie on top and watched it burn.

She'd gotten lulled into a false sense of security having Sean there, but she couldn't count on him. Not without putting him at risk.

After working all afternoon and then picking up the girls from the library program, she was tempted to stay in town to eat at the little diner, knowing how dark and deserted the Sea Pine Cottages got at night. But she didn't really have the money for meals out. And she needed to be brave.

She hadn't realized, until now, that the isolated resort had felt safe because Sean was there for protection. But that wasn't good. Relying on a man was a mistake.

They'd be fine there, she and the girls, even without Sean around. But even though the box hadn't come directly from Beau, but from Sheila, it had spooked her. It would be better to be safe and sound inside the cabin before it got dark.

By the time they'd stopped to get gas and groceries, darkness was falling. Her nerves tensed, but then she glanced down the row of cottages and she saw a light on in Sean's place.

Hope rose within her. The fact that he was still here made her feel a hundred times more safe.

It also made her want to talk to him, be near him. He'd kissed her so tenderly, so sweetly and with such promise. She'd never felt so cherished.

As she helped the girls bathe and get into their pajamas, she dithered about whether or not to text him. She'd insisted that he leave because she didn't want to put him at risk from Beau's jealousy. But how likely was it that Beau would find them here? And how likely was it that he could somehow hurt Sean—giant, competent, muscular Sean?

*Be a grown-up. You decided to back off from him.*
*But what if I made a mistake?*

Before she could lose heart, she sent a note:

Could you come over for a few? Need to talk.

Almost immediately she got a text back:

I'm in Columbia. Something wrong?

Fear clamped her insides. If it wasn't Sean in his place, then who was it? She was pretty sure she'd seen a light go off and another go on.

She searched around and found her pepper spray—
how lax she'd gotten, that she didn't have it handy—
and shoved it in her pocket. Made sure the doors were
locked, the windows, too.

Then she texted him back:

There's someone in your cabin.

I asked Tony to stay.

Oh. Relief coursed through her, to learn that it wasn't
some stranger or intruder inhabiting Sean's cabin.

Know you don't like him, but he's reliable. Texting his
contact information in case you need something.

A few seconds later the shared contact came in.

Got it. Thanks.

She clicked her phone off.

Her emotions were in turmoil. She was grateful that
Sean had cared enough to plant a bodyguard when he
was gone, even if that bodyguard was Tony. But there
was no warmth in his texts, no emotion.

She sighed. It seemed like he'd taken her coolness
to heart, when in fact it had been manufactured out of
worry about him. But maybe he'd been relieved by her
distance. Maybe he hadn't wanted to stay connected.

All her old feelings of not being enough, of being
in the way, of no good man wanting her, came back to
her, making her heart ache in a familiar, hollow way.

She ignored it and read to the girls, tucked them into

bed and kissed them good-night, and as always, being around them made her priorities crystal clear.

Her own longings notwithstanding, she couldn't focus on Sean. She had to figure out some ways to make herself and the girls safer at home, whether home was this cabin or somewhere else down the road.

First step: she contacted her friend Sheila, again, to ask about the package. This time, she got a sheepish message back. Yes, Beau had approached her about sending gifts to them. She hadn't seen the harm. He didn't have the address, no way—she hadn't given it to him.

But he really was sorry about their last fight, and he missed them all terribly.

Sheila, Sheila, Sheila.

Anna reiterated that Sheila wasn't, under any circumstances, to reveal Anna's location. But when she clicked away from the message she was still worried.

Beau was obviously getting to Sheila. Gaining her sympathy, and he was good at that—he had his charming side.

And Sheila had weaknesses: she liked drinking and partying and handsome men. Beau could appeal to those tastes for his own ends.

So she had to stay ready to move at any time. And she had to rely on herself. Just like always.

She used her phone to search online, and once she'd scrolled past all the ads for home security alarm systems, she got into list after list of safety measures you could take on your own. Most of them were for people who owned their own homes: install lights and motion sensors, remove outdoor hidden keys, hide objects attractive to thieves. Things she couldn't do.

But she could install locks or bars on the windows

here. And maybe, she could get a dog. Not a purebred puppy, of course—she couldn't afford that—but a rescue who needed a home.

The thought of that filled her with hope. She'd always liked dogs, had befriended neighborhood ones and covertly fed strays. Beau had refused her request to get a dog, but she knew his secret reason: he was afraid of them.

She called Miss Vi and then Ma Dixie, figuring they'd know how she could get a dog on the cheap. Sure enough, both had some good leads. And then, after checking the doors and windows one more time and fielding a text from Tony, checking on her, she climbed into bed.

And lay there hoping against hope that her fears were wrong, that Beau was getting over her, and that they'd be able to stay in Safe Haven.

SEAN'S WORK KEPT him away the entire week, but by Saturday morning, he'd settled back into his cabin. He needed to double down on the renovations. The owner had toured the place last weekend and gotten excited: maybe they could have a grand opening later this summer, get some business for fall.

Which meant he had to hustle. But the good news was, it was the weekend. Anna wouldn't be here working with him.

He'd checked in with Tony and learned that Anna and the girls were fine. No strange visitors, no graffiti or other threatening messages, at least not that Tony could see. They all seemed fine, happy.

It was unseasonably hot, and before long he'd

stripped off his shirt and was taking satisfaction in digging out a row of heavy-rooted shrubs.

He'd dodged a bullet with Anna. He'd been so close to getting involved. Her ex's package had arrived at just the right moment to remind Sean of lessons he'd learned in the past.

He'd seen his mother return to his father, time after time. He couldn't bear to see Anna do the same, putting herself and the twins at risk.

He was on the last shrub when he heard it: the high, happy laughter of the twins.

He'd hoped to avoid them, still planned to, but he couldn't resist walking over to where he could get a clear sight line to the beach where the sound had come from.

The girls were there, playing happily in the shallow water, digging with buckets and dancing with the surf, dressed in matching red swimsuits.

And Anna was in her swimsuit, too: a black bikini. Modest by some standards, but as she laughed down at one of the twins, and then lifted her high in the air, Sean swallowed hard.

He'd sort of known she had a gorgeous body under the baggy clothes she wore. He just hadn't known *how* gorgeous. He dropped his shovel and walked a few steps closer, drawn like a magnet.

Any husband would be an idiot to let a woman like Anna go. No wonder her jerk of an ex had seen sense and decided to woo her back by sending gifts.

He forced himself to turn away from the sunshine and beauty and cuteness before him and go back to his manual labor. Got into it harder, working up a sweat.

He felt good ripping things out of the earth, using his muscles.

It kept his mind away from the question Ma Dixie had asked him earlier today: If you're not going to let love into your life again, what exactly do you have to look forward to?

The truth was, right now, not much. But everyone was entitled to a down stretch. Normally he looked forward to playing poker with his buddies, or, now that he was back in town, having a beer at the Pig with old friends, or breakfast at the café with Liam and Cash. Normally, he enjoyed running his business and felt satisfied turning plain wood into buildings, homes for people, new decks and porches. Taking things that were old and ugly and making them nice again, whether in Knoxville or here in Safe Haven.

An earsplitting scream pierced the dense, humid air and he dropped his shovel and sprinted toward the ocean, toward the sound. Had her ex gotten to them, done something awful?

When he saw the three females alone and looking unharmed, his heart rate settled, but still, he jogged toward them. Anna was holding Hope on her lap as she sobbed, while Hayley stood pointing at something on the beach and screaming.

Anna said something sharp to Hayley and she stopped screaming—thank heavens—lapsing down instead into a sobbing heap.

"What happened?" he asked when he got there.

Anna jolted, her arms tightening around Hope, and looked up at him. She drew in a breath, her shoulders relaxing a little.

"She stepped on a jellyfish and it stung her," Anna

explained, examining Hope's foot. "I don't know what to do about it, and I left my phone in the cabin, so I can't google it. Do you know?"

He knelt, examined the sting and nodded. "We got stung all the time, as kids. Most of the jellyfish around here aren't dangerous. But it hurts, doesn't it, honey?" He ruffled Hope's hair.

Hope looked up at him, teary eyed.

"I'll pull the stingers out," he offered.

"No!" Hope tucked her feet under her, which must have jiggled the stingers, because she cried harder. "Mommy do it."

Sean glanced at Anna. "Better if I do, because there's a trick to getting them out without getting stabbed yourself." He smiled at Hope. "Did you ever see a movie that had a magician in it?"

She nodded, tears rolling down her rosy cheeks, lower lip sticking out.

"And did you know it's really important to believe in the magic?"

She narrowed her eyes, then nodded once.

"Well," he said, calling up a trick from elementary school days. "I have a little magic, and it's because I have eleven fingers. Want to see?"

Hope frowned, forgetting to cry. "You have *ten* fingers. Everybody does."

"Not me." He counted, using his forefinger: "One, two, three, four, five—" he switched to the other hand "—six, seven, eight, nine, ten. That's funny." He twisted his features into a puzzled frown. "Let me try again. Ten, nine, eight, seven, six… Okay, six on this hand." He switched to the other. "Five, four, three, two, one. Five on this hand. Six and five is eleven."

Hope's forehead furrowed as she studied his hands and tried to puzzle out what he was saying.

"That extra finger means I can make things not hurt." He glanced at Anna, who was fighting a smile. "Distract her?"

"Yeah." Anna gently straightened Hope's leg. "What we're going to do," she said, reaching up to include Hayley in the circle, "is to make up a story about a jellyfish. We'll start it here, and then finish it at home, and you can draw pictures. When we're done, you can show it at Ma Dixie's tomorrow so everyone can see what happened."

"And that we were brave," Hayley said. "That's how we should start it—we were brave." She patted Hope's hand. "You're brave."

"That's a good idea, and you're both very brave," Sean murmured, plucking out stingers. He'd had a ton of practice doing this, having helped his younger brothers many times, and done it to himself, as well.

"I don't want… Ouch!" Hope cried.

"All done," he said.

Anna turned toward him, a relieved smile creasing her face. "Really? Already? Thank you so much! What else should I do for it?"

"Nothing better than salt water. Some antibiotic ointment when you get back home, if you have some."

"Come on, Hope. Let's go in the water again!" Hayley was done being sympathetic.

Hope's lower lip stuck out, and then she looked up at Anna as if assessing how much attention she could get by making a big deal of a sting that Sean could guarantee barely hurt anymore.

"Go on," Anna said. "You're all better. I'll walk down with you."

"Okay," Hope said, and walked down with her mom holding hands, Hayley several yards in front of them.

Sean just sat there in the sand, watching. He couldn't take his eyes off her, couldn't help checking her out.

She was so pretty. And such a good mom. And, yeah, there was a chance she'd end up back with her husband, but even knowing that, Sean was only human.

He wanted her, not just her body but the whole package, the person she was.

After watching the girls for a few minutes, Anna turned and came back, brushing the hair out of her eyes with a self-conscious gesture. "Thanks for helping Hope," she said. "I didn't have a clue what to do. I was scared it was poisonous." She grinned. "Although, since you have eleven magical fingers..." Her eyes skimmed over him and darkened.

At that point he realized he had no shirt on and that he was slick with sweat. As was Anna.

When their eyes met, heat and desire sparked between them.

Finally she looked away and cleared her throat. "Um, so. Do you think that critter is poisonous?"

He pulled his mind back to the present moment. "Not so much, not around here," he said. He forced himself to look down the beach, out to sea. "Happens to every kid," he added. "They'll watch out for the jellyfish now."

"I think they're disgusting," Anna admitted, wrinkling her nose. "That's one thing we didn't have in Montana."

"Yeah."

Their conversation went on, but Sean could barely

focus and he had the feeling that the same was true for Anna. He kept stealing glances at her, and a couple of times, he caught her looking at him, too.

It even seemed like she was *enjoying* looking at him, and that tantalized him, in addition to being a little flattering.

And that made him think back to kissing her, practically on this very spot. She'd seemed to enjoy that, too.

"Sean?" Her curious expression made him realize he'd dropped the thread of the conversation.

He'd been thinking with his body, which wasn't cool. "You know what? I'm going to dip in the ocean, wash off the sand." He stood quickly and jogged down to the water and right in until he was waist deep.

It was the cold-water jolt he needed. His brain reactivated and with it, his sense of caution.

He'd rinse off, make sure Hope's foot was okay and then head back to his work and then his cabin. No harm, no foul.

As he walked out of the water, though, Hayley grabbed his hand. Not to be outdone, Hope ran over to his other side and grabbed that hand.

And God help him, he couldn't bring himself to shake them off. "How's your foot feel?" he asked Hope.

"My foot?" She looked at him blankly. Best sign possible.

"Your jellyfish foot, silly!" He restrained a laugh. She'd forgotten. Kids were amazing that way, so resilient, so in the moment.

"Oh!" She frowned down at the wrong foot. "It's fine, I think."

He nodded gravely. "That's good. You have a very fast-healing foot."

Hope beamed and squeezed his hand, and the simple confidence in that gesture made Sean's breath stutter.

They were approaching Anna, who was watching with eyes wide and shiny. And then he realized that the girls were talking to him as naturally as if they'd been doing it their whole lives.

He'd made it into the inner circle, apparently.

"Guess what?" Hayley tugged at his hand. "We're getting a dog!"

"Yeah!" Hope dropped his hand to dance around in excited circles. "For 'tection, so a big one."

"Want to come look at it with us?"

Anna clapped a hand to her forehead. "I am so sorry. I should have checked with you about whether dogs are even allowed here."

Sean was still processing the for-protection idea. "Tony got permission to bring his dog, when he stayed here a while back," he said. "Eldora loves 'em. If a dog will make you feel safer, go for it."

The girls cheered and danced around, giving Sean the chance to move closer to Anna. "Any more packages?" he asked.

She shook her head, tiny wrinkles appearing between her eyebrows.

Hayley sank down in front of him. "Will you come with us to get the dog?"

"Yeah, will you?" Hope added, flopping down beside her twin. Then both girls stared at him with wide eyes, obviously planning to put on the pressure until he gave in.

He glanced over at Anna.

She shrugged, a grin tugging the corner of her mouth, probably because she could see the twins' tactics were working on him. "You're welcome to come. We're going around four this afternoon."

"Well…" The thought was appealing, but he shouldn't get any more involved with Anna and the twins.

"You can give us feedback on a good Southern dog, one that'll be okay here."

It sounded like she really wanted him to come, and that undid him. And after all, it wasn't as if he had something else to do on a Saturday afternoon. Maybe he'd even take them to dinner.

*Just don't get too close*, he reminded himself.

"We should go back up to the cabins and shower," Anna said to the girls. Then she glanced over at him. "I should have brought us cover-ups. I was thinking we had the place to ourselves."

He met her eyes, held them. "Believe me, I'm not upset."

Her cheeks went pink. "Girls! Come on."

He scrambled to his feet and followed. "And I'd be glad to come along on your dog shopping trip," he added.

Even as he scolded himself for being a fool.

THE NEXT SATURDAY, dressed in her waitress uniform, in front of her apartment building, Rita hugged her friend Norma with mixed feelings. "You've been a royal pain in the behind this week," she said, "but I'll miss you."

"Same." Norma hugged her back. "Look out, or I might get sick of that cold Maine weather and move here."

"I wish you would. I could help you find a place." Rita put her hands on Norma's shoulders and studied her. Norma would be so pretty if she'd make half an effort. But Rita knew better than to bring that up.

Around them, the streets were busy with Saturday-morning activity. Up the street, someone who looked like Claire was headed in their direction.

"If you don't get moving on your own behalf, I will." Norma glared. "You know what I mean. Take some steps to find out what happened to you."

The very idea made chilly fingers squeeze Rita's insides. And the dread was getting worse, not better. "Not your problem."

"It *is* my problem." Norma frowned. "You stood by me when I was sick with cancer, and I'll stand by you now. Whether you want me to or not."

"Get on out of here." Rita forced a laugh and gave Norma a gentle shove. "I gotta get to work."

Norma closed her car's trunk and walked over to the driver's side. "Speaking of your job, you ought to take the plunge with that Jimmy," she said. "He's interested. I could see it."

"I doubt that." Rita said it automatically, although she knew he was; he'd asked her out. And the notion hyped up her pulse a little bit. "Go on! I'm sick of your advice."

There was the sound of a gulp and crying behind her, and Rita turned to see Claire hurrying down the sidewalk, tears streaming down her face.

Strange sight, when Claire was usually so upbeat. Rita moved toward the younger woman, one arm extended. "Honey, what's wrong?"

But Claire didn't look in Rita's direction. She practically ran by, headed toward the main street of town.

Rita looked back down the street from which Claire had come, and the likely source of the problem was right there: Brandi. Along with a couple of other women, all thin and blonde, looking after Claire and talking and laughing.

Norma was looking in the same direction. She lifted an eyebrow at Rita. "Mean girls?"

"Uh-huh. Move here, and you can help me get rid of them."

"I'd like to." Norma reached out and gave Rita another hug, the smell of cigarette smoke matching her husky voice. "I miss you, girl."

"Miss you, too. Now, go on. And quit smoking, okay?"

Norma snorted, slid into her car and drove off.

Rita continued the rest of the way to work, soaking in the small-town vibe she was coming to like: a group of old men talking on the sidewalk, two teenagers walking identical little white dogs, an old truck proclaiming the merits of Shrimpy's Shrimp Company puttering down in the direction of the docks. A soft sea breeze kissed her face.

She could like it here without delving into the past, couldn't she? There was no need to dig up all kinds of old news and finished business. Lots of people visited Safe Haven, or moved there, drawn by the nearby beaches and the friendliness. She could just be one of those people.

But her own stream of thoughts made shame burn in her. Cowardice, that's what it was. Fear of what she might discover about herself. What if she found out who her child was and barged into his life, or hers, and disrupted everything? What kind of mother was she, anyway, that she didn't even remember whether she'd birthed a boy or a girl?

She shook off her thoughts as she reached the café and saw Claire sitting at the counter. That was Rita's station today, so after she put on her apron and clocked in, she headed over. "Anyone wait on you yet, honey?"

"No, ma'am." Claire forced a smile.

"What can I get you?"

"Pie à la mode. Pecan."

"Good choice. Abel puts a little extra magic into his pies. Coffee to go with?"

"Sweet tea, please."

That sounded like a horrible combination, but there was no accounting for tastes. Rita brought Claire her pie and tea, and then leaned on the counter. "You okay? Saw you headed this way and got the impression you were upset."

"Nothing sugar won't cure." Again the younger woman forced a smile, but Rita could hear the hurt in her voice.

"Sometimes women are the worst," Rita said as Claire took delicate bites. "I don't want to pry, but I saw that little clique hanging around in front of the boutique. That kind doesn't have anything better to do than pick on other women. They ought to be ashamed."

Claire sighed. "Well, and I ought to lose weight. They're right about that…"

"Is that what they were on you about?" Rita huffed out a breath. "That's ridiculous. There's all kinds of beautiful, and seems to me there's a man to appreciate every kind." Her heart ached for the young woman. "I remember when I worried about what I looked like. Chipped teeth and a broken nose, and I felt like everyone who saw me knew the rough way I'd been treated."

"You?" Claire looked disbelievingly at Rita. "You're

so pretty." She finished the last bite of pie and shoved the plate away. "I shouldn't have eaten that. I gotta go to work. No doubt the skinny gals will come in to buy their yogurt and Diet Coke and they'll have plenty to say."

"Then go fix yourself up before you leave," Rita said. "Wash your face. You don't have to dress to please anyone but yourself, but you do need to wear what you like, and hold your head high. A little makeup wouldn't hurt, either."

"Thanks, *Mom*." Claire stood and turned toward the ladies' room, then glanced back at Rita. "Seriously. I'm glad you moved here."

As Claire walked toward the ladies' room, Rita came around the edge of the counter and sank down onto a stool. That word—*Mom*—had hit her like a knife, ripping open her guts.

Someone had called her "Mom" before.

Someone she'd taken care of that way—told how to behave, given advice and a pat on the shoulder.

She'd been a mom before.

She'd known it intellectually, but she'd never *felt* it until now. Pain cut through her, taking her breath away with its sharpness. What had happened? What had she lost? And who had nurtured her child once she'd gotten her amnesia?

Had she done something awful, to lose custody of her own child?

Shortly after waking up in Maine, she'd learned that she'd given birth. The hospital that had treated her could tell, and later, her gynecologist had confirmed it. But she'd never known if she'd raised the child, never remembered anything about it.

Until now.

And all because a friend had made an offhand joke: *Thanks, Mom.*

"Taking the afternoon off?" Jimmy's teasing voice brought Rita out of her reverie.

She slid off the stool, shaking the memories away. "I'm sorry. Just spacing out."

"You're allowed." He stood beside her, close, and she could see every hair on his muscular arm, every bit of ink in his tat, and it made her warm. "We're not busy. Sit down. What's giving you that million-miles-away look?"

"Just…the past." There was no way she could explain her issues to Jimmy. It wouldn't make sense to anyone, except possibly Norma.

He squeezed her shoulder, quick and somehow personal. "Just don't hang out there too long. There's a whole world in the present moment and a whole future ahead of you."

Good advice, but hard to put into practice, she thought, watching him walk away. He shared an easy laugh with Rip Martin, a next-to-homeless guy who stopped in often for coffee and a hot meal. For free, she'd learned when Jimmy had taken Rip's check from her and ripped it up, one day when she was waiting counter.

Jimmy was a good man.

She was wiping off the counter when she noticed one of her customers, a younger guy named Sean, walking by with a woman and two cute girls, along with a big black Lab that kept pulling on the leash.

Funny, she'd had the impression Sean was single.

Not so funny: seeing him and his young family made her feel somehow sadder.

She blew out a sigh. She had to find out what had happened to her. Had to take more steps to figure it out, because Norma was right. For her own peace of mind, she needed to know the truth, even if the truth made her completely miserable rather than setting her free.

Hard to know where to start, but the image that kept popping into her mind was Abel's face, his wise, all-knowing eyes. She couldn't put off talking to him forever, out of cowardice.

She'd find a time to speak with him, she told herself firmly. Sooner, rather than later. Maybe even today.

# CHAPTER THIRTEEN

ANNA AND THE twins were walking out of the grocery Sunday afternoon when a high-pitched scream pierced the air, sending bolts of panic through Anna's chest.

"My car! Somebody trashed my car!"

It was the friendly cashier, Claire, examining her car almost directly in front of them. "Stay here and watch the groceries," Anna told the twins, and hurried a few steps to reach the distressed young woman.

Her car was spray painted with ugly words—the same words that had been on Anna's cabin, plus additional slurs related to Claire's weight—and her tires were slashed.

Anna's stomach churned at the similarity. Had Beau been here? Had he mistaken Claire's car for Anna's?

"That shrew! I can't believe she went this far!"

Belatedly, Anna took in Claire's angry words. "Who do you think did it?"

"I *know* who did it. It's Brandi."

"Why do you think so?"

"Because she hates me." Claire was crying, kneeling to run a finger along a ruined tire. "We have a history a mile long. Plus, she thinks I'm out to steal Tony."

Anna put a hand on the younger woman's arm. "Stop touching it. Don't destroy evidence."

"Oh, what does it matter?" Claire sat down on the curb, wiping tears. "She'll get away with it."

"Not necessarily." Anna glanced back to give the girls a thumbs-up—they were sitting beside the groceries, watching the scenario with interest but without apparent fear—and turned back to Claire. "I had similar vandalism on my cabin out at the park. I just got everything fixed without talking to the cops, and Liam yelled at me. Said he could've done something with prints and paint if we'd waited."

"Everyone will see!" Claire buried her face in her hands.

"I'm calling the police." Anna pulled out her phone, dialed 911 and explained the situation.

Behind them, people were starting to gather around, including one of Claire's cousins, who hurried to put an arm around the crying woman. Anna returned to give her girls a simplified explanation. Within two or three minutes, Liam was on the scene.

After he'd spoken to Claire, he surveyed the crowd for witnesses. When there weren't any, Anna spoke up, reminding him of the almost-identical vandalism against her.

As she was talking to Liam, Anna's eyes were drawn to Sean's truck, driving by and then pulling into a parking place. She scolded herself for the little jump in her chest.

But she couldn't help it: she was exquisitely conscious of him climbing out of his vehicle and walking in her direction. He wore an olive green work T-shirt, but she couldn't forget the way he'd looked without it, when he'd come to help them at the beach.

Something must have shone in her eyes, because Liam glanced back just in time to see Sean approach them.

"Everything okay?" Sean asked. "What's going on?"

"Look at my car," Claire said. "It's ruined!"

Sean looked at the car, gave a low whistle and then looked at Anna. "A little too familiar."

"Right?" She was grateful that he saw the same thing she did. "Claire thinks it's Brandi."

Could Brandi have vandalized Anna's car, too? Could it have been her, not Beau, all along? But that didn't make sense.

Sean cocked his head to one side. "But what would she have against both you and Claire?" Then he and Liam looked at each other. "Oh."

"What?" Anna demanded.

"She's pathologically jealous," Sean said. "Always thinking someone's after Tony. That's what three-quarters of their fights were about. She always thinks he's cheating."

Liam turned to Claire. "Have you had any contact with Brandi?"

"Yes, sir," she said. "She's been harassing me for the past few days."

"Did anything happen before that?"

Claire frowned. "He helped me change my tire last week, and then we went for a drink. Totally as friends."

"That would do it," Sean said. "Brandi's kind of... one-track about that stuff."

"'One-track' is a nice way to put it," one of the by-standers said. "That girl's simple."

"We'll investigate." Liam turned to Anna. "What dealings have you had with Tony's ex?"

"I don't really know her," Anna said. "I saw her once,

when she and Tony were fighting outside a bar." She looked over at Sean. "You were there, remember? And she came back down the street and spoke to me in front of the library."

"What did she say?"

Anna frowned. "She said something like... Oh." Realization dawned. "She said to stay away from her man."

Liam and Sean exchanged glances. "I'll be in touch," Liam said. He waved a hand. "Nothing to see here, folks. Carry on with your lives."

"Us, too?" Sean asked.

Liam nodded. "I'll give you a call later."

Sean walked over to the twins, even ahead of Anna, knelt down and made like he was going to take something from their grocery bags.

"Mr. Sean, stop!" Hayley said, giggling. Then she clapped a hand over her mouth, looking around at the bystanders.

Anna approached them then, her heart full. They hadn't gotten scared. In fact, Hayley was inches away from being able to talk in a general public situation, and Hope wasn't far behind her.

And a good part of it had to do with the gentle giant before them.

The best news was that the vandalism hadn't been done by Beau. Relief rolled over her like cool ocean waves.

If the vandal had been Brandi, then she'd be caught and Anna was free.

Beau had sent that package, yes, but when she thought about it, the approach there had been penitence, not violence. Was it possible that he'd changed?

That their leaving had affected him, made him see the error of his ways?

She couldn't completely let down her guard, and no way would she contact him, but now she had hope. Hope that she'd be able to start over without the shadow of his anger looming over her forever.

Sean gestured toward her car. "Go ahead. I'll grab these groceries and follow you home."

"We can get our own groceries!" She smiled down at Hayley and Hope. "We're strong women, right, girls?"

"Yeah!" Hope said.

"Well, but he can carry *my* bag." Hayley smiled up at Sean and handed it to him.

"Let me carry them all. I want to help." His eyes were warm on Anna's, and their gazes tangled.

*Uh-oh.*

"Come on, Mommy. Let's go home and make our hamburgers!" Hope said, then looked around at the people on the street, biting her lip.

She *was* close to speaking in public. "We're going now," she said, reaching down to give Hope a supportive little hug.

"I'll follow you," Sean said, picking up all the grocery bags easily, in one big hand.

Driving home, between glancing back in the rearview mirror, seeing the twins chatting and, behind that, Sean's truck, Anna felt the semipermanent knot in her stomach finally ease.

Coming here had been the right decision.

Beau hadn't followed them, apparently. And the twins were recovering.

And there was a good man who, miracle of miracles, seemed to be interested in her.

The thought brought a quick twist of shame. Beau had told her no decent man would love her, and to an insecure girl, her father's neglect had implied the same thing.

She'd carried that feeling of unworthiness with her for years, but now she put down the burden, at least some of it. She *wasn't* the names that had been painted on her cabin and Claire's car, any more than Claire was. And she didn't deserve to be called those things, any more than Claire did.

She'd never approve of someone treating a sweet woman like Claire badly. And maybe, finally, she was ready to stop allowing that treatment for herself.

Maybe she could even permit herself a little bit of happiness.

When they got to the cabin, it was only natural to invite Sean in to share their humble dinner, and it seemed natural for him to agree, and to help with the preparations.

And of course, he had to roll around on the floor with Blackie, the dog he'd helped them pick out, and show the girls how to throw a stick for the big Lab.

After dinner, it was only natural that he'd build another bonfire. That they'd all roast marshmallows and make gooey, messy s'mores again.

And once the twins started yawning, it was natural that he'd help to carry them inside, that he'd tuck Hayley into her side of the bed while Anna tucked Hope into hers.

That he'd go out and wash the dinner dishes while she read the girls a story, a short one, and they couldn't even stay awake through that.

She came out of the bedroom and closed the door behind her.

Sean was putting the last dish into the drainer. "Are they out?" he asked.

"Already sleeping hard." She felt suddenly shy. What would happen now? Would he stick around or leave?

Which did she want him to do?

He walked a few steps toward her, then stopped. Looked off to the side, rubbed the back of his neck and laughed self-consciously. "I should go."

She didn't say anything, and slowly, he turned his head to face her again. "Shouldn't I?"

Her heart rate accelerated, and she couldn't take her eyes from his. "It would probably be the smartest thing."

He half smiled, eyes still intense on hers. "I've never been considered the smartest guy."

"I didn't even graduate from high school." She barely recognized the breathy sound of her own voice. "Nobody's ever called me smart." And then she smiled a little, unable to believe she could make a joke about something that had mostly embarrassed her in the past.

He knelt to rub Blackie's head, then stood again. "I think you're smart," he said, looking at her seriously. "And I think you're a wonderful mother. And if you want me to leave, I'll leave."

"I'm not..." She hesitated. "I'm afraid."

He took another step, held out a hand and brushed a lock of hair back behind her ear. "Of what?"

She shrugged and looked down.

"Are you afraid of being close to me?"

She crossed her arms. "That—the physical side of things—has never been exactly fun for me. Maybe there's something wrong with—"

"Hey," he interrupted, running a thumb along her cheek. "Did you like it when we kissed, before?"

She met his eyes and nodded.

Blackie's tail thumped as if to agree, and then the dog settled down onto his blanket with a big sigh.

"That's all we have to do," he said. "And we don't have to do that, if you'd rather I leave. I know your girls are in the next room. I'd never ask you to do something that might disturb or upset them."

Tears rose to Anna's eyes as she read the sincerity in Sean's. She'd never have expected a rugged man like him to have this kind of sweet sensitivity. Never expected to be treated so gently, with such compassion.

"How about I just hold you a minute," he said, "and then I'll leave, and you can have a nice cup of tea and read your book." He gestured toward the armchair with a reading lamp and bookmarked library book beside it.

"Um…okay," she said faintly.

"Come here." He pulled her against him then and stroked her hair as she laid her head against his chest, listening to the solid, steady beat of his heart.

After she'd relaxed into his embrace and relished its tenderness for a long moment, she looked up at him.

He touched his lips to hers, oh so gently. Then his mouth brushed hers, back and forth.

Sensations, warmth and tenderness, flashed through Anna's body, making her toes curl against her flip-flops. She made a tiny noise.

Sean growled a little and pulled her closer, cupping the back of her head in a big, tender hand.

She drew in a gasping breath and stood on tiptoes, wanting to be closer, wanting it with a part of herself that felt new.

Later, Sean let himself out the front door and she sat down in her reading chair. But she didn't read. She just wrapped her arms around her knees and touched supersensitized fingertips to her lips, her heart racing, her whole body warm, her mind walking a tightrope from joy to worry and back again.

THE NEXT DAY, Sean headed for the Safe Haven Women's Center, finally to fulfill his obligation to fix their roof and start looking at the plumbing.

He needed a little distance from the cottages. From Anna. Being with her last night, kissing her, holding her—it had been physical, yes, but also emotional. He'd felt a depth of caring beyond anything he'd felt with Gabby, with anyone.

He turned up the country music and drove faster. That melting look in her eyes as they'd said good-night. That "see you tomorrow," filled with promise.

What was he doing? What was he getting himself into, and what expectations was he setting up?

The last thing he wanted to do was to hurt Anna. She'd been hurt too much already.

He let himself into the old church where the shelter was housed, and immediately memories assailed him, all tied up with a musty, old book, candle wax smell.

He ducked his head into Yasmin's office. "Here to work on the roof," he said, and left before she could ask any questions. She looked preoccupied, anyway, and when a frazzled-looking mother and her young teenage son—a big, gawky kid—emerged from one of the other offices, he could see why. He'd make himself scarce.

He climbed up on the roof, using the ladder and tools from his truck, and started nailing on shingles.

He thought about how Anna had held the ladder for him on that first day of working together. Then, they'd been just getting to know each other. Now they worked as a comfortable team.

Then, he hadn't trusted her. Now he thought nothing of leaving her alone with his files or having her process invoices for him.

He heard a truck with a bad muffler pull up and looked over the edge of the roof. A plaid-shirted man emerged and strode toward the church's front door.

Something about him didn't sit right with Sean, so he finished nailing on the last shingle and climbed down the ladder.

"Benny!" The woman he'd seen before had yanked open the church's door and was standing there, breathing hard, eyes wide. "What are you doing here?"

"Hoping to get you back," the man said.

"Look what you did to me!" She held out her arm, and Sean was too far away to see it but he could already guess that bruises ringed it.

"Babe, I'm so sorry."

This was disgusting. Sean cleared his throat, took a step closer and crossed his arms over his chest, giving the man a dirty look.

Plaid-shirt glared at him. "We can't talk here, baby," he said, and urged the woman inside.

Sean shook his head as he put his ladder back on his truck. Stuff like this made him crazy.

He heard Yasmin's voice, loud, firm and angry. No doubt scolding the man for coming, or the woman for revealing her location.

He lingered to trim a couple of overgrown bushes, hoping to avoid the scene inside.

And then, through an open window, he heard crying.

The choked, harsh sound of a young boy who didn't want to cry but couldn't help it.

With a muttered curse, he grabbed his toolbox and headed inside. The adults were talking and arguing out in the main part of the building, but the crying had come from one of the side rooms.

While Mom and Dad worked out their problems, who was helping that kid? He knocked lightly on the door of the shelter's little library and rec room, then let himself in.

"Don't mind me," he said as soon as he saw the boy, scowling, brushing fingers under his eyes. "Just working on the carpet here."

He knew, instinctively, how much the kid would hate having his tears observed. He remembered his own frustration and anger, in the same situation, as if it were yesterday. He'd just wanted to be a teenager, free to cope with his own emotions. He'd had feelings for girls at school and worries about how his body was changing, and yet he'd had to repress all that and act like a man, leaving town under cover of darkness as his mom had planned. He'd had to be a support for her.

As he used the fork of his hammer to pull up carpet, he chatted with the boy. "I came here myself when I was about your age. What are you, fourteen?"

"Thirteen," the kid said.

So. Big for his age.

"You hoping your parents get back together?" he asked, still not meeting the boy's eyes, still working with his hands. "Here, hold that for me a minute, will you?"

The boy took the proffered hammer, looking at Sean suspiciously.

"Give me a hand if you want." Sean dug around in his toolbox until he found an X-Acto knife. "That your dad?"

The boy was silent for a moment, and then he started yanking up carpet.

"No," he said. *Rip.* "He's my stepdad."

Sean cut a long slit in a section of carpet and didn't say anything.

"I'm not hoping they get back together." *Rip.* "But they will." *Rip.*

"Bummer," Sean said.

"I hate him." Venom laced the boy's cracking voice.

"I hated my dad." And feared him. He remembered the few nights he'd stayed in this shelter, once with his mom and brothers, then later with just his brothers, then just Cash, then alone. He'd been so angry.

Before the anger, though, there'd been fear. He remembered that awful day, squatting on the sidewalk outside one of the little stores here in town, reading a book, trying to escape all the chaos. When he'd looked up and seen his father, terror had coated his insides.

Of course, he'd forced himself to jump up and head their way. Protecting his mother was what he did, who he was.

But in truth, he'd wanted to run away. When his mom had jerked her chin toward his brothers in the store, communicating to Sean that he should go to them, he'd rushed inside with relief.

He was sweating just thinking about it. Just hearing the couple arguing outside while the boy sat in here, ducking his head, muscles rigid.

When the voices modulated, the kid didn't relax. If anything, he looked more tense.

And Sean knew exactly why.

His own mother had returned to his father multiple times before their final great escape.

The question of whether she'd gone willingly, that last time, came back to gnaw at him as the movie of that last day with her played out in his mind.

He'd looked out the door and seen what looked like his dad shoving her into the truck. As if it had happened yesterday, he remembered the guilt of not being able to protect her, the heavy weight of responsibility for his brothers, Cash cursing and Liam crying as they'd stumbled back to the shelter.

But now, for the first time, he remembered when the adults at the shelter had gone through their things. Their mom had put together a packet for each of them: birth certificate, medical records, school records and a request that they go into foster care here, rather than back in Alabama.

Almost as if she'd planned the whole thing out, almost as if she'd known she was going to abandon them. In fact, he now remembered, he'd overheard a couple of the shelter workers speculating about that very thing.

One had maintained that she must have wanted freedom from the responsibility of three boys. The other had thought she was probably just resigned to being found, that she couldn't get away.

But if Sean had managed to protect her, if he'd gone forward into the fight with his father instead of backward to take care of his brothers, his mother might still be here.

It had haunted him his whole life, a black cloud chasing after him, the idea that it was his fault. His brothers had never said one word of accusation, they mostly looked up to him, but that just made his guilt worse.

"Rocky. Get out here." The door opened. "We're going home."

The boy gave Sean a desperate look. He stood, fists clenched, and walked toward the couple.

Yasmin sat at her desk, obviously fuming. The kid skulked slumping past them, ducking away from the hand his stepfather reached out to him.

"Thanks for your help," the woman said to Yasmin, sounding embarrassed. "We'll be leaving."

Sean opened his mouth, but a headshake from Yasmin stopped him. The trio went out the door.

Yasmin swore.

Sean narrowed his eyes, then walked out behind them. Put a hand on the guy's shoulder and spun him back around. "If you lay one hand on her…" He forced himself to stop, not to issue the threat he wanted to. He knew his own short fuse too well, and feared his own potential for violence. "If you lay a hand on her, you'll answer to me."

The man puffed up his chest, started to sputter and then seemed to think better of it.

Sean pulled one of his business cards out of his pocket and leveled a glare at the man. "I want to talk to your son. Got a problem with that?"

"It'd be okay if he talked to Rocky for a minute, wouldn't it?" the woman asked nervously.

"Sure, hon. Whatever you want."

*Fake, fake, fake.*

He waited until the couple had gotten into the truck and then squatted in front of the boy. "Put this in your pocket," he said, handing him the business card. "My name's Sean, and my number's on the card. If you need help, you can call me anytime."

The boy took the card, looked at it and then looked at Sean, lip curled. "You like boys?"

A flush of anger rushed through Sean. Not because the boy had said it, but because he knew what that meant, at his young age. The child had already seen too much. "Nope. But I've been in your shoes, and people helped me. Just returning the favor."

"Huh." The boy sneered a little more.

"Come on, honey!" The woman's voice sounded anxious, and Sean could just imagine that the man's niceness was already wearing thin.

"I gotta go." The boy turned away. But at least he slid the card into his back pocket.

So there was some chance he'd call for help when he needed it.

Sean stood glaring after the truck until it disappeared, and then returned to the shelter. "I'll finish with that carpet and haul it away," he told Yasmin.

"What did you tell the kid?" she asked.

"That he could call me."

"She's been here before, when the kid was about ten. And eight." She crossed her arms. "What kind of hope does a kid like that have? What kind of man will he turn out to be?"

*One like me. Broken, angry, short fuse. Not fit for a family of his own.* Sean ducked into the side room. There he ripped up the rest of the carpet with unseemly force and a lot of cussing, way too much for a church building.

When he ripped his finger open on a nail, he didn't stop. The pain felt good. Deserved.

He'd been a failure at protecting his mom. He hadn't managed to keep his brothers all together in one family, either.

So what right did he have to get involved with Anna?

What hope was there that a guy like him, with a past worse than that young boy Rocky, could grow up to have a normal family, a normal life?

Mothers should protect their kids. They shouldn't let loser men ruin kids' lives. They had a responsibility.

He barely understood the rage that coursed through him.

He carried his supplies back out to the truck and drove too fast to the diner, because he didn't want to go home and risk a repeat of the hamburger-bonfire-kissing scenario that had gotten him into trouble last night.

But he'd just sat down and growled out an order to the redheaded waitress when he heard voices behind him, felt little hands tugging at his arm.

"Mr. Sean!" Hayley whispered, probably loud enough for the whole restaurant to hear. "Come sit with us!"

"This is a nice surprise," Anna said, her voice warm behind him.

And in a flash, he knew what he had to do. He had to let Anna and her daughters go before things between them got any more complicated, any more serious. Before they relied on him or he got too used to being with them.

*Maybe you could do it. Maybe it could work,* his heart cried as the twins leaned trustingly against his legs.

But no. Exactly *because* he cared so much, he couldn't take that risk.

And the kindest way to break it off was quickly. He spun on the counter stool. "Do you have a minute?" he said to Anna, not modulating the brusque tone of his own voice. "I'd like to talk to you."

# CHAPTER FOURTEEN

SEAN'S ANGRY, ALMOST-CRUEL tone stabbed into Anna, bursting the happy bubble she'd lived in all day.

Ominous clouds settled in around her heart. "You want to talk now? Um, the girls…" She looked away from his stony face. She really didn't want to hear what that face had to say.

One of the waitresses, Rita, leaned forward. "Your little girls are welcome to sit at the counter for a few minutes. I'll get them chocolate milk and crackers while you two talk."

"Can we, Mommy?" Hayley whispered.

Hope didn't speak; her pleading expression said it all. Both girls would be thrilled at the chance to sit by themselves at the diner counter.

"Okay," she said. "I'll be right outside, keeping an eye on you," she warned the girls. "You listen to Miss Rita." Then she glanced at Sean. "We won't be long, right?"

He shook his head, his eyes never leaving hers. Never warming up, either. "Nope. This will be quick."

She helped the girls climb up onto the counter stools while her mind raced. Things had been so good last night. When he'd left, he'd seemed so caring, so warm.

She got the girls settled and looked up at him.

He jerked his head to the side, indicating she should lead the way out.

Once outside, where they could see the girls through the windows, he turned to her. "Last night shouldn't have happened," he said abruptly. "I don't want you to think it meant something it didn't."

His words pressed down on her chest, heavy weights that made it hard to breathe.

Why had she let herself be a silly girl, young and excited and hopeful? She swallowed hard. "Okay."

He lifted an eyebrow, looked away and then looked back at her. "That's all you're going to say?"

She shrugged. "Did you want me to cry or something?" There. She'd managed to sound as cold as he did.

Although what good that would do when her heart felt like it had been scraped out of her chest, she didn't really know.

"I expected some reaction." He gave her a fake smile and held up his fist for a bump. "Glad we're on the same page."

"It meant nothing to me," she lied, fist-bumping him back, maybe a little harder than was necessary. "I'm surprised you felt like you had to say something." There. Throw it back at him. Make *him* feel like the loser.

This angry part of herself was new. With her dad, with Beau, she'd internalized their neglectful actions and harsh remarks, figured it was her fault.

Sean's cold rejection made her furious.

His eyes went hooded and he crossed those brawny, sexy arms over his chest. "You feel okay about working for me still?"

*Oh Lord, no. No way.* But she glanced back inside at

the girls and knew she couldn't give in to her impulse to run. Not yet, anyway. "Been thinking about moving on," she said. It wasn't a lie; she'd thought about it when she'd been afraid about Beau.

He was watching her with cool, assessing eyes. She couldn't find the caring, kind man she'd been falling for, not in those eyes.

"I've applied for some jobs nearby, made some calls." She forced the words out past a tight throat, through lips that kept wanting to tremble. "But I'd appreciate staying on at the cottages until I find something."

"No problem. I'll give you a good reference." His voice was cool, but he shifted from foot to foot, glancing in at the girls.

Was it just her, or was this conversation exquisitely painful? They were being *so* polite with each other now. Going back into their boxes, crushing the bit of happiness they'd found together last night.

Well, let this be a lesson to her. Following her instincts in love was a disaster. She never made good choices. Being attracted to a man ought to send her running in the other direction.

Her eyes burned and she let her forearm sweep across her stomach, which had started to ache. Like she'd had surgery there and something crucial had been removed.

She cleared her throat. "We done here?"

An ancient Buick pulled into the parking space just in front of them with a little honk. Miss Vi emerged and walked energetically toward them.

"Just the people I wanted to see," she said. "Or rather the person. Anna, the girls talked to me today!"

Anna sucked in a breath. "That's so… That's wonderful, Miss Vi."

"Power of books," the older woman said. "I was reading with them and they just got too excited to remember
to shut themselves off."

"Thank you. So much." Anna wanted to inject excitement into her voice, but the lump in her throat
made it hard to even get the words out. This town was
so good for her girls, and they were settling in. How
would they react when she made them pull up stakes
and leave? Blinking back tears, she reached out and
gave the woman a quick hug. Cleared her throat. "You're
the best."

"They've had good mothering." Miss Vi looked
around. "Where are they?"

Anna gestured toward the restaurant, where the girls
were seated at the counter. Rita, the waitress, leaned
forward, admiring the place mats they were coloring.

Miss Vi did a double take. "Who's that waitress? Is
she new?"

"Within the past few weeks, I think," Sean contributed.

"She looks familiar." Miss Vi frowned, and then her
face cleared. "When you're as old as I am, you start to
think you've met everyone in the world. I'll see you
folks later. Going to say hello to the little ladies and
pick up my dinner to take home."

"I'll follow you in," Sean said. "I need to pay my tab
and get on out to the cottages." He turned, then looked
back at Anna. "You okay?"

"Why wouldn't I be?" she snapped.

He lifted his hands, backed away and turned.

Anna took a couple of deep, shuddery breaths and
followed him into the café.

"Miss Vi!" Hayley practically yelled, jumping off

her stool and running to the older woman. She gave her a hug, then spun away toward Sean. "Mr. Sean!"

Hayley was *talking*. In a restaurant full of people.

Sean peeled her arms off his leg, gently, and turned away without speaking. He nearly bumped into Hope, who'd followed her twin to do the same thing, just a bit more timidly.

He lifted his hands to avoid touching her, but she hugged him anyway.

"Hey, honey, not now." He stepped away from her.

Hope backed away, turned and ran to Anna, clearly hurt and confused.

"What's got into *him*?" Rita asked.

"You know better than to take out your mood on a child," Miss Vi said to his back, her tone scolding.

Anna didn't speak, couldn't. She just stroked Hope's hair and made a quick, firm decision: they were out of here, just as soon as she could find another job and place to stay.

TWO DAYS LATER, Rita urged Claire toward a big, fancy house at the edge of Safe Haven. Afternoon sun shone down on pink azaleas that lined the iron-fenced back courtyard. Music and talk and laughter filled the air.

Women with hats and men in light-colored suits crowded the spacious yard. A bit intimidating—these were Safe Haven's beautiful people—but no way was Rita letting Claire back out.

"I can't wear this." Claire gestured down at her red dress. The swirly skirt hit her at the knee and the neckline was a deep V, emphasizing her curvy hourglass figure.

"You look beautiful!"

"It's old-fashioned," Claire fretted. "Not like my normal style at all. People will laugh at me."

"It's very becoming." Much more so than the short, tight dresses Claire usually wore. Rita raised an eyebrow. "It emphasizes your assets."

Claire rolled her eyes. "Just what I *don't* need emphasized. And these earrings? Seriously, cherries? I look like I'm straight out of the 1950s."

"Like a *vamp* out of the fifties. Come on."

Rita didn't feel especially secure about her black sheath dress, straight off the rack at Target, but it did hug her figure while still feeling age appropriate. And the strappy heels she'd borrowed from another waitress hurt her feet, but she had Claire's word that they looked fantastic.

Rita opened the wrought-iron gate, ushering Claire inside with a firm, motherly arm around the shoulders. She'd been having so many maternal feelings lately, and sometimes they hurt like a fire in her gut, pain without any apparent focus.

Mothering Claire, though, didn't hurt. It made her feel good, so she was indulging in it.

"Welcome, ladies!" Miss Vi stood near the entrance, dressed in purple from her hat to her dress to her shoes. "Come get food and drinks. Unless you'd like to look at the displays first?"

"We'll do that," Rita said. "Thank you for including me." Claire had been on the original invitation list, no doubt because she'd grown up as one of Miss Vi's protégées, but Rita was a last-minute add-on.

"And I might add, young lady," Miss Vi said to Claire, "you look absolutely lovely."

"Thank you kindly, Miss Vi!" Claire flashed her big

smile, but the minute Miss Vi had moved on to greet another customer, she leaned close to Rita's ear. "So far, I've got the fifty-through-seventy-something females wowed with my outfit. Not exactly my target audience."

"Just you wait." Rita wove through the buzz of chatter and reached the row of display tables set up on one side of the lawn.

They talked to a woman who paired up adult readers with at-risk kids, and she was so convincing that both Rita and Claire signed up for volunteer training. Maybe, Rita thought, helping out little kids would give her some peace, or absolution, about her unknown sins toward her own child.

Next, they approached the table focused on the GED program run by the library. Behind it, Anna George stood next to a good-looking man about her age. "Ladies, welcome!" the man said, with a wide, charming smile. "We're spreading the word about our GED preparation classes. Know anyone who might be interested?"

Claire glanced back at the well-heeled crowd and snorted. "Pretty sure all these folks have their high school diplomas and then some. The upper crust of Safe Haven isn't allowed to drop out."

Rita noticed that Claire's comment made Anna look away and fidget. Interesting. As for herself, she was guessing she'd finished high school, but had no actual memory of it and no record, either. "You'd be surprised," Rita said to Claire, but loud enough for the other two to hear. "Formal education doesn't necessarily go along with wealth or success."

"Definitely true," the man said, "but the lack of a high school degree can be a hindrance to getting a good job. Our program has helped twenty people pass the test since we started last year." He nudged Anna. "About to be twenty-one, yes?"

Anna lifted her chin. "If all goes well," she said, and looked from Rita to Claire with something like defiance.

"Oh holy smokes, Anna, you don't have your diploma? Look, I didn't mean one thing by that comment I made." Claire's voice was contrite. "If you're working toward your GED, I'm happy for you. And impressed that you can find the time as a single mom."

"Second the motion," Rita said. She felt proud of Claire for her blustery, warmhearted people skills, and of Anna for her quieter determination to improve her own life and the lives of her girls.

"Thanks, ladies." Anna's smile became more genuine. "I'm excited. I've wanted to do this for a while."

Rita and Claire headed toward the last table—featuring the women's shelter, which had a small library linked to Safe Haven's main branch—but Claire gripped Rita's arm. "Uh-oh." She nodded toward the entrance.

Brandi had just walked in. She stood, flipping back big hair, looking around speculatively.

"I have to go hide," Claire said, her tone half joking, half alarmed.

"You have every bit as much right to be here as she does, and a lot more to offer," Rita reminded her.

"Yeah, tell that to the hospital that stitches me together after she rips me apart."

"You can take her. Plus, I have to warn you, hiding in that dress isn't really an option."

"Thanks a lot." Claire frowned, but for all that, Rita was pretty sure she felt good in her dress—almost as good as she looked.

"Hold your head high," she reminded the younger woman as she disappeared into the crowd.

That left Rita standing alone at the table staffed by Yasmin, the woman who ran the women's shelter.

"You have any books to donate, let us know," Yasmin said, going into a practiced spiel about the value of books as escape. "We focus a lot on children's books, since we work with a lot of kids. But we also have books for women."

"Escapist or self-help?" Rita asked.

"A little of both." Yasmin looked out at the crowd. "I'm hoping to get some of these folks to make a donation. Even if it's just to improve the library, that would free up our funds for other things. We're hurting."

"I'm sorry to hear it." Rita picked up one of the brochures. "I'm not exactly flush, since I just moved, but I'd like to donate something."

"Every little bit helps." Yasmin indicated the donation jar, which stood in front of a poster showing the history of the women's shelter.

Rita dug in her purse while perusing the old pictures. Did they look familiar, or was it her imagination? "You used to have a bigger building?"

Yasmin nodded. "The shelter used to actually house women and families, but there was some big incident and they stopped. The place became just a resource spot to visit after that, and it went downhill. Women in trouble don't want to talk about their options until they feel safe and have a place for them and their kids to go."

"Makes sense." Rita was holding herself still, listening hard, trying to understand the tug she felt toward this place and this conversation.

"After all, protecting women and kids is what a shelter is supposed to do." Yasmin sighed. "I don't know how much longer we'll stay open, and I don't know how hard to work at it. Seems like we don't do a whole lot of good these days." She pulled up a stool and sat down, frowning at her own display. "I threw this stuff together when Miss Vi asked me, but I don't seem to be attracting a lot of interest here. It's probably me."

The discouragement in Yasmin's tone tugged at Rita's heart. "Do you work alone there? Do you have any support?"

Yasmin shook her head. "No money for another employee, and I'm only part-time."

"Volunteers?"

"We have a few, but our program's kind of limping along. I can't find the time to organize it, what with my family issues." She sighed. "Honestly, I love what the shelter does, but I'm burned out. I'd really rather do something else."

"Like what?"

Yasmin looked embarrassed. "If I could, I'd work with teenagers. Teaching, coaching, whatever. But I don't have the background for it."

"God love you if you're willing to deal with kids that age," Rita said. "I can't imagine." Inside, the question nagged at her: Would she have been a good mother to a teenager, if she'd managed to stay near her child?

"Thanks for listening, anyway." Yasmin's shoulders sagged, just a little.

"Listening I can do. If you'd like to go get a drink or coffee sometime, give me a call." Rita took one of the shelter's cards and scribbled her name and number on the back of it.

"That's nice of you!" Yasmin offered up a small

smile. "It's not that often somebody thinks about how it's all affecting me."

"Gotta take care of yourself before you can take care of other people," Rita said.

Other visitors approached then, and Rita wandered off into the crowd. She felt a little out of place. For one thing, she was new in town, and had only been invited because she'd been waiting on Miss Vi the other night and the older woman had insisted. Then, when Claire had been vacillating about whether to come, Rita had agreed to come with her.

Which left her not knowing many people.

Besides that, this wasn't the type of gathering she and T-Bone had frequented. They'd tended toward backyard gatherings of a different sort, where everyone wore jeans and there was a keg instead of a nice bar.

Whatever. People were people, she reminded herself, and sure enough, when she eased into a couple of conversations, she found them friendly. She even ended up with an invite to a book group that met once a month and was, the woman who'd invited her promised, very casual and fun.

The smell of barbecue was getting stronger, and Rita's stomach growled. She looked toward the grills and sucked in a breath.

There was Jimmy, manning the grills along with a couple of other guys, but clearly in charge. He wore a chef's jacket. The diner must be catering the event, or else Jimmy—like most everyone else in town, it seemed—was a friend of the library.

He scanned the gathering with a practiced eye. Rita's gaze must have drawn his attention, because he smiled and beckoned her over. Warmth spread over her.

Young people might think romance ended when you hit forty or so, but Rita could make a strong case that it wasn't so. She felt as breathless as a teenager.

She took her time getting there, admiring the view. Jimmy was good-looking in just the way she liked. Well-groomed, but a little rough around the edges, with muscles from real work, not from working out.

She wondered what his tattoos represented. Kind of wanted to trace one with her finger and ask, but that would be *totally* inappropriate.

When she reached the grill, she saw that the cooks were removing ribs and chicken pieces and loading them up on plates. "Anything I can do?" she asked.

"You look more like a guest than a waitress today," Jimmy said, "and believe me, that's not a complaint. Why don't you just keep me company?"

"I can do that." She climbed up the single step to the grill platform and leaned back against the wooden railing, facing him.

"You having fun?" he asked as he laid out a row of burgers on the grill.

"Sure," she said, "considering that I don't really know anybody. It's a nice group. High-end, but not too snobby."

"That's Miss Vi's influence." Jimmy added long strips of zucchini and eggplant to the grill. "She gets everyone involved, whether they're rich folks from Safe Haven's founding families or poor families who come to use the library's computers."

"Good for her. I like to read, and I've had times when I was too poor to afford books." More like T-Bone hadn't valued them, but whatever. "Libraries are important."

Jimmy nodded. "To kids, too."

"Do you have any kids?" she asked, suddenly curious. She'd been working with Jimmy a few weeks, but hadn't heard him mention them.

"Two," he said. "One's an engineer out in California. The other..." He sighed. "We don't see eye to eye. I have a hard time reconciling his lifestyle choices."

Rita lifted an eyebrow. "Is that code for he's gay?"

Jimmy shook his head. "That, I have no problems with. No. He's a real womanizer and a bit of a scam artist. I wouldn't want him around my daughters, if I had any." He studied her. "How about you? Do you have kids?"

The question froze her. What was she supposed to say? *Yeah, I think so*? *Yeah, but I don't know what happened to him...or her...or them*?

If she were to get involved with Jimmy, she'd have to tell him that truth. But what would he say? What would he think of her, let alone anyone else?

"Hey, Rita!" Claire hurried toward them and stepped up on the platform. "You were right! I am getting so many compliments on this dress."

*Saved. For the moment.*

"Let me add to the pile. You look great," Jimmy said. "And that's as a guy who's old enough to be your dad, but still appreciates a pretty woman."

"I told you," Rita said to Claire. "And the good news is, you're a great person inside, too. Any problems with Brandi?"

"No, ma'am." Claire shook her head. "I'm avoiding her, and for now, she seems to be avoiding me."

"Smart move."

One of the younger guys manning the grill took the

opportunity to chat to Claire, his interest obvious, and Jimmy winked at Rita. "Come on. Let's carry some of this food over to the tables. Give them a little privacy."

"Good idea." She picked up a couple of platters and he took two more, and they moved through the crowds to the tables.

At which point they saw Sean, sitting in front of a group of middle-school-aged boys, looking miserable.

The boys looked as miserable as Sean did, and nobody was talking. "Wonder what's going on there?" Rita mused.

Jimmy chuckled. "Miss Vi, again. She got Sean and his brothers to do a program encouraging boys to read, since they're a demographic that doesn't do enough of it. Apparently they're supposed to be role models, but Sean doesn't look too happy about it."

As they watched, two more young men came over and took the chairs on either side of Sean. One wore a police uniform—Liam, whom she'd seen around town a lot as well as in the diner. The other man wore an expensive-looking, up-to-the-minute suit and fancy shoes.

The sight of the trio gave her an odd chill.

"Pretty strong family resemblance, eh?" Jimmy said as the two newcomers started joking around with the boys, clearly defusing the tension. "I hear they all three came through the foster care system in Safe Haven, and Miss Vi was instrumental in keeping them off the streets. In return, she extracts her pound of flesh every few months. She's intent on getting them to help the community, specifically young boys."

"Miss Vi is a force of nature," Rita murmured, studying the three men.

Jimmy put a hand on her neck from behind. Gentle but so very sexy, and the feel of his hand pushed other thoughts from her mind. "We're not at work now," he said, "so what would you think about going out with me one of these days? Totally no obligation, your job is safe, et cetera, et cetera," he added.

Her skin heated under his touch and she longed to lean into it. Even started to. But she stopped herself.

She wasn't looking for a one-and-done, which was about the only thing she could have, until she'd figured out her past.

Reluctantly, she stepped away from his touch and drew in a breath. "Jimmy, I like you, but there are things standing in my way."

"What kind of things?" The low growl danced along her nerve endings. His eyes were intense on her face.

She shook her head a little. "Can't talk about them, not really. Not yet," she added, because, God forgive her, she didn't want to close the door entirely on this man.

He studied her. "You brushing me off?"

"No." She looked steadily into his dark eyes, awareness of him speeding up her breathing. "I'm interested. But I need to figure stuff out first, so…" She leaned forward and planted a featherlight kiss on his cheek. "Don't feel like you have to wait for me, honey, but I'd like it if you did."

She turned regretfully away from him, ignoring the raised eyebrows that meant at least some of the guests had seen her bold, unwise move and would no doubt talk about it.

But Jimmy put a hand on her arm and leaned in. "I

can wait," he said, "but not patiently. If I know you're interested, I'm following up."

It felt like a promise, and Rita couldn't help the tiny smile that curved her lips as she walked away.

# CHAPTER FIFTEEN

ANNA WATCHED SEAN scowl while his two brothers hammered it up in front of a group of kids.

What was *his* problem?

She'd had no contact with him since he'd basically dumped her outside the café. He'd left her notes about what work needed to be done, and then spent his time in whatever part of the Sea Pine Cottages she *wasn't* in.

Which was fine, because she had no desire to be around him. None at all, thank you very much. A morose, difficult, hot-and-cold man was exactly what she *didn't* need, and if she'd forgotten that for a little while, well, that was her mistake.

Thanks to the way he'd acted the last time they'd seen him, the girls were mostly resigned to staying away from him, too.

She could have forgiven him being cold to her, pulling away. She knew she wasn't the most sophisticated woman around, nor the most gorgeous, and she came with two kids and plenty of baggage, as well. If he'd had second thoughts about getting close, that was his right. Not even very surprising, really.

But when he'd turned away Hope's careful, tentative hug, that had pretty much sealed the deal. She wanted nothing to do with a man who would hurt her girls.

"What's going on inside your head?" Rafael asked

her. "You've been preoccupied this whole time we've been working this table."

"I'm sorry." She adjusted the tablecloth and straightened a stack of brochures. "I volunteered to do it and I want to do my part. I'll focus better."

"Go out and socialize if you want. I'll hold down the fort. You don't have to do this."

"No, I'll stay." She looked out at the growing crowd, getting louder as people sucked down the pretty pink concoctions that waiters were carrying around on trays. Not really her kind of thing. "You've done so much for me. I'm just thinking about all I have to do. Looking for a job and a new place to live, taking the GED exam… making sure my girls are doing okay…the normal racing thoughts of a poor single mom." She smiled when she said that last, so she wouldn't sound so pitiful.

"Speaking of the little ladies, where are they?" Rafael had been nothing but kind to the twins, but they were still wary of him. Wary of any man, really.

Except for Sean.

Or at least, they hadn't been wary until he'd gone cold on them.

"They're having a playdate with one of the kids from the library program," she said. "It always worries me, because they won't communicate with other adults besides me. What happens if they need something?"

"What does happen?" he asked. "I've read about selective mutism before but I've never seen it in person."

She pursed her lips. "They usually manage to get their message across. Hayley, especially, is a great little mime. But anything complicated, they just have to wait until they have me to translate for them."

"Did you ever think you might be too overprotective?

Being away from you might motivate them to communicate more."

She stiffened at the implied criticism. "Pressure seems to make them more anxious, not less."

He put a quick arm around her shoulder and squeezed it. Impersonally, like he'd do for any student.

At least, she *thought* it was impersonal.

"I for one am very impressed with your mothering skills. I didn't mean you were doing something wrong." He was looking at her warmly.

*Very* warmly. Her face heated. "Thanks for the vote of confidence," she said, and walked to the end of the table to adjust the tablecloth where it had blown out of place.

She'd never been exactly a hot commodity, so what was going on with her and men in Safe Haven? If Rafael was actually interested in her, that made two men in the space of two months.

Too bad the one she really liked had decided she wasn't for him.

A shadow fell across the table. "I guess you weren't lying," Sean said quietly.

His gravelly voice woke up everything inside her even as his tone made her wary. "About what?"

"That what happened between us meant nothing to you."

She *had* been lying, of course, but his tone made her bristle. "What's your point?"

He frowned toward Rafael. "Just…be careful, okay? Sometimes men are out for one thing."

Her eyebrows rose almost to her hairline. "Are you seriously telling me how to handle my personal life with men?"

She felt rather than saw Rafael stepping toward them. He put a hand on her shoulder. "You okay, Anna?"

Sean's eyes narrowed and he straightened. In a big man like him, it felt threatening.

Rafael straightened, too, and glared.

"I'm fine," she said, stepping out from under Rafael's hand. "I think I *will* go do a little socializing, after all. It feels kind of oppressive in here." She unfastened her name tag, practically flung it down on the table and marched past Sean and into the crowd. Then, because she didn't see anyone she knew, she circled back to Yasmin's table.

The other woman raised an eyebrow. "You don't look happy. What's wrong?"

Anna glanced back toward the table she'd just left. Sean and Rafael were having a heated conversation. "Nothing that living in a convent wouldn't solve," she muttered.

"Come on back here," Yasmin said with a chuckle. "This isn't a convent, but you won't find many males approaching this table."

"Fine with me." Anna stepped behind the table. "You need help? I'm done working with Rafael for the day, and I don't really feel like mingling."

"Matter of fact, I do need help." Yasmin smiled at her. "I was just mentioning to Rita that I'm having trouble finding volunteers."

Anna walked behind the table and perched on a stool beside Yasmin. "I wish I had time to volunteer. Single mom...two little ones... I have to stick pretty close to home when I'm not working. If you have a job that I could do from home, I'd be glad to help. Lord knows, I believe in your cause." Then she could have slapped herself. She wasn't one to admit the embarrassing way she'd been treated by Beau.

"Actually…" Yasmin tapped a pencil against her lips. "One of my big needs is someone to recruit and coordinate our hotline volunteers. You could do most of that by phone. Any interest? Being a volunteer coordinator would look great on your résumé."

"Are you serious?" Anna stared at Yasmin. When had anyone ever wanted Anna's help with something so professional? "Why would you ask me to do something like that? I don't even have a high school diploma."

Yasmin shrugged. "You're smart. Good people skills, and you must be organized to be doing a good job with two special-needs kids, while setting up in a new town and working a new job."

Anna blinked. It was the second time today someone had said she was doing a good job at her life. "Tell me what's involved," she said, taking out her phone to jot down notes. "I'll see what I can do. Next week, the girls are doing some full days at the library's Spring Break program, so I might have a little extra time."

SEAN WAS HEADED toward the exit of this not-his-type-of-party when he heard his brother call out to him. "You're leaving for real?"

Liam's voice held censure and Sean really just wanted to keep walking. But he made the mistake of half turning back toward the gathering. He should have just left after that encounter with Anna and Rafael, rather than coming back to let his brothers know.

"We made a commitment." Liam glared at him.

"You and Cash are handling the kids fine. Better than I can do. I scare 'em."

"Whose fault is that? Can you blame anyone but yourself?" Liam was winding up into full lecture mode, which would have been funny considering how Liam used to idolize Sean, except that Liam's words were true. "You could dress nicer and smile once in a while. It wouldn't kill you."

"It might," Sean said, just to egg Liam on and dodge the real issues.

"Miss Vi stuck her neck out for us all the time when we were kids. We owe her."

"I'll do something else. Maintenance work at the library, or something. I'm no good with kids."

Liam cocked an eyebrow. "You seem to do okay with Anna's twins."

"Leave it alone." Sean spun and stalked out of the gated yard.

He'd had the sense that she cared, but he'd obviously been wrong.

*You were the one who told her it couldn't work.*

Yeah, but saying that had practically choked him, because he'd wanted it to work so bad. Because he'd grown to care for Anna and her little girls. He'd hated hurting her, hated hurting them, even if it was for their own good.

A late-model SUV squealed to a stop at the curb, just close enough that Sean could read its BMW logo. Rich people drove like maniacs, and for what? So they could show off their suits and dresses in somebody's back garden?

The window lowered. "Sean O'Dwyer. I need help. Can you give me a hand here?"

The voice belonged to Bitsy Mercer, one of Cash's many high school girlfriends. Her school nickname,

Ditsy Bitsy, wasn't nice, but it had always fit her so well that it had stuck. "Hey, Bitsy, what's wrong?" As he walked closer, he heard children crying from the back seat.

Bitsy got out of the car and opened the back door. "Okay, okay, I'm getting you out. You can see Mommy in a minute."

When he saw Hayley climbing out of the back seat, Sean's gut clenched. The twins shouldn't be spending even an afternoon in Ditsy Bitsy's care.

"Hey, Hayley." He approached her slowly, kneeling to her level, but she cringed back against the car. Hope emerged next, crying, and when she saw Sean, her sobs intensified.

Their reaction made him feel about six inches tall, because he knew he'd caused it himself. "What's going on?" he asked Bitsy.

"Can you just take them in to their mom? I left my twelve-year-old in charge of my girls." She lifted her hands, palms up. "They were doing fine. I thought it was going to be okay that they didn't talk. Poor little things, they need to play with some normal kids their own age."

Sean frowned at her. "They understand every word you're saying, Bitsy."

"Well, I don't understand them. The kids were all playing outside, and I guess something spooked them. They freaked and ran in and were hiding. I had a terrible time getting them into the car, and I have no idea what upset them."

Sean looked toward the girls. "What happened?"

They met each other's eyes and pressed their lips together in identical silent frowns.

"Tell Anna I'll call her. And that I'm sorry." Bitsy took Hope's hand and urged her toward Sean, then followed suit with Hayley. "Thanks a bunch."

Then she was gone with a squeal of tires and the purr of a very fine engine.

And he was left with two scared little girls to take care of. "Come on," he said. "Let's go find Mom."

They stood frozen to the spots where Bitsy had placed them. Hope was still crying.

It was a standoff that couldn't be maintained forever. "Who wants to ride on my shoulders?" he asked.

Hayley didn't speak, but her eyes lit up, and his heart lifted. He'd been harsh to her before, or at least cold, but she had a short memory, apparently.

Kids were so quick to forgive. Adults would do well to follow their example.

He swung her to his shoulders. "Hold on tight," he said, and then grimaced when she gripped onto handfuls of his hair.

"Come on, Hope." He held out a hand. "Let's go find Mom."

She didn't extend her hand, but her crying settled a little.

He knelt low enough to take her hand, careful to be gentle. He gave her the slightest of tugs, and she fell into step beside him, her arm extended so that there was as much distance as possible between them.

When they reentered the party, conversations died down and he realized people were probably wondering why Hayley was on his shoulders. Or maybe that murmur going around the crowd had to do with how cute the girls were.

He looked around and spotted Anna, standing beside Yasmin at the women's shelter table.

Talking to Rafael.

The sight jolted him, made him queasy and tense, even though he had no business being jealous.

He tugged Hope toward the table, without thinking how it would affect her, until she resisted and cried. Remorseful, he knelt and pointed. "Your mommy's over there."

Then it was Hope tugging him toward Anna.

When they got close, he called, "Anna." His voice was sharp—he heard it, and so did a lot of the surrounding people. She heard it, too, and looked at him, her face impatient.

"Your girls need you." He bit off that sentence lest he say something inflammatory to Rafael.

Anna gasped and hurried around the table, opening her arms, pulling Hope close.

Sean lifted Hayley from his shoulders and set her down beside her mother. "Are you sure it was a good idea," he asked quietly, "leaving the twins with Bitsy Mercer?"

"What happened?" She was wiping Hope's tears, her eyes alert, examining the twins for any injuries.

Mostly, the surrounding conversations had gone back up to normal by now.

"She's a little ditzy, that's all. Not exactly responsible enough to take care of girls like yours."

Anna bit her lip, her face troubled. "Hayley. Are you all right? Did anything bad happen?"

Hayley frowned and leaned into Anna's side.

"Hope?" she asked. "Are you all right?"

Hope just buried her face in Anna's other side.

He felt like a jerk, but it was important for Anna to know how upset the girls had been.

Anna looked up at him, visibly struggling to control herself. "Do you know what happened?"

"Bitsy pulled up in a big hurry and handed them off to me, even though they were crying." And it was ridiculous, but he'd gotten scared. Scared she would neglect her children for the sake of a man.

Like his own mother had done.

The thought surfaced and was as quickly submerged.

"Did she even know we were...acquaintances?" Anna's voice rose in apparent disbelief. "I can't believe another mother would leave my girls with someone she thought was a stranger."

The word *acquaintances* echoed in Sean's mind.

They'd had potential to be so much more. "She said she'd call you and explain," he forced out through a tight throat, "before she drove off."

Anna stood and straightened her shoulders, holding each girl by the hand, and leaned close enough that only he could hear.

"Thank you for bringing them to me," she said. "I'm sorry you had to deal with them. It won't happen again."

"Anna..." He searched her eyes for the connection they'd had. But it was gone, and he was the one who'd destroyed it.

For good reason, and at least partly for the sake of Anna and the twins. "Never mind," he muttered, and stalked away from the trio and then out of the party.

LATER THAT DAY, when hard work hadn't quelled the fierce hurt inside him, he got in his truck and headed for town. He needed a drink or six, and he needed not to be alone with his thoughts.

And not to be on the same acreage as Anna and the twins, who were now back at the Sea Pine Cottages.

He parked and got out, and saw Rita, the waitress from the diner, coming down the street with tall stoop-shouldered Abel, the cook.

They entered an old-style souvenir shop and Sean stopped in his tracks as if some larger force were pinning him to the ground.

He stared after them as his stomach churned.

He hated that souvenir shop, because it was the last place he'd seen his mother before she'd abandoned him and his brothers. He always avoided it.

Now, having seen Rita and Abel go inside, he felt oddly compelled to follow them. See what they were doing, what they were talking about.

But that didn't make any sense. He was through with getting involved with outsiders and trying to help solve their problems. That kind of behavior got you exactly nowhere. Take Anna's coldness toward him this afternoon, for example.

*Coldness like yours toward her.*

He forced his feet to move past the shop, past the spot where he'd been reading a novel when he'd last seen his mother.

He moved faster and faster. By the time he got to the bar three doors down, he was practically running.

He felt like tearing up the place, breaking windows, doing the kind of vandalism he'd been known for as a teenager. The kind that had gotten him a sentence of doing volunteer community service, building things up rather than tearing them down. Service that had gotten him into the construction field, where he'd done all right for himself.

Just like back then, he had to stop this racing mind and these crazy impulses. What was wrong with him? He knew he was the product of an unstable mom and a violent, impulsive, abusive father. Was all that stuff finally coming out in him, as Gabby had sometimes theorized?

It took two shots and two beers before he finally started feeling like himself again. And before he could have one single, rational thought about the events of the day: What had happened at Bitsy's to upset the twins so much?

# CHAPTER SIXTEEN

*IF YOU'RE GOING to move ahead, you have to do this.*

Rita followed Abel into the little gift shop on Safe Haven's Main Street. They made a funny pair, both of them in their working clothes, Abel tall and thin and dark, she a roundish redhead. Plus, they were being a little furtive, since they'd sneaked out on a fifteen-minute break.

"You don't remember this place at all?" he asked as they walked through the aisles, squeezing past tourists.

She looked at the tacky souvenirs. "No."

He indicated a bin of kids' toys, alligator heads on sticks, long water guns, pretend light sabers.

She felt a flicker of something, but she couldn't tell what. "Nope."

They reached the front of the store, where a young cashier looked up from her phone. "Can I help y'all?"

"We're just looking around," Abel said. And then he held up a necklace to her. "Remember this?"

She studied it and her heart started to pound. "I have that necklace."

He nodded as if he already knew it, then shoved a dollar across the counter and took a thin wrapped package from a bin. He opened it and held it out to her. "Ever taste a praline?"

"It looks good, but no." They stepped away from the

cashier and she touched his arm. "Abel, what's going on here? What do you know?"

He studied her. "I've been praying about you," he said. "I met you before. And I don't want to tell you anything you don't ask me about."

That set her heart to pounding harder. She wanted to ask so much, but was she ready to know the answers? "Why'd I buy that necklace?" she asked. "Why was I in the store?"

"You didn't buy it," he said slowly. "I was working here at the time, and I gave it to you."

"Why, Abel?"

His phone buzzed before he could answer, and he studied the screen. "Jimmy say we're gettin' backed up. We better go."

She should follow up with her question, but her stomach burned at the thought. Getting back to work sounded like a relief, a bandage over a wound, a return to her everyday reality. "Sure."

They left the shop and started toward the restaurant, and then Rita stopped and looked back. The storefront with the bright concrete sidewalk outside, shimmering in the noontime heat—it was like she could see shadows there.

Abel watched her closely, but he didn't say anything more.

They walked the rest of the way back, sharing the praline, which should have been delicious, but instead made her feel slightly nauseous. And she thought about what Abel had said and about the necklace.

She'd been in that store before, in another life. Abel had given her the necklace she still treasured. Memories seemed to hover just out of reach, tugging at her.

He hadn't wanted to tell her. Why not? What did Abel know about her?

Inside the café, they were swept up into the dinner rush, burgers sizzling, fragrant onions frying, customers waving her down. She was glad for the distraction. Sometimes, she just needed to let things sit for a bit and she could figure out what to do.

During a little lull, Jimmy touched her arm. "You're not upset I asked you out?"

She smiled at him. That, she felt sure about. "Not at all. I hope I'll have an answer for you soon."

Truthfully, Jimmy's asking her out had propelled her into trying to dig into who she was, to follow up on hints that Abel had dropped.

But once inside the little store, with Abel looking at her in his quiet way that seemed to see deep inside her, she'd lost her nerve.

Was it guilt? Had she done something terrible here, in this town, in this store? Or some minor, petty misdemeanor like stealing? But if it were that, why had she been beaten so badly that she'd almost died?

T-Bone had gotten her emergency hospital care, and then driven her to his home in Maine while she was still half out of it. When she'd recovered enough to think, in a clinic in Maine, she'd been frantic. The sensation of having no idea who she was or what had happened to her had disturbed her continually, day and night. Moreover, she'd had a terrible ache inside, independent of the physical injuries, that had made her feel like she needed to find something, do something, fix something.

T-Bone had told her he'd found her on a highway in a remote part of West Virginia. She'd searched the area via GPS and online, made phone calls, but she'd gotten nowhere. There was no legal record of a woman by the side of the road in the whole state. After she'd gotten over her initial fear, she'd befriended a police officer and gotten her to run her prints, both in national and West Virginia databases. But there were no matches.

After a while, she'd settled into a life with the kind man who'd rescued her. Started to make new friends and build new memories. For weeks at a time, she'd forgotten that she didn't know the first twenty-some years of her life.

And then something would remind her: talk of an old TV show or of high school days, women reminiscing about their children's babyhood or their first dates, questions about whether she'd ever owned a pet or what was her employment record.

And she'd be right back to the realization that she didn't know, that the early years of her life were a blank.

The pain had gotten less each time. Over the years, she'd admitted the truth to a few people, but mostly she kept it to herself. She'd even invented a fictional biography to use with strangers she didn't want to discuss it all with.

When T-Bone had finally admitted that he'd found her outside of Safe Haven, South Carolina, she'd been furious. She'd railed against him, drunk too much, complained to Norma.

But the truth was, T-Bone had been good to her. He'd saved her life, paid for her medical expenses and treated her well.

His motivation for secrecy hadn't been all bad. Not knowing anything about her past or how closely she knew whoever might have done this to her, he'd given her a fresh start. He hadn't owed her anything, and she was grateful to him.

Jimmy took the coffeepot out of her hands, refilled cups along the counter and then came back to her. "What's going on?" he asked.

She looked at his kind, curious face, his square jaw, his thoughtful eyes. Something in her chest—she guessed it was her heart—wanted to reach for him, get closer. It was building to an ache inside her. But she'd have to tell him the truth if she wanted even a chance at building something with him.

And to tell the truth, she had to know it.

"It's to do with my past," she admitted.

He leaned a hip against the counter. "Want to talk about it?"

She did. But she didn't know what to say. What if he hated her for what she'd been? What if she hated herself? "Better not," she said.

He shrugged philosophically. "Remember, I'm here for support if you need it. I can be a friend." He leaned closer and spoke into her ear. "It's not *all* about my being hot for you."

Her face warmed and she pulled back, shaking her head. "You've got a devilish side, don't you?"

"Yeah." He winked at her, and then his face went serious. "But I mean it, Rita. I'll help if I can."


THE NEXT MONDAY, after work, Anna pulled her car close to Ma Dixie's house, sending gravel spraying. "Stay," she said to the dog panting eagerly in the front seat. And then she hurried inside, her mind racing with everything she had to do.

Immediately, Hope ran to her. Hayley put her hands on her hips, clearly displeased.

"I'm sorry I'm late," she said to Ma Dixie, who sat in her recliner crocheting what looked like a baby blanket. "I had a phone interview I didn't expect, and it ran long."

"That's a good sign, ain't it?" Ma smiled at her. "It's no problem from my end. I'm not going anywhere."

Hayley tugged at Anna's arm and Anna bent down to hear her, discouraged that the girls were back to not speaking in front of nonfamily members—even Ma Dixie, who was practically family.

Sean had done that, set them back. Her jaw clenched.

"We hafta go to the library right now," Hayley said.

"I'm sorry, honey." Anna spoke so Hope and Ma could hear her, too. "It's too late today, but you can go to the library program tomorrow." It was spring break in the local schools, and the twins had been looking forward to attending the longer program the library was offering this week.

"I wanted to go!" Hayley punched out at Anna, and Hope threw herself on the floor and began to sob.

"Hayley! We don't hit." Anna glanced over at Ma Dixie, then back at Hayley. "I'd like for you to sit in the chair for a time-out."

Hayley sulked, but went. Then started to cry.

Hope's cries intensified in volume, becoming screams.

"Tell you what," Ma said over the racket. "Let's you and I go out on the porch. Sometimes taking away the audience is the best thing." She put aside her crocheting and pushed out of the recliner.

Anna followed the older woman out the door. "I'm

really sorry to be late," she said again, "and I'm sorry for their behavior."

"They've been in a mood all day," Ma said. "Lots of acting out. This isn't the first tantrum, nor the first time-out."

"Oh no! They were doing so well."

Ma shrugged philosophically. "Their misbehaving can't hold a candle to some of what I've seen in my years as a foster parent," she said. "Including from our friend Sean. He was a wild one."

Sean. The mention of his name made Anna's stomach churn.

She didn't want to care about him, but she did. Her skin ached for his touch. Her fingers longed to smooth the furrows from his forehead. Every day working near him, while not speaking, was taking a piece of her heart and making it shrivel and die.

"Why was Sean so bad?" she asked, just because she longed to hear more about him. A weakness she shouldn't indulge, but couldn't resist.

"Angry. He and his brothers were abandoned here in town, and he'd been that older kid who takes charge, you know? So when he was placed here without his brothers, it was a complete role change for him to be a kid again. And he felt like he'd failed, because he couldn't keep his brothers together."

"Wow." Anna thought of the upright, hardworking man she'd been falling for. No wonder he had a dark side. "He's turned out well, for all that."

A million creases formed in Ma's face, her striking version of a smile. "I'm proud of that boy," she said. "I always told him he could make something of himself, with God's help. Took a while, but he did it."

"Well. I'm sorry my girls were acting out. I guess it's to do with how this week is different at the library program, because of the schools' spring break. That, and the things they've overheard with my job search."

"Kids don't like change," Ma said easily. "They were talking to me a little bit, last week. Today, nothing."

Anna's heart ached. Her girls were going backward, and it was her fault. She'd gotten involved with Sean, and that meant they had, too. And then he'd rejected them all. Leading her to look for a job, and think about a move, and they had to feel that tension.

Her heart hurt. She wasn't giving her children the life she wanted to give them. She'd thought she was getting closer, but she'd been wrong.

If the slight changes they were now experiencing hit them this hard, then what would it be like if—when—they actually moved?

"I worry so much. If we have to move, or…" She broke off, not wanting to reveal too much to Ma.

"Hey," the older woman said. "Life is change. The girls will have to learn that, sooner or later."

Impulsively, Anna put an arm around Ma and hugged her. "You're the best," she said. "I don't know what we'll do if we move. We'll never find a better babysitter than you."

On the swamp road, headlights broke the twilight, and Blackie started barking from the car.

"What're you going to do with your dog if you move?" Ma asked.

Anna stood and sighed. "I don't know. I really didn't think that through. Okay if I let him come in a minute?"

"No problem," Ma said. "How about I get the girls a little snack for the road?"

"Great." Anna went out to the car to get her hysterical dog on leash and out of the car.

She was squatting in front of the dog, trying to attach the leash and calm him at the same time, when Sean's deep voice sent shivers down her spine.

"Anna." At the same moment, Blackie leaped joyously toward the voice, knocking her onto her hip.

She didn't look up at him. "Hey, Sean." She got to her knees and brushed the dirt off her jeans.

He cleared his throat. "I didn't think you'd be here."

"I was running late." She still hadn't looked at him, but she could just imagine his expression. "And, no, it wasn't because I was socializing or being a bad mom!"

"I didn't say that."

"You didn't have to." The dog was tugging to get to Sean, practically pulling her off balance again, so she stood and let him go.

She'd thought maybe Sean would apologize for the way he'd acted at the library event. If he did, she thought maybe she'd accept the apology. And then *maybe* they could go back to being at least a little bit friendly.

But it didn't happen. Instead, Sean clucked his tongue to the dog, who bounded over and stood on his back legs, paws on Sean's chest.

Sean gave the dog the loving, friendly greeting he hadn't given to her.

The greeting went on longer than was natural.

Then there was nothing. Nothing more for them to talk about. They, who'd had easy conversations almost since they'd met.

Anna supposed that, on his part, it was a case of "if you can't say something nice, don't say anything."

For her, it was "if I talk, I might cry."

How had they gone from friendly, warm, even intimate, to this coldness? Her heart gave a sharp little twist. For just a short while, love and happiness had seemed to be within her reach.

She needed to stop thinking. She stood and headed inside, leading the dog. She tried not to pay attention to whether Sean followed, but of course, she couldn't help noticing that he closed the door of his truck and then came after her.

Well, he was here to see Ma, and that was his right. He had more right to be here than she did. "Girls, let's go," she said, embarrassed that her voice sounded hoarse.

Hayley and Hope came running from the kitchen, cookie crumbs and smiles on their faces.

The smiles died when they saw Sean.

But then the silly dog jumped at them, joyous and simple, and that made them laugh. He licked their faces.

"Well, look what the cat drug in," Ma said, coming into the room and beaming up at Sean. She held out her face for a kiss, and he gave it obligingly, then put his arm around the woman and rested his cheek on the top of her head.

Anna's heart gave a twist. Sean didn't have to come visit Ma Dixie. She wasn't his biological mother, and she'd raised him only during his teenage years. He'd been a handful, gotten in trouble with her.

And yet he visited every week. Right now, he had a toolbox in hand. Probably he was going to fix something Ma and Pudge couldn't fix themselves.

He was a good man.

No doubt he thought he was too good for the likes of her. Maybe he was right.

Hayley giggled and tugged at Anna's hand. "She said the cat dragged him in. But she doesn't even have a cat!"

"And he's too big to be dragged by one anyway," Hope whispered from her other side.

Their improved moods were probably sugar induced, but so what? She'd take it. At least they were talking again. She put an arm around each and hugged them fiercely.

"Ready to go home?" she asked them.

Hayley pointed at the dog and laughed, and Anna almost did, too. Blackie was jumping at Sean, and then Sean sat down in a chair, picked him up and cradled him. The girls' laughs got louder, high-pitched.

Anna almost laughed herself, at the sight of the big man holding the big dog like a baby.

But just as quickly, worry pushed its way in. Would she be able to keep the dog in their new place? How would she find a good caregiver?

If only she could've stayed here. She flashed back on Ma's Friday evening gathering, knowing she'd love to be a part of that going forward. Then, watching Sean cuddle the dog, she remembered the evening they'd picked Blackie up. How patient Sean had been with the girls, answering all their questions.

She cleared her throat. "We have to go," she said to Sean, proud that she could speak without emotion. "Thanks for keeping the girls extra, Ma Dixie."

"Not a problem," she said, and Sean set the dog down on his feet.

Anna and the twins headed outside, and the dark immediately seemed to sink around them. Frogs chirped a rhythmic chorus, punctuated by the hooting of an owl.

The dog lunged toward the river and barked, almost pulling Anna off her feet.

"Come on—calm down!" She tugged him back toward her car.

In the swampy river where he'd been barking toward, there was a light and the splash of an oar, and then the light went out.

A shiver ran down Anna's spine. "Get in," she said sharply to the girls, and fortunately they did as she said. But she heard them whispering to each other, rapid and concerned.

The dog lunged and barked more hysterically.

What did he see?

She longed to go back inside and ask Sean to check the area. But that would be stupid. There were probably fishermen here who were plenty annoyed at a dog scaring away their catch. She just needed to leave.

She urged the dog into the car and then climbed in herself. In the illumination of the dome light, she felt strangely like a target, so she quickly slammed the door shut.

The dog lunged at the darkened window and barked more.

That was weird. She started the engine, and her foot heavy on the gas pedal made it roar.

She definitely felt a case of the creeps coming on.

"Mommy, it's too dark!" Hope whimpered from the back seat. "I'm scared!"

"There's nothing to be afraid of." Anna said it too sharply, and Hope launched into a full-fledged sobbing spell, joined soon by Hayley.

Sugar high officially over. She clicked the locks shut and put the car into gear.

Again, the dog barked and lunged at the passenger window. Anna couldn't see anything outside except the dark outlines of trees and a glint of moonlight off the swampy river.

*Was* it moonlight, or a struck match, or a flashlight?

Anna executed the quickest three-point turn she'd ever managed and headed out the dark road through the swamp toward their cabin, stomach churning, nerves tight as violin strings, trying to still the agitated beating of her own heart.

# CHAPTER SEVENTEEN

"WHAT WAS WRONG with Anna?" Cash asked as he came into Ma's house. Like usual, he was dressed in a tailored, expensive-looking sport coat, dress pants and leather shoes, ridiculous clothes for the low country.

"When did *you* see her?" he asked, not bothering to conceal the jealousy that constantly seemed to claw at him where Anna was concerned.

"Dude. She drove past me on the way in. She was driving kind of crazy and looking scared."

"What did you do to her?" Liam punched Sean's arm, not lightly. He'd arrived just before Cash. Since Cash would be overseas—another big business deal— on their usual gathering night, they'd come early to celebrate their birthdays, as they'd all been born in late April or May.

"Why are you chasing a good woman away?" Cash asked. Then he held up his hand. "Don't answer. I know why. It's what you do."

"It's what *we all* do," Liam corrected.

Sean banged down his soda can just a little too hard. He wished it were a beer, but Ma didn't allow alcohol in the house. True, sometimes they or Pudge sneaked it in, but only if she was outside, or after she'd gone to bed. "Maybe, but I'm not so sure she's a good woman."

Liam frowned. "Why would you say that?"

Sean looked around Ma's familiar front room, the crocheted comforters and ragged furniture and windowsill full of thriving houseplants. He was trying to cool down. To *be* cool, but it wasn't happening where Anna was concerned. And with his brothers, he didn't have to pretend he didn't care. "I think she's already with someone else."

Liam and Cash glanced at each other. "That implies that you were together," Liam said. "That you had some claim on her."

"Which I didn't." And couldn't; couldn't make a commitment to Anna and her girls, no matter how much he wanted to. Gloom as deep as the darkness in the bayou pressed down on him. "Never mind. Drop it."

"Who's the guy, anyway?" Cash asked. "I thought all she did was work her butt off at the cottages and take care of her kids."

"Her GED teacher." Sean's gut knotted at the very thought of the grinning guy.

Liam tilted his head to one side. "Rafael Rodriguez? Really? I thought he was after Yasmin."

"Sure you're not just looking for cheating where there isn't any?" Cash asked, his tone mild. "Anna's not Gabby, last I looked."

"And she's not your mother, either," Ma said as she came in with a huge sheet cake, homemade, with all three of their names on it.

Sean glanced at his brothers, and then focused on Ma. "What do you mean, Ma? Our mom wasn't a cheater."

"No, but she left you boys high and dry, whether intentionally or not," Ma said. "And that's what scares all of you, when you start to get close to a woman."

LEE TOBIN McCLAIN

Cash put his hands over his ears in mock protest. "No psychoanalysis, Ma."

"That's a door you don't want to open," Liam said. "Though you're probably right." He put an arm around her.

"You're all three good boys. I just want to see you happy." She reached across the table to squeeze Cash's hands, then Sean's, beaming at them. "Now, let's sing."

Sean thought about what she'd said while she and Pudge sang "Happy Birthday," Pudge picking along on his ukulele. He made himself smile and go along with the little party. Ma and Pudge were good to the core, and a true family to him and his brothers. That wasn't something to take lightly.

Nor was the big piece of cake topped with ice cream in front of him. He dug in.

"What do you think, Ma?" Liam asked. "Do any of us have a chance to get it right with a woman?" He threw the remark out in a casual tone, as if it didn't matter, but Sean knew differently. Liam had been in love with Yasmin way back in high school, might still be. And for some reason he wouldn't talk about, everything had gone south between them.

He glanced over at Cash and noticed that he was pushing his cake around his plate, listening.

Despite the fact that they were all grown men, they all held utmost respect for Ma Dixie and her wisdom, especially where people were concerned.

"On your own?" Ma looked from one face to the next, her expression serious. "Not a chance. But if you stick together and say your prayers, anything's possible. Faith and family can heal anyone, and that's a fact."

"Amen," Pudge said.

It was too simple. Simple, homespun low country wisdom, completely at odds with what his marriage counselor had said.

"How'd you get us all figured out so well, Ma?" Cash asked. His tone was joking, like he didn't believe what Ma had said, but Sean knew his brother. That hope and longing in his eyes, that was the truth.

"Oh, we foster moms talked," Ma said. "We practically had a hotline going, trying to raise you three right. Just ask your other moms sometime," she added to Liam and Cash, and then looked back at Sean. "As for you— just know what color lenses you're looking through. Ask yourself if you're seeing clearly. Especially when you're looking at that sweet woman and her daughters."

"I saw what I saw," Sean said, knowing he sounded just like the stubborn teenager he'd once been, sitting at this very table.

"Your eyes have been blurry before. Wait here." She headed toward the back of the house, gesturing toward Pudge to join her.

They ate cake and helped themselves to more. "Listen to your ma," Cash said to him. "Out of all of us, it's you who tends to jump first and ask questions later. Remember when Liam was getting bullied?"

Liam scowled at Cash. "Or how about when *you* got in trouble selling ramen noodles at a five hundred percent profit?"

"I was selling convenience," Cash said with an easy smile.

Sean remembered that same smile when Sean had beaten up the kid who'd ratted Cash out.

Ma returned and plunked down a box.

Sean's stomach tightened. Their mementos. "Thought I put that in the burn bin."

"I pulled it back out," Pudge said.

"You boys have little enough of your past," Ma added. "I wasn't going to have you destroying what you do have."

Sean looked at the box, complete with one charred, blackened flap. Maybe he did jump first and think later; maybe that was why all his relationships got destroyed.

He thought of Anna's face, tight with betrayal. The hurt in the twins' slumped shoulders.

"Figuring things out is the first clue to fixing it," Ma said. "I think you boys should go through this together."

"I wouldn't mind." Liam looked intrigued, like the investigator he was.

As Liam started to pull out that wretched old photo, though, Sean grabbed his arm and pushed the object back into the box. "I'll do it later."

Liam didn't get mad, as Sean would have expected. Welcomed, even. "Listen, buddy, you helped us. Let us help you."

"I'll go through it later," Sean said.

Cash lifted an eyebrow. "You gonna burn it again? That's our history, too, you know."

"I won't burn it," he said, and practically groaned. Having made that promise, he'd have to keep it.

"I remember the day we lost Mom," Cash said unexpectedly. "It was like she knew it was going to happen."

"Did you ever think maybe she did know? Planned it out, even?"

Liam looked at him, astonished. "You mean planned to leave us here? She would never have done that."

Cash nodded agreement. "I don't think so, either. It's not her you should be mad at, bro. It's him."

They all went silent, remembering the father who'd abused them and their mother so horribly.

Whose genes they all bore, and when the conversation halted right there, Sean figured that was in all of their minds.

He'd never used his fists on a woman, wouldn't dream of it. None of them would, or at least, he prayed not.

But there was no doubt he'd hurt Anna and her girls, badly. Was *that* how their father's blood came out in him? In inflicting hurt with cold withdrawal, rather than with blows that left physical bruises?

Enough thinking. He tuned Ma's old television to a baseball game, spring training, and dished them all out more cake. Part of their birthday tradition was that the three of them ate the whole thing.

This year, Sean tried to be nice and give a piece to Pudge, but he waved it away. "Too much sugar," he said.

"Why don't you talk to Anna?" Cash said out of nowhere, after they'd watched the game awhile. "Give her at least a chance to explain. She looked pretty upset."

"Don't be the same knucklehead you always were," Liam said. "Anna's way better than Gabby."

Suddenly the little cabin was too oppressive for Sean. He kissed Ma on the cheek, shook Pudge's hand and hit both of his brothers on the shoulders, friendly-like. They were making him think more than he wanted to.

And all the thinking led to one conclusion: he'd hurt Anna and the girls. No matter what free choices Anna might have made about Rafael or anything else in her life, she didn't deserve that after all she'd been through. And the girls were innocent victims.

When you screwed up that badly, there was only one thing to do. He swung the box to his shoulder and headed out to his truck. Maybe, just maybe, he'd see if Anna was home. Apologize, at least.

Tonight, before he lost his nerve.

AFTER SHE CLOSED the door on her sleeping girls, Anna looked around her quiet cabin. Even though the dog lay curled up beside the chair she usually sat in, a chill started at the base of her spine and crawled to her neck and back down again.

She shook it off, turned on an extra lamp and sat down. She'd read her library book, that was what she'd do.

Except what had she been thinking, checking out a thriller about a woman living alone in an isolated forest? She read a paragraph and then slammed the book shut, her stomach churning.

Had there been someone in the river when she'd left Ma Dixie's? Someone outside her car?

Had Beau found her? Was there some other creepy person who'd realized she was a woman with kids, alone?

The dog got up, shook restlessly and uttered one sharp bark.

Her breath came faster. She wanted to close the curtains, but she was afraid to approach the windows. Her heart was ready to race out of her chest.

Too anxious to feel shy about it, Anna made a phone call.

THIRTY MINUTES LATER, there was a light tap on the cabin door. Yasmin's voice: "Anna?"

Anna opened the door and the sight of Yasmin's friendly, concerned face was a huge relief. "Come on in."

"Are you okay? Are the girls okay?"

Anna nodded. "Yes, they're asleep. Thanks so much for coming." She gestured Yasmin inside and waved a hand. "Sit down. Can I get you some tea?"

"Tea sounds good if it's decaf. I haven't been sleeping real well."

Two minutes later they were seated kitty-corner from each other on the cabin's two most comfortable seats, cups of tea steaming on an end table between them.

"Want to tell me what's up?" Yasmin asked.

Anna felt heat creeping up her face. "I'm sorry to bother you, but I just had this creepy feeling. Felt like someone was watching me, following me, and I figured you'd understand."

"Better than most. Tell me what's got you spooked."

So Anna explained about the lights and noises out at Ma Dixie's. "It was probably just some night fishermen, but the dog got really upset and, well, so did I."

"Understandable. Do you think it was your ex?"

Anna stared at her. "I'm surprised you'd go there right away."

"I work in domestic abuse," Yasmin said. "It's the first thing that comes into my mind. Do you think he's around?"

"I do and I don't," Anna said. "At first I thought he was the one vandalizing the cabin and my car, but then that turned out to be Brandi, most likely."

Yasmin sighed. "Yeah. I heard she might get off on the charges if she agrees to do counseling."

"That *might* work," Anna said doubtfully, thinking of

the rageful woman she'd met and the destructive, hurt-ful vandalism. "Anyway, I thought he wouldn't come here, but lately…like I said, I got the creeps."

"I believe in paying attention to your intuition," Yas-min said. "I've got my overnight bag in my car, and I'm glad to stay here if it'll make you more comfortable."

Anna felt embarrassed for bothering the poised, pro-fessional woman, but the thought of the company filled her with relief. "I would be so, so grateful," she said. "But it's way beyond the pale. You don't owe me any-thing."

"Anna." Yasmin reached out and touched her arm lightly, which stopped Anna's words in her mouth. "It's okay to need help and to ask for it. I want to be your friend."

Anna stared at the woman for a minute and tears pushed the backs of her eyes. She could count on one hand the number of times someone had reached out to her so kindly.

Yasmin, perceptive, seemed to see. "Hey, what's wrong?"

Anna took a deep steadying breath. "I just…haven't had a lot of that, that's all."

"Want to talk about it?"

Anna opened her mouth to say her automatic "No!" and then shut it. This, sharing yourself with others, was the way to be close and part of a community. She'd made a small start at doing that, with Miss Vi. And maybe another one with Rafael.

The biggest, of course, was with Sean and that had backfired.

But Yasmin wasn't Sean, and she wasn't Beau.

"I just grew up without a lot of friends," she said,

stumbling a little with the unfamiliarity of talking about herself. "My dad...well, he had a hard time getting it together after my mom died. He moved us around a lot, trying to find work."

"Was he the one who abused you?"

Anna shook her head, not even questioning why Yasmin knew about her abuse. "That was my husband, the twins' dad."

"Pay attention to your instincts," Yasmin said. "Lock your doors and keep an eye out. Angry abusers are no joke."

Yasmin's voice was passionate. "Personal experience?" Anna asked. "Or just professional?"

"Both," Yasmin said grimly. "I've seen a lot at the shelter, but I have a...personal stake."

As if knowing they needed a distraction, Blackie came up and put his nose on Yasmin's lap. The woman laughed and petted him as he was begging her to do. "My sweet little Josie girl—she was my fifteen-year-old Chihuahua—just died two months ago."

"You've had a hard time of it." Anna felt a little better about inviting Yasmin over. The other woman seemed to need a friend, as well.

They drank more tea and talked, and when Anna mentioned working on her résumé, Yasmin offered to take a look. So Anna got her laptop and showed her what she'd written, and they talked about ways to make it stronger.

"I'd hate to see you leave Safe Haven," Yasmin said, still scratching Blackie's neck. "Any reason you couldn't stay in the area, if you found something suitable?"

Anna hesitated. "I'd like to stay," she said, "except…" Involuntarily, she glanced in the direction of Sean's cabin.

"Except for Sean O'Dwyer." Yasmin seemed to know exactly what Anna meant. "Believe me, I know what it's like to have a man in town you're at odds with."

Anna lifted an eyebrow.

Yasmin looked at her, then away, then nodded. "Liam and I had a…thing."

"And it's over now?"

"Very. But Safe Haven is a small town, so nothing's ever really over." She brushed her hands together as if washing them of her whole history. "Anyway. I'm glad I looked at your résumé. I might be working on one, myself. Thinking about making a change."

Suddenly, Blackie started barking, and a loud knock on the door made them both tense.

"Anna!" came Sean's voice. Annoyingly loud, and it was also annoying the relief she felt. What kind of a girlie wimp was she?

"I'll get the dog and close the girls' door," Yasmin said.

"Thanks." Anna stalked over to the door and pulled it open. "What?"

"I just wanted to apologize," he said, making no pretense that he wasn't looking past her into the cabin. When he saw Yasmin, his shoulders relaxed.

Anger rose in her. "Listen, Sean," she said, low but hot, "checking on me to see what company I have is *not* cool. I'm a free woman."

"I'm sorry," he said. "And mostly, I'm sorry I was so cold to you and the girls. I didn't mean to hurt you. I just…" He looked off to the side as if trying to figure out what to say. "I just have some issues, but I'm sorry they caused pain to you and the twins."

She wanted to believe his words. But he hadn't said he wanted to be close again, just that he was sorry his distance had hurt. The thought of getting together with him and being hurt again was terrifying. "I'm fine." She heard the stiffness in her own voice. "Working on ways to get out of Safe Haven." She shut the door in his face, gently, but not before she'd seen the white, tight, stricken look of it.

## *CHAPTER EIGHTEEN*

SEAN COULDN'T MAKE himself go directly back to his cabin. He had way too much energy.

So he strode down to the beach and walked. And walked, and walked some more. Listened to the waves crashing against the shore, and felt like his emotions were crashing and churning right along with them.

Why had he acted so caveman jealous around Anna?

Why was she leaving, and where was she going, and would she and the girls be okay once they got there?

He caught a piece of driftwood and threw it into the water, hard. A couple of shells and sea-polished rocks followed.

Why had he pushed them away, made her unwilling to be close to him?

What was wrong with him?

That was what it came down to: there was something wrong with him. He'd always known it, but Ma's wise words had given him a reason why. His mother's leaving had scarred him.

So it wasn't just about him protecting others from his own bad blood. It was him being afraid, afraid of being left.

He hated to admit such a wimpy way of thinking, even to himself, but admitting it was the only way he could start to heal. Now, for the first time in his life, he

LOW COUNTRY HERO

was truly motivated to change. He wanted to be able to be close to Anna. To protect her and—he swallowed as he realized it—to *love* her.

He walked a while longer, thinking about his family, reaching for faith that he could change.

When he arrived back at his cabin, he remembered the box of mementos from the past. Before, he'd tried to burn them.

But Ma had said they were important, and now he'd promised his brothers that he wouldn't destroy them. Moreover, he felt a slight pull of curiosity. He went and got them out of his truck.

He picked through the photos and papers, and as he did, his chest began to ache. They'd had happy days with their mom, before the terror had started.

He studied a picture that showed him and Liam fishing with their mom. They all loved fishing now, especially him and Liam, and this was where it had come from: their mom. She'd looked happy about it, too, holding a big fish up for Liam, while Sean grinned beside her with an even-bigger fish of his own. Cash had undoubtedly snapped the picture; he'd never liked getting his hands dirty.

He leaned closer to study his mother. She was pretty, slim, with long hair, dressed in jeans and an old T-shirt. A lump rose to his throat as he remembered how much he'd loved her, and how awful it had felt not to be able to protect her.

Not to be able to save her, that last time.

He thrust the photo away and dug on through. When he unearthed a devotional book and cross necklace, that brought up the fact that they'd used to go to church together. Not with their father present, not ever, but somehow his mother had gotten three young boys acceptably dressed and over to the little church down the road from their house. She hadn't mingled a lot; they hadn't gone to Sunday school or Bible school or activities, but she'd made them sit in a row and pay attention.

Ma Dixie had done the same, when he'd come to live with her. She'd dragged her motley crew of foster kids to church every Sunday. He grinned to remember the ear-pinch technique she'd used to keep them quiet, his hand going to his own ear in remembered pain. You'd only had to experience it once, and you sat up straight and at least pretended to listen to the sermon.

At the bottom of the box was a dictionary. He pulled it out and more memories came. His mother had loved words. She'd made up games where they had to guess a definition. If they'd ever asked what something meant in a school reading, she hadn't answered, but rather had sent them to this book.

Later, when he'd moved in at Ma Dixie's and gone into his near-delinquent stage, he'd shoved the dictionary into the box and forgotten about it. Now he flipped through, looking at the tiny illustrations and remembering how he'd studied them as a young boy.

He kept flipping and came to an envelope. They must have used it as a bookmark. He pulled it out.

His heart stopped.

On the front was written three names: Sean, Cash and Liam.

In their mother's handwriting.

SEAN ARRIVED LATE to the Southern Comfort Café the next morning, his steps slow and heavy, his truck exerting an almost-magnetic pull to keep him away from the place.

Normally, when he met his brothers, Sean was first to arrive.

Today, he'd barely made it at all.

As expected, the others gave him a hard time about being late.

"What's got you in a mood?" Liam asked.

"You look like crap," Cash added.

Sean slouched into the booth, banging his knee on the too-low table, glancing around at the usual crowd, inhaling the scent of coffee and pancakes. "Anna's leaving town," he growled. "And this." He slapped the envelope onto the table.

"What is it?" Cash grabbed the envelope and pulled out the handwritten letter inside.

Liam stared at Sean. "Anna's leaving? How'd you find out?"

"I went to her place last night and—"

"Did you apologize for freaking her out at Ma Dixie's?"

"I tried." Sean reflected back over the scene, and it didn't sit any better this morning than it had last night. "She basically slammed the door on me." He scrubbed a hand down his face. "Somewhere in there, she also mentioned she was leaving." He hesitated, and then added, "She looked at me like she was afraid of me."

At that, both Cash and Liam looked up. Scaring a woman, even accidentally, was no joke to any of them, not with their genetics. "Why would she be afraid of you?" Cash asked.

"Because she could tell I wanted to know who was visiting her." Sean waited while Rita, the waitress, poured their coffee. "There was a car outside her place I didn't recognize. I guess she thought that was intrusive."

"Depends on your motive," Liam said. "Did you want to make sure she was safe, or did you want to keep her away from other men, other people?" They all remembered their father's insistence that no friends—theirs, but especially, their mother's—come anywhere near the house.

"Both," he growled.

"Makes sense." Cash tapped the letter he'd been scanning. His skin was pale. "And apparently you were always like that. She has me pegged, too, and Liam."

"*Who* has us pegged?" Liam grabbed for the letter. "Gimme that."

Sean blocked Liam's arm as Cash held the letter out of Liam's reach. "Careful!" they both snapped at the same time, too loud, and the murmur of voices in the café died down for a moment. "We only have the one copy," Sean said in a quieter voice.

Cash handed the letter to Liam. "From our mom. It doesn't say much. Seems like she was writing fast." His voice sounded a little choked.

"This was in the box?" Liam asked.

Sean nodded. "In an old dictionary. I guess that's why we never saw it. I know I didn't crack a reference book in high school."

Liam unfolded the letter carefully. "We could run forensics on this, see if we could find her based on handwriting."

"We're not going to find her," Cash said.

"She probably didn't make it." Sean forced out the words. "We've always thought that."

"I want to." Liam took the letter and scanned it. "She

says here that if anything happens, she'll move heaven and earth to…" He broke off, shrugged, looked away.

Sean clapped a hand on Liam's shoulder, gave him a rough squeeze. Yeah. It wasn't like there was much to say about a letter like that. A line about each boy, advice to them based on their personality. She was sorry about their father. She loved them so much. All in messy, scribbled-across-the-page handwriting.

But it was a link they hadn't had before.

"Here you go, boys." Rita placed a breakfast in front of each of them. "I'll get you more coffee, too. And—" she pointed at Sean "—ketchup for you, hot sauce for the other two. Right?"

"You got it." They all dug in, or pretended to. Liam kept looking at the letter, and Sean and Cash watched him. At a time like this, they both worried about him; he was the youngest, had always been the most vulnerable.

"Hey, I saw Tony at the Pig again last night," Cash said before putting a forkful of eggs Benedict into his mouth. He was trying to distract Liam, Sean could tell.

It worked. "With the Mahoney brothers?" Liam glanced up from the letter.

"No, he was alone. But the place was full of low-lifes." Cash shrugged. "Nobody I knew, but a couple of 'em were from out of town. Montana plates."

Sean's entire body tensed. He looked at Liam. "That's where Anna's from."

Liam pushed the letter away and, just like that, snapped back into police mode. "Why don't you give her a call?"

"I would," Sean said ruefully, "only I don't think she'll answer it. She's pretty mad at me. Could you call her?"

"Will do." Liam scrolled through his contacts and clicked. When she answered, he asked, "You okay?"

There was a rapid exchange, and Sean wished he could hear Anna's side of it. Liam didn't tell her about the Montana plates, only that there were some strangers in town, some rumors.

"Okay, well, call me if anything comes up." Liam looked up at Sean. "Or even better, call Sean. He'll be close by." He clicked off the call. "I did what I could for you, man," he said, giving him a fist bump. "You'd better live up to it. Keep an eye on her."

The hairs on the back of Sean's neck tingled. He intended to do just that.

THE CAFÉ WAS QUIET, aside from the three brothers talking so intently, so Rita gathered up her courage. No time like the present to finish her talk with Abel. She checked in with her few customers, brought checks and carried out a meal, and then headed into the kitchen.

Abel's cleaver moved rapidly over a heap of peeled potatoes, chopping them into small, symmetrical slices. He turned to the grill, drizzled oil from a plastic bottle and then set the potatoes to sizzling. He was picking up a large tin saltshaker when he saw her standing there watching.

"Want a turn at cook?" he asked, offering her the spatula.

"No way. Can't live up to your reputation. But I'd like to talk to you when you get a minute."

He shook seasoning onto the potatoes and then gestured to a young guy in a baseball cap. "Keep an eye on these, would you?" Then he waved a hand toward the back door. "We can chat outside."

They got out there and he looked at her in that all-knowing way of his. "What's up, Miss Rita?"

She forced herself to open her mouth. "Was there anyone with me?" she asked through a tight throat.

He studied her for a moment and then gave a slow nod. "Yes, ma'am, there was."

Her heart leaped. "Who was it? What kind of person?"

He looked off down the alley and then back at her. Patted her shoulder with a long-fingered, bony hand. "You had three young boys with you."

She stared at him. "Three boys... How young? Were they mine?"

"Boys about, I don't know...ten? Twelve? Fourteen? They were stairsteps." He held up a flat hand to indicate successive heights, as high as her chest, then her shoulder, then her chin.

She felt like she was choking. "Abel. Were they mine?"

"I have no way of knowing for sure," he said quietly. "But if the way you looked at them was any indication... then yes. I'd have to guess they were yours."

A voice called from the kitchen, and Abel called something back. Then he took her arm and led her inside, through the kitchen, to a counter stool at the back of the café. "Sit down here and get your bearings. You've had a shock."

She sank onto the stool at his gentle push. The world seemed to reel around her, and her stomach burned with anxiety and hollowness.

She crossed her arms over it and leaned forward, staring at the restaurant's tile floor, trying to breathe.

Finally she caught her breath, but kept her arms

clutched across her middle, the realization nudging its way throughout her body.

*I carried three boys in here. Not one, but three.*

*And then I lost them.*

Confusing emotions and images swirled through her mind, kaleidoscope-like. She swallowed and looked around for a glass of water, but of course, there wasn't one. Terrible help here.

She gripped the edge of the counter and leaned forward. Mustn't fall, mustn't create a scene.

Mustn't upset the boys, no matter how much it hurt… Mustn't upset the boys…mustn't upset the boys…

"Rita!" The voice next to her ear was low and kind. Jimmy.

"Let's get you back to my office. Abel said you were sick." He slid an arm around her and lifted, and she tried to get her feet under herself, but still ended up leaning most of her weight on him as he helped her through the door that led into the kitchen. They walked through the frying and boiling and curious stares, and then into his office.

He eased her down onto his padded desk chair.

Abel, his face wrinkled with concern under his white chef's hat, looked in. "She okay?"

"Could use a glass of sweet tea." Jimmy threw the remark over his shoulder, felt her forehead and then knelt beside her, hand on her wrist. "Do you have a doctor in town yet?"

She shook her head. "I'm fine. Not…that kind…of sick."

"Here you go, boss." Ice cubes clinking, a few low words she couldn't understand.

The next moment, Jimmy held a straw to her lips. "Take a little sip."

She did, and swallowed, and then all of a sudden tears were coming out of her eyes. A *lot* of tears. Tears like she hadn't cried since way before T-Bone died.

She felt Jimmy's arms go around her. "Hey, it's okay. Whatever it is, it's okay."

"No, it's not!" She shut her mouth against the confession that wanted to come choking out.

His arms tightened, and he stroked a hand down her hair, which had to be altogether out of her ponytail at this point. "Whatever it is, I'll help you deal."

That made her cry harder. Who *was* this man, that he was so good to a woman he knew nothing about? That he was letting her cry onto his white work shirt, now a mess of mascara and lipstick and tears?

Finally her tears slowed and she pulled her head back. He reached over his shoulder and found a box of tissues and held it out to her.

She blew her nose and wiped her eyes and gestured at his shirt. "Sorry about that."

He shrugged, smiled a little. "I've had worse things happen than holding on to you."

That was when she realized how close together they were, and something primitive took over. She leaned forward and pressed her lips to his.

Just a gratitude kiss, but he gave a little growl and cupped the back of her head, pulling her closer.

Her wrung-out, cried-out body woke up and begged for notice. And then there was nothing but this man, his strong arms, his warm lips.

Finally, he came up for air, turned his head to the side and pulled her to his chest. "I'm sorry." Then he put her away from him, holding her by her shoulders. And then he backed away and stood.

She wiped her eyes and nose again, not sure where to look. Not sure what to feel. All her emotions were a big tangled mess inside of her.

Jimmy cleared his throat. "Take the rest of the day off," he said. "I'll walk you out to your car when you're ready."

"I didn't drive," she managed. "I can make it home. Just…give me a minute."

She went to the ladies' room and got herself cleaned up enough that she could walk down the street without people calling the cops. And then she headed out the almost-empty diner's front door, hoping Jimmy was too busy in the kitchen to see her leave.

Outside the restaurant, the biggest of the brothers she'd waited on, Sean, stood beside his truck, looking like he was trying to decide something.

Jimmy came striding outside the restaurant, putting an arm around Rita. "I can walk you home."

Sean looked over. "You live at Magnolia Manor, right?" he asked. "I'm going that way. I can give you a ride."

"Thanks—that would be great," Rita said, adding to Jimmy, "Go back to work. They need you in there."

Jimmy looked back at the restaurant and then at her.

"I'll be fine," she said, and squeezed his arm. "Thanks for giving me a hand in there."

His gaze was steady and warm. "I'm here for you. Hope you know that."

She nodded, and as he strode back into the restaurant, she turned to Sean. "Thanks for this," she said.

"Sure, no problem." Sean held the door for her.

Once inside, it only took a moment. That smell. She *remembered* it.

Was she hallucinating, or was that the scent of her own child?

Covertly, she watched Sean as he drove, comfortable and capable, someone to be proud of. She had no memory of any child she'd borne, just a few flashes and feelings.

And this sweet scent, and the awareness that, yes, Sean had two brothers and had been eating breakfast with them. She cleared her throat as hope rose in her. "What were you and your brothers arguing about back there?"

"There's someone I need to help out," he said, "only she's not speaking to me." He flashed her a rueful grin. Making light of a situation that must be heavy on his heart, in the joking way you did that when talking to an acquaintance, not a real friend.

Not your mother.

A deep, sorrowful ache spread through her chest. If he were her son, surely he'd remember her.

"Want me to help you up the stairs?" he asked as he pulled up to her apartment building.

"No. I'm fine. Jimmy's a worrier." And she was about to start bawling.

"Stay there. I'll get your door."

When he opened it, she let him help her out, and something compelled her to address him seriously. "Listen, none of us knows how long we've got. If there's something you need to say to your friend, some way you need to help her, don't wait. Do it now."

He grinned. "Thanks for the motherly advice," he said. "You sure you're okay to get yourself inside?"

She couldn't speak, so she gave a little wave and hurried off toward her apartment door. Cleared her throat hard so she could call a respectable "thank you" over her shoulder.

Then she went into her apartment and fell apart.

ANNA PUSHED THE wheelbarrow of seedlings in garden-store flats toward the cottages' newly restored kids' playground, hoping the heavy physical activity would calm the anxiety that had licked at her stomach ever since Liam's phone call two hours ago.

Why had Liam called her? What was going on? He'd been completely vague, said there was *probably* nothing to worry about, which had freaked her out more than if he'd said what he was really thinking.

*Had* someone been watching her as they'd left Ma's last night? Were she and the girls safe?

Where was Sean?

She stopped the wheelbarrow beside the strip of garden she'd prepped yesterday and scratched Blackie's head, grateful for his peaceful presence. He'd warn her of any trouble, and for sure, at his size, he'd scare off Beau.

Then she dug another hole, took a purple vinca seedling from the wheelbarrow and patted it carefully into the sandy soil. It was a perfect South Carolina day, the sun warm, the breeze from the sea keeping the humidity away, the sky a rich azure blue. It was satisfying to plant flowers around the benches and play structures, to imagine guests enjoying the beauty once the seedlings had grown into flowers.

But instead of relaxing into her work, she had a sick

feeling in her stomach. She kept stopping to look behind her, squinting into the dark low country vegetation.

Which was ridiculous. Beau didn't know this part of the country; he wouldn't be able to sneak around like some native hunter. He'd be arriving in a loud truck and stomping through the brush, cursing when he tripped over a root or got a boot sucked into the mud.

She was so glad the girls were safe at the library program, not isolated here. Last night in the car, when she'd thought there was someone in the swamp near Ma Dixie's, had been ten times more terrifying because she'd felt the girls were at risk.

Come to think of it, no way could Beau have been behind the light and boat out at Ma Dixie's place. He didn't know how to sneak around the swamps and bayous in a rowboat or canoe. He was Montana born and bred. He could barely swim.

The thought cheered her. She'd been happy that they could stay away from Ma's isolated place, since the library program was all day for the length of spring break. But actually, they were probably safe out there, too. After this week, they could go back.

Unless they all moved on.

She continued planting, thinking about her upcoming Skype interview. Rafael had shown her the job description, and Miss Vi had agreed to be a reference; with Yasmin's help, she'd finished the application last night and emailed it in. Amazingly, they'd already called her this morning.

So if she passed the GED exam and did well in the interview, Anna had a chance at a job as an aide in a GED support program in Charleston. Something way more professional than she'd ever dreamed of doing.

In Charleston. So she could get away from Sean O'Dwyer and all the pain he brought just by being near her.

As fast as the worry had faded and the relief had come in, tears arrived, making her blink away the blur before she could place another plant. She'd fallen hard for Sean—she could admit that now. He'd seemed so kind, so good to her and the girls. So sexy, when you got down to it, with his muscles and his rugged looks and his gentle, slow touch.

Just over there, at the cottage visible through the pines, they'd started getting to know each other, clearing away brush and doing renovations.

How had they gotten so at odds so quickly?

*Stop thinking about it.*

She tried, but couldn't. His face, his deep-pitched voice, the way it had felt when he'd touched her—all of it washed through her mind, as repetitive as the distant surf she could hear pounding rhythmically against the shore. Her heart filled with a terrible loneliness.

She'd valued his friendship and she'd loved working side by side with him. She'd never met anyone so companionable in her isolated life. That he was handsome and sexy and about as male as you could get, that was awesome, but it was the loss of his friendship she was going to miss the most.

Blackie gave a friendly bark of greeting, lifting his head but not getting up.

"Anna?" came a voice from behind her.

She brushed dirty knuckles underneath her eyes and turned. Yes, it really was Sean. She hadn't conjured him out of her imagination. She cleared her throat. "Hey."

He didn't speak, but tilted his head to one side, studying her.

"I'm almost done with the plants for the playground." She rose to her feet and pulled the wheelbarrow back so he could see. "Is that okay?" Her voice sounded almost calm. Thank heavens he couldn't hear how rapidly her heart pounded.

"I just wanted to check on you." His voice sounded oddly formal.

"On my work, or..." She trailed off. What else would he want to check on? He'd made it clear he had no interest whatsoever in her as a person.

"Where are the girls? At Ma's?"

"No, they're at the library program. It's all day this week."

"That's probably...good." He stood there, looking off into the surrounding trees, looking at the plants. Anywhere but at her.

What on earth was going on?

She replayed what he'd said in her mind, and her heart started a dull, heavy thudding. "You said you wanted to check on me." She stepped closer, to where she was right in front of him. "Why are you checking on me and the girls? Why did Liam, earlier?"

He met her eyes for the briefest second and then looked away. "It's just a precaution."

The pounding in her heart sped up, making it hard to breathe. "You didn't ever check on us before, so what gives?"

"I... Liam didn't think we should worry you."

Her jaw about dropped. "Sean, if you don't think I've been worried every minute since I've arrived here, you'd be dead wrong." *With the possible exception of when you were holding me.* She drew in a breath, held it a second, let it out. "Tell me what's going on. If it concerns me and my girls, I need to know."

He pressed his lips together, still looking indecisive.

He was trying to gauge how much to tell her, and it made her want to punch him. "Would you stop being all sexist protective male and just let me know what's happening?"

He looked at her then, directly. "A truck with Montana plates is a rare thing to see in Safe Haven."

Her whole body went cold. "What did it look like?"

"Newish, red, Chevy."

She sighed with relief. "That's not Beau's. Besides, his would never make it this far."

"Good." He still studied her. "Do you think he'd have borrowed one?"

Tension rushed back in. Beau had a number of low-life friends, and trucks were the obsession of a couple of them. "Maybe," she said slowly. "I've felt like someone was watching us a couple of times, but I just attributed it to me being paranoid."

"When?" Sean was instantly alert. "Where?"

"Here, a couple of times," she said. "And out at Ma's."

"Why didn't you tell me?"

"Because you were barely speaking to me?" She couldn't keep the sarcasm out of her voice, but she couldn't focus on those feelings, either. "I'll check on the girls." She slid her phone out of her pocket and found the library's number. The familiar voice at the other end reassured her. "Miss Vi? It's Anna. Are my girls there and okay?"

Miss Vi laughed, deep and cackly. "Oh my, yes.

They've been outside having a scavenger hunt all over the library grounds, finding clues from a story. They seem to be having a wonderful time."

Relief surged through her. "Thanks. I guess you're right. I'm overprotective."

"They're lovely girls," Miss Vi said. "You're welcome to call anytime."

She clicked off her phone, the tension leaving her body to the point where she had to sink down beside the plants. "False alarm. They're fine."

"That's a relief." He stood there, not moving to go away.

"Was there…something else?"

"Look, Anna." He knelt to her level, reached over to scratch Blackie's head. "About the other night…the way I've been acting…" He trailed off.

Her heart almost flew out of her chest but she made herself keep looking into his eyes. "Yeah?"

"Look, I'm sorry if I—" He broke off and turned toward the thick vegetation that separated the play area from the cabin next door. "What was that?"

She narrowed her eyes at him. "I didn't hear anything."

Blackie looked in the same direction Sean had been. He let out a low, rumbling growl.

Sean got up and walked to the edge of the trees, looking into the dark interior of the narrow forest. Blackie followed.

Uneasy, Anna stood and tiptoed over to where he and the dog were standing. If Sean had heard something, then maybe she wasn't imagining things after all.

Her phone buzzed, making her jump.

Sean looked once more into the trees, then shrugged and turned back to her.

She clicked to silence the phone, then glanced down at the lock screen. "It's the library," she whispered as she clicked it on and walked away from Sean, back toward the cabin.

"Anna?" It was Miss Vi's voice, worried this time. "I went to double-check on the girls. They're actually *not* here."

## CHAPTER NINETEEN

MINUTES LATER SEAN was driving toward town, Anna beside him, taking the curves at the highest possible speed.

To Sean, it didn't seem fast enough.

Anna had buckled in at his orders, but she gripped the edge of the seat and leaned forward as if she could make the car go faster.

Ahead, a guinea hen and her chicks meandered across the road, and reflexively Sean slammed on his brakes.

"Hang on!" he yelled, and cut the wheel sharply, veering into the swampy ditch and then back out on the other side of the little procession. Mothers and kids, you didn't interfere with them. But they had human kids to save. He gunned it and they went on.

He dug for words of comfort. "The girls might be hiding...or maybe they took a walk off the property," he said around the sick feeling in his gut.

Anna made some kind of a sound, a wounded animal sound that broke his heart.

He reached for her, then pulled his hand back, accelerating on a straight stretch. "What are you thinking?"

"They don't do that. They don't walk away from places. They're..." She stopped, drew in a shuddering breath. "They're too afraid."

She pressed a fist to her mouth.

He swallowed a giant lump in his throat, because he knew what she was thinking. They had to be afraid now.

She'd called Liam, explaining the situation in terse, anxious phrases. Now Sean nudged his phone toward her. "My brother Cash. Call him. And anyone else in my contacts with an 843 area code."

"Why?"

"Because they'll *help*." How had she lived in Safe Haven for even a few weeks without realizing that?

He gunned it down a straight stretch. "If your ex…if their father…" He trailed off because he didn't want to say it, but when he glanced over he knew that nothing he could say would be as bad as what she was thinking. "If their father took them, abducted them, what would be his purpose? What would he do with them? Where would he go?"

She cleared her throat. "He'd want to get back at me."

*Oh.*

He squealed into town and toward the library. When he saw Miss Vi and Yasmin hoofing it toward the Southern Comfort Café, he turned sharply into a diagonal parking place. "Any word?" he called through the open window.

"We've searched the library from top to bottom," Miss Vi said, distress and anxiety in her normally calm voice. "No sign of them. We've called parents and they're coming to get their kids. Some will stay to help search."

Scenes from his own history flashed through his mind, scenes he'd remembered before, but now with more color and sound attached. Shouting to the store

clerk that his mother was gone. Cash yelling, Liam crying, the pedestrians on the street rallying around.

It hadn't helped her.

But he couldn't go there. "Let's set up at the café," he
said, because it was hot and they couldn't stand here on
the street, and the police station was small and cramped.

He clicked Liam's number and suggested it. "Good
idea," his little brother said promptly. "Be there in five."

"I don't know what to do, I don't know what to do!"
Anna's voice was edging toward hysterical.

Miss Vi put a firm arm around her. "Come on. We'll
gather together and make a plan. We *will* find those little girls, Anna."

Sean led the way, pretending to know what he was
doing when in fact he was berating himself. He should
have protected the twins. He cared about them, all of
them, and it was his job to make sure they stayed safe.

He jogged ahead, looking into alleys and behind cars,
desperate to do something, to find Hope and Hayley.
He hated that he'd been harsh to them the last times
they'd been together. If he did find them, they'd probably be afraid of him.

They hurried into the café just as Liam arrived.
There were Rita and Jimmy, Claire and a few others he
vaguely recognized as local parents of young children.

Everyone was talking at once. Cash—praise God, he
was still in town—was talking to another uniformed
cop.

Liam was on the phone, giving information in a low
voice, but when he saw Anna, he gestured her over. "I
need to talk to you. We may be able to file an Amber
Alert, but we need to establish whether they're in im-

minent danger of bodily injury or death. If it's their father who has them, we probably can't file."

He ushered Anna toward a back table and they sat down, talking fast.

Sean looked around the room. Aside from his brothers, the group was mostly women and older people. It was a ragtag, inexperienced crew. All were sympathetic, but nobody seemed to know what to do.

What hope did they have of finding two little girls?

*Think.* He'd organized teams in the military and on the construction site. He was the one who knew how, and he had to take charge.

He put fingers to his mouth and whistled. "Listen, everyone. We need to divide up and find Hope and Hayley. Let's take the town in quadrants. Biggest focus is the area close to the library."

"I'll do the neighborhoods from here to the shelter," Yasmin offered.

"Teams," Liam called, looking up from his phone.

Sean instantly understood that his brother meant no one should go out alone. "Claire, can you go with her?"

"Yes, sir." The normally cheery cashier looked serious and determined.

"Miss Vi," Sean continued, "I'm going to send you back to the library. You and the parents know all the areas inside and outside. I'm talking the woods and playgrounds surrounding the library, as well."

"Will do." Miss Vi straightened, but not before Sean saw that her chin was quivering. No doubt she felt responsible.

Jimmy lifted a hand. "Rita and I will do the shops

up and down Main Street. Lots of appeal for little kids there."

Sean knew that all too well. His brothers had begged their mom to go into the souvenir shop on that long-ago day, the last time any of them had seen her.

He looked at Rita and saw her go pale, then nod. He cocked his head to one side, feeling an odd connection to the woman. She stared into his eyes for a long moment, too.

Sean blew out a breath and looked away. No time to figure that out now.

Ma Dixie and Pudge came through the front door, both breathing hard, faces creased with worry.

What to do with them? Sean didn't want to put them at risk. "We need someone Hope and Hayley know well, staying put in this central area," he said. "Ma and Pudge, that's you."

Pudge started to protest.

Sean bowled past it. "Everyone, get Ma and Pudge's phone numbers so you can keep them posted on anything you see. Anything suspicious or dangerous, you call the police."

Liam clicked out of his phone call. "We've got people watching all the roads out of town, and a description of the girls statewide, but…" He trailed off, looked at Anna and didn't say what he was undoubtedly thinking.

If their father or someone else had taken the girls, they might be too late.

Liam pushed on, calm, speaking with authority. "Before we start searching, let's get photos of the girls and also of their father, since we believe he could be behind the disappearance." Liam looked at Anna. "If you could send pictures to my phone, I'll get some printed up, but meanwhile, I'd like everyone to take a look."

Anna pulled up pictures of the girls on her phone and everyone looked quickly; they were already familiar with the girls, but Anna had taken a picture of them that morning, one that showed the outfits they were wearing. Just seeing those two innocent faces gave Sean even more determination to find them, get them to safety.

Next, Anna pulled up a picture of Beau, her ex.

Sean hadn't really thought about the fact that she'd have a picture of her girls' father at the ready. And he definitely hadn't expected James Dean–style good looks. "He's always armed, and a good shot," Anna was saying. "And he's volatile. Please—" she choked up, then got ahold of herself "—please be careful, everyone."

"Anything else we should know about him?" Liam asked.

Anna thought. "He grew up in Montana, so he doesn't have a lot of experience with the low country. I doubt he'd go off into the delta or anything."

"I saw this guy," said one of the moms. "Talking in the back of the Palmetto Pig last night. I didn't like the way he looked at me."

"I saw him, too," Cash said grimly. "With the Mahoney brothers. If he's teamed up with them, he could be anywhere."

Concerned voices rose around the room. The Mahoney brothers were no one's idea of good people. And they also ran a low country guide service. They knew every creek, river and inlet in the county.

"Why would the Mahoneys have connected with her husband?" Miss Vi asked.

"Those boys will do anything for a few bucks," Pudge said, his tone disgusted, and Liam nodded agreement.

Anna's eyes turned to Sean, looking panicked. He put a hand on her shoulder. "We'll find them. Me, Cash and Liam can find our way through the low country way better than those guys."

He prayed he was telling the truth.

Quickly, the groups dispersed, and he automatically went with Anna, hurrying from the café through town, past the library and toward the docks. The sun slanted westward, and overhead, seabirds flew; a rich, murky, fishy smell increased as they got closer to the water.

"Are Hope and Hayley familiar with this area of town?" he asked.

Anna nodded miserably. "They fed ducks here a couple of times, with the library program. If their dad asked them about places in town, they'd show him this."

"Do you think he'd do that? Act…fatherly?"

"Maybe. I don't know," Anna said, her voice hopeless. "If it would get him something. All I know is that he's strong, and fast. There's no way we'll find him."

"We will. We'll catch him."

They reached the docks. There was a hair bow, red with white polka dots. He picked it up.

"That's Hope's!" Anna cried.

Sean scanned the area. "The Mahoney brothers' fishing boat is missing. You call Liam. Meanwhile, we'll get in the old canoe we keep here—it's quiet—and head out into the bayou."

ANNA HAD NEVER been in a canoe, but she climbed in with Sean's steadying hand to balance her. He took the back—apparently that was the steering position—and pushed off.

As soon as they got out into the little bay that led off toward the grassy channels of the bayou, she started paddling hard. She welcomed the strain to her muscles. She had to get to her girls.

What was Beau doing to them? How scared they had to be! Although he was their father, and they'd had a few warm times with him, for the most part it had been fear and yelling and dodging his anger.

"Stop paddling." Sean's voice behind her was quiet, but firm.

"I want to go faster!"

"You're throwing us off. Let me do it. You text back to the café and let them know what we found."

She lifted her paddle and turned to protest. But Sean's face was steady and firm, and so were the strokes of his paddle. The canoe cut quickly through the dark water.

She tucked her paddle beside her and called Ma Dixie, who agreed to relay the information to Liam, Cash and the other groups.

"We're not sure they came this way," Anna said quickly. "Everyone should keep searching. It's just… we found Hope's favorite hair bow."

"The red-and-white one?"

"Yes."

There was a beat of silence. "You keep on going, honey, and be careful. I'll get someone to come back you up as soon as I can."

Moments later, Liam called, promising to come as

soon as he'd followed up on a possible sighting of the girls out on the Delta highway.

Anna didn't know what to hope for: that they were on the highway or the water. She squeezed her eyes shut and shot up a desperate prayer for the girls to be safe and comforting each other, wherever they were.

Then she turned back to Sean. "How can you guess where they might be going?"

"There's a little island up here," he said. "Deserted, except the Mahoney brothers have a shack and dock there. They've hidden out there before." He hesitated. "Just try to sit and relax. Breathe. They'll need you at full capacity when we find them, not hysterical."

So she tried to focus on the black water and the Spanish moss, the play of light as Sean paddled the canoe through deep shade sprinkled with patches of sunshine.

There was a plastic bag floating in the water, and she pointed it out to Sean. Was it something the girls had dropped, or just ordinary litter?

And then, on the shadowy bank, she saw movement. "Sean!" she hissed.

Then she realized it wasn't Beau and the twins, but two adult men, standing on a short wooden dock that extended out through the grassy marsh.

One lit a cigarette. The other cocked a gun.

Anna's heart fluttered, her throat closing.

"What's y'all's business here?" came an unfriendly voice.

"Looking for a couple of missing kids," Sean called, back-paddling to stay in the same place. He sounded perfectly calm, and that reassured her a little. "Seen anyone pass this way?"

The smoker, a heavyset man, frowned. The other, the one who'd asked their business, spit into the water, and his gun glinted. Neither man spoke.

"Please," Anna pleaded. "They're young and afraid. We won't bother anyone. We just want to find my daughters and go home."

The two men looked at each other. Then the heavyset one gestured with his cigarette. "That way."

"Thanks," Sean rumbled, and took up his paddle again, going faster.

Once they were out of earshot, she half turned. "Do you know them? Are they reliable?"

"I've seen them before, but I don't know more than that. Depends if they're related to the Mahoney brothers. They could be sending us in the wrong direction, but it's all we have."

Gratitude for this steady man flashed through her. They could have been a team, if things were different. Could have maybe found happiness, if Beau hadn't ruined it for them.

"Look!" Sean pointed to a plastic bracelet floating by. "Is that Hayley's?"

"Yes!" she almost shrieked, pulling it out of the water. "They're leaving us signs. Like Hansel and Gretel!"

"And the guys directed us right. You can help paddle now. Gentle strokes on the left until I tell you to switch."

She followed his instructions, and the canoe sped through the water.

In the deep shadows ahead she saw a dark shape. "Look out," she called back, "there's a log, or—"

"That's not a log. That's a gator." Sean paddled hard

and the boat swung around it, but not before Anna saw its large glinting eyes.

Her stomach clenched. She just prayed the girls hadn't seen anything of the sort, because it would terrify them. Or do worse, if they somehow fell into the water.

"We're approaching the island now," he said. "Let's be real quiet and see if we can find them. It's been a while since I've been there."

Anna looked ahead at the clump of trees that rose out of a wide spot in the river.

"You think they're—"

"Shhh." Sean laid his paddle across the canoe and they coasted silently toward the shore.

"You girls better talk to me," came a thunderous voice out of the darkness.

*Beau.*

Her stomach cramped so hard she felt like she was going to be sick. But then she heard a whimpering sound.

It was Hope. Maternal instinct took over and she was out of the boat, which rocked wildly. Beneath the knee-deep water, thick muck sucked at her shoes as she splashed her way toward the shore, toward her girls.

She was panting when she reached dry land and saw two small shapes. She knelt and they ran and hugged her. "You came, you came," Hope whispered.

"Anna, I'm almost there." Sean was paddling, trying to keep the canoe in place close to the shore.

The sweet, sweaty smell of her girls was heaven. Anna stroked their hair, the silky texture interspersed with twigs. "Are you all right?" Her eyes scanned the water, the trees, the cabin-like structure barely visible through the leaves.

No Beau. Where was he?

"We're okay, but Daddy's mean." Hayley looked back into the thick vegetation of the island.

"Come on. I want you to get in the boat with Mr. Sean." She wrapped an arm around each girl and hustled them to the canoe, which Sean had steered close to the shore. She lifted Hayley in. "Sit down, honey."

"I've got her." Sean knelt forward and put a hand on Hayley's shoulder, moving his weight to steady the canoe. "Hurry," he said to Anna, low and urgent. "Let's do this."

She lifted Hope next and tried to set her in front of Hayley, but the child clung to her.

"Get in, honey. Sit with your sister in the middle of the boat, and then I'm going to be right in front of you." She glanced back toward the trees. Where was Beau? Why wasn't he chasing after them?

"Get in." Sean's voice was urgent as he helped position Hope, struggling to keep the boat from capsizing. Finally, they steadied it and Sean looked up and held out a hand to help her in.

Suddenly, his face changed. "Anna! Behind you!"

She started to turn, to duck away, and then a heavy hand clamped on her shoulder.

"They can go, but you're staying," Beau said. "Thanks for taking my bait."

Horror and revulsion swirled inside her but there was no time to process that now. Anna used her foot to push the canoe away from the shoreline. "Get them to safety, please," she said.

"Let Anna go," Sean said to Beau, paddling to keep the canoe from going farther downriver. His voice was steady, but Anna could hear the fear in it. "You can get away."

"Oh, I'll get away," Beau said. "With her. She's what I wanted anyway. I have no use for whiny little girls."

Anna's stomach twisted, because her girls had heard their own father say he had no use for them. "Sean, please, take them away from here."

Beau yanked Anna backward and she nearly fell, but he caught her. By the hair, and man, did that hurt.

He uttered a few choice curses into her ear and then looked in Sean's direction. "Get outta here. I have a gun pointed right at her brain."

It was true. Anna felt the cold, hard pressure dig into her temple.

"Go!" she begged as the girls cried. "Please! Get them home."

"I'm not leaving you here." Sean drew himself up and paddled the canoe closer.

He was strong, so strong. But he couldn't shield her from Beau's weapon, and if he used his own, the girls could be caught in the cross fire. "Please. Please, Sean. Get my girls to safety. It's the only thing you can do for me." She nearly choked on the words.

Her heart was breaking at the thought of leaving her girls motherless. But at least they'd be safe. Sean would know what to do.

And no way would Beau allow her to live after she'd escaped him, and then dared to connect with another man.

Sean paddled strongly, heading the canoe back in the direction from which they'd come.

And Anna turned to face her outraged ex.

# CHAPTER TWENTY

SEAN PADDLED THE canoe with all his might while Hope and Hayley cried. His heart was torn in two.

How could he leave Anna in the presence of that monster? But how could he *not* do his utmost to get the twins to safety?

The girls' sobbing diminished, so that was a good thing. But when he took a breath and focused on them, he saw that they were whispering. Then they both stood up in the canoe.

"Sit down!" he told them firmly, but they didn't obey.

Instead, they held hands, scrunched their eyes shut and chanted: "One, two, three..."

The significance of their words dawned on him and he dived for the girls, grabbing Hope and shoving her into the bottom of the canoe, catching the back of Hayley's shirt as she catapulted over the edge and into the brackish water. The boat rocked wildly as he hauled her back in, soaked and sobbing. He plunked her down beside her sister, and both girls wailed.

He steadied the boat, heart pounding, kneeling in the center with the girls. But now the canoe was drifting toward the grassy, mucky waters near the shore. Getting stuck there would be a disaster.

"Be still while I get my paddle." He made an effort

to gentle his voice. "You have to cooperate and do what I say. That'll help me keep you safe."

"And Mommy, too?" Hayley's voice trembled.

"Yes. And your mommy, too." He leaned back, grabbed for his paddle.

Gone. It must have fallen out when he'd dived for the twins. He looked around, wildly, and saw something pale and flat glinting in the dappled sunlight, floating downstream at a fast clip.

Hayley tugged at his arm and pointed toward the front of the boat.

Anna's paddle, tucked along the side.

"Good." He managed an approving smile at Hayley while he slid out the oar and used it to maneuver them out into the center of the river.

Out of immediate danger, he stopped paddling and looked seriously at the two girls, whose teary eyes were fixed on him. "You girls can't jump out of the canoe, understand? There are scary things out there. Fish, and snakes, and alligators."

Hope whimpered. Hayley wrapped her arms around her twin and glared at Sean.

He started paddling again, guiding the boat into the strongest current. "I have to get you to safety, and then I'll go back and help your mom, okay? Work with me here."

Hayley's glare faded. She and Hope looked at each other as if trying to decide whether he was telling the truth, was to be trusted.

He kept paddling, now at a steady rate. "You have to stay in the boat," he continued, figuring his voice might soothe them, "because the river is hard to swim in even if you're a good swimmer."

He glanced down and realized both girls were shivering. Of course. Hayley had gotten herself soaked in the river, and then she'd hugged Hope.

He paused and stripped off his jacket. "Wrap yourselves up in this, best you can," he said. "And just hunker down in the boat, try to rest and I'll get you home."

The sun was slanting lower, and the shadows along the river deepened. He paddled hard.

Hope screamed. Then Hayley did, too.

They cringed to one side of the canoe, rocking it hard, screaming and pointing and crying.

He saw it a few feet away from the boat: a giant alligator, probably the same one he and Anna had seen, eyes glinting at water level. Then the canoe moved into a deeply shaded area and Sean lost sight of the creature.

The girls screamed and sobbed.

"Hey, listen. He's more scared of you than you are of him," Sean told the girls. Still, he paddled away from the spot where the creature had been, making noise, splashing with his paddle. If this gator had been fed by people, then it was dangerous. And it would be looking for food.

He paddled hard, and when they emerged from shadows into sunlight, there was no alligator to be seen.

They were far enough away from the island to be temporarily safe, and he felt for his phone and was relieved to find it in his back pocket. He clicked Liam's number.

"Yeah?" Liam's voice was curt.

"I have the girls. Up Santee Mill Creek."

"They okay?"

"Scared, but okay. Can you send a boat up to meet

me? Either you or Cash? And bring Miss Vi, or Ma. Someone who can make them feel safe."

"That'll take a few minutes but...yeah. Where's Anna?"

"That's the bad news," he said grimly. "I had to leave her on Ricochet Island." He paused, swallowed. "With her ex. Hurry. We have to go back and find her."

"Right. Stay on the line." Liam shouted some orders, and Sean heard Miss Vi's voice.

He glanced down at the girls, and found them quiet, staring hopefully at him. He checked their position in the water and then tried to smile reassuringly. "It's going to be—" He cut himself off. He didn't know if it was going to be okay, and he hated to say that and then have everything go horribly wrong.

And things *could* go horribly wrong. Who was to say Beau would stay on the little island until he could get back and rescue Anna?

Who was to say he wouldn't just kill her? It had happened to his own mother, most likely.

He swallowed against the sudden thickness in his throat. "Miss Vi or Ma Dixie is gonna come help you," he said to the twins. "It'll be good to see them, won't it? And then I'll go back and help your mom."

They didn't speak, but they seemed to be hanging on his every word.

He paddled steadily now, but not as fast. A tap-tap-tap came from a tree and they both looked up, so he pointed. "Downy woodpecker. He's hunting for his dinner of bugs."

That made them both wrinkle their noses, so he knew they were listening. Maybe he could glean some information from them, but only if they trusted him.

"Listen, did your...?" He swallowed bile. "Did your father say anything about where he was staying? Where he wanted to take your mom?"

They just looked at him, no answer.

If only he hadn't upset them before, maybe they'd talk to him now. "Did he have a boat?"

They glanced at each other, then nodded.

"A boat like this?"

Hayley shook her head and spread her hands wide.

"A bigger boat? I wonder where he was headed?"

They looked at each other, both with lips pressed tight together. Almost as if they knew something. "Did he say where he was going?" He assumed Beau would want to take Anna back home, if he didn't kill her on the spot. But then, too, Montana was far away. A volatile man wouldn't have the patience for several days' travel before taking his revenge.

He opened his mouth to ask another frustrated question, and then a trembling started in his hands and worked its way up his arms and into the core of his body.

He'd been in this situation before.

*"Where would your dad take your mother?"*

*"What's the name of the nearest big city to your town?"*

*"Was there a place your mom and dad liked to go around here?"*

But he and his brothers hadn't known the answers. Would it have helped if they did?

He tried to put himself back into those shoes, those days. What would have prompted his memory? What might have saved his mother?

Getting to her faster.

Knowing the make of truck.

Giving a full description of his father.

Paying attention during their fights rather than shutting it out. But that, he knew, was a terrifying thing for a child.

He had to try, though. "What were some of the things your daddy said when he found you?" he asked, keeping his tone conversational.

The girls glanced at each other. Hope's lip started to wobble.

"No," he said, "uh-uh. Don't cry." He thought about what Anna did to keep her girls calm and happy. "Let's play a remembering game—it'll help you help your mom."

Amazingly, the mention of a game made Hope's lip stop shaking and Hayley's eyes perk up.

"Who can remember one thing your daddy said?" he asked.

Hayley raised her hand as if she were in school.

"Hayley?" He kept paddling, not putting too much focus on the child.

"He said he spied on us." She glanced at Hope. "When we stayed at that lady's house while Mommy worked at a party. Hope saw him in his truck but I didn't."

Bitsy's. "Why didn't you tell your mom?" he asked.

"We 'cided not to," Hayley explained. "Mommy would be sad."

Guilt swept through Sean. He'd wondered what had scared the girls at Bitsy's, but he'd never followed up. "One point for you, Hayley!" He was forcing it, faking it, this role of a game master. "Where's his truck now?"

Hayley shrugged.

It couldn't be on the island—no roads led there; it was boat access only. He noticed Hope bite her lip and hug herself. Time to continue the game. He reached for patience. "Did he give you food?"

Hope glanced at Hayley and then opened her mouth as if to talk.

"Go ahead—tell me what it was," he encouraged her. "Then you'll get a point."

"Biscuit," she whispered.

He narrowed his eyes. That wasn't helpful; the guy could have gotten biscuits anywhere. Although at least they were both talking to him.

Fear rose inside at the thought of what might be happening to Anna right now, but he shoved it away.

"He was going to take her dancing," Hayley said suddenly.

Sean lifted an eyebrow. "Really?"

Hope shook her head. "Not dancing. To a place that's a dance."

That made no sense.

"I get a point," Hayley reminded him.

"Yes. You do." He just hoped they wouldn't ask him to tally them up.

"A place that's a dance," he said. "I don't get it."

The twins looked at each other and grinned. Then they passed their hands back and forth in front of their knees, crossing them over.

Hayley was looking at him like she'd turned the tables. Now he was going to have to guess.

Could they know about…? How on earth…? "Are you doing the Charleston?"

They both erupted into giggles, which just as abruptly went away.

His mind reeled. Someone had taught them the Charleston.

Beau wanted to take Anna to Charleston.

A place where the Mahoney brothers had ties to organized crime, if local scuttlebutt was to be believed.

A place that was reachable through the rivers and delta country, if you had the right boat.

A place where it would be almost impossible to trace Anna. He called Liam again. "The twins think he's taking Anna to Charleston."

He could hear the sound of Liam's exhaled breath. "Okay. I'm on it."

A sound in the water: the quiet hum of an airboat motor. Sean tensed, scanning the surrounding area.

The boat that appeared was a state-of-the-art mud boat, flat bottomed, wide and fast. At its helm was Miss Vi. In the back were Cash and Ma Dixie.

He waved and shouted and the boat pulled alongside the canoe. Then it was a quick decision: the mud boat would be too loud to rescue Anna; it should be used to take the girls to safety.

Moments later, the girls were tucked in on either side of Ma, blankets around them. Miss Vi expertly turned the boat. "Headed back to town," she said. "You boys. What are you doing?"

"Liam says he's going to block off roads and waterways to Charleston," Sean said. "And meanwhile…" He looked at Cash. "The two of us are going to sneak up from this end and see if we can rescue Anna."

ANNA'S HEARTBEAT SETTLED into race pace, not quite as high as before. The girls had been out of sight for a while and no one had bothered to chase them.

Beau and those awful Mahoney brothers had gone off into a wooden shack. They were arguing, leaving her tied to the protruding roots of a tree. She couldn't get loose, and she couldn't get comfortable.

But at least her girls were safe. She shut her eyes and prayed as hard as she ever had in her life: *Please help them. Let Sean get them to Safe Haven.*

Suddenly, Beau burst out of the shack. Dread clutched her stomach as he hurried over to her. He cut the ropes that bound her and yanked her along by the arm, pulling her toward a moored boat. It looked like a cross between a flat airboat and the type of shrimp boats she'd seen in Safe Haven.

Instinctively, she resisted. A boat like that could travel much faster than Sean's canoe. "No, Beau. You have me. You don't need to have the girls, too."

"Don't you get that I don't want them?" He slapped her face, offhandedly, not even hard. But it was a sign of how far she'd come that the blow offended her, angered her.

For years, she'd been used to that treatment, nearly immune. She could only hope that she'd gotten out of the situation before her girls had internalized that women should be treated that way.

He hauled her onto the boat and threw her down onto the deck just as the Mahoney brothers emerged from the shack.

They climbed onto the boat. "Well, lookee there," the bigger one said. "Yankee boy brought us a present."

"She's just as pretty as she looked at that old biddy's house."

She could barely breathe, but she thought: *Aha. So that was why Blackie went crazy barking at Ma Dixie's place.*

If only she'd found a way to flush them out and face them there.

Now what hope did she have?

Desperate longing rose in her: to be free to raise her girls, raise them in a community like Safe Haven.

She knew that now. Now that she was in trouble, she saw how valuable an asset a good community was. Even in this horrendous situation she had some peace, because she knew Sean would get her girls to safety, and she knew that people like Miss Vi and Ma Dixie would make sure they found a home, good people to care for them.

Except *she* wanted to be the person to care for them.

She wanted it so bad she bit through her lip, tasted blood and surged to her feet. The men's startled cries were behind her as she plunged into the murky water beside the boat and started to swim.

Slimy plants and who knew what else tangled with her legs, and when she ventured to put a foot down, the bottom of the river was pure, deep muck. She recoiled, gasping. The black water had a salty taste.

But whatever lurked in the swamp water was safer than the land creatures now turning the boat to come after her.

She lifted her head and looked around. Now that she was away from them, where could she go? What direction offered even the slightest opportunity of escape?

There. The other shore, away from the little island. If she could get to land and run, run through the trees, maybe she'd come to civilization, a house, a road with cars on it.

It was her only chance.

She struck out toward the middle of the river, arms

windmilling, legs kicking fast. It had been years since she'd done any swimming, and her breath started coming hard. But the thought of her girls, of their desperate need for her, lent strength to her stroke.

A sound behind her, a splash. Another. They must be using the small rowboat that had been tied to the back of the motorized one.

Something grabbed her by the back of her T-shirt and she thrashed away, causing the rowboat to rock wildly. Beau fell into the water.

Good. He couldn't swim well. She kicked hard, then started crawl-stroking away.

"Get her!" one of the Mahoney brothers yelled, and when she looked back, she saw that the little rowboat was gaining on her.

"Help!" Beau's voice was faint, gurgling.

Hands grabbed her by the hair and then the back of her shirt. She looked back, kicked and thrashed, but one of the brothers leaned out and grabbed her around the middle, flipping her into the boat with what seemed like superhuman strength.

Despair washed over her. She lay gasping while they more lazily rescued Beau, who sputtered and kicked out at her. They paddled back to the bigger boat and carried her aboard, leaving Beau to climb in behind them.

She'd failed.

She'd never get to raise her girls.

Defeat brought tears to her eyes, and when Beau leveled another savage kick at her, they flowed down even as she used her legs to leverage herself out of his reach.

"Hey, now," the younger brother scolded, mildly. He made quick work of tying her to some kind of silver protrusion on the boat's deck.

Beau leveled another kick at her. It caught her in the ribs and she couldn't restrain a cry.

"Ya know…" The older brother looked at the younger one.

The communication between them was as instantaneous as it was between her own girls.

"Right," said the younger brother. And with a quick elbow to the neck, he hit Beau's windpipe.

Beau went down like a collapsing inflatable.

The brothers glanced at each other, again with the silent communication. One took his shoulders and the other his feet, and they dumped him into the rowboat.

"We taking him with us?" the younger brother asked.

"No. Because…" The older brother leaned down to the rowboat, flipped Beau onto his stomach and pulled something out of his back pocket. A wallet, and he quickly looked inside and counted the bills. "It's all here. Wet, but here. Pull over to shore and we'll tie him to the island. Let O'Dwyer find him."

The idea was swiftly carried out, and Anna watched, her mind racing. She couldn't regret seeing Beau overpowered. This man had terrorized her and her children for so long. It was stunning that he could be vulnerable, could be beaten.

But there was no time for reflecting on the past; she had to focus on this moment, and these men who now held her captive.

"If you've got your money now," she said, "you could just leave me here, right? I won't say anything to anyone."

The older brother snorted out a laugh.

"You're coming along," the younger one said.

"What are you going to do with me?"

The two looked at each other.

Then the younger brother went to the helm of the boat and started steering it into the bayou.

"WE SHOULD'VE GONE to Charleston," Cash said. "If that's where he was headed, I've got all kinds of connections there."

"So does Liam." Sean paddled steadily.

"You think they'll still be on Ricochet?"

"Or close. Maybe." He glanced back at his brother. "When I found out the Mahoney brothers were there, it's like a wild card."

"Yeah," Cash said slowly, "or not. Because we know 'em."

It was true, and it gave them some kind of advantage. The Mahoneys, though younger than Sean and Cash, were from a family known to most of the area. They lived deep in the bayou, grew weed and made meth, and generally terrorized the region.

The thought of the family made Sean paddle harder, and behind him, he felt Cash do the same.

The sun was sinking in the west, painting the sky pink and gold. If Anna were alone with those two—and her abusive ex... It didn't bear thinking about.

"We're getting close," he said a few minutes later. "Muffle it."

They had done this as kids, sneaking around the delta. They paddled silently.

When they reached the island, though, the Mahoneys' big boat was gone. Only a small rowboat floated, tied to a protruding root.

Cautiously, they came alongside it. Saw a limp, face-down body, thankfully male. Sean swallowed, nudged him to his side with his paddle.

Anna's ex. Unconscious, or… "Is he dead?" Cash asked.

Sean felt his neck and detected a pulse. "Just knocked out."

"So the Mahoney brothers took Anna somewhere."

A chill went over Sean. "Yeah."

"We have to bring him along."

"He'll slow us down."

"Not by much, and having him out in the world is a bigger risk to Anna."

"The *Mahoneys* are a risk to Anna." But he saw Cash's point, and reluctantly, he took Beau's feet while Cash took his shoulders. They lifted him into the bottom of the canoe, and he started moving restlessly, coming back to consciousness.

"Where do you think they took her?" Cash directed the question at Sean.

But Beau's eyes flickered open. "Their fishing camp," he said, his voice foggy. He started to struggle upright.

Sean took a lot of pleasure in socking him in the chin, knocking him out again.

"You think he's right about where they took her?" Cash asked.

"It's as good a guess as any." As they paddled swiftly, silently, in that direction, their boat riding low in the water, Sean felt like he was reworking the past with every movement of his muscles. Now he wasn't the helpless kid whose father was out to destroy his mother.

Now he had some power, and God willing, he was going to use it to fix things for the twins and for Anna.

FROM HER AWKWARD position over the bigger Mahoney brother's shoulder, Anna looked around the small fishing cabin and tried to think.

She had no chance of overpowering these two hulks, and escaping them in the midst of the dark swamp was almost worse than being here. All she could hope was that Sean or Liam would find her, somehow, before Beau did.

Her eyes lit on the cookstove at the same time she heard the bigger brother's stomach growl. Suddenly, she knew exactly how she was going to buy herself some time.

"Put me down," she ordered, and to her surprise, he complied. She put her hands on her hips and faced the two men. "When was the last time you ate?" She was quaking inside, but she tried to channel the strong women she'd met in Safe Haven: Ma, Miss Vi, Yasmin.

The younger brother looked at the floor and rubbed the back of his neck. "This morning," he said.

"That won't do. You boys sit right down at that table and let me fix you some food."

They looked at each other, and she held her breath.

"Ain't no food here," growled the bigger one. He started toward her.

She spun away and opened the cupboard, found cornmeal and a bag of potatoes, white strings growing off them.

If there was one thing she knew, it was how to make a dinner out of what seemed like no food. She'd done it often for her father, and the skill had come in handy with the twins occasionally, as well. "I need lard," she said, "or butter."

They looked at each other again. Then the smaller

one opened the cupboard beneath the sink and pulled out a tin can. "Bacon grease," he said, thrusting it at her.

"That'll do. Now either sit, or go get me some fish or greens."

"Ain't no time to fish," the younger one said.

"Ain't no time to eat," the older one growled.

"But I'm hungry!"

She ignored the squabbling and tried to still the shaking in her hands. A moment's rummage through the drawers and cupboards yielded a spoon and a cast-iron skillet.

She put the bacon grease to melting and then looked around the rest of the kitchen. Found an onion and a knife, thought briefly about stabbing the two men with it and decided that appealing to their senses was the wiser path. Speedily, she chopped the onion and threw it into the bacon grease.

Even she, who felt sick with fear, recognized the appeal of the fragrance that quickly arose.

The younger Mahoney went out the cabin door and she saw him outside slicing up greens with a hunting knife.

The older Mahoney went to the freezer, pulled out something and thrust it at her.

It was meat. Skinned. In the shape of a squirrel.

She swallowed the gag that wanted to rise in her. "Oh, that'll be good," she said to him sweetly. "It might not thaw for a while, but we've got time, right?"

"No." He took the frozen squirrel out of her hands and thrust it back in the freezer. He gave her an assessing look.

*Hurry up, Sean*, she telegraphed mentally as she turned back to the chopping board.

Would there be any way he could find her here, though?

Soon enough, the potatoes were chopped and frying. The younger brother brought in the greens, and she chopped them carefully, and as slowly as she could.

"Get a move on," the older brother said.

"I'll have to cook the greens after the potatoes fry," she said, trying to keep her voice calm.

He opened a cupboard, pulled out another cast-iron pan and handed it to her. "Do it now."

Carefully, she flipped the potatoes and onions and then set another blob of bacon grease melting in the second pan. Sprinkled the greens in. Found salt and pepper for seasoning.

If these two were anything like Beau and her father, they'd eat fast.

And afterward, who knew what they'd do to her? Desperately, she looked out the window, hoping to see Sean, Liam, anyone.

"Serve them up."

"They're not crispy yet."

"Serve them." The older brother narrowed his eyes at her.

He knew she was stalling. "Where are your plates?"

He nudged his younger brother, who pulled a couple of tin plates from the cupboard. He held them out, and Anna piled both of them high with greens and potatoes.

They both sat down at the table and she got them beers from the fridge. Looked out the window again.

Nothing.

She drew in her breath, prayed for strength. And then she started melting another blob of bacon grease.

It took a minute before the chewing sounds stopped. "What are you doing?" the older one asked.

"Cooking more," she said.

"Don't."

The bacon grease was sizzling now.

"Okay," she said. Turned off the gas heat, took the pan off the stove. And flung the hot grease into his face.

He screamed and clawed at his eyes and stood up in a rage, but he was blinded and in pain.

His brother wasn't. He stood and came toward her.

She grabbed the chopping knife and held it up. "Keep your distance," she ordered.

But her voice trembled.

He came at her fast, grabbed her hand and, with one squeeze, made her drop the knife. "You hurt my brother," he said, and smacked her face.

It hurt. But she was used to hurting. "Look at him," she cried, the oldest child's trick in the world, but he fell for it. While he was distracted, she yanked her trapped hand away—a skill born of long experience with Beau—and ran for the door.

He was behind her, grabbing her, but she flung it open. Ran out toward the river.

There was a rustling and crashing in the vegetation beside the Mahoneys' dock. She saw a shadowy form.

Sean! And Cash, right behind him.

Sean gripped her shoulders for the briefest second, looking into her eyes, then scanning her. "Stay out here. We've got this covered as long as I know you're safe."

"The girls?"

"Safe with Ma and Miss Vi."

"Come on!" Cash jerked his head in the direction of the cabin, and they rushed inside like a two-man army.

There was some thumping and falling then, and the sound of blows. A shot was fired.

Who'd been shot? She rushed to the propped-open window and looked inside. One of the Mahoney brothers lay on the floor, but the other was swinging a gun wildly.

"Anna!" Sean yelled. "Get out of here! Call Liam!" He tossed her a phone. And then he and Cash dived for the brother who was still standing.

Anna ran for the boat and half collapsed beside it, then punched the button for an emergency call.

As she explained the situation, she saw movement in the boat. Beau was there, unconscious, but starting to wake up.

As she ended the call, Beau sat up in the boat. He looked woozy, but angry, and he reached for her.

Behind her, she heard Sean shouting. Heavy running feet. He'd help her, save her.

But she wanted this one for herself. For herself and her girls.

She stood, drew back her fist and hit Beau in the chin like some TV boxer. As hard as she could, with all her anger behind it.

It was exceptionally shocking—and gratifying— when he went down.

Sean reached her and wrapped his arms around her from behind, laughing and dancing her in a circle. "I'm crazy about you," he said, his voice more exuberant than she'd ever heard it before.

His excitement had to be the aftereffects of adrenaline, but she'd take it. As Cash wrapped thick ropes around Beau's hands and feet, Anna let herself lean back into Sean's arms.

"You're everything to me, Anna George," he said, his voice roughening as he pulled her close. "Everything, you hear? And I'm not letting anything bad happen to you, ever again."

If anyone could fulfill such a promise, it was Sean. She turned in his arms and pulled his face down to hers and kissed him.

# *EPILOGUE*

*Three Weeks Later*

ANNA TIED HAYLEY'S hair ribbon and adjusted Hope's. "Good. You both look lovely. Now, play with Blackie until I'm ready, and we'll go out to greet our guests."

"You look pretty, too, Mommy," Hope said. And then both girls rushed out into the cabin's living room. An excited series of barks let Anna know the girls had followed her instructions.

She studied herself in the mirror. *Did* she look good?

Her hair was still on the short side, but she'd gotten it shaped so it framed her face better. Her figure—she turned sideways and studied herself critically—well, she'd put on a couple of pounds, but she'd needed to. Pretty soon, if things kept up the way they'd been, she'd have to start watching the pasta and pastries.

Her face was the biggest change. For once, she actually looked rested. Felt that way, too.

She sent up a silent prayer of thanks for her girls' safety and well-being, for her own, for the blessings she'd found in this community.

For Sean.

And she didn't need to go there, because she'd start daydreaming. She leaned forward to do a quick bit of eye makeup, then straightened her lightweight shirt and denim capris.

"Come on, Mommy. Mr. Sean's here!"

*And that blush gives everything away.* She rolled her eyes at her own pink face in the mirror and took a few deep breaths before coming out of the bathroom to face her girls, her dog, her life.

And her man.

His eyes darkened when he saw her. "You look nice."

She struggled to keep the wide smile off her face. "You clean up nice, yourself." Sean had shaved off his beard, and he was wearing a collared knit shirt.

Faded, ripped jeans, and of course he was still huge, but he looked considerably less scary than when she'd first seen him just a couple of months ago.

"Are we ready?" he asked, holding out his arm to her and winking at the girls.

"Yeah!" they cried, and they went out to the Sea Pine's main driveway, where half the town, it seemed, was already lined up and waiting for today's grand re-opening.

As soon as they opened the gate, things got hectic. But they all knew their roles. Tony and Sean showed people around, and Anna took photos to post on their new website and social media pages.

The girls and Blackie took charge of the kids who arrived, many of them new friends from the library or from Ma Dixie's. There was soon a small army of youngsters running from the beach to the renovated playground to the rustic shack that would be a combination office, concession stand and general store.

As she talked to people and posted pictures, Anna felt light, focused, clear. She hadn't known how oppressive even the distant threat of Beau had been to her, but now that he was behind bars along with the Mahoney brothers, she finally felt safe.

"Anna!" Sean beckoned her over, and she joined him, Rita and Jimmy at the pair of huge cook pots. "I'm going to bring out the reserve supplies, because we've got twice as many people as we expected."

"Which means you can take over shucking corn, if you don't mind," Jimmy said, pointing to three bushel baskets of it.

"Or you can do shrimp." Rita's face was flushed as she stirred pieces of sausage into one of the pots, but she looked happy.

Anna worked comfortably with the others, and their low country boil went off without a hitch, people eating giant bowls of food over newspaper-covered tables. Even the twins learned how to peel shrimp and throw the shells into the big heap in the middle of the table.

"We've got so many people from out of town," Anna marveled to Miss Vi during a moment's break.

"I put out the word to all the libraries in the surrounding counties," the older woman said. "Let them know you're planning to have reading corners in most of the cabins, and information about local library events. They were happy to share the information with their patrons."

"Thank you!" Anna hugged the older woman, who looked startled, but soon hugged her right back.

"I want in on this," Claire said, coming over, resplendent in a red swimsuit, sarong and high-heeled sandals. She looked like a 1940s film star and was catching a lot of attention.

Obligingly, Anna hugged her, too. "I know you

spread the word among your family and friends. Thank you so much."

"We gotta keep you in the area," Claire said. Then she turned and beckoned to Rafael. "He says he wants to hire you as an assistant. Isn't that right?"

Rafael put an arm around Claire. "That's right, and you would still have time to help Sean manage the Sea Pine Cottages."

Sean, who hadn't strayed far from her all day, ambled over. "What's going on, now?"

"Rafael wants to hire Anna to help with the GED classes," Claire said. "Isn't that great?"

"Um…"

Claire leaned over and kissed Rafael's cheek, then clung to his arm. "I may have told him to do it," she said.

Sean's expression went thoughtful. "She'd be good at it," he said finally, smiling at Anna.

A small worry Anna hadn't realized she was holding lifted off her shoulders and floated away.

Sean was nothing like Beau and never would be. That part of her life was over. He was protective of her and her daughters, yes. But he'd never stand in her way or prevent her from being who she was.

Cash approached them from behind and tapped Sean on his shoulder. "Good job, man, but I'm outta here."

"Oh no!" Anna turned toward him, hands on hips. "You can't leave already!"

She'd grown fond of Cash, and not only because of the role he'd played in rescuing her from the Mahoney brothers. He'd started treating her like a sister, teasing her about her freckles and buying way-too-indulgent gifts for her girls.

"'Fraid so," he said. "This small-town stuff makes me crazy."

Sean narrowed his eyes at his brother. "Work through it, man," he said.

Cash let out a disgusted noise. "Just because you turned into a homebody, that doesn't mean I have to."

Liam approached in time to hear Cash's remark. "Sean was always a homebody," he said. "It's just that now he has a good woman beside him."

"That's for sure." Both Cash and Liam looked at Anna fondly, causing heat to rise in her face.

Because no matter what his brothers said, no matter how warm and connected he'd been acting in the past couple of weeks, Sean hadn't spoken to her yet about a future.

After they saw Cash off, and Liam went over to join a group of people—as far away from Yasmin as possible, Anna noticed—Sean cleared his throat. He was looking at Anna with an odd expression on his face. "Come over here," he said, nodding toward a picnic table a little away from the crowd. "I want to talk to you a little."

Something about his face made her nervous. "Um… there's still some corn left to shuck."

"We did enough. Rita and Jimmy can do what little's left if they need to."

Anna glanced over to see the older couple standing close together, renewing the supply of fresh corn on the cob to roast on the grill.

Perching on the top of the picnic table, Anna opened her mouth to comment, but when Sean knelt on the ground before her, whatever she'd been about to say flew from her mind. "Sean? What…?"

"I love you, Anna. I'll always love you."

Anna's heart stuttered, then came back beating hard and fast. "Come up here and sit by me," she said, reaching out to him. "You're too far away."

He smiled and nodded. "I want to be close to you, too," he said, and rose gracefully to sit beside her on the picnic table. "And I respect and admire you, and I want to ease your burdens." He put an arm around her and stroked her hair, her cheek.

She'd never felt such tenderness in her life.

Her eyes filled, but she didn't want to cry. She looked to the side and saw Hayley and Hope, holding hands, running down a sand dune, their hair shining golden in the sun.

Sean leaned close and took her hand. "I love them, too. If you'd let me, and if they'd accept me, I'd like to try and be a father to them."

A tear did escape then, rolling down her cheek.

He was fumbling in his pocket, and then he took her hand. "Look at me."

She did, and the love in his eyes radiated from him like ocean waves, taking her breath away.

"Marry me, Anna," he said.

She bit her lip and tried not to cry.

He turned her hand over and slid the ring onto it. "Just try it on," he urged, speaking faster now. "I know it's quick, and you might need time, just try it and I'll know if I got the right size, because maybe later, after you've—"

She put a finger to his lips. "Sean."

He lifted his eyes to hers.

"I'll marry you," she said.

He pulled her into his arms.

There was a whoop from the crowd she hadn't

known was listening, and suddenly all their friends were around them, congratulating them, hugging them, shedding tears of their own. Hayley and Hope pressed forward through a crowd that willingly parted for them, hands ushering them toward Anna.

"Is Mr. Sean gonna be our daddy?" Hayley asked.

Sean knelt before the twins in full marriage-proposal stance. "I would like to," he said. "Would you have me for your daddy?"

They looked at each other, and broad smiles broke out across their faces. "Yes!" they shouted together, voices clear and strong.

Sean opened his arms to both of them, and Anna knelt down to get in on the hug of her new family, her heart swelling with gratitude.

Safe Haven. She and her girls had found it, at last.

\* \* \* \* \*